A BLOODY HABIT

ELEANOR BOURG NICHOLSON

A Bloody Habit

IGNATIUS PRESS   SAN FRANCISCO

Cover illustration by Matthew Alderman

Cover typography hand-lettered by Eric de Llamas

Cover design by John Herreid

© 2018 by Ignatius Press, San Francisco
All rights reserved
ISBN 978-1-62164-206-0
Library of Congress Control Number 2018931240
Printed in the United States of America ∞

For Father Thomas Joseph White, O.P.,
who told me to take a nap and brought on nightmares.
For Julia, who likes vampires.
For Anne, who isn't one.

With eternal apologies to Bram Stoker
and to the Order of Preachers
for taking such liberties.

In the Order's conflicts with the Albigensians, a blood-stained habit was that of the martyr, a sign that the adversaries of Truth were spurred on to violence. Most remarkable in our recollection is Peter of Verona. Today, in contrast, a scarlet-stained habit is popularly conceived one of the familiar attributes of the battle whether it ends with martyrdom or a staking. Metaphorically speaking, of course. Some have posited the theory that the bloodiness of the scapular was indicative of the ability of the supposed vampire slayer. This supposition is likely apocryphal, or, at best, gravely mistaken.

Rev. Thomas Edmund Gilroy, O.P., D.C.L.,
Catalogue of the Preternatural

PROLOGUE

It is a literary convention proper to the more sensational genres that a narrator attempt to explain, justify, or render believable his account of something truly *un*believable. "This is completely unlikely and even impossible," the narrator admits, "and I wouldn't have believed it myself, but it actually happened, and I saw it with my own eyes! Consequently, you ought to believe every ridiculous thing I say!"

As I write this apology to the reader, I feel keenly the implausibility of my tale. Beyond the usual experience of Robert Louis Stevenson and others in my youth, and intermittent forays into the Gothic (the most important of which is chronicled here), my training has been less in the niceties of these literary practices, and more in the concrete and practical exercise of the law. It is perhaps a sign of my legal training, more than the impulse to imitate that literary convention I described above, that I wish at the start to produce my credentials both as a sane man and a skeptic. I am not a writer of fiction, and the ease with which I have shifted into that role alarms me. In fact, I have spent a great deal of time in recent years questioning myself (and my sanity) because of this whole business.

When a close friend encouraged me to write a personal account of my experiences in connection with certain well-known incidents just after the turn of the century, I had too great respect for that friend to laugh in his face, but I did articulate my doubts. As I say, many of the events told here are known to the public and are duly recorded in official volumes that chronicle crime and urban unrest. Theorists of a spiritualistic bent have had their say; even politicians have weighed in. I have no desire to proclaim the back-story of those bloody, headline-worthy incidents—partly because it was all so strange and need not be revisited, and partly because it exposes so much that is personal to me. In fact, I hope no one (except the friend who requested it) bothers to read this. In case, by some cruel machination of fate, this book stumbles its way into popularity, I have changed all of the names of those involved.

To one other deliberate literary liberty I must confess. My own narrative is completely intertwined in my mind with that other novel. In fact, I found that Stoker's demonic Count—rather in the manner of Copperfield's Mr. Dick and the head of Charles I—would intrude himself upon my story whenever and wherever he pleased. To combat this assault, I have granted him his own due place, and set brief quotations from *Dracula* at the head of each chapter. I hope no evil may come of this calculated hospitality.

Beyond this, my motive is twofold: first, to provide my friend with the account he requested, which will be inter-esting to him as related to his work as a historian, with a particular focus on (and I feel absurd as I write it!) vam-piric activity since the seventeenth century; and second, to garner for myself a clear picture of what did happen, and through it to exorcise the emotional, mental, and even spiritual remnants that still haunt me.

—B. R., Esq.
(hereafter "John Kemp")

Chapter 1

1 May 1900: Somewhere between Budapest and London

(From Jonathan Harker's diary) *She then rose and dried her eyes, and taking a crucifix from her neck offered it to me. I did not know what to do, for, as an English Churchman, I have been taught to regard such things as in some measure idolatrous, and yet it seemed so ungracious to refuse an old lady meaning so well and in such a state of mind. She saw, I suppose, the doubt in my face, for she put the rosary round my neck and said . . .*

"Pardon me."

That was precisely the thing I was most unlikely to do, I thought to myself with wry bitterness as I looked up from the page and into the face of the little man who had invaded my course of light literary recreation. I did not often venture into the realm of Gothic absurdity, but when I did I certainly did not like to be interrupted by round-headed little men with pink faces and beady black bespectacled eyes, attired in flowing white dresses, with rattling beads strapped to their sides.

"Yes?" I replied, making a meager effort at keeping the irritation out of my voice.

"May I pass you, please," asked the little man—he was some sort of a Roman priest or a monk, I could tell by his outlandish dress—"to open the window?"

I suppressed the urge to tell him that he would not be overwarm if he didn't go about in that quaint ritual garb; instead I grunted a vague assent.

He smiled and began laboring with the heavy window. It *would* be stuck, I thought with a self-pitying sigh. There was nothing for it. I put my novel aside (taking care to keep the title hidden, as there is nothing more irritating than having strangers comment on one's choice of reading material, especially when it happens to be the latest and most sensationalized work of a melodramatic Irish novelist) and stood up to do battle in his stead. A few fierce heaves and it was open the desired smidgen. Meanwhile my coat sleeve had acquired a nasty-looking black smear—of grease, I had no doubt.

The priest thanked me and sat back in his place, nodding politely toward the elderly Frenchwoman sitting in the opposite corner. Her relief was visible.

My face flushed, partly from irritation at the ridiculous exchange, and partly from shame. I had not noticed the old woman's discomfort and should have been observant enough to bring her relief without being pressed into service by the smiling Papist. It was a consequence of travel—trapped in that compartment, surrounded by five strangers (the elderly Frenchwoman, heavily shrouded in mourning; a Romanian or Hungarian man with black teeth, a goiter, and a plump wife; a thin woman severely attired in gray, probably a governess; and the Roman-English priest), and with an unusually uninspiring tract of Hungarian countryside hurtling by, I had been relieved to have Bram Stoker's book into which to escape. At this time, it had been published a few years earlier, but an acquaintance—a young lady, with a charming smile—had foisted it on me before my departure from London with the urgent demand: "John Kemp! You must read this!"

Thus: I soon recovered from the momentary self-criticism for such ungentlemanly inattention to my feminine companions by retreating back into my novel. I was seemingly far away from the train carriage, on a horse-drawn coach winding on a serpentine path past a bewildering mass of fruit blossom; I spared a moment or two to smile ruefully at the enthusiasm with which the fictional traveler took in the wild grandeur of scenery through which he was passing. We were traveling along much the same route, but it was a dirty gray day and even majestic mountaintops looked unremarkable. A host of local people littered the pages, full of superstition and dread. I glanced up from my book at my black-toothed companion to see if he were nervously fingering a cross or other talisman, but found he was asleep with his mouth open and nostrils flaring with each gurgling exhalation. I returned to my novel with a shudder. Several pages later, when the calèche with four horses arrived, bringing with it, I had no doubt, the full Gothic force of the supernatural, I became conscious of pangs of hunger.

I looked up again.

The carriage was already partially empty, and I hoped they were not all simply removed to the dining car, or if they had, I hoped they would prove silent dining companions. As I well knew, traveling made me irritable, and I was already rather embarrassed at my earlier petulance. If I met one of the witnesses to my mood, I might feel compelled to be friendly, and I would prefer to let my mind wander. I should sort through those Kilbronson papers, I thought, with a mild pang of guilt. It was an unappealing idea. The last few days had been chock-full of that sordid affair of Kilbronson's marriage to a sultry Hungarian temptress. I was weary of it and contented enough to find distraction in the strange and wondrous things dreamed up in the feverish brain of Bram Stoker. At least, I thought wryly, I would be keeping nonsense where it belongs—in cheap fiction.

With my hopes of social nonengagement, the scene in the dining car was not a pleasant one.

All of the white-clothed, tightly cramped tables were completely full—full to brim over—except one, beside the currently north-bearing windows. And there a single seat remained opposite the round-faced priest.

For a brief moment I considered escape, considered a willing bout of fasting to escape that company, but a steward arrived with untimely expedition and, between his eagerness to serve, the brokenness of his English (which undermined every subtle repulse), and the fact that I could not squeeze past the large tray he carried in his hand without crawling under it, I was pushed with all but physical force into the empty seat.

I nodded in recognition over the range of glasses and cutlery and hoped the nonverbal communication would suffice.

"Why, hello!" said the little priest with friendly enthusiasm. "I thought you might be joining me."

As this was a silly hypothesis to have formed when we were perfect strangers (and, I hoped, would remain so), I did not deign to answer.

"I've nearly made up my mind," he said to the attentive steward. "I should be ready to order along with my friend here."

It was worse than I could have imagined—he had not even begun to eat and obviously considered me as the companion (or, as he put it, a *friend*) ordained by heaven for his entertainment. I could only pray, with a sense of foreboding, that the meal was sufficiently satisfying to atone for so much suffering.

I ordered chicken and he did the same.

I requested more water and he requested more water.

"A little pitcher would be lovely, in fact," he added.

When he asked for tea I became rather stubborn and ordered coffee, despite the fact that I wanted tea. When the coffee came it was bitter, and I harbored an added resentment toward my newfound comrade.

"It is a lovely day," said the priest.

I agreed monosyllabically, though inwardly I thought the adjective recklessly applied.

"Look at the intensity of that sky! It is the sort of color one sees in really vivid landscape paintings."

Agreement was even more difficult here as I thought the sky was decidedly unattractive and any landscape painter who endeavored to capture it must be a maudlin sort of fellow. Luckily the same noncommittal monosyllable seemed to satisfy my companion.

"There is something enchanting in such a view," he continued. "I do often find, though, that people are inclined to doubt that intensity of color. Man is always happiest to ascribe that force of brilliance to the mind of the artist. Reality is often seen abstractly as a sort of vague dreariness. As if there could not be such intensity in the natural world. As if God Himself were not capable of creating more brilliant vividness than we could ever comprehend."

I could not assent as I had never really thought of the point. I liked art galleries well enough and had considered myself rather a connoisseur in early days, but theology was quite beyond my ken.

"It's the kind of paint they use, I believe," I said dryly, and felt I had made a real point.

The merry cleric did not seem bothered by my crude pragmatism.

"Oh, yes," he said. "Cobalt. Its history is rather interesting, you know."

And he launched into a brief lecture on the geniuses and processes involved in the formulation of the stuff. He finished, gazing out the window. I was not sure whether he expected a response or not. In any case, he had pressed my practical knowledge of things artistic to its breaking point. I once again took refuge in a vague grunt.

For a few brief moments, he continued in silence, looking earnestly out the window. When he spoke again it was with embarrassing fervor: "The world is charged with the grandeur of God," he said, speaking to my profound discomfort as if he were pronouncing a prayer. And then, before I could recover, he turned to me, looking at me with embarrassing concentration, and said in a matter-of-fact tone: "But, then, you fancy yourself rather an agnostic, don't you?"

Considering it was a term I had embraced willingly enough among my friends, and even defended with a degree of self-importance at several important society luncheons, I really should not have begun babbling self-explanatory speeches as I did (all the while inwardly writhing at the catechism).

"I would not quite say an agnostic. Perhaps I was simply waiting for ... My father was a Calvinist preacher, you see, and his sort of enthusiasm did not really resonate for me. And my mother ... In colleges these days, with science ... Any young man of spirit ..."

I trailed off and hoped to goodness that the food would come soon and I could eat it with haste and escape this zealous lunatic.

"I've been away from London for some time, you know," said the little round-faced fellow—as if I really did know. "Preaching a course of lectures on the doctrine of Christ. I do a great deal of that now—training young friars."

"Are there many English priests in Hungary?" I asked.

He looked at me sharply—or at least I thought he did. In a moment he was again cheerful and silly, prattling away, though not, I noticed, in a direct answer to my question. "The youngest friars ask a great many questions, some of them because they really want to know, others because they want to assure themselves that they understand by formulating something or other to say. Challenging the instructor is always invigorating to youth—as you found with your father."

(Good God! I cried inwardly. Is the man human?)

Meanwhile, he prattled on: "Yesterday the conversation drifted rather." He smiled. "I tend to digress more and more with old age. We spoke at length of the sins against charity." His voice assumed an orotund tone: " 'But if you bite and devour one another, take heed you be not consumed one of another.' So sayeth Saint Paul. Have you been enjoying that book?"

Surprised at the sudden change of subject, I blushed violently. Like a fool, I had brought the scarlet-encrusted volume along with me.

"I haven't read very far," I said.

"It's rollicking good fun," he said. "All quite ridiculous, of course."

I was glad we were agreed on that point, but wondered if it were a good thing ever to agree with such a fanatic.

Our food came. For a moment we were distracted in the expected exchange of polite nothings with the steward. When he left I once again hoped to escape, this time in the Englishman's powers of politely ignoring his fellows when they happen to be engaged in anything so animalistic as the consumption of a paprika-crusted chicken with bouncing peas in the dinner car of a moving train.

The priest obviously was not restrained by such considerations of false etiquette. His face became pinker as he ate, and he blinked emphatically after swallowing a large quantity of scalding tea, but after a few moments he returned to the discarded topic.

"Yes, all quite ridiculous."

"You don't believe in blood-sucking Romanian counts?" I asked in mock surprise.

"Oh, I don't mean that," he said with great seriousness. "It's all that other business that is so ridiculous. Little things. Like that business of the consecrated host and the putty. Rome would never grant a dispensation—and it would be a dispensation, not an indulgence, but then the author is not yet a Catholic and so wouldn't know. His wife is Catholic now. But it's all silly nonsense—harmless really, but silly. I laughed out loud when I read it. Then there's the larger point. That business of consummate evil. Well, it is, of course. There's no denying it. But you can't go about saying that there is consummate evil and it is somehow an equal force to the Good. That's Manichaeism."

I looked at him blankly.

"Oh, dear," he cried, sincerely penitent. "You haven't reached the bit about the putty yet, have you? Well I shan't say anything more about it. I wouldn't want to ruin the surprise for you. But when you reach that point, you'll know it's all nonsense. Oh, dear. Very careless of me. Quite thoughtless. Another demonstration, I fear, of the danger—or even the wickedness—of frivolous talk."

He was so earnest about it that I felt compelled to assure him that I was sufficiently forewarned and would at the same time be appropriately surprised by the business with the putty.

"How long have you been away from London?" I asked, more for the sake of relieving his distress at the inadvertent revelation of the putty passage than out of any desire to become better acquainted.

"Four months. And you?"

"Three weeks." But I did not want to talk of myself. Catholic priests were all inclined to be gossips, I knew. It came from the thrill of having their deluded sheep unburden all of their secrets in the dark of a confessional.

I never liked sheep.

"Will you return to the Continent again this year?"

"That all depends on the orders of my superiors," he said cheerfully. "We are itinerant, you know. I generally go where I am told."

More sheep. Sheep leading sheep, in fact. I did not respond.

"Do you like being a barrister?"

So he had seen the address of my legal chambers in London at the top of one of the documents bulging from my briefcase. Once again I was punished for the casual nature in which I treated my papers. Further, a new thought started to creep into my head—was he pumping me for information? I hadn't thought of Kilbronson's affairs as inspiring lurid interest, but perhaps this bizarre little man was somehow in league with the wife?

Looking at him again, I was a bit embarrassed at the thought. Such an absurd little man couldn't be in league with anyone—he couldn't be an effective ally, especially to a conniving femme fatale. In any case, discretion was the best course so I nodded soberly but volunteered no further information.

He was not to be put off. "Our work is rather similar. You collect evidence to persuade in a legal case; I amass evidence to persuade souls into eternity."

If he liked to think our work of equal importance, I was content to let him believe so.

"In fact," he said, with the corner of his mouth twitching mischievously, "as you are a minister of the law, I might be called a minister of the"—he coughed—"Law-d."

It was not a remarkable pun, but it was rather unexpected, and I laughed in spite of myself.

My companion continued to chuckle amiably. "If you want a really hearty laugh at your jokes, you should tell them to a group of nuns in a cloister. They will laugh uproariously at a simple witticism. It's really charming."

"Why is that?" I asked—rather uncomfortable with the subject but curious at the same time.

"Extraordinary spiritual sensitivity," he replied. "You see, they have only the liturgy and the community. They have none of the noise and speedy chaos we see in the world. Instead they have a heavy, a profound silence. That brings extraordinary peace and the capacity for incredible holiness—and a special appreciation for those little jokes that we so frequently take for granted. And often the most mystical are the most practical. They can recognize evil more quickly than other people, and can appreciate Goodness because they are intimately united to Him."

The reply was rather preachier than I had desired, and my mind began to glaze over the moment he began to speak of holiness in that knowing tone. I wondered, in passing, if the rumors about Papist priests and their illicit cavorting with nuns were true—and once again felt embarrassed for the thought. The silly man probably knew nothing of the passions.

I changed the subject. And changed it again. And again. Each time he deflected my attempts to avoid undue religiosity.

A discussion of the weather brought us back to God as Creator.

A discussion of our meal prompted him to a Eucharistic discourse.

A mere mention of politics brought him to the history of the Church, with more names of popes than is probably inflicted on the average young Catholic.

It was growing dark. I began to display ostentatious signs of exhaustion. I could not yawn openly into his face, but I came as near to it as I felt good manners allowed. He was an amusing enough eccentric, but his tendency to see me as his dear friend would become exceedingly tedious if it carried on for much longer. He might even be traveling by the same boat as I was. I had studiously avoided requesting greater detail on his future plans for fear that he might take this as an overture to unite with him as a semipermanent traveling companion.

Finally, after several minutes of stifled yawns and declarations regarding the lateness of the hour and the fatiguing effect of travel, he made movements to rise from his seat.

I allowed him to precede me out of the dining car and, at the door, turned to allow several other passengers to enter or leave as they wished.

I rather thought he would be gone, so when I turned around to find his little round hand extended toward my face, proffering a visiting card, I started violently.

He did not seem to notice. "For when you come to see me in London," he said with a smile. I could think of nothing to say, and so took the card. He nodded at me in an affectionate manner and said, "God keep you, Mr. John Kemp!" Then he turned and rumbled down the wood-paneled corridor, waddling like a little duck encumbered by a sea of flowing white fabric, and rendered an eerie yellow every time he passed through the light streaming out of each succeeding compartment door.

Were all Papists quite mad? I asked myself. But I shook the thought away, dropped the card into my pocket without looking at it, and made my way toward my sleeping quarters.

I loathe berthing with other people above and below and to the side of me, and so make a habit of pampering myself with a private sleeping compartment when I am obliged to make long journeys by train. As the train portion of my trip would be followed by several days of travel by boat—which I despise for other reasons—I hoped to have at least one night of sound sleep.

I have always prided myself on my integrity as a sleeper. When I sleep, I sleep. I have never been bothered by the sorts of disorders that torture the nights of unhappy victims—neither afflicted by nightmares as a child nor by insomnia as a young man. While close friends confessed themselves kept awake by residual terrors drawn from the silly books they insisted upon reading, I could read anything with a healthily skeptical mind and sleep the sleep of the just upon closing the book. So I reopened the novel at the point I had left it and, wandering through an absurdly sinister castle with an overwrought young man named Jonathan Harker, soon fell deeply asleep.

My eyes opened into imperfect darkness. For a moment, I could not have said where I was. The shadows surrounding me were unfamiliar—this was not my bedroom. As my eyes adjusted, so too did my ears. Rhythms of mechanical regularity, so constant as to have been nearly forgotten, sounded suddenly deafening. A train. I was on a train. Memory returned, and I knew the sleeping compartment for what it was.

And yet, what was that strange sound? It was discomfortingly close to the berth where I lay—the noise of determined scavenging. Was it a mouse? No, it was too big for a mouse.

Now my mouth followed my eyes and ears—I tasted the odor of rotten eggs before my nose could fully detect it.

The train lurched into a new direction, throwing open the window shade to admit a deluge of moonlight. Now I could see it, eerily glowing in the new light, as if it were on a stage in a cheap, grotesque theatrical.

It was a figure in ragged, if not rotting, clothes. Its limbs were misshapen into unnatural length, so that it stooped into a crouch to complete its work. The hands, actively rummaging through my belongings, drew forth something light and delicate from my small attaché case. The brightness of the moon danced about the fingers and the hairy palms of the hands.

At my feeble noise of protest, the thing turned to stare at me. The moonlight, freak and eccentric, struck it anew, illuminating a horrific absence—a large, jagged hole through the thing's chest. I could not look long at this remnant of violence; my eyes were pitched to the face. It was so pale as to be nearly yellow, housing beetling black eyebrows furrowed down as if in a rage over a pair of perfectly blank pink eyes. The mouth was a streak of crimson, like you might see on a French clown. Now the lips parted, revealing shining, sharp, animal-like white teeth. Glistening fangs.

Bewilderment and terror paralyzed me. The thing moved toward me, and teeth, ever prominent, bent down over me.

Then I cried out and threw the first thing that came to hand—my billfold—toward its face. As it whirled through the air at my attacker, the billfold burst open in midair. Something flew out—something small and white, luminous in the darkness.

This secondary projectile hit it full in one of those pink eyes. The creature let out an unearthly shriek. There was a dazzling flash of whiteness, blinding me, shutting out that unholy sight.

The train lurched again and I fell back against my bunk, my head slamming violently against the outjutting wood of the shelf above me. For a moment I sat in stunned silence, rubbing my throbbing temple, then reason flooded back over me. The room was empty, though the door was partially open. I rose to close it and locked it—and checked the lock three times . . . and once more again.

It was a dream. It had all been a dream. I laughed aloud then; I must have awakened my comatose neighbor in the next-door compartment because he rolled over in his sleep and muttered an incoherent protest.

Then I glanced toward my bag and, after a moment's hesitation, leapt up to make my own search. Only one thing was missing—the lacy blue handkerchief Adele had given me as a love tribute. I must have lost it somewhere. Shaking my head a little, as if that could right it, I remembered my billfold. As I stooped to retrieve it, a little piece of white—too small to be mistaken for the missing handkerchief—on the ground caught my eye. For a moment I caught my breath then laughed at myself. Here was no discarded holy wafer, left by a careless young zealot to ward off evil spirits. Nor was it the remnant of the torn raiment of a besieged young maiden, fleeing a demon lover. It was merely the visiting card handed to me by the relentless little priest the evening previous. The card must have been ejected from my billfold when I flung it from me in my half-dreaming alarm, and was now lying patiently, but slightly crumpled, on the floor, waiting to be picked up.

I picked it up with some impatience; it reminded me of that strange interview, of the unwelcome interruption to my reading, and reminded me too of my dream. It was all nonsense and grotesque fairy stories to fright children and overly emotional young women. It was decidedly unsuitable reading for a mature young barrister. I decided to leave the Stoker novel behind me in the compartment. Perhaps the conductor would enjoy that sort of silliness. In any case, I must have forgotten Adele's handkerchief somewhere else. It was not really that important. She might be petulant at first, but would forgive me. Or not. It did not signify much.

It was not undue curiosity that made me look more closely at it, but rather the ingrained habit of examining something once I had willingly picked it up.

What I read made me blink my eyes rapidly to cast off the lingering and bewildering dream that was my own way of accounting for the absurdity of the thing. No, I was no longer sleeping, and there, in letters of unnatural (and rather unnecessarily bloody) redness, was displayed the name of

---

REV. THOMAS EDMUND GILROY, O.P., D.C.L.
Vampire Slayer

St. Dominic's Priory
London, NW5 4LB

Chapter 2

25 May 1900: London, the Inns of Court, Belgravia, and South Kensington

(From Jonathan Harker's diary) *I raised the lid, and laid it back against the wall; and then I saw something which filled my very soul with horror. There lay the Count, but looking as if his youth had been half renewed, for the white hair and moustache were changed to dark iron-gray; the cheeks were fuller, and the white skin seemed ruby-red underneath; the mouth was redder than ever, for on the lips were gouts of fresh blood . . .*

"Just a moment—let me clean that for you, Mr. Kemp, sir."

Francis Carstairs, my clerk, leapt from his stool (knocking over a pot of ink in the process) and feverishly attacked the swelling drift of red tea that I had absent-mindedly tipped across my desk.

I murmured an apology.

The weeks after my return to London were passing by swiftly. Business demands were heavy. Details regarding the Kilbronson case still demanded my attention. The man had married ill—very ill indeed—and now sought refuge in a divorce. That was the central theme of the case, but the surrounding details were convoluted and often contradictory. I questioned more than once the sanity of the man—what had possessed him to attach himself to that sensuous Hungarian in the first place? Lust was seemingly at play (this thought came somewhat primly to mind), and yet it hardly seemed in keeping with the thin, ascetic, Gladstone-like appearance of Edgar Kilbronson. The sensationalism of the case was all superficial, of course. The work was predominantly dull.

Truth be told, I did not mind dullness. I was sleeping ill, but attributed it mostly to the weather, which was principally defined by a heavy gloom. Even my chambers— of a restricted if not cramped size, but envied by many of my colleagues for their small but respectable window— were now rendered increasingly suffocating as each unsavory gust galumphed its way from the street into the professional prison where I and Carstairs were unhappily confined together.

I bent to examine my stained papers. Their matted confusion had been substantially worsened by Carstairs' ineffectual efforts. An hour's labor followed in rehabilitation. Briefs were clipped up along bookshelves, and letters hung stolidly in the solitary window—as if anything could dry in that torpid air.

At the very bottom of the soiled stack I discovered a discarded invitation to a ball at Fitzalan House, held that very evening. After a moment, I was decided upon it. Though my *répondez* was decidedly late, even a ball would be a welcome escape from my chambers, now a caricature of a washroom, with tea-soaked papers everywhere. I left Carstairs to manage as best he could. Really, I think he enjoyed the chaos. He certainly combated it more diligently than ever he addressed his regular work.

If it were at all a sign of selfishness in me to quit him so suddenly, I was soon punished. I hurried home to dress for the evening and, reemerging from my rooms suitably attired, my trousers were effectively splattered by mud and filth flung up by a passing carriage. An urchin in the street guffawed at my plight but dashed away speedily to avoid the vengeful tap of my cane.

Fitzalan House, ablaze with light and bustling activity, proffered me no improvement of fortune. My failure to inform my hostess that I would be in attendance was not accepted as lightly as I would have wished. Moreover, Adele was at the ball and was in rare form, teasing and pouting and rather tiresome. And with her blonde hair so decidedly overcurled—large and frizzy, a fashion I loathed.

"You naughty man," she said (a phrase stolen from a petty feminine novel, I had no doubt). "I am sure you didn't read the book I gave you."

"I haven't the time," I lied stubbornly and without apology.

A long pause followed before she attempted again.

"Lady Masten's soiree was *really* the party of the *Season*, Mr. Kemp; you *should* have been there ..."

I had been told so ten times and was becoming increasingly unconcerned at my loss with each passing second. I had never known Adele to be so confoundedly repetitive.

"Well," I said curtly. "I wasn't."

This seemed to put somewhat of a damper on our conversation.

A moment later, when a smart young lieutenant strode manfully across the room and asked Adele to dance, I watched her whirl off with scarcely a pang.

The ball was moderately well-attended, with throngs of London's second-brightest lights of the Season assembled—the brightest were taking advantage of the lateness of the date to rest at home under the guise of being otherwise engaged. Lovely young women, many of them armed with mothers, had begun to wax rather desperate as the weeks passed. The debutante hunger for matrimony was so strong it was almost tangible.

Still, it was a pleasant scene and well lit; the decorations were not oppressive, though there was an extraordinary amount of diaphanous green fabric draped throughout the room. The food was excellent. The wine was respectable enough.

Why I was out of humor, I could not have said. I had come to escape from my tea-drenched office and had slipped into a more insufferable prison. I was bored before the evening began. The surroundings were strangely obnoxious. The wide blue eyes of Adele suddenly seemed more vacant than luminous, and her bell-like laugh struck a strangely tinny note I had not discerned before. Something was awry, either with me or the world. I did not care to consider further to determine which, having an instinctive feeling that the results of a self-examination would not prove flattering.

The world was dull, the party was dull, and I was dull.

"Why, Kemp. You're back," said a well-cultured and ostentatiously indolent voice (oppressed with a slight, false accent, the affectation of the decadent Englishman who wishes he were foreign).

"So it would appear," I replied.

Charles Sidney's mouth twisted into a crooked smile— a smile known to make unsuspecting women swoon if it came upon them unawares. His evening clothes were an ill-advised shade of purple—violet, he would have called it. With disgust I noted smudges of rouge across his high cheekbones.

"Your travels have certainly left you a pleasant and friendly object."

"I have not been sleeping well of late."

"What on earth did you do to Miss Lawson? She looks positively irritable."

I grunted in response, and he continued—Sidney was well known to have carried on conversations for hours without outside assistance. I did not like the bounder. He was too meticulously dressed and wore sickening perfumes.

He continued his evaluation of Adele: "Not that it isn't an improvement. She always has that glazed look of well-crafted innocence. It would be intriguing to learn that she is capable of emotions other than docility and contentment. Lovely, of course. No one would deny that. But decidedly uninspiring." Then, with an arch look and a tone of mock penitence: "Oh, but I nearly forgot! You're an acknowledged admirer, aren't you?"

Once again it was born in upon me how much I disliked Sidney. He was far too much like a stock character—the satirical dandy—of one of those sickening romantic novels written by unfulfilled female writers of the present day. He had not always been such an obnoxious dandy. He'd been rather interesting when I first met him. Now he was just a gossipy old woman in absurd clothes.

I muttered something about "family friendships" and tried to look dismissive of any rumors of a romantic entanglement—it might be more accurate to call it "entrapment". At this point I did not honestly see how I could avoid marrying Adele if she were of a mind to the union, but that was no reason for me to be forced to admit to the situation—not to that self-satisfied popinjay.

"Changing the subject as you so obviously desire me to," Sidney continued urbanely, "and for the moment setting aside the question—if it is a question—of your romance with the fair Adele, have you met the tantalizing young American lady who has so explosively broken in on the pageantry of the Season? A Hellenic beauty, a dark and lusty goddess, with rapier wit and incapacitating charm—potent even when delivered in the snide, grating tones of her native tongue ..."

A rich, deep, though feminine, laugh broke out behind me.

"My dear Mr. Sidney," said the lady with both amusement and a faint colonial twang plainly audible in her voice, "you really are the most delightfully rude person I have ever met."

I turned toward her.

Was it the effect of Sidney upon me that I continued to feel as if I were caught in some strange new universe—one only possible in the most lurid terms of the popular novelist?

I have often remarked upon the propensity of novelists of the last fifty years (usually those desperate female writers I mentioned before) to describe their heroines in absurdly self-indulgent terms. Every heroine must be soul-shatteringly beautiful. Every first encounter must be a soul-thundering experience. Love—always achieved at first sight—is supposed to be earthshaking, the sight of the beloved causing the heart to stop or to leap or otherwise to gyrate with exceptional irregularity. The soul is mercilessly battered about in this way, the heart is positively disemboweled with overblown emotions, and even the world is rocked on its axis. All in all, romance has the same effect on man and on society as an overzealous anarchist with an endless supply of gunpowder. Love, it seems, acts upon the soul as Guy Fawkes would happily have acted upon the Houses of Parliament. (I had often observed that the effect of Adele upon me was in no way prone to this theatrical, psychosomatic destructiveness.)

Of course, this new encounter was not love. It would be silly to call it so. Only madmen, poets, and immature young women of the middle classes believe in such things as love at first sight. And yet when I saw that woman, my heart lurched in its frame; a strange giddiness filled my head as a host of new sensations flooded over me.

Slim and shapely, with clouds of rich dark hair framing a clear, bright face. Dark, deep, wide eyes, with a hint of green in them. An honest face. An expressive face.

"I am not averse to hearing myself praised," she continued, "but praise is thoroughly undermined when you use such terms."

"Most profuse apologies," he replied with a degree of obsequiousness, which I thought totally unnecessary. "I shall make obeisance to the gods of American speech and moreover throw myself upon your mercy."

"Oh," she said, laughing once again, "I don't object to that. Next to your melodic linguistic strains, we sound like consumptive livestock. But 'charm', which must be as hollow as your own gallantries—to that I do most heartily object!"

"Mercy, dear lady, mercy!" cried that perpetually theatrical ham, wafting more scent at us with each overdone gesture.

"I know that you all laugh at us behind our backs, and we accept it. We really do. In fact, we find it rather amusing. Have you ever heard one of your renowned British stage actors attempt to speak as an American? The result is hilariously absurd. Take, for an example, a book I happened upon a few days ago. The one American character spent his time going about saying the most ridiculous things that only one of your writers could possibly conceive. Out in the uncivilized wilds of the great West, you understand, a man would be shot for talking like such a buffoon."

"Once again, I throw myself on your mercy. As a peace offering, I proffer an introduction."

And so I found myself formally presented to Miss Esther Raveland, currently of Belgrave Square, under the patronage of a distant cousin—the relation was too distant and too convoluted for me to understand, much less describe articulately.

At this juncture, with many significant undulations of his eyebrows and murmured phrases of Lady-this and the Duchess-of-that, Sidney quitted us.

By this time I had perfectly regained my equilibrium. I knew well the proper conversational form for that particular moment.

Was she enjoying London?

She was.

Had she visited any of the parks?

She had.

I refused to descend to the level of commenting about the weather. So we stood in uncertain silence for several moments. All the while I was vaguely suspicious that she was laughing at my inability to guide the conversation in a more authoritative manner.

If so, I was not going to be baited.

"Well," I said lightly, "I hope you continue to enjoy your time here." Then with a careless smile, I excused myself rather abruptly and quickly crossed the room to speak with Dr. Grant—a stodgy, elderly physician who had been tormenting his patients for an obscene number of years. He was one of the people I usually endeavored to avoid at parties.

That evening I was deeply interested in all he had to say, even regarding the fainting spells of the youngest daughter of Lord and Lady Pendleton. I was fascinated by his comments on the adenoidal problems of the Honorable Philip Young.

It was a full ten minutes before I ventured a glance toward Miss Raveland.

She was being quietly charming to an aging, stately countess. I thought the younger woman appeared rather subdued.

But I hardened my heart. I had been abrupt and perhaps even rude, but I was not going to be trapped in an insincere flirtation just because the world felt like the plot of a penny dreadful. Perhaps someday ...

Then I heard Miss Raveland laugh—an untroubled, merry laugh—and I felt mildly foolish.

A moment later, Sidney was at my elbow again, glancing at my face and back to Miss Raveland with an irritatingly knowing glance. But he said nothing of her.

"You have not told me of your trip, my friend," he said. "But that is quite in keeping with your character. Whether you stayed dully and safely on the path of righteous business or whether you ventured out into the thrilling and intoxicating dangers of unknown darkness, you would still have that imperturbable and thoroughly British air about you."

I was nettled in spite of myself. "I was away on business, Sidney, damn it. I wasn't off tripping through opium dens and dank dens of iniquity."

"Nor would you have been," he said primly. "You wouldn't have known what to do with yourself in such exciting places."

"And you would, I'm sure."

"Quite thoroughly. I flatter myself I have plumbed the depths of sin as adequately as any self-respecting Paterian apostle."

As usual, I did not really know what he was talking about. I tried to change the subject.

When was the last time he was on the Continent?

He dismissed my attempt with a quick response—a month—then proffered a question of his own: Had I not been in Budapest?

I acknowledged a weekend spent in that city (a tedious weekend, focused upon court-related business with Kilbronson's discarded Hungarian wife—a lurid detail so decidedly out of the ordinary in my usually uneventful professional career).

"I do wish I had known of it before," lamented Sidney. "I might have recommended adventures for you." Then, when I did not respond beyond a careless shrug of the shoulders, he smiled broadly, mockingly. "Had you told me of your travels to Budapest, I might well have directed you to see wonders—"

In his enthusiasm, he began to gesticulate self-indulgently. People around us were beginning to notice. A few openly stared.

"Oh! Such wonders! Wonders that would make your spine tingle with excitement! Terrors that would overwhelm your mind and bring your very soul to bursting point!"

I saw an obvious spinster nod in our direction and whisper, giggling, to an older woman, dripping with diamonds and with a most disapproving facial expression.

As I stood there squirming, Sidney waxed eloquent of wonders that would teach me not to dismiss the fascinating depths of evil, the zenith of pleasure to be found in the arms of the occult, astrology, divination, alchemy, even dabbling in necromancy, the glories of the Black Mass— all the while enjoying my discomfort as much as he was thrilled to be the object of censorious fascination to society.

"The thrill of *das unheimliche* ... ," he was saying, "the bloody horrors of the ..."—he leaned close to my ear and hissed it—"*nosferatu!*"

"Damn it, Sidney," I said with annoyance, pushing him away.

My torturer made a great show of looking surprised. "I don't believe it!" he exclaimed. "So upright and forthright and downright an Englishman and ... he believes in *vampires?*"

I began to protest, but he went on.

"Ah, I see that you do, though you would rather not. My dear friend—"

"Sidney," I interrupted unceremoniously, "you are the most unmitigated and overdressed ass of my acquaintance."

I walked away rapidly, trying to ignore the ringing sound of his laughter, which followed so closely upon my back.

I left for home a few minutes later and greedily drank in the stale, horse-ridden, but free, air of the open street. This was real, this was safe, this was sane.

I hailed a cab and hurried home.

My head ached but I was determined to be businesslike and diligent. I entered my flat with a firm step; greeted Jenson, my valet; tossed my hat and coat carelessly on a chair for him to retrieve; loosened my cravat and threw it too into a corner; and seated myself at the desk in my small study, ready to bury myself in the stack of thoroughly uninteresting case papers—papers that were unstained by spilt tea and, thanks to Jenson's diligence, unencumbered by dust. I had stumbled across a copy of Browne's *Religio Medici* earlier in the day when I wandered into a bookshop near Charing Cross—I tossed it casually aside and wondered to myself what had possessed me to buy it in the first place.

My rooms were a place of great solace to me, especially in contradistinction to the closet-like containment of my legal chambers, which had seemed so much more unsupportable to me that day than usual. I lived in one of those tall row houses near South Kensington, a few streets from the bustle of shops and businesses that culminated in the gargantuan glory of Harrods. There were three rooms at my disposal—a large, comfortable sitting room with a fireplace, two sizeable windows that looked out upon the street, a small bedroom next door, the window of which opened onto the back of the house and looked out upon a small garden and the backside of a house that faced a parallel street, and a smaller room upstairs in which my man resided. The kitchen downstairs was also at his disposal. The lower level of the house bore another tenant—a retired Army colonel with whom I had scarcely ever spoken. I saw his cook sometimes, for she hovered watchfully about the stairs. Perhaps she and Jenson were friends of a sort.

Jenson was an odd figure in the pantheon of the valets of high society, owing to his singularly unprepossessing face and figure. Five feet tall with a hint of a stoop to his shoulders, he displayed a long nose, notably large ears, small, thin eyes under drooping lids, and a broad birthmark on his forehead (resembling the stain that would be left by a fistful of rich pudding thrown against a white wall). His hands were beautiful and finely crafted, like those of an exquisite marble sculpture.

He had come to me as an informal inheritance upon the death of an uncle with whom Jenson had traveled throughout Europe, India, and the Orient. Jenson was impeccable in his work and maintained a quiet contentment of demeanor, a piquant contrast to his hideous physiognomy. He was a figure as diametrically opposed to that of Sidney as a single race can conceivably be expected to produce.

That night he was in an uncharacteristically communicative mood.

"A good evening, sir?"

"Mm."

"You came home rather earlier than I expected."

"Mm."

He cleared his throat loudly (it was the one thing he seemed incapable of doing silently, leading me to wonder once or twice in the past whether the bones of his neck were properly aligned). "Miss Lawson is well, I hope, sir."

"Mm."

A lesser man would have been dissuaded from this conversational campaign by my dogged unintelligibility; but Jenson was not a lesser man.

"Would you like some of the port, sir?"

I accepted the offering, bade him good night in a tone that quashed (I hoped) further conversation, and stared fixedly at the papers in front of me.

For a time I sat there staring, though seeing nothing. I doggedly avoided thought of my day or the weeks previous. I avoided thought of Adele, avoided thought of Esther Raveland, and avoided thought of the repellent Sidney. My mind wandered.

But I could not sit still for long. Every page of the brief seemed to have a face imprinted on it—sometimes Adele, with strange paleness and preoccupation; at other times it was the face of Esther Raveland, with those unnervingly dark eyes; sometimes too there was another face, a smiling pink-faced priest . . .

But such thoughts I dismissed as nonsensical, the work of an overtaxed brain made feverish by the stress of travel. Soon I was back on my feet, wandering the room distractedly in pursuit of some other form of distraction. Had the light of the streetlamps been more inviting, I might even have ventured forth again in hope that the exertion might settle my mind, but I was comfortable and loathe to fetch shoes and hat once again.

I would not quit the comfort of home, but I was not yet tired enough for sleep. I needed something to drive all thoughts away.

There, by the bookcase, hidden from view by a stack of books I had moved myself—not with any deliberate purpose of concealing the book, of course—I thinly discerned the lurid colors of the Stoker book. I had not glanced into it since my return to London.

The words of Sidney came hauntingly back to me. Vampires, I thought derisively. What utter rubbish.

Reading might well provide the necessary diversion. Any sort of absurd Gothic tensions introduced by the novel could easily be dismissed. No prey to night terrors was I—I reminded myself of the fact once again. As if to prove the point, I took up the book with a satirical grimace and set to reading.

Chapter 3

26 May 1900: London, Mostly in Mayfair, with a Little Time by the Serpentine in Hyde Park

(From Jonathan Harker's diary) *I lay quiet, looking out from under my eyelashes in an agony of delightful anticipation. The fair girl advanced and bent over me till I could feel the movement of her breath upon me. Sweet it was in one sense, honey-sweet, and sent the same tingling through the nerves as her voice, but with a bitter underlying the sweet, a bitter offensiveness, as one smells in blood . . .*

The next day, which was a Saturday, I made a purely obligatory visit to Adele—and went most unwillingly.

The house had a tired look, as if it and not its inhabitants had been out marauding the night previous. I was tired too and could sympathize. I had sat up reading far too late.

Adele came to the drawing room when she was summoned, and looked strangely pale and listless to my eye. Last night's curls, so offensive to me in the splendor of the ballroom, now looked rather pathetic, like children endeavoring to appear cheerful when they would much rather weep alone in their nursery. Adele greeted me with limp sobriety. Her grandmother—with whom she lived, being an orphan—did not accompany her.

For a brief moment I was alarmed that this unexpectedly private interview, accompanied as it was by her blanched features and bright eyes, was a harbinger of an emotional scene that I could not very well avoid. The Mayfair setting was perfect too: the drawing room was decorated in blue and pink flowers, full to brim with lace stuffs, porcelain shepherdesses, and other knickknacks. It might have been a stage constructed for a matrimonial dialogue. But another moment allowed a closer look and dispelled all such concerns. Even the most unconscious male victim has a natural instinct for a pending nuptial crisis. This was not the face of a young lady about to provoke a proposal. Adele was unwell—perhaps overexerted or perhaps really ill.

The realization made me more tender than I had meant to be, though I was doggedly restrained even in my compassion. A brief indisposition would pass in time, and it could prove absolutely cataclysmic to be remembered for marked gentleness or concern. Sweetness today could be the doom of tomorrow.

She was indeed unwell. She looked it. She admitted as much. This was no pretense of feminine frailty.

She was rather pettish too and unflatteringly dismissive even of my qualified concern.

For a few minutes we engaged in uninspired small talk, then she unceremoniously broke through a prolonged moment of awkward silence (one of many) with: "I am going upstairs."

And she went, failing even to say goodbye as an afterthought. It may have been rude, but I was far too thankful to her for bringing the interview to an end to be in a position to criticize her manners.

I left the house without regret and stepped out of the front door with a sense of relief that was singularly lacking in gallantry.

It was a cold, crisp November day, with wisps of sunlight visible through the thick mantle of familiar clouds. The heaviness of the air had lessened overnight.

The streets bustled with business and activity. I weaved my way through a market, listening to the cries of shopkeepers and tradesmen, noting the occasional twang of a country accent. I passed a respectable-looking young man in tweeds who was endeavoring to steal his arm about the waist of a pretty girl who was plainly torn between her irritation over some small quibble and her own desire to give in to his affectionate caresses.

After some little while, I found myself walking along the Serpentine with a distracted air; though it was a Saturday and my office was closed, there was business that might be done, and if I were not set upon business, why not venture homeward? And yet I walked, thinking of everything and nothing, all the while pervaded by a feeling that there was something I could very nearly articulate to myself—but not quite.

This time I saw Esther Raveland before she spoke, and indeed before she saw me.

She was standing beneath a large, spindly-looking tree, quietly watching the ducks—predominantly mallards—and the geese endeavoring to negotiate the lake quietly in the midst of a teeming host of argumentative coots and moorhens. A graceful figure in a dark, trim, fashionable dress, topped with a fetching, black, wide-rimmed hat. A large swan rose from the multitude long enough to ascertain that the watchful lady had nothing edible to offer, then swam off with noble scorn to seek better-supplied spectators.

"Good afternoon, Miss Raveland."

She looked up and graced me with a polite smile. Another woman, recalling my bizarre behavior of the night before, would have flounced at me with a missish and offended air or pretended not to know me, forcing me into the awkward position of reminding her that we had met during the previous evening.

Esther Raveland did neither.

"They're lovely, aren't they?" she said, gesturing lightly toward the birds. "The ducks, I mean. Not the swans—they are too pompous and self-satisfied—and not the little ones, though they're entertaining in their horridness. Rather like people—greedy and choleric. Self-seeking, bloodthirsty, and ruthless."

It was a dark commentary on society and I said so.

She laughed at that. "I am no Darwinist, my friend. I am not even a pessimist. The birds often make me pensive, prompting rather melodramatic musings on the state of man in the modern age. But I do love to watch them."

"You are not a sentimentalist either?"

"No, I suppose not. But I am an avid reader of novels and perversely take delight in the happiness of home and hearth which a Dickens or a Trollope presents."

"Have you known much happiness of home and hearth?" I asked without thinking.

"No," she said simply, "I have not."

In the awkward silence that followed, my mind raced to find a safer avenue of conversation. "Have you read much, then?"

"Yes, indeed," she replied with amusement. "Occasionally books are brought by stagecoach to comfort us in our unsophisticated isolation—in the vast and vacant reaches of Manhattan."

At that, we began to argue on literary themes—chatting amiably and comfortably. For twenty minutes we stood together beside the lake. She was carrying some packages of books along with her dainty purse; I feared they might grow too heavy and so took them from her gallantly. This led to a detailed list of her purchases, a continuation of our previous literary conversation. Then, without consciously discussing the matter, we began to walk down one of the nearby paths. For over an hour we sat on a park bench addressing the finer points of political questions currently discussed in the papers. Sometime later, when we suddenly realized a mutual desire for tea, we ventured arm-in-arm (a lady who had endured so long a conversation must be in want of sustenance) into a nearby shop, daring the most elemental expectations of propriety in our continued impromptu tête-à-tête. I had a momentary qualm when I saw a dour lady of rank, armed with an unmarried daughter, eying us sharply, but Miss Raveland appeared quite untroubled by it, perhaps protected by her less rigorous American standards. She was not unmaidenly; on the contrary, she was a perfect personification of feminine virtue, but in the very confidence of her manner she was somehow free of the concerns that so clearly characterize the husband-hunting ranks of unmarried socialites. A man would as soon offend her with a dishonorable thought as he would do battle with an undefended tigress.

For a moment I thought of Adele and felt something like a guilty pang, but I was happy enough to dismiss a false sense of unmanly betrayal and attend to my charming companion.

When questioned, Miss Raveland spoke freely of her present home and her situation, dropping a host of first names carelessly (as a woman will), as if she assumed I would be able to follow the network of relationships thereby implied. She appeared to know everyone in New York and to be on a campaign to know everyone in London as well.

There were few details of her past or, really, herself: she was an orphan and an heiress, though from what source I could not entirely determine. She was old enough to be considered essentially a free woman in her own right, and rich enough for such liberty even if age were not on her side. She could not be more than four and twenty, I decided.

I had been so distracted by my calculations (which would prove, by the by, to fall short of the truth—Miss Raveland was, at the time, twenty-seven), that I fell a few seconds behind her in the conversation. Consequently I was surprised when she mentioned Sidney.

"Sidney?" I said (and with a touch of annoyance as I remembered his idiotic mockery the night before). "What about him?"

"He is a rather odd man," she said.

I laughed dryly at the understatement. "Odd? He's a conceited, pompous, dandified fool. An embarrassment to his fellow countrymen." (The freedom exhibited in this comment must not be held against me; it was symptomatic of our entire conversation, which would have horrified a well-trained chaperone by its amiable comfortableness.)

"Is he English, then?"

Now my laughter was derisive. "Unfortunately for England, yes, he is. He would like to be thought cosmopolitan but he was born and, I think, bred, in Yorkminster. He lives here in some strange house left him by his great-aunt or some other unlikely person. His father was some sort of wealthy merchant, and his mother was the daughter of somebody-or-other—the natural daughter, perhaps, considering the sort of man her son is."

"How well do you know him?" she asked.

"Not well at all," I admitted. "But I knew a fellow who was up with him at school. He was rather clever and impressed all the dons, but he had a habit of thinking himself even more clever than he really was. He joined up with a self-satisfied set, and they took to profligacy just to impress everyone else."

"What did he do after taking his degree?"

"I don't think he actually took his degree, you know. I think he stayed around long enough to tarnish the stones of scholarship by the association and then left to squander his riches."

"Is he very rich?"

Once again, I was forced to retreat. "I don't know, actually. He is wealthy enough to support his silly notions of dress and to buy his way into a number of clubs where he really isn't wanted. His house is supposedly a decadent monstrosity. He's under the thumb of half the money-lenders in town, I've no doubt."

"Is he well-traveled?"

"He claims to be and very likely is."

"What sort of man is he?"

"A sorry sort of excuse of a man. He's probably committed more sins than are recorded in the Newgate Calendar and is rather proud of them. He's usually popular with women—though why he would be, I couldn't say. He's ruined a few reputations and irritated husbands, but he's too puny and uninspired to achieve anything like original sin. Still he thinks he has attained the height of sophistication by dabbling in spiritualism."

She was silent and thoughtful, and I began to feel a little uncomfortable at my own warmth of expression. I was speaking quite emphatically—as if I were some sort of authority on the man's character, when really he was merely an unimportant though irritating fellow I sometimes encountered in society. And how was I to know whether she did not believe in the whole business as well—séances were rather popular in some circles.

I looked back at her, then laughed at myself. This sensible, blooming woman, playing with spirits in dark rooms? A foolish notion!

"Of course," I said by way of reparation, "I don't know him well. And he *is* invited a good many places. He wouldn't have been at Fitzalan House if he weren't relatively respectable."

She hummed meditatively.

I was about to ask her what interested her about Sidney, but she shook herself out of whatever thought had so possessed her, flashed a smile at me that turned my soul to water, and spoke brightly of theatrical topics. She was an avid theatrical aficionado, it seemed. She would even have ventured upon the stage herself, but it would have driven her relations quite mad with distress. She had made up for the lack of formal artistic experience by joining in amateur theatricals at the homes of friends upon many occasions.

"It was an abysmal failure," she admitted, laughing. "I could not act to save my life. I lack the skill and the patience and perhaps too the capacity of being silent long enough to learn any lines—or allow anyone else to deliver theirs!"

She went on to discuss all of the most recent happenings of the West End. Had I heard of the planned reappearance of Sir Henry Irving at the Lyceum Theatre?

I owned that I had not.

She was impressively well-informed on the topic: Irving, absent from the stage because of illness, was to return to perform in Sardou's *Robespierre* in just a very few months.

"You know," she remarked eagerly with a charming lapse into Americanism, "I would love to see it but not only because of Irving. I think the man I would really love to meet is Bram Stoker. You know—the author of *Dracula*."

Vampires again, I thought. So she did play with spirits. It was to be expected, of course, with the popularity of the book—but then, I had not thought it was so very popular when I had first picked it up (well, accepted it as an offering from Adele, anyway).

"I read it in three days," went on Miss Raveland. "I really could not put it down. Millicent"—that was the distant cousin with whom she was then living—"was quite unhappy about it and said it was quite disagreeable. She would have stopped me from reading it, I am sure, if she could have. She just followed me about for a few days and told me that it was unnatural and would probably corrupt my young mind." She laughed. "She really is a dear and, in truth, it was a ridiculous novel. It could not corrupt even the most innocent and unspoiled of girlish minds, and it certainly couldn't have an ill effect on someone as well versed as I am in the realms of the sensational. I pride myself that I have read everything from Radcliffe to Braddon, and Polydori and Shelley too."

She paused. "I must confess, though, I was frightened enough after reading it to sleep in Lydia's room." (Lydia, I was left to conjecture, was a young lady somehow under the supervision of the aforementioned Millicent, and probably therefore her daughter.) "She thought my pregnant terror was quite silly and even pretended to be a vampire to frighten me more, but I told her to read the book herself and see how well she liked it." She smiled broadly and her eyes sparkled mischievously. "She has been sleeping in my room ever since."

Here was a welcome relief. To be a connoisseur of the Gothic was not, I owned to myself, to be caught up in all of the nonsense of the spiritualists. For a moment I considered mentioning my own reading of the novel, but determined instead to smile with manly indulgence at this revelation of feminine timidity.

"Stoker is Irving's manager, you know," she continued. "Someone told me that the character of Count Dracula was really based upon Irving himself. I am not sure if it is entirely flattering to have your friend depict you as a vampire ..."

"It seems a gamble on which to *stake* your friendship," I said before I could stop myself.

She was startled, but laughed. A brief pause followed (during which the remembrance of my mad clerical companion of the train came upon me with uncomfortable vividness), then we launched safely into analysis of the vanities of the theatrical world.

Miss Raveland knew a great deal of the theatre, it seemed. Had she been an English young lady, it might have been deemed unwholesome, rather like her attachment to Gothic novels. But she was an American and rich, as has been noted, and consequently was forgiven many things by her indulgent hosts.

It was quite late in the afternoon when we parted at her door, exchanging a friendly good evening. I could see the face of a respectable older woman with well-groomed gray hair—Millicent, I supposed—peering with unabashed curiosity through one of the downstairs windows. After a few moments, a younger face—Lydia, I thought—appeared beside her.

As I was walking toward the street Miss Raveland called me back. "Perhaps," she said with a charming flush to her cheeks, "perhaps we might meet up again in the park sometime?"

It was an entirely inappropriate proposal, and thoroughly charming.

"Perhaps, indeed," I said with a smile.

She smiled in return and, bidding me once again to have a good evening, hurried into the house. On the step I remembered her books and turned back to hand them into the waiting arms of the maid. My last glimpse of Esther was her friendly interaction with that same maid, laughing and apologizing even as she showered the poor girl with hat, gloves, and all the sundry accoutrements that burden young ladies who venture out into the London street. I thought I heard too a rush of interrogating female voices. If there was timid concern in the elder voice (young ladies should not venture forth into the street and remain out in the company of young men without a chaperone), there was unconcealed interest in the younger. Miss Raveland—Esther—was, I felt sure, more than a match for both of them. Without a clear reason to support me, I was certain of seeing her again and before many days had passed. The world was a wonderful place, full of delights.

I returned to my rooms with a light heart and received the polite welcome of the ugly Jenson so warmly that he was left rather confused and—I flattered myself—even alarmed. I was glad of it; it was a fitting revenge for his uncharacteristic and ill-timed chattiness of the night before.

Amid the slew of uninteresting letters—invitations, reminders of business appointments, notices from clients— I found a note from Sidney, written on expensive parchment-like paper and sealed with purple wax, with the words "MOST URGENT!" inscribed in scarlet ink across its front. I smelled its odor before I found it, so saturated was it with the man's scent. Usually, the swirls of his distinctive script formed a suffocating filigree that was almost illegible; this abjuration to alarm and attention was uncharacteristically clear.

Nevertheless, I dismissed the urgency and tossed the note to the side. Sidney could wait until morning—or until the end of time, for all I cared.

That night I settled comfortably to sleep, the Stoker novel lying forgotten beside the cold fireplace. Before I closed my eyes I thought of Esther Raveland and smiled. A succeeding thought of Adele faded the smile somewhat, but I dismissed concern. For now, all was well and all was strangely pleasant. All things would resolve in time. I was not formally engaged to Adele, after all, and I would not become so if I could possibly avoid such a fate. If she were really ill, perhaps she would go off to the country to rest. While in that convalescent retirement, she would surely catch the eye of some stolid, upright, manly fellow, and be carried off to some manorial holding complete with a squad of servants, vast lands, and a bottomless bank account.

With this happy picture of Adele's matrimonial contentment (and my own subsequent release) still in mind, I drifted off.

I slept soundly until the clock struck three. Then I awoke and heard the chime and knew—though how could I know?—that this was the witching hour. Strange visions were upon me, of ghouls and blood-sucking fiends with blank pink eyes and hairy hands, of the bloated, satiated corpses of the undead, of dark, sultry women, their faces white and strangely menacing, and their lips scarlet red, dripping. I could not recall the dream that had been broken with the chiming of the clock, but felt sure that it had been important. The vague remembrance of a figure—a figure in white—teased at the borders of my mind but, try though I might, the form eluded me.

I lay, restless in my sleepless captivity, incapable of further rest until the dawn began to dance nervously about the fringes of the night sky. The sun rose to reveal a London transfixed with horror. The news had spread rapidly, waking the rich and the poor alike with the frenzied fascination that always accompanies the bloodiest of murders.

At a little after three o'clock Sunday morning, a wandering vagrant came upon the body of a man at the edge of Hyde Park, illuminated by a dimly lit streetlight—his face grotesquely contorted, his eyes lifeless, still staring upward with wild and illimitable terror. The grass was bathed in thick blood. Dear God—that smell.

The man's throat was torn open—as if by the claws of some ravenous beast—and the broken ends of his spine stuck up in uneven, jagged points, irresistible to the brutal gluttony of the rooks.

The man was Charles Sidney.

Chapter 4

28 May 1900: Hyde Park Police Station, the Inns of Court, and South Kensington Again

(From Dr. Seward's diary) *I presume that the sanguine temperament itself and the disturbing influence end in a mentally accomplished finish; a possibly dangerous man, probably dangerous if unselfish. In selfish men caution is as secure an armour for their foes as for themselves. What I think of on this point is, when self is the fixed point the centripetal force is balanced with the centrifugal; when duty, a cause, etc., is the fixed point, the latter force is paramount, and only accident of a series of accidents can balance it.*

"Your name again, sir?"

The young constable peering down at me over the desk at the front of the police station appeared to take a dim view of my character. The harsh cleanliness and orderliness of the station was a poignant rebuke to all but the most organized and law-abiding of citizens—and he was its harshest adornment, from his pointy chin to his annoyed gray eyes.

I identified myself for the third time.

"Hmph." He ruminated, tapping his pencil against the desk to punctuate the passage of thought, but appeared to like me no better on this third introduction. "Kemp. Mr. John Kemp."

I acknowledged this to be the case.

"And your business here is . . . ?"

I patiently explained—*again*—that I had come by appointment to speak with Inspector Harris regarding the investigation of the death of Charles Sidney.

"Hmph," said the young man with an affectation of a meditative manner. And tap, tap, tap again.

Moments passed, with the silence broken only by occasional tapping and the grunts of a filthy, drunken reprobate, strewn across a bench in the hall, indulged in stentorian slumbers. I was about to announce my intention of attempting a visit at another time, leaving Inspector Harris to sort out his own calendar and his own subordinates, when a door down the hallway opened and voices issued thence—the gruff, slightly bored voice of a man, and the unforgettable voice of a woman. The man and woman in question followed upon the heels of their respective voices.

"Good afternoon," I said to them both.

Esther Raveland greeted me with a smile, but her face was pale and her tone appropriately subdued to match the solemnity of the occasion and unwholesome setting for our meeting.

"I hope you are well," I said, trying to suppress the note of concern in my voice—it would be insufferable to expose any degree of tenderness to the constable's attentive, critical ear.

"I am. I am indeed," she replied. But her white face yet belied the brave assertion.

There was no mention of a possible meeting, but then it was hardly the place to schedule a romantic rendezvous, especially with the full force of official curiosity upon us.

I escorted her to the door and made a little gallantry of the office, then returned to face Inspector Harris, whom I had not, until that moment, really observed. He was not a tall man, but neither was he short. His hair was of a nondescript color, clipped short, and displayed in a well-regimented beard and mustache. I am sure his eyes were some color or other. I could never really tell. He was, in point of fact, one of the most unremarkable and unmemorable figures I had ever seen in my life.

That he had observed me was immediately apparent; when I turned around, he was staring back at me, his eyebrows raised, and his eyes and mouth perfectly expressionless. The next moment, I began to wonder if he had noticed me at all. He was looking down at a fly crawling around on the floor at our feet—gazing upon it in an abstracted manner, as if his mind were fixed on an abstruse point of philosophical inquiry.

"Inspector Harris?" I queried.

He glanced up from the fly then down again.

I explained my errand.

"Very good, sir. Peters!"

This last was, it seems, addressed to the constable. It was delivered, however, with so little emphasis and concern that I wondered the young man had been able to follow the inspector's shifting focus.

But follow he surely had. "Yes, sir?" he replied with a promptness that was somehow a condemnation of my person and habits.

"I want to speak with the doctor the moment he arrives."

Then, without changing his position or looking away from the fly, Inspector Harris addressed me once again.

"I appreciate you taking the time to come and see me, sir. If you might spare a moment for me in my office ..."

I followed him down the hallway, carefully avoiding contact with the sot—who was dreaming of a female named Nellie—and ever conscious of the disapproving gaze of Constable Peters boring into the back of my head.

The room was well suited to the man. It was rustic, rigid, and perfectly lacking in personality. A more nondescript assemblage of walls, window panes, wooden furniture, papers, and miscellaneous souvenirs of police business could not be imagined.

Inspector Harris settled into the chair behind his sturdy, unremarkable desk, sitting up so straight that I wondered if his coat had somehow been sewn of planks of wood. He picked up the envelope I had sent to him that morning from my office and, extracting its contents, examined my letter, quoting from it as he spoke as if reminding himself of the purpose of our interview.

"Now, sir," he began repetitively, "I do appreciate you coming to see me 'on a matter regarding the death of Charles Sidney'. I do indeed, sir. You have 'information which may prove of interest to the investigation'. Well, sir, I should be glad to hear of it. You are 'happy to help in any way'—we do appreciate the cooperation of the public, sir, especially when we can be sure that it is a mature public, a responsible public, not the sort of public that just wants to make something out of the tragedy, you know."

I said that I did, indeed, know.

"Now, sir, that 'letter written by Sidney on the night of his murder'—how did you come to figure it was a murder, sir? And the timing too?"

The eyes rose quickly from the paper.

I shrugged and murmured something about the news in the paper.

"Ah, yes, the papers." The eyes fell again. "And you would 'bring the letter here this afternoon'—have you it with you, sir?"

I handed over Sidney's note.

He raised his eyebrows and peered down at the purple wax seal and the scarlet inscription—"MOST URGENT!"—as if over a pair of invisible glasses, then squinted and held the envelope close to his nose.

Then he extracted the single piece of notepaper contained therein, unfolded it, and began to read the contents aloud. The note opened without greeting and proceeded into a series of seemingly unrelated statements:

You must find them all. Will you even understand it? I did not—fool that I am.

You. Victor Montrose. Adele Lawson. Kilbronson. TEG—but that is more foolishness.

The house in Bloomsbury? Unlikely.

You were in Budapest. You must have known.

I am mad with fear. Shall you believe now? Why do they haunt me? I do not know. Perhaps they will haunt you too—perhaps they already do. There is no way to escape.

Esther Raveland—beware.

I do not even know what I write, but I shall see you in the morning. We shall—we must talk then.

The page, I knew, was punctuated at the bottom by a strange, scribbled symbol in which were encircled the initials "GD".

Hearing it aloud confirmed my earliest reaction—the whole thing was the melodramatic product of a man in advanced state of drunkenness. Perhaps Sidney really had toyed with opium—it would have been in keeping, I supposed, with his general character. It was only the fact that the writer had been brutally murdered shortly after writing it that elevated the note to anything beyond an embarrassing display. A gentleman would have pretended never to have received, much less read, such a self-exposing screed.

Inspector Harris held the note gingerly for several more seconds. Then he pursed his lips, clicked his tongue, and set the note down upon his desk.

Silence reigned for several minutes, during which Inspector Harris examined the sharp left-hand corner of his desk with intense concentration.

When he finally spoke—softly, though gruffly—I was startled, as if he had suddenly shouted in my face. "Do you mind if I hold on to this, sir? Evidence of the state of mind of the victim, sir."

I told him he could keep it for as long as he liked. It had no meaning for me.

He glanced up at me, then returned to his resolute study of the desk corner.

Moments passed.

"You *did* recognize the names mentioned, sir?"

I acknowledged an acquaintance with Miss Lawson and Miss Raveland. Kilbronson was the name of one of my clients. Sidney should have had no knowledge of the relation between me and Kilbronson. He had certainly not received any such information from me. If Edgar Kilbronson had seen fit to disclose information regarding the case, that was his business.

"And that business was, sir ... ?"

"Personal to my client."

"Quite so, quite so."

The rest was quite beyond me.

Once again, he was silent.

"You *were* in Budapest recently, sir?"

I acknowledged my recent travels without entering into further detail. His manner was beginning to irritate me.

When that awkward pause followed yet again, I became rather frantic. As if instinctively knowing that the limit of my patience had been reached, Inspector Harris broke into my thoughts (which were waxing murderous): "Well, sir, knowing that it has no meaning for you, sir, I would still suggest a copy ..."

In the end I was forced out of sheer politeness to scribble down those bizarre phrases onto a scrap of paper and to enclose them in my billfold.

As I wrote the words, the strangeness of the murder suddenly came vividly upon me. I tried to shake it off, but found I was strangely reluctant to write down the names listed. It was quite absurd, of course, and probably had nothing whatsoever to do with Sidney's death. I had been overeager in my uprightness as a citizen when I conceived of the notion of handing it over to the authorities. Why shouldn't Sidney mention the two women in his note? He knew them as well as I did—perhaps better in the case of Miss Raveland.

Still I disliked my task intensely and hurried through it, like a boy eager to finish his lesson so he can escape from the confines of the schoolroom to the freedom of the outdoors.

I slipped the paper in my billfold, and as I held that object, I recalled the incident of the train—but that memory I dismissed as quickly as I could.

When I looked up, I found the eyes of Inspector Harris on me, but they removed themselves so quickly that I was again left wondering if his attention were a figment of my imagination. How could he have been watching me when he was so clearly fascinated with the symmetrical shadows cast through the mullions on his glazed window?

Someone knocked at the door. I jumped, though I tried to pretend I hadn't.

"In!" barked Harris.

A thin, pale, clean-shaven, tow-headed young man entered, followed by an even younger man, nervous and pimply, with a shock of unkempt orange hair. Both were attired in simple, gray suits, evocative of institutionalized professionalism. The older of the two was not unattractive, but his face appeared to be frozen into a bored frown—so pronounced that I even wondered if he were partially paralyzed.

The inspector introduced us briefly. "Dr. Martin Lewis is engaged on an investigation of the body of Mr. Charles Sidney. Mr. John Kemp is ... an interested party."

I didn't like the sound of that at all, but I still strove to look unconcerned.

"Well, Doctor?" The inspector seemed inclined to hear a report in my presence; when I rose and made a vague movement toward the door, he gestured me back into my seat.

"Deceased met his death through a violent and somewhat unorthodox attack." The doctor delivered the report in so clinical a tone he sounded half asleep.

"A throat torn into jagged points," I murmured, the horror washing back over me.

"In fact, sir," the dour mortician replied with a hint of enthusiasm brightening his dull eye, "the news reports were misleading. A broken neck is unlikely to present 'uneven, jagged points' as the vertebrae of the spine articulate by design. We have determined this through meticulous analysis. What then is our conclusion?" He turned unexpectedly to me and waited.

I blinked. "So ... it wasn't jagged," I ventured.

He was openly smiling now, as a teacher might indulgently beam upon a subintelligent student who, in his ignorance, has afforded the instructor with yet another opportunity to showcase his vast, specialized knowledge.

"Oh, yes, sir," he disagreed happily. "Indeed, yes, it was. How can this be possible? That is the question in your mind, I know. I have just told you something remarkable: it is not possible for the vertebrae to behave in that way, and yet, I say such was the case. How ... *how* ... is this so?"

I stared at him. A few awkward moments passed. Then he chuckled and said: "My dear sir, the answer is simple. It was *not* the vertebrae!"

"Not the vertebrae?" I replied, bewildered.

"Not the vertebrae," he repeated. "I've made a focused study of the situation and I have found that, if the attack included a severe, downward, crushing thrust by a blunt object through his left collarbone into the *base* of his neck ..." He illustrated in pantomime, using his nervous little assistant as his subject. "As I said, hitting the *base* of the neck with enough force, you might be fortunate enough to expose jagged ends of the aforementioned bone and furthermore the first rib ... which, technically, would be closer to being a chest wound than a neck wound."

Once again, he smiled at me, seemingly expecting a response.

"That sounds ... very plausible," I said lamely.

He frowned then, and his eyes glazed back over into dour dullness. He turned back to the inspector, his very form expressive of his despair as a Superior Mind doomed to exist among the Stupid and Unappreciative Herd. "Is that all, Inspector?"

The inspector nodded, and the doctor stomped out of the room, with his little assistant scrambling along after him.

I made my goodbyes promptly and left.

I ignored the glare of Constable Peters as I departed the station. I returned to my office and determinedly thought no more about the entire business. It was certainly no concern of mine. It was the concern of the police. I had done my duty and behaved much more graciously toward the dead man than our relationship warranted.

I threw myself into my work with a degree of focus that appeared to offend my clerk, Francis Carstairs.

My work for Edgar Kilbronson had a new interest. What Kilbronson could have had to do with the dandy Sidney I could not even begin to imagine. I reviewed the facts, which had thus far brought me to a complete impasse. The wife—Elisabetta—had disappeared. The husband's dour recalcitrance was a positive handicap. How could divorce proceedings go forward without further details? Everyone would assume that Elisabetta Kilbronson (née Vadas) had been unfaithful, but if Edgar Kilbronson refused to acknowledge his wife's infidelity, we could never proceed. An English court would privately sympathize with his plight, but was hardly likely to sever that imprudent union without proof of adultery.

It was, indeed, a gruesome topic to absorb the time of a respectable English barrister. At the same time, the renewed melodrama of the case was a happy respite from inescapable ponderings regarding the dramatic death of Sidney.

The morning passed quickly. That afternoon, however, the death of Sidney came once again to my notice, bringing with it a handful of strange and troubling thoughts.

At around tea time I received an official visit. I knew it was an official visit from the moment I heard the heavy and uncertain step on the stair that anticipated the arrival of a somewhat doddering but profoundly respectable old practitioner. Sparing half a thought to wonder if such demonstrations were exacerbated by a desire to give one's host plenty of time to compose himself and his rooms before actually crossing the threshold, I hurriedly bade Carstairs pull down a few scraggly sheets of tea-soaked paper that had been left hanging beside the window, stuffed unfinished correspondence into my desk, knocked a stack of books into great orderliness, and settled down at my desk with a few eminently respectable-looking papers as props to my pretense of well-organized professional diligence.

Carstairs made quite a business of meeting my visitor at the front door and returned to my own room, opening the door with a flourish and announcing, "Mr. Augustus Flossingdon to see you, sir. Are you free?"

I cursed Carstairs under my breath—he really was the most obnoxious little object—and rose to receive my guest who was, as I had predicted to myself, an elderly legal figure with all the respectability of our trade stamped upon his visage, his hair stealing out wispy and white from under his thoroughly respectable hat.

"Mr. Augustus Flossingdon," said the aged practitioner. "Yes, yes." And he shook my hand.

By way of welcome, I bade him a good afternoon.

"What's that?" he said irritably. "What's that you say?"

I repeated myself.

"Confound the boy!" remarked my guest to himself (at a volume that was readily audible to passersby in the street). "Whispering!"

"Good afternoon!" I roared.

"Now then, sir," he replied with an air of slight offense, "there's no need to shout. There's really no need to shout."

With a feeling of foreboding, I gestured him toward a chair. He seated himself, smoothed his thin, ghostly hair across his forehead, and shifted his limbs, rattling them about as if to resettle his bones into a more comfortable arrangement. I waited in patient silence, hoping that an attentive look would suffice in inspiring him to deliver his message.

"I am here on behalf of my client," said Mr. Flossingdon, "the late Charles Sidney. Mr. Charles Sidney, now deceased. Yes, indeed. Mr. Charles Sidney, who died upon the *sixth inst.*, as it were."

Then, with a rapidity of which I had not imagined him capable, he held forth on the point that had brought him to my door: it seemed that Charles Sidney (repeatedly clarified as the late, now deceased, who died upon the *sixth inst.*) had made the unlikely selection of me as the legal executor of his estate. All relevant documents would be open to my perusal if I would but inform my respected counterpart (Mr. Flossingdon indicated himself) of the date upon which I intended to visit the home of Mr. Sidney (the late, now deceased, etc.) and look through the documents.

"Tomorrow morning would suit my schedule," I said politely.

"What's that?"

"TOMORROW?" I bellowed.

"What an impetuous young man!" he cried to himself. "Very well. Very well. Tomorrow morning at eight. At the house of Mr. Sidney. The late Mr. Sidney ..." He trailed off in a musing etcetera.

Then, gathering up his scattered bones and rising with the respectable air of an aged legal practitioner standing in preparation to depart, Mr. Flossingdon extended his hand, shook mine with bone-crushing emphasis, and left me.

I was somewhat meditative after his departure, reminiscing in the most unexpected manner about a man whom I had rather distinctly disliked. A memory stirred in my mind, taking me back to my first meeting with Sidney, some years earlier.

I had just come down with my degree and was studying to take the bar. A green, unsophisticated young man with a rigid sense of decorum, a puritanical air left over from childhood anxieties that my father's preaching of hellfire was directed solely toward me (which even thoughts of his kindly, shortsighted face could not dispel), a patent anxiety that I would fail to appear sufficiently professional, and a secret awe at my surroundings that I would have been loathe to admit to anyone. An elderly matron of a most severe breed invited me to a musical evening at her home. She described herself as an old friend of my mother's, but I rather thought she meant my grandmother's. They both came from a long line of rigid matriarchs who had each had conventions driven into them by devoted though unfeeling mothers, stretching all the way back (I suspected) to a prim woman who had read *Don Juan* as a girl and never recovered from the experience.

"How *is* your dear mother?" asked my matriarch of matriarchal hostesses.

I was just considering whether it would be more appropriate to say that she was quite well or to admit that she had been dead for three years—I presumed she was quite well in any case and my father's staunch Calvinism would admit of no other possibility—I was just considering it, as I said, when I was spared the onerous task of response by the entrance of a most extraordinary figure: Charles Sidney, resplendent in velvet, jeweled necklaces, and multicolored ribbons, with silver buckles on his shoes.

The young woman next to him looked to my eye rather sinful, but it soon appeared that she was merely a singer and not even remotely connected with the stage.

And when she sang, I nearly wept at the sound. At the sound of that brilliant voice, trembling with passion and tripping blithely over French and Italian love songs, my soul expanded, and emotional vistas opened up to my uninitiated heart. I almost trembled with exhilaration. (In retrospect I thought I had made rather an ass of myself, but no one had noticed, save Sidney.)

Charles Sidney was sitting close beside me, to all appearances as closely engaged in listening to the performance as was I.

At the end of the evening, when I gathered my hat and my gloves and readied to depart for my lowly rooms, he appeared at my elbow.

"Now, my friend," he said, doffing his own lavender gloves, rich with scent, "come along, for the evening is not finished."

And I went, stifling my feelings of transgression even as I accompanied him and his musical companion (whose name was Stella) to a small, densely packed café near Soho. I expected to see sin in innumerable manifestations, but instead I encountered color and excitement, scenes and odors, rackets and music far beyond my experience.

For some weeks I spent my evenings with Sidney, listening, watching, and wondering. My religious convictions became increasingly conflicted. Sometimes Sidney would speak for hours on end; other times he would sit in silence or with his eyes closed, drinking in our surroundings. (Or perhaps he was asleep, my more mature mind suggested.) The girl Stella disappeared. Sometimes there were others, but none of them strikingly wicked.

One night, after a horrendous, bastardized Shakespearean performance came to an end, Sidney seemed preoccupied. Some dilettantes around us openly lamented the wretchedness of the performance, but Sidney turned to me and said: "There was something essentially human in its miserableness, don't you think?"

I lied and agreed with him rather than appear aesthetically stupid.

As we walked together in the street, Sidney began to wax eloquent on that theme—the wretchedness of man—and to pass from it to something that I found vaguely, inexplicably disturbing—the greatness of a few, mixed in with a whole lot of nonsense about powers and circles and mystical bindings.

Then he grew irritable. "You're not listening! You're standing there with that stupid, dullard look on your face, and you're not listening!"

I turned on my heel and left him in the street, my face pink with mortification.

Two weeks later I passed the bar.

Sidney never invited me again and I never invited myself. Neither of us ever mentioned that evening or even indicated that for some weeks we had spent a great deal of time in each other's company. Sometimes when I saw him he would seem to be more extraordinary than ever—sometimes brooding, sometimes full of teasing good humor as he had been that night at Fitzalan House. Thus I more than once wondered if he took opium. But over-all I had been busy with work and far more occupied with the comforting realities of divorce cases, wills, and miscellaneous little legal problems. There were no more daring ventures down dark streets, no more music. I was no artist, and the temperament was far beyond me. I was made of that same stuff that had produced armies of unemotional, undramatic Englishmen.

Shortly after I had fully grown out of any Evangelical fervor to which I had previously remained faithful out of loyalty and fear toward my father. When he died—how odd it was that Charles Sidney had come to the funeral, and how clearly I recalled how glad I was of it!—all the desperate energy of religion just melted away. It was not profligacy that destroyed my faith; it was reality. I was no dreamer, just as I was no artist.

And now Sidney, the strange and colorful dreamer, was dead.

The memory passed, and I found myself standing beside my inadequate window and looking down at the street, my eyes focusing on a figure leaning beside the unlit lamppost. He had been standing there for some time, I thought—I must have marked his presence there unconsciously before my eyes cleared.

As I watched, another man came up to speak with the first man—and with a start I recognized him. It was Constable Peters.

Was it my imagination or were they looking up at my window? Was I—what an absurd notion!—was I a suspect in the investigation into Sidney's murder?

Let them watch. They would discover nothing. There were no mysteries in my life.

What motive could they imagine? I asked myself somewhat irritably. That I murdered him for the privilege of being his legal executor? Perhaps I was a legatee—the thought provoked a wry smile.

In any case, it was late and I should return home. Business could wait until the morning.

That evening I found it impossible to relax. I even tried to read a chapter of the Stoker novel, thinking it might bring some relief and distraction, but my mind would wander back to that other—that real—tragedy. I was irritable and restless. There was blood on every page, turning my stomach with the recurring thought of Sidney's bloody carcass.

Finally, worn out with fruitless wondering and discontented flipping of pages, I climbed into bed and tumbled immediately and deeply into sleep.

It is an eerie, moonless night. Restless and preoccupied I wander through the heavy darkness of the park—Regents Park? Hyde Park? Where am I? I pass down one pathway, then another. Noises crowd in around me—the bushes crowd in too, as if they grow with abnormal, with horrifying speed. Who keeps these grounds?

Dear God! What a cry! And at my elbow.

I turn, and the world turns with me.

The bushes, the trees, the path have all vanished. I am alone upon the moonlit heath—no, not alone.

A dark creature in a black cloak huddles on the grass before me—huddles over a fallen figure. A figure dressed in velvet and bright, shiny silver buckles on its shoes.

The grass tangles desperately with a stream of ribbons—grass and ribbons soaked together with blood.

Charles Sidney. Blood at his throat. Blood everywhere.

The creature looks up. Eyes pink and staring, and dry, yellowing skin dyed in scarlet.

I open my mouth to scream, but the blood is there too, clogging my throat, choking the voice, the very life out of me.

"What a bloody mess!" chuckles a cheery voice at my elbow.

I turn again, and the face of Father Thomas Edmund Gilroy looms out of the darkness at me, smiling benevolently.

"Beware of the putty part!" he adds with an affectionate whisper. "It is all nonsense, you know."

I awoke shivering.

Chapter 5

29 May 1900: Primarily Belgravia, and Briefly the Inns of Court and South Kensington

(From Jonathan Harker's diary) *In the library I found, to my great delight, a vast number of English books.... The books were of the most varied kind—history, geography, politics, political economy, botany, geology, law—all relating to England and English life and customs and manners. There were even such books of reference as the London Directory, the "Red" and "Blue" books, Whitaker's Almanac, the Army and Navy Lists, and—it somehow gladdened my heart to see it—the Law List.*

I arrived early at Charles Sidney's house the following morning. My legal friend of the preceding evening was nowhere to be seen. This was not a black mark against the prestigious record of Mr. Augustus Flossingdon—I was nearly three quarters of an hour too early to be categorized as prompt. I determined to wait for him to arrive before I ventured down the drive and into the house. It was an unseasonably frigid morning and uncomfortably damp but somehow I felt reluctant to pass through the gates before it was absolutely necessary. For a few minutes I paced, my hands in my pockets to keep the chill off, looking at the houses that lined the other side of the street, and largely ignoring the outer walls of the Sidney grounds that loomed at my side.

Then movement caught my eye—a police constable standing with an affectation of carelessness by the entrance to the drive. Well now, I could imagine him saying to himself. What's this fellow up to, lurking about the house of the murdered man? Don't let him see you mark him— these sorts of fellows incriminate themselves by their suspicious behavior. Let him hang himself with his own rope.

If the constable were indeed pretending not to notice me, he was doing a marvelous job of it. In any case, I thought to myself, it was cold and I should simply make my way into the house and begin my work. The sooner I began, the sooner I would be free to return to my chambers and concentrate on other things.

"Good morning, Constable," I said in what I hoped was a confident tone thoroughly undeserving of official police suspicion.

"Good morning to you, sir," he replied and nodded amiably.

I introduced myself. "I am to meet Mr. Augustus Flossingdon here to look over some of the legal papers of the deceased ... of Mr. Charles Sidney."

I unconsciously drew a few of my own papers out of my briefcase and held them out, as if a few legal documents would furnish the necessary proof of my identity and of my thoroughly respectable motives in loitering there.

"That's quite all right, sir," said the constable. "We've had word you would be coming by this morning."

So I was spoken of by the police. Was this a cause for concern? I thought not. I nodded my thanks to the constable and, as he unlocked the gate and moved back for me to pass through, stepped over into the drive and made my way toward the house.

It was a large, heavily Gothicized residence in Bloomsbury that had come to him through some family inheritance. I had never been inside, but had heard of the gross decadence of the interior from a passing acquaintance at my club.

"All plush and perfume," he scoffed, choking on the memory and on the cigar in his mouth. "Strange-looking flowers and pottery and curtains and hideous paintings. The house is as cluttered as an old maid's."

Another man—who was known to have artistic tastes but in a decent rate of moderation: "Sidney has taken upon himself the role of a libidinous aesthete. He's quite a collector of the bizarre. I've even heard there is a chapel in the cellar—a monstrous, dark, gold-encrusted closet, with Popish paraphernalia scattered about."

"I don't know about any bead-mumbling chapel," returned the first man (in a rather irritated tone, as he had been setting himself up as a Sidney authority), "but the place is damn disturbing. So's the man."

As I made my way down toward the house, I wondered about the chapel.

The house was set back from the road some fifty yards and segregated by a tall stone wall, for which a line of unfriendly fir trees had been added as an almost impenetrable second. I say "almost" because the house could be clearly seen through a gap between two of the trees. To realize the full potentiality of this gap, one would have had to twist one's body over the wall and stick one's head through the branches—a singularly undignified position I had been unwilling to assume, especially with the constable standing there watching.

74

Walking down the drive, I noted the trees and bushes, surprisingly well-tended foliage. My eye fell on one large tree, which might well prove floral in a past springtime but would never flower more: its twisted, knobbed grandeur was now wizened and dead, black, and with its trunk twisted and split open like the ravaged body of Charles Sidney, as if the tree had been struck down by the sort of Divine smiting power my father had often described. A recent act of Providential destruction it seemed—there were still pieces of charred black bark and branches scattered beneath the blighted giant.

"'Twas a bolt of lightnin' wot done it," said a grizzled voice at my elbow.

I swallowed my heart, which had leapt to my throat at the unexpected sound, and hoped that my own voice was untroubled when I replied to the man: "Lightning?"

The man—the groundskeeper by the look of him, though how Sidney could have afforded staff I could not imagine—nodded with sage importance, perhaps rehearsing for an interview with representatives of the press.

"Happen' the same night as was that Mr. Charles died ...," he went on.

I was silent.

After a few moments and another sober nod, he tilted his head toward the house. "I'll take you to Mrs. Mallery, sir."

Inside the house was dimly lit by the meager sunlight that streamed through the windows—multicolored light, I noticed. Sidney had been fond of stained glass. The entrance hall rather had the look of an elaborately decorated church on the Continent—perhaps this is what had begun the rumors of a private chapel.

Mrs. Mallery, an elderly woman in black, her eyes small and red, met me kindly. "Good morning. I shall show you to Mr. Charles' library, sir. Mr. Flossingdon left you some papers there in case you arrived before him."

As I followed her, I curiously noted my surroundings: lovely wood paneling; painted molding along the tops of the walls; faded tapestries draped between large, colorful paintings, some of a pre-Raphaelite tint while others were stark and garishly stylized sketches; exotic vases; strange carvings and statues; a thin, flat-faced Madonna with the paint chipping from her nose but her lips still vibrant, rubious; a faint air of cobwebs all around, but no such signs of negligible housework were visible. But it was not as splendid as I had come to expect. Not as bedecked and burdened and cluttered. In many ways, the house felt spare and empty. Perhaps Sidney had been forced to sell many of his richest belongings. Perhaps his finances were indeed in the wretched state that I had sometimes imagined.

The library rather disappointed me. It was neat, tidy, well stocked with books, but not as dramatic and colorful a place as I had anticipated. In fact, it looked rather stodgy, with an uninspiring rug on the floor, the books all neatly arranged, and Sidney's desk at its center. The desk was likewise not at all what I had expected. It was meticulously neat. Mrs. Mallery did her work well. Notes on one side of the desk—once again, oddly not in the condition I had expected in Charles Sidney. The scarlet ink was there, but I had expected rambling notes, scarlet scribbling scattered all over the place in wild confusion, signs of a desperate man. But there was nothing here of desperation, no sign of an awareness of his approaching doom. Beneath the record of "Sunday tea, Lady N——'s", I found a few playbills and a small flyer announcing the pending performance of a Swedish soprano. The letter to me must have been an anomaly. Or a forgery. But it was in Charles Sidney's hand.

He must have been killed by a madman. He had an eccentric taste in decoration, certainly, but there was no mark of anything worse here. This was the house of a collector, an aesthete. Nothing more. If the man had been dangerously vicious, he had concealed it methodically. I wondered if his necklaces and ribbons were as tidily stored in the upper rooms of the house.

The papers left for me by Flossingdon were carefully stacked, with the will at the top, followed by the deed to the house and miscellaneous other dull legal documents. It all appeared to be in good order. The property passed to a distant relation—an elderly cousin in Glasgow. A few small bequests were listed, including little gifts for Mrs. Mallery and for Mr. Josiah Hopplethwait (my groundskeeper friend). Then came the following surprising note:

To my dear friend John Kemp, I leave my ornamental peacock box and its contents.

A peacock box. As if it had suddenly appeared, like something out of *Alice in Wonderland*, the box caught my eye. How could I have missed it, sitting there on the small table by the door, a distinctly vibrant object in comparison to this regimented, uncharacteristic room? The box was certainly Sidney's, even if this room seemed to belong to someone else.

I walked over and gazed down upon my inheritance.

It was of middle size, painted with gold and illuminated with purple and turquoise peacocks in an elaborate, even dizzying pattern of orientalized beauty. I should not open it, I reasoned, until Flossingdon arrived. But, Pandora-like, I could not resist the lure of "and its contents". I carefully raised the lid and looked down: a book (Sabine

Baring-Gould's *The Book of Were-Wolves*), a cross, and one scarlet ribbon tied in a bow around a lock of dark, rich hair.

After the book (the title of which rather embarrassed me), the cross caught my attention. It was small and elaborately designed, made up of a myriad of multicolored tiles arranged in careful patterns, and inscribed with a host of strange symbols and ciphers, some of which were letters I thought I recognized as Hebrew. Squares, green rays, pentagrams—a thing of striking brilliance and enigmatic complexity. Yes, this box and its contents were surely the property of Charles Sidney—the late Charles Sidney.

"Yes," said my visitor of the day before. "That is your legacy, young man."

I shut the box hurriedly and moved back toward the desk with Flossingdon. I tried not to wonder how long he had been standing there watching me.

I wondered too if he had been called "Flossie" in school. With flaxen, limp, airy hair like that, a nickname was inevitable. I did not dare call him "Flossie", of course. Not even in my mind.

"Come now, my boy," he said, "if you've quite finished playing with that pretty box, we can begin our work."

For some hours we delved together into the papers of Charles Sidney, going over them so methodically and painstakingly that the world seemed a well-regimented legal concern and every mystery the result of undisciplined, imaginative persons whose illusory confusions were easily soluble by the professional mind. Even the violent death of Sidney began to seem like a secondary or even a tertiary concern. That was not business. Probate was a far more pressing matter than murder.

Sidney's finances were not in as wretched a state as I had begun to anticipate. He was not a gambler, it seemed.

There were a few debts that had been effectively canceled by his death (though Mr. Flossingdon and I deemed it appropriate to satisfy the debts, which, being small and concerned with local tradesmen, were therefore moderately respectable). The residual estate was not grossly affluent but it was sufficient. In fact it appeared that Sidney had proved an able and a discriminating manager of his inherited wealth. If he had done nothing to increase it, he had certainly done nothing to damage it inalterably.

The house and grounds were a large consideration. It was left to the Glasgow relative along with the majority of his estate. She would be unlikely to want to keep it or to live in it.

I did not much care what the fate of the house would be, so long as I could somehow gain an opportunity to explore it more fully. Indeed, it was only the fear of appearing completely unprofessional (what interest could the house have for a respectable barrister, executor or not?) that kept me from requesting a tour outright or, even better, announcing my intention of looking around on my own.

I do not know if I expected to see obscene paintings or the skeletons of discarded dancehall girls—or, worse, their living forms imprisoned in dark, sinister chambers—but there was no sign of those sorts of things in the rooms I had barely glimpsed as we walked toward the library. No sign of a chapel either, beyond those colored windows in the hall. But there must be more to the house than what I had seen—more of Sidney than decorations, and more than that single peacock box. Perhaps there had been a chapel once. Perhaps the rumor of the basement was correct. I wondered what the Papists did when their chapels were destroyed or redecorated.

Meanwhile Flossingdon continued to forge ahead with the business at hand. We would speak to the other legatees at our convenience. Mrs. Mallery and Mr. Josiah Hopplethwait could be dealt with immediately. As to the doorman at the Lyceum Theatre (to whom a twenty-pound note was left) and the miscellaneous friends and enemies to whom various items were left (including a silver pen and an antique brace of pistols left to Edgar Kilbronson and a painting by an artist whose name I did not recognize left, along with a ruby ring, to a Mr. Victor Montrose)—these could all be dealt with either in person or by letter.

The house would be let or sold. We must determine the most appropriate options for Mrs. Agnes Puttock (the Glasgow relative) so that we would be able to facilitate her preferences in this matter.

"Advertise?" queried Flossingdon tremulously, as if I had suggested that avenue. "I do not think that advertising would be quite proper or even effective. There has been some notoriety in connection with Mr. Sidney's death, I believe."

Some notoriety. That was one way of putting it. Had he noticed the police guard stationed outside the gate? Did he too wonder who had done that vicious and horrific deed? Did he fear that he might be a police suspect as well?

No, such things required imagination, and Mr. Augustus Flossingdon was singularly lacking in that faculty. With a wry humor that was quite unlike myself I wondered if the smell of cobwebs was from my companion rather than from the house.

In the end we arranged it among ourselves that the Glasgow relation would be properly notified and, if she so desired it, discrete steps would be taken to hand over the house to a respectable realtor—a fellow sufferer of the contagion of respectability of which Flossingdon was so strong a carrier—in hopes of finding a modest, respectable lessee or purchaser.

The box I would take with me. Flossingdon insisted. In any case it would spare me the trouble of returning to the house to fetch it.

"Perhaps ... yes, it *is* rather noticeable. Rather conspicuous you even might say. Perhaps ... perhaps it would be better ... some degree of concealment might be discreet ... Why, yes, thank you, Mrs. Mallery. Always so thoughtful. Such a kind woman."

That afternoon I returned to details of the Kilbronson case but once again found it all as obnoxious and absurd as a French novel. I made little progress with my papers that day. All the while thoughts of Sidney's house seemed to plague me. I frequently caught myself wondering if I had been too anxious—if I should have requested to see the rest of the house and chanced Flossingdon's odd look or Mrs. Mallery's suspicious glance. To have known what was concealed in the upper rooms would have been reward enough. Anything was better than wondering in a highly sensationalized manner whether there were dark, sinister secrets—my vocabulary of the fantastic was too limited to imagine anything more definite—left unknown and undiscovered. Perhaps even Mrs. Mallery did not know of them. Perhaps Charles Sidney had locked his secret upper rooms and carried the key about on his person.

Perhaps perhaps perhaps.

Perhaps I would never accomplish a satisfying afternoon of work again in my life.

On my way home, I thought I saw Esther Raveland walking along the Strand and quickened my pace to join her. Once I was within a few feet of her, I called her name.

She was visibly startled.

I felt suddenly presumptuous and awkward, but went on doggedly.

Was she quite well?

She was indeed.

Had she recovered from the ordeal of her recent visit to Inspector Harris?

The allusion to the police official was apparently unwise. She turned pale. I wondered if she, like Adele, might be ill. "Yes, yes. It was no ordeal, really. Indeed, I do beg your pardon, but I must leave you. I have ... Millicent is expecting me."

And, with a brief nod of farewell, she hurried off with a deliberate step that did not brook the possibility of being followed. As she walked an impertinent gust of wind reached in under her hat and pulled loose a single dark lock of hair. I remembered the lock of hair left as part of my legacy and felt irritable—and even foolish, though I could not have explained why. I found too that I was relieved that I had not had the opportunity to speak to her of Charles Sidney. It had been an unprofessional impulse in any case, especially in the light of her unwillingness to converse. I shifted the package under my arm—Sidney's box, still cloaked in black cloth. I wished I had left it at my legal chambers. I would stow it somewhere in my rooms where I would not see it and remember Sidney. Would it be disrespectful to the dead to sell it? I wondered.

That night I was strangely reluctant to go to bed, but I defied this foolish neurosis and went about my evening routine as usual.

"I was so sorry to hear of Miss Lawson's illness," said Jenson as I lingered over my glass.

So Adele was still unwell. I felt some twinges of conscience, but could surely remedy my ungallant neglect in the coming days.

When I finally reclined upon my bed, I was unconcerned. It had been a busy day and tiring. For all my incredible wonderings regarding Sidney's house, it had been a comfortingly mundane day. Even with the disturbing patterns of poor rest that characterized my nights of late, sleep was ever my ready friend.

My immediate descent into a dark dreamlessness seemed to confirm this friendship.

I am once again in the park. Hyde Park. Yes, indeed, it is Hyde Park. Along that same path ... then another ... then another.

The trees and bushes pressing in densely upon me. That cry—

I am on the heath once more. The heath. Hampstead Heath? Of course. I am not in Hyde Park. Or am I?

The creature bends over its victim.

The blood. The blood. The blood. Before my eyes, soaking the grass, the velvet, and the tangled ribbons, and rising in my stomach, into my throat. Sparkling shoe buckles. So out of place. So bright.

The creature turns toward me ...

This time, though the scream once again sticks in my throat, I lunge away bodily, leaping out of dream even as I would have leapt away from that horrifying sight—

Esther Raveland, her dark hair lustrous and rich about her face, a single lock of it stark with the mark of a recent cutting; her mouth dripping with the blood of Charles

Sidney, and lingering pieces of his neck's flesh flecking her cheek, her sharp, white teeth shining like the shoe buckles, brilliant as stars in the midst of the darkness.

I did not sleep again after that and rose from my bed with the sun, miserable and sick.

Chapter 6

30 May 1900: South Kensington, the Inns of Court, and South Kensington Again

(From Mina Murray Harker's journal) *When I got almost to the top I could see the seat and the white figure, for I was now close enough to distinguish it even through the spells of shadow. There was undoubtedly something, long and black, bending over the half-reclining white figure. I called in fright, "Lucy! Lucy!" and something raised a head, and from where I was I could see a white face and red, gleaming eyes.*

After that night I was too indisposed to go to my chambers—feverish and plagued with what appeared to be a mild case of influenza. The doctor, summoned by Jenson, assured me that there was nothing to worry about. I simply needed a little bit of sleep and rest and would soon be myself again.

And it seemed that his prognosis would prove quite correct; I woke the following morning after an uneventful, dreamless night and felt eager to be at work once more. I was not fully rested, and the illness of the previous day had left me sore and without an appetite (in which latter condition Jenson was irritatingly unsympathetic, plying me with food as if my life depended upon me gorging myself), but I was restless and happily escaped back into the street to make my way toward the Inns of Court.

Before I reached my chambers I stopped by to visit with Inspector Harris.

I had nothing further to report, but felt the need to inquire as to what progress was being made in the investigation into Sidney's death.

"Well, now," said Inspector Harris to the window-sill, "it would seem that progress is being made, but such things take time. They do indeed."

"Have you any theories or suspects?" I demanded directly—rather too directly, it seemed, for Inspector Harris looked at me sharply, then returned to his casual observance of the window casing.

"We have our ways of doing things," he responded after several moments of silence. "Of course ...," he added, offhandedly, "there are those members of the press eager to have answers as quickly as possible. Some of them are even speaking of evil forces at work. I heard talk from one newsman about ... *vampires*."

I laughed quickly. He looked up from the window, stared fixedly at me for a moment, then smiled and looked away.

Constable Peters glared at me as I left the station.

As I made my way through the streets, I thought I saw a glimpse of the form of Esther Raveland, but I turned away and did not inquire further. I had begun to envision her everywhere, I told myself derisively.

I returned to my chambers and focused determinedly on my work. I wrote letters to all of the remaining legatees of Charles Sidney's will to inform them of their inheritance. Financial bequests were easily dealt with. Carstairs carried Kilbronson's silver pen and antique pistols to his house along with a note regarding recent letters I had received that had confirmed my suspicions—Elisabetta Kilbronson had not been in Budapest and she was not in France. There was no way of proving that she was on the Continent in any case. Further inquiries were being taken up immediately. The painting and the ring left to Mr. Montrose I sent to his club, the only address I had been able to obtain for the man. These were returned to me within a few hours with the information that Mr. Montrose was no longer a member. I was referred to a hotel in an unsavory neighborhood, and there I assume Carstairs found the elusive Mr. Montrose, for he returned without the painting and the ruby ring and did not complain of robbery.

I concluded the day with a feeling of having achieved a great deal.

That night and for several nights following the dream returned, though now it had undergone a metamorphosis: the creature still revealed itself as Esther Raveland, but now the little rotund priest did not merely gambol about the scenery placidly; he did battle with the fiendish maiden, sometimes with a sword, sometimes with a rifle, sometimes with a host of unlikely things—spears, trowels, candlesticks, crosses, the beads at his waist, or myriadic religious pieces I could not identify, such as a swinging chain with aromatic smoke issuing forth from the ball at its end. That night he wrapped the chain about the creature's neck, choking its unholy life away.

"You might say," he said, this execution concluded, "that such things rather *incense* me!"

I became so unwilling to return to my rooms—and there relive the nightmarish existence that would come when I shut my eyes—that I took to wandering the streets for hours on end, anything to prolong the time away from that inevitable dream.

It was absurd. It was ridiculous. And yet I found myself behaving in this irrational manner, as if I really did believe in such supernatural, blood-sucking menaces.

Several days passed in a miserable pattern: mornings at my office, sometimes a visit to the Lawson home in the afternoon, where I was always greeted with the news of Adele's continued ill health, then a reluctant return home.

Work proceeded apace and without significant incident. The legal representative of Mrs. Agnes Puttock, the Glasgow relation to whom Sidney's house had passed, notified us by post that the lady was perfectly contented in her own home and had no intention to transferring her residence to that den of iniquity (though whether she referred to London or to Sidney's home, I could not say). We were therefore directed to dispose of the house to an appropriate renter or buyer as soon as possible and forward all income from the transaction to her bankers.

The lady, I noted to myself as I read the letter, could stoop from her moral high ground to retrieve a profit even if she found herself incapable of descending to the level of living in Sidney's house. Probably an old Scottish bat, I thought, canting and censorious. The sort who would have barred her colorful young relation from crossing the chaste threshold of her own home ...

No, I mentally shook my head at myself for that. I was becoming an irrationally surly fellow, harsh in my judgments of a poor old lady and bizarrely defensive of Sidney. It was the consequence of composite exhaustion. Indeed, day after day I grew more irritable and sick. Night after night I kept a horrifying vigil. I shunned sleep. I would haunt my rooms—sometimes walking, sometimes writing, sometimes reading. I avoided fiction altogether.

And every night, when I fell unwillingly into sleep, I would fall into the arms of that same vile nightmare. Sometimes Esther Raveland would rise and walk toward me. Usually I would awaken at the sight of her face.

Always the little figure in white was to be seen—sometimes wandering about some yards from the ghastly spectacle, gazing up at the sky with a quizzical expression, sometimes reclining in the grass beside the vampiric feast, lazily flipping through an open book—a garish book I knew too well.

Occasionally there were other figures—Inspector Harris and Constable Peters, the latter incongruously attired in the voluminous white robes of the Papist priest.

I began to behave rather like a mad, superstitious fool—avoiding the Stoker book as if it were possessed of a strange, unearthly power.

I met Miss Raveland in the city many times—at least, I saw her. As often as I could, I hurried away before we could speak.

She still seemed pale, and even reluctant to see me, but with a strange perverseness, as I began to dread the sight of her, her appearances became more frequent.

Once, when a meeting was unavoidable, we spoke with cool politeness and briefly.

"It is tragic, is it not—the illness of Miss Lawson," she said.

I agreed and detached myself from the conversation swiftly, this time leaving her to watch my steadily retreating back.

Adele was indeed quite unwell. She was paler and weaker. She was listless and dull. The light had quite gone from her eyes. Even the meager exertion of walking across a room exhausted her, leaving her breathless and sometimes even tremulous. She complained of headaches. She would not eat. She grew thin.

Now she was practically a prisoner to her bedroom. My visits to the house became more frequent. Every day the report was the same: her condition was unimproved. One doctor murmured of greensickness, but looked rather as if he were thinking something rather worse.

Every evening I returned home with a growing disquietude, reeking of discontentment and vague dread.

Another issue arose that should have distracted me from every other preoccupation: Elisabetta Kilbronson had been found—had been seen in any case. There were reports of a lady roughly fitting her description who had sold a small, delicate garnet ring that had been itemized on a list of jewelry provided to me by Kilbronson. It was an odd aspect of the case—regarding which, had my client been a more approachable man than the dour Edgar, I would surely have asked certain questions—that Elisabetta had only taken with her jewelry that had belonged to her before her marriage. The garnet ring, I had been led to understand, was a different matter. Its provenance was somewhat unclear: Kilbronson said it did not belong to him, and yet he insisted it was not hers and was eager to follow up this lead as a possible means of tracing her. It was of course a distinct possibility, and yet I was led to wonder what sort of immoral Hungarian would balk at taking with her the numerous jewels that Kilbronson himself admitted to having given to her? But I set such wondering aside. If the report were true the errant Elisabetta had been in Naples, Italy, only a few days earlier. There was no sign that she had any traveling companion at this time—that is, there was no sign of an adulterous lover.

I wrote of this development to Kilbronson and assured him that further steps would be taken to determine the accuracy of the report and, if possible, identify where Elisabetta had gone upon leaving Italy.

While I awaited his response, I read over a legal publication a friend had sent on to me for my opinion. The whole world melted away, and I had quite forgotten about vampires, murders, and unfaithful Hungarian wives, lost in consideration of property laws, when Carstairs announced the arrival of Edgar Kilbronson.

I removed my feet from where they had perched comfortably on my desk and stood up to receive my client.

As I shook his cold, slightly clammy hand, I wondered—not for the first time—if he had been born looking like a cadaver or had only attained this appearance through long years and diligent effort.

"I received your message," he said as he seated himself. "Mrs. Kilbronson is, you say, in Italy."

"We have evidence to support that idea, yes," I said—when those large, ghoulish, staring eyes fixed upon me I found myself reflexively qualifying statements. Perhaps I feared that if my statements were even partially disproven—if the errant Elisabetta had been in Salerno rather than Naples, or even worse had been in Sicily—his grim, eagle-like face, with that emphatic nose and that drooping chin, would loom up before me like an eerily emotionless ghost and denounce my lies in sonorous tones, as if he were reading a list itemizing the cargo delivered by one of his ships.

"Fifteen crates of dust—you are doomed eternally to listen to this dreary, droning voice," the ghost would say.

"Thirty-two boxes of moldy bones, for you have lied to me—lied to me. Twenty-seven baskets of lost teeth from assorted mouths ..."

I shook myself from this morbid fantasy and endeavored to refocus upon my visitor.

"You must find her—you must—and find her quickly," he was saying, his voice a slow, ponderous hum. "Every day she is lost is a day of infamy and pain."

"Do you suspect a connection with some man?" I asked (more in an effort to demonstrate attentiveness and concern—albeit falsely—than out of any concrete suspicion).

He was silent for some time, leaving me to wonder if he had heard me or properly understood the question. Then he looked up, fixing me with a steely, forbidding glance, and I faltered out: "Any connection which might prove helpful in identifying Mrs. Kilbronson's state of mind and what might be directing her current trajectory of travel?"

He pursed his lips. "Mrs. Kilbronson ... I would have remained patient with her. Patient for some time with her ... *inappropriate* ... behavior and ... *unseemly* ... manner. Indeed, I was patient with her for a long time. I would never have spoken of it. Indeed, I did not. It was most painful. Most painful."

A long silence followed during which Kilbronson brooded in a dry, dull manner, leaving me to squirm and to listen to the tick ... tick ... tick of my clock.

Finally, as if in desperation, I inquired as to his receipt of the items left to him by Charles Sidney.

He roused himself from his meditative coma. "Yes, yes. I received the objects."

I waited to see if he would elaborate—I rather hoped he would give some explanation to clear up the mystery of that inexplicable pairing. What did the gifts signify? A close relationship? A passing acquaintance? Perhaps business had drawn them together?

"We must find her," said Kilbronson.

No explanation then, it seemed.

I inquired whether he wished me to venture over to the Continent again (and prayed that he would not—the mere thought of another trip so soon after the last journey and with my intervening bout of sickness made me tired).

Once again he did not reply directly. He spoke of the family name and of vaguely unfortunate circumstances.

When I gently asked once again if he wished to divorce her quietly, he closed his eyes.

"I would not have this ... this lost child of God, this ... this wandering lamb ... to be so deserted to her fate ... to the fate that she has brought upon herself ..."

Then his tone changed; he spoke sharply and (for him) quickly: "And what of the garnet ring? Can it be recovered?"

I felt like Tubal to his Shylock—which did he lament, his daughter or his ducats? But I said nothing of this to him. "I have instructed an agent in Italy to inquire further and to seek to regain the ring," I assured him. "This will, I hope, lead to further intelligence regarding her current whereabouts."

What on earth could have driven her to marry the man? Though Kilbronson could produce no paintings or even photographs of her, she was widely accounted a beauty. I could well understand what had prompted her to flee him.

Kilbronson rose, having achieved nothing in our interview, and readied himself to depart. He put on his gloves with a meticulous care that nearly drove me hysterical and yet was oddly fascinating.

As he adjusted his coat to make room for his overcoat (each new layer required ever slower and more laborious movements), he remarked in a calculatedly offhanded tone: "I believe you are acquainted with a young lady from America—recently arrived. Miss Raveland. Miss Esther Raveland."

I coldly replied that I had enjoyed the honor of an introduction to Miss Raveland.

Then there was silence.

"Goodbye," said Kilbronson with a sigh, and lumbered out with a stately and bleak step.

I was left, as I had been left so many times before, wondering if there were more to say—something Kilbronson was reluctant to tell me. Why did he seek her so devotedly?

Perhaps he was obsessed with her.

Perhaps he truly loved her.

Perhaps his religious convictions were really motivating him to this.

Perhaps she had taken more than jewelry with her.

Perhaps there was another woman in the case.

The mention of Esther Raveland had left me irritable. Was she the "other" woman? Was he overwhelmed with a passionate love for the unattainable American beauty?

"I cannot marry you!" she might have said, gently repelling his suit. "I cannot marry you, Edgar, for you have a wife still living!"

And Edgar, returning home to be confronted with the infamous woman with whom he was trapped in a loveless marriage, so frightened her by his passionate insistence on a divorce that she ran out into the night. Had he struck her in his fury and frustrated desire? And Esther Raveland wept at night, refusing his letters and cursing the ill fate that had filled her heart with love for a man burdened with a monstrous wife? Was Sidney their intermediary—endeavoring to soothe the lady and bolster up her lover with manly courage?

I shook myself. The narrative in my mind was becoming increasingly like that of a trite romance. The idea of Sidney as Cupid to the dry and cadaver-like Kilbronson was grotesque enough in its absurdity to be possible. And that cold, unfriendly man was incapable of anything so dramatic or as human as love. But beyond all of this, the thought of Esther Raveland accepting the emotionless advances of a half-dead lover was too repugnant to entertain seriously.

Half dead, I thought. Half dead or undead.

Vampires indeed.

I threw down my papers with disgust, growled good evening to Carstairs, fetched coat, hat, and gloves, and left my chambers.

I trudged back along the cold, lonely streets, nursing my ill humor.

It was not really a swifter route to pass through Hyde Park, but that was the excuse I gave myself for venturing into that unwholesome, nightmarish stage. A few brave waterfowl could be seen shivering along the banks of the Serpentine, but I had no crumbs with which to encourage their frigid bravery and would not have spared them had my pockets bulged with crusts. I was irritable and the whole world could freeze or starve to death for all I cared.

On the edge of the Bayswater side of the park, beneath a streetlamp, I met Esther Raveland. Her face was pale with the cold, her lips rich with an unhealthy color. But she was beautiful—heaven help me! She *was* beautiful.

"Good evening," she said with a gentle smile.

I frowned at her. Confound the woman for thinking it was a good evening. It was a hideous, atrocious sort of evening.

I grunted a reply and walked on.

I thought she looked hurt but I was unmoved. She might not be the lover of Kilbronson, but she was certainly something unsatisfying. She must be, connected as she was with both Kilbronson and Sidney.

"Damn, damn, damn!" I cried aloud, frightening a young baker's assistant who was closing up the shop.

I hurried down the few remaining streets toward home and the oppressive attentions of that ministering angel, Jenson.

Jenson finally left me—at my demand—at a quarter to one. I was restless, as always.

I do not know what possessed me to take up the Stoker novel again—a casual whim or an evil thought. Perhaps a compulsion. Vampires indeed.

It was such profound nonsense, really. I found that I could ill remember the plot thus far and was forced to retrace my steps by several pages.

I recalled the final scenes in the Romanian castle and even revisited the horrifying vampiric crypt without curling my hair in the slightest. Rubbish indeed.

Regaining my place, I passed through the record of the romances of an innocent maiden—and reached a point of chilling description, with one heroine discovering another, the victim of sleepwalking, and of some strange black figure with a white face and red, gleaming eyes, when a feeling of vague familiarity interrupted my concentration.

My brow wrinkled with the effort at remembrance. What was it that so struck me about the passage?

It was certainly not worth worrying about. I shut the book and set it on the table with a nonchalant air.

I was just drifting off to sleep when realization came, and my eyes flew open with mounting terror.

Adele Lawson was Lucy Westenra incarnate.

It was a long time before I slept, and when I did, the dream returned with horrifying intensity: the shining, mesmerizing face of Esther Raveland looming out at me, scarlet blood dripping ... dripping ... dripping from her evil smile.

Chapter 7

31 May 1900: Belgravia Again

(From Dr. Seward's diary) *The attendant tells me that his screams whilst in the paroxysm were really appalling; I found my hands full when I got in, attending to some of the other patients who were frightened by him. . . . It is now after the dinner-hour of the asylum, and as yet my patient sits in a corner brooding, with a dull, sullen, woe-begone look in his face, which seems rather to indicate than to show something directly. I cannot quite understand it.*

On Thursday afternoon—the day following my epiphanic association of Adele and Stoker's doomed heroine— I attended the funeral of Charles Sidney. It provided a striking contrast to the wild, supernatural wonderings I entertained so unwillingly each night. I remembered my father, that mild, unremarkable man, preaching hellfire and damnation at us over breakfast and concluding with, "Anne, my dear love, would you pass me the marmalade, please?"

Even that memory, that strange conflation of alarm and comedy, was strangely comforting. Here was the old-fashioned stolidity and unemotional common sense of the English rendered liturgical. Here was safety. Here was reality. And it was reassuringly boring.

The church was a recent monstrosity, built in an anti-Gothic style by an unimaginative designer. It represented the very lowest of the Low Church, with a dogged resistance to decoration. Sidney would have mourned its simple style, its unadorned lines. No stained glass, no soaring arches, no heavy darkness, no flickering candles, no exotic, stern-faced Madonnas. An uneventful nave, heavy with Methodist placidity. Nothing fine, nothing ornate. Nothing that captured the character of the odd man who had died in so strange a manner. Dull dull dull.

The church was crowded with fascinated onlookers, each one more macabre than the last. There were many faces I recognized. I suspected that Esther Raveland was there, but refused to crane my neck to confirm the suspicion. Inspector Harris was there, looking rather like a distracted tourist, more absorbed in the thoroughly uninteresting architecture than in the proceedings.

The church was roomy enough in its construction, but the day was abnormally humid, making the crowds of people all the more unendurable. The air was close and rank, with the strong scent of stale perfumes.

The clergyman was having a hard time of it; he had obviously dismissed the subject of Sidney himself as too complicated for a sermon, and so dedicated his efforts to an in-depth analysis of various thoroughly uninteresting Psalms. The congregation clearly expected a great deal more; after so sensational a murder, they expected something dramatic from the pulpit.

A few brave souls at the back whispered their revolt.

One man napped openly. I envied him.

The highlight of the service came when a bat fluttered down from the rafters and circled the coffin.

The crowd gasped. A woman at the back screamed. Three debutantes fainted—perhaps an affectation, and perhaps from that strange, disgusting odor. (It really was stomach-turning.)

The bat flew around the coffin four times before a diligent churchwarden dispatched the errant rodent with a well-aimed hymnal, prompting applause from the back pews and causing the clergyman to lose his train of thought and to take refuge in twenty minutes of meandering through the book of Job.

"We have 'em sometimes evenin' times," said the churchwarden to me when I stopped as I left the church to congratulate him on the killing. Then he shook his head. "Straaaange," he added, lingering dramatically over the word. "Never 'ad one on 'em creatures come in daylight …"

When the newspaperman jogged my elbow to inspire me to move out of his way, I realized that the churchwarden was preparing to perform for a wider public. Not wanting to stand in the way of publicity so keenly desired, I obligingly removed myself.

The churchyard was far more interesting than the building it contained—the original church had stood there for some centuries before an enterprising seventeenth-century general decided to raze its quiet prettiness in a moment of religious enthusiasm. Or perhaps it had taken place during the Gordon Riots. I could not say. In any case, the church that had once stood in that place had been (someone had said) much more worth a visitor's attention. But perhaps that was merely the myth concocted by nostalgic locals.

Whatever the case, the churchyard remained from several centuries back and was well stocked with antique graves, many of them contorted by the slowly shifting earth in which they dwelt. More than one tombstone lay collapsed on its side.

"Not the sort of place you'd like to be in the middle of the night," said a voice at my elbow. I turned to face a smiling, bright-eyed young man in a pea-green coat and with a nonchalant moustache.

I agreed and attempted to walk on.

"The bat was a rum touch, don't you think?"

I agreed once again and once again made a motion to escape.

"Toby Barnes," announced the young man, extending his right hand firmly into mine. "*Pall Mall Gazette.*"

I accepted the handshake (as there was nothing else to do) and reluctantly returned my name for his.

"Delighted to make your acquaintance, Mr. Kemp. You're the executor of the estate, I understand. My business to know. Will you be going to the graveside?"

With a start I realized that, much as my thoughts had lingered on Sidney, I had almost forgotten the reality of his death and the fact that his corpse—his mangled, bloody corpse—had been present in that coffin. It was not merely a prop to delight lurid spectators; it was a real functionary of death. And it must be laid to rest—to rest in peace—somewhere.

"Is he to be buried here?"

"Not here—out in Kensal Green. I don't know why the funeral was here. I don't think it was his parish. But, then, he didn't seem to have much family. Perhaps Kensal Green did not want all the notoriety."

"Perhaps not," I said.

"Well," said Toby Barnes with a smile, "ta for now."

Inspector Harris and Esther Raveland were standing close together just outside the gate. I nodded to them both and would have continued on my way peacefully, but Miss Raveland moved in a very deliberate manner and blocked my path.

I could not escape conversation without being openly rude.

"Miss Raveland," I said in reluctant greeting, then took refuge in a half lie. "I did not see you."

She was no longer pale and preoccupied. She was as beautiful as ever, as uncannily alive as the vile creature of my dreams. The color had returned vibrantly to her cheeks, and there was a playful light in her eyes, which seemed oddly sinister to my perception.

"You seem to be rather inclined to blindness lately," she said briskly. "But never mind that. An odd funeral for an odd man, wouldn't you say?"

I made a noncommittal noise, though she was expressing my very thought.

"Perhaps," she continued, turning to Inspector Harris, "you came in hopes of finding your bizarre and bloody killer?"

He chuckled good-naturedly. "Indeed, Miss Raveland, such a thing would make my job all the simpler."

"I should think it would rather take the fun out of things. You would lose the thrill of the hunt. But you could still have a sense of the dramatic. Isn't there an old legend that a corpse will begin to bleed if touched by the hand of the murderer?"

"I have heard tell of such a superstition, Miss Raveland. Dramatic, yes. It is rather more the stuff of novels than it is of the police courts."

"Come now!" she laughed. "You are too hard on the novelistic tradition. I suppose you dismiss as offhandedly the more fantastical prognostications of the newspapers.

Was Charles Sidney indeed the victim of a supernatural beast?" She turned to me. "Help me defend the dramatic, I beg you, against the pragmatic brutality of this policeman!"

I managed a brief smile—that was all.

"Alas!" she cried. "The defense counsel has abandoned the case! I am left to withstand this unimaginative onslaught by myself—an undefended and innocent maiden against the full weight and brutality of this arm of the law!"

Inspector Harris chortled with obvious amusement at her waxing hyperbole (which seemed so ill-timed and so out of keeping with the atmosphere of dry death and boredom I had brought with me from the church, that I was almost angry with her).

She waited, as if expecting me to interject myself into the conversation. When I failed to do so, she spoke again. "Well, the afternoon is passing. I must go home. I have already offended a multitude of conventions by attending the funeral on my own. Millicent will be frightfully upset."

"Shall I send for a carriage?" asked the inspector.

"I can take a carriage, of course, or"—she paused and looked at me—"perhaps I can find an escort home ...?"

The question lingered on the air for a moment. Suddenly I felt trapped, desperate to escape.

"Indeed," I said hurriedly. "I would happily do the office myself, but ...," I murmured something of an appointment, nodded an abrupt farewell, and quitted them.

I sensed rather than saw Inspector Harris take her arm and guide her politely toward the street, hailing a cab as they went.

I wandered slowly home, not paying much attention to what roads I chose, hoping to lose myself and clear my head through the exertion.

I thought I had rid myself of the stench of that bizarre funeral service which stayed with strange persistence upon me, but, when I awakened from daydream and looked around to discover where I was, I found that I was so deeply embroiled in that preoccupation that it had unconsciously guided my steps.

I was once again in Charles Sidney's old neighborhood, standing before his house. There was still a constable standing guard—not the same man as I had met previously. His glance indicated that he had labeled me as a morbidly curious member of the public, eager to catch a glimpse of the murdered man's house.

Eager to distance myself from such a suspicion, I bid this representative of justice a pleasant good afternoon.

"And to you, sir," he replied politely.

I noted that this was the former home of Charles Sidney.

"Yes, indeed, sir."

I observed that the funeral had taken place this very day.

"So it did, sir."

I posited that the house must have caught the attention of many ghoulish passersby.

"Yes, sir."

The patience of the police force must, I continued, have been sorely tried.

"I wouldn't say so, sir, certainly."

I began to wonder if Inspector Harris specially trained his men to be as obtuse as he himself appeared to be.

I was about to make another conversational foray when we were interrupted by the arrival of three large carts, each laden with furniture and luggage, and heading in the direction of Sidney's house.

When the carts had passed, I was spared the humiliating ordeal of inquiring outright what their business was at the house by the less self-conscious crowd that had gathered around us—with alarming rapidity, I might add. Where they came from I could not say, but they were a motley crew, a generic sampling of an everyday London crowd, ready to impose the most sensational interpretation on any mundane happenstance.

"Coo! That's the house of the murdered man!"

"Look 'ere, you!" one bold man said, addressing the constable. "What's this all about, then?"

"Goodness! Do you suppose it's his family come to take possession of the house?"

"I shouldn't like to live there. They say his body was torn into pieces and scattered all over St. James Park."

"It was in Kensington Gardens, wasn't it?"

The constable shooed them away, but managed to admit (as if against his will) that the house had been let and the new tenant was due to arrive very shortly.

So it had been let, then. Mrs. Puttock triumphed. I wondered to myself how Flossingdon had managed it so quickly and wondered who it was that had appeared with seemingly miraculous promptness and offered to take the house.

The rest of the crowd would readily have empathized with my surprise and my inquisitiveness. The business was roundly denounced as having been undertaken with inordinate and even unseemly haste. Not that such disapproval was demonstrative of a larger dissatisfaction. On the contrary, some members of the crowd were so enlivened by this information that they appeared to be readying themselves to remain indefinitely so they could greet the new tenant with fixed stares.

I had no intention of being one of the welcoming party and so quitted the street, but not so quickly as to avoid the sight of a large, ornate brougham, elaborately ensconced in scarlet and red trimmings, driven by a morbidly pale-faced man wearing a wide-rimmed hat and a pair of darkened spectacles. The passenger was not visible, save for one, black-gloved hand, resting against the edge of the window. As the brougham passed me, I shivered and attributed the involuntary shudder to the briskness of the air.

Jenson was waiting for me. He offered me dinner and stood glowering hideously over me as I pretended to eat it.

That night I was too restless even to capture the few, troubled hours of sleep as was my wont. I thought of but avoided my bed, knowing the fruitless tossings and turnings that would follow from any attempt at sleep—dread of that familiar nightmare would make sleep quite impossible. I would lie in the dark endeavoring not to think about my inability to sleep—and all the while thinking about it in a most perverse and indirect manner. There was nothing for it. Sleep and I would yet remain strangers. It was better that way.

I sat for a long time before the window, my mind wandering—streetlight, street, and the infrequent passersby all blurred together into the indistinctness of my distracted perception. A faint murmur of movement caught my attention. My eyes focused. A fly had collapsed upon the windowsill and was wriggling in spasmodic misery. I watched, fascinated, as it went through its death agony, its legs whirring madly, then freezing in the paralysis of pending death. I fancied I could even hear its heart—if such things have hearts—throbbing faintly ... slowly ... and stop.

The creature was dead. A horrible death. But bloodless.

I looked away toward a nearby bookcase. Perhaps reading would help. Then my eyes fell upon the rejected Stoker book.

"That way madness lies," I quoted to myself out of context.

Refusing to give in to the temptation (though rather feeling that my strength of will would be weakened as the hours passed), I dressed myself again hurriedly and left my rooms, left the house, left the street where I lived.

I walked south for what seemed like hours, weaving through the silent, cold streets, bathed as they were in the eerie blue light of a moonlit night.

My limbs ached from nervous exercise—I had walked miles that day, miles that week. I could hardly imagine a time when I had not been walking, or when my body had not cried out in its exhaustion for some brief respite.

I had been standing for some time, gazing fixedly at a tree without seeing it, when my eyes suddenly cleared and, as if awakening from a dream, I looked about me, blinking and trying to discern where I was. I had walked for hours it seemed, and in the darkness, my surroundings looked vaguely familiar—a trick of the night, perhaps, which can as easily turn a bush into a bear and the familiar into the unfamiliar as it can imbue the unknown with a sense of vague familiarity.

No, it was certainly a tree I knew, and knew well. I was standing outside the house of Adele Lawson.

As I stood there, wondering at the strange circumstance and even toying about with little scientific notions that might explain it—Adele had been so much in my thoughts that I had walked there, directed by my anxious subconscious—something else caught my eye. Something that I felt I recognized. The moonlight seemed to pale from blue to gray to an unearthly, a luminous white.

A miscellaneous assemblage of phrases came to me—a cacophony of voices on a single theme.

All quite ridiculous ...
You don't believe in blood-sucking Romanian counts?
Evil forces at work ... vampires ...
Esther Raveland—beware ... beware ...
Shall you believe now?

It was only a shadow outside one of the upper-floor windows, a deeper darkness concentrated against the wall and up against the windowsill. I watched, transfixed by mounting terror, as the shadow crept upward until it pressed against the glass. My eyes seemed to gain a supernatural sort of clarity as I looked, and I discerned strange, ghostly, and yet concretely reptilian limbs, appendages of the thing that clung to the side of the house.

I cried out involuntarily.

That hideous, lizard-like form contorted itself into a still more horrible shape, turning so that the white, ghoulish face was full upon me. As I watched, the blank pink eyes blazed red—a piercing, infernal glance that well I remembered, that nightly haunted my most impenetrable dreams.

"Help!" I cried—a cry that was the merest whisper.

A rustle of leaves was upon me and someone—some*thing*—emerged from the bushes at my side. A dark cloak, with white robes flurrying out below. But this was not the face I expected. This was not the Father Gilroy of the train nor the elusive friar of my dreams; this was the face of a lanky youth, with startled blue eyes and a shock of unkempt black hair.

"Oh!" he cried. And as I stood there in shock, he stared closely in my face for a moment. Then he smiled—*grinned*—as if in recognition, nodded, bid me a cheery "Good night!" and moved with a light step to disappear into the darkness.

I cried out again—this time with shrill urgency: "Help! Help! Rouse the house! Help!"

Murmurings. Sounds of windows and doors. Bright lights.

I looked up, blinking.

The creature at the window had vanished.

And I stood surrounded by inquisitive and moderately annoyed men in various stages of nighttime attire—with a constable possessed of a particular disapproving countenance at their head: the young man Peters.

Chapter 8

31 May 1900: Mayfair and South Kensington

(From Lucy Westenra's diary) *Perhaps it is the change of air, or getting home again. It is all dark and horrid to me, for I can remember nothing; but I am full of vague fear, and I feel so weak and worn out. When Arthur came to lunch he looked quite grieved when he saw me, and I hadn't the spirit to try to be cheerful. I wonder if I could sleep in mother's room tonight. I shall make an excuse to try ...*

It is hard to describe the humiliation one must naturally feel when, having risen with chivalric nobility to the defense of a lady about to be assailed by a sinister bloodsucking fiend, one is castigated for disturbing the peace and generally supposed by all one's acquaintance (for the story of my "nighttime serenade" of the neighborhood spread far through many ghoulishly gossipy circles) to have been thoroughly intoxicated at the time.

Such a supposition was exacerbated by my failure to explain the situation well.

"Wot's all this, then?" Constable Peters had demanded—unnecessarily like a stock character in a penny dreadful detective piece.

I just stopped myself before I launched into a frank description of the threat I had perceived at Adele's window.

"A bat!" I cried. "Or some other creature. There! It was near the window!"

Peters looked at the window. Then he looked at me. He appeared to be summing up my character by my appearance. I own I must have been somewhat disheveled from my lengthy walk. And, after all, it was nearly two in the morning.

He looked at me closely, then his eyes cleared with recognition and narrowed into slits.

My identity was known.

The situation only deteriorated after that. By some unhappy fortune (unhappy because I would have welcomed even deportation had it come with the preservation of my anonymity) a rather influential judge of my acquaintance—Alasdair Jorgins by name—happened to be present at the station to which I was taken. He had once enjoyed a reckless youth (or liked to think that he had) and consequently was inclined to receive my display with overly jocose indulgence. Through his persuasions, I was at liberty with a firm reprimand ringing in my ears and the lasting punishment of an irretrievably tarnished reputation.

In the halls of that place of judgment, I encountered Inspector Harris. He acknowledged me with a nod and a smile—which was, I fear, rather at my expense.

As I left the station, I thought I saw a moustache atop a pea-green coat but I fled a possible meeting with Toby Barnes, eager representative of the press. I could imagine the headlines: "Mayfair Uproar! Drunken Barrister Plagues Residents! Batty Barrister Terrorizes Town!"

That same morning, after a few hours of sleepless self-torture, I rose, dressed, and set out upon the streets with a determination much intensified by compounded exhaustion.

I made my way to the British Museum—the resplendent Reading Room, that Victorian bastion of self-improvement, seemed a logical place to begin an investigation, and that was precisely what I meant to take up. Priests and fanatics were all alike, putting their faith in overburdened fantasy. There must be a logical, scientific explanation for these weird and disturbing events, and I refused to be reduced to an overreliance upon a sensationalized bit of nonsense dreamed up by some unbalanced Irishman. Another night like last night would drive me completely mad. Perhaps then I too would take to attacking epicurean dilettantes in Hyde Park.

I discerned a handful of gray and white heads bent among the books and felt a slight sense of embarrassment. They were all, I was sure, occupied with classical subjects—economic factors of the Peloponnesian War, artifacts of ancient Greece, minute biographical details of the life of Henry Fielding ... and there I was, about to delve into the *Encyclopædia* volume in which an entry on blood-sucking fiends resided, and to glance—with a very cynical eye—into a woman named Gerard's treatment of "Transylvania Superstitions". But I swallowed my feelings of mortification and, in an effort to preserve my privacy and my reputation, fetched a respectable-looking treatise on the early history of British coinage and propped it up ostentatiously to block any inquisitive eye.

I was just beginning with the *Encyclopædia Britannica*—doggedly refusing to shiver over the notion of a corpse, fresh and rosy from the blood that he has sucked from the living—I was just beginning, as I say, when a heavy, paunchy hand was laid upon my shoulder, causing me to start up violently from my chair.

I looked up into a fat and distinctly unpleasant face, in which a set of singularly small teeth was self-consciously displayed.

"I could not help noticing," began the teeth mincingly, "that you are delving into a rich and fascinating world and, knowing my own close acquaintance with the things of that world, make bold to present myself as an able guide."

Before I could curse his impudence, he extended a hand (which I correctly suspected to be damp). "Victor Montrose," he said with a flourish, "at your service."

One of Charles Sidney's legatees. I murmured something that he took as a greeting in response. I did not proffer my name, but he did not seem to require it.

"A rich and fascinating world indeed," he continued. "The world of dark powers, the world of shadows, the world of demons, ghosts, and corpses who rise from their graves when the sun sets, and walk out into the darkness of the world to wreak dark vengeance upon the living, satiating their demonic lusts and desires in a glut of blood and terror."

As he spoke, he waxed enthusiastic, concluding at so great a volume as to inspire an elderly man with spectacles (who had hitherto appeared so deeply focused upon a dust-encrusted tome as to seem a Reading Room fixture rather than a visitor) to raise his venerable head, frown, and hush us both with some annoyance.

Montrose looked rather as if he appreciated the attention. It certainly did not inspire him to greater subtlety of motion or voice.

"I could tell you stories, my friend, tales that would chill your bones to their very marrow. Not the stuff of legend and folklore—true accounts of things that have been, things that even now are. I am, I think I may pride myself, a modest scholar on the subject."

He produced from his bag a large portfolio on which was inscribed in bold and garishly scarlet lettering: HISTORY OF THE UNDEAD. I squirmed and wished we were not so noticeable. I wished someone would come and silence this mind-boggling bore—I could not do it myself. It was as if exhaustion and some strange power inherent in his very abominableness had paralyzed me, an unhappy victim and spellbound audience.

"I have studied the subject from its inception in ancient mythologies—where the tread of the ghoul and the revenant and the vampire is undeniable. The subsequent history I know all too well. I have read Charles de Schertz's *Magia Posthuma*, and made my way through the absurdity of Davanzati's *Dissertazione*—the fool! He sought respite from the reality of demonic forces because he had not the courage to face the intoxicating realities so clearly demonstrated before him. Dom Calmet I have also read. He dared defy the stodgy denial of the Church—championing the cause of truth in the face of Papal tyranny!"

Once again he had exceeded polite boundaries for noise. We were shushed emphatically for the second time.

"I too have suffered the oppressive weight of that august body," Montrose declared proudly. "For I am in fact a priest, consecrated and ratified. You think I do not appear like any priest you have seen? Very likely so. How could you?"

He spoke almost pityingly, but before I could clear my mind to comprehend the revelation of his apparent clerical status, he had resumed the larger topic.

"The evidence is incontrovertible—that is the message of Calmet. The ancients knew it. Primitive people

dark and glorious marvels are contained within the mind of man! And, indeed, of some men in particular."

He leaned forward to place his wet lips beside my cringing ear.

"We are drawn close by an extraordinary series of events, my friend," he whispered. "Not least of which the sad passing of our mutual and very dear, dear friend"—here his whisper became a wet hiss—"Charles Sidney ..."

He held forth his left hand and displayed the ruby ring that Charles Sidney had left him. I half expected him to produce the painting that had been included in his bequest from somewhere beneath his wide black cloak, but instead he waggled his fingers, scattering scarlet light recklessly about.

I remembered him then—not as a person, but as an overwhelming scent that had made the suffocating closeness of the crowd in the church all the more revolting. So the legatee of the painting and the ruby ring had ventured out for the funeral as well.

With the memory, my body was freed from its paralysis. I would have drawn back in disgust, but he held me tightly by the arm so that nothing less than a dramatic and full-bodied lunge could have freed me.

"Yes, I do know you, and you know me," he continued. "And our paths will yet cross again, my friend. You cannot escape your own dark destiny. Sidney knew it as well as I do. Sidney was close to the darkest of dark mysteries. But he weakened in his resolve. He was, at heart, a coward. He could not see the full potential of the forces in which he dabbled. That was what destroyed him. There can be no dabbler here, my friend. You must plunge fully into the mystery, intoxicate your very soul with it, choke upon it, drown in it. Give in to the call of pleasure, my dear. For you know that desire already haunts your dreams with dark, bewildering urgency ..."

As if in a flash, I saw the blood-stained face of the Esther Raveland of my nightmare, freshly glutted with blood. On her face was a look of seduction, chilling my very soul. With a stifled cry, I shook off Montrose's restraining hand, picked up my briefcase and a few scattered notes, and hurried away without a word of farewell.

At the door I realized I must have left several papers behind. For several moments I debated with myself. I wanted to retrieve my papers, but was terrified that I would be trapped once again by the disgusting Montrose.

After more than five minutes of unsatisfying deliberation, I cautiously reentered the Reading Room and made my way back to the table where I had undertaken such futile studies.

Montrose was nowhere to be seen. Perhaps he had gone to seek his elderly victim to finish the task of tormenting the poor creature into an early (or long delayed) grave.

I found my papers where I had left them, neatly stacked and with Montrose's portfolio at the top, a note affixed to its cover: "You may return this to me when next we meet. —V. M."

Almost against my own will, I gathered up the portfolio along with my papers, shuffling them about to try and conceal the lurid title.

It was the most extraordinary encounter of my life, I concluded. Charles Sidney had been bad enough—poor, tragic soul—but he was an innocent and harmless little man in comparison with Victor Montrose. I returned home reeking with discontentment and shame—as if I had somehow been soiled by contact with that repulsive object.

Jenson met me at the door. He would have assisted me with the collection of papers and items in my arms, but I resisted his assistance sharply.

On another occasion, he might have been offended by my rudeness, but that night he appeared preoccupied. "You have had a visitor, sir. It was the doctor—he had just come from the Lawson house. I was so bold as to inquire as to Miss Lawson's health. I'm sorry to inform you, sir, that her situation has worsened. The doctors ..."

The rest was lost to me. Jenson continued to speak for some minutes but I heard none of it. I was lost in painful, horrible reverie.

I vaguely heard the knock on my door but did not consciously attend to it until I found Jenson once again at my elbow.

"An Inspector Harris to see you, sir."

I rose quickly from my seat to face my visitor squarely, meanwhile scattering some of the books in an effort to try and cover the title Montrose had so generously deposited upon the cover of his portfolio.

I needn't have bothered. Harris was characteristically unconscious.

"As you have been so kindly interested in the Sidney investigation, sir," he said, addressing the lamp on my desk, "I thought I might stop by and inform you of the arrest we made this morning."

"Arrest?"

"The murderer of Charles Sidney, sir," he said quietly, glancing away from the lamp toward me, and then back again.

"A strange sort of fellow, sir. The doctor called him Zooaphagus—he goes about eating flies and spiders and birds. His family had him committed to the asylum when he began to slaughter cats and dogs and drink the blood of his victims."

Once again, a Stoker parallel. The Zoophagus lunatic of the novel. What did he cry? The Blood is the Life! The Blood is the Life!

Though my stomach churned, Harris appeared completely untroubled. I suspected he was privately enjoying this ghastly description. He was probably a reader of penny dreadfuls on the sly. The man must have *some* horrible secret indulgence, and that seemed as likely as any other.

"He escaped from the asylum several hours before the murder took place. We only found him yesterday when we found another body."

"Another body?" I echoed queasily.

"Yes, sir, another body. Young woman. Name of Stella. In the Whitechapel district. We found her in a back alley. Sorry business. Quite unpleasant." Harris looked up. "You wouldn't happen to know any Stellas from the Whitechapel district, sir?"

I shook my head slowly. "A madman," I said once again.

"Yes, sir. A madman." Once again, Harris observed the lamp with pointed interest.

"Then your investigation is at an end?"

"It would seem so, sir."

Several moments of silence must have followed—I cannot know for certain. I was once again lost in thought. When I looked up, I nearly caught Inspector Harris watching me—nearly, but not quite.

I roused myself to thank him. His presence had suddenly made me self-conscious and nervous, and I was eager for him to leave. The murderer had been found. I need not think of it at all further. Harris was a reminder of everything I longed to forget, a strange, silent rebuke that brought Charles Sidney back into mind. Charles Sidney was dead. It was tragic, but it was fact. And the entire business was over. My nightmares were the result of over-exertion and the idiotic Gothic fantasies of a theatrical manager.

As he made his way obligingly toward the door (making a careful study of that portal in the process as if it were the most fascinating object he had ever encountered), I asked, in a momentary afterthought: "What will happen to the poor wretch?"

"Oh, well, sir," Harris said to the door, "if he's truly mad, he'll go into a special asylum."

"And if he isn't mad?"

"Why, sir, then he'll surely be hanged."

And Harris left, bidding the door farewell with a polite nod of his head.

For several minutes after the door closed behind him, I stood where he had left me, quietly reflective of nothing. Some time passed—I could not say how long—then I suddenly became conscious of Jenson once again standing before me. In his hand was a newspaper.

"The *Pall Mall Gazette*, sir. Delivered specially by a Mr. Barnes. He would not stay to trouble you, but thought you might find a story on page three worth your attention."

I flipped to the page in question and easily found the desired headline. "HYDE PARK MURDER SOLVED?" was printed in emphatic dimensions across the top of the page.

HYDE PARK MURDER SOLVED?

Readers, who will recall the bloody murder of Mr. Charles Sidney, and the terrifying effect of the tragedy on our fair city, will be relieved to hear of Scotland Yard's recent arrest of the man who may be responsible for this appalling crime. Inspector Harris, who has been at the front of the investigation, acknowledged the arrest but refused to make further comment, but the Gazette's inquiry revealed further details. The possible murderer is a Mr. Isidore Perry, recently residing in St. Luke's asylum in B——.

Mr. Perry, once a respectable postman and now reportedly an unstable personality with a penchant for animal disembowelment, escaped from the asylum two weeks ago.

What drove this deliverer of letters to strike down his victim so violently upon that grassy park knoll? Is he, indeed, the perpetrator of this foul crime that has brought the horrifically memorable excesses of the Ripper so vividly to mind? And what will the police have to say about eerie rumors concerning yet another corpse—that of a young woman in Whitechapel?

If the poor lunatic is exonerated—and many expect him to be—will this atrocity be left unsolved, like the murders of bloody Jack? The Gazette thinks not—and hereby devotes this column to the unfolding of the mystery of the Hyde Park murderer. Watch for news of further revelations . . .

I threw down the paper with disgust. This was the work of Toby Barnes to be sure. I had pegged him for a sensationalist from the moment we first met. The *Gazette* would endeavor to transform the business from a simple tragedy into living Gothic romance. And that hint of the disreputable. Torrid and unseemly. Men like Sidney had recourse to women like Stella. Not the sort of thing one spoke of—unless one was a brazen newspaperman.

There was nothing more to fear, nothing more to dread. It was but a murder—a murder at the hands of a madman who had escaped from an asylum.

Horrible places, asylums.

There was no real connection with Sidney. He was simply an unfortunate victim. It might have been anyone—like the girl Stella in Whitechapel.

Stella. Stella and Sidney. It was an odd pairing, and yet it seemed somehow familiar. Recognition flooded over me, bringing in its wake a faint feeling of panic. Stella was the name of the girl in whose company I had first met Sidney. A quiet creature. Eyes were light blue. She was the sort of girl who didn't seem to have a surname—and yet there must be many Stellas in London, and even many Stellas of that particular variety of female.

It was all coincidence and insanity. In any case, there were no such things as vampires. There was no such thing as the living undead.

I was a sane Englishman living in a London of modernity, of enlightenment, free from the taint of superstition. Free—except in some of its seedier corners—of the revolting corruption in which Montrose delighted and Sidney had "dabbled". Montrose was an offense to England herself. An object for disgust. For scorn. He deliberately courted such censure—he thrived upon the attention, I was sure. He was a diseased, a tragic, a repulsive creature.

The whole thing was more a subject for Freud than for an exorcizing priest.

With the thought of Freud, I glanced toward Montrose's portfolio, visible on my desk despite my better efforts at concealment.

I would not read it. It was all absurd and offensive. The driveling of an unbalanced, disordered buffoon.

I would not read it.

I would not.

Chapter 9

1 June 1900: South Kensington and Camden

(From the log of the Demeter) *There came up the hatchway a sudden, startled scream, which made my blood run cold, and up on the deck he came as if shot from a gun—a raging madman, with his eyes rolling and his face convulsed with fear. "Save me! Save me!" he cried, and then looked round on the blanket of fog. His horror turned to despair, and in a steady voice he said, "You had better come too, Captain, before it is too late. . . ." God help me! How am I to account for all these horrors when I get to port? When I get to port! Will that ever be?*

"Sir? Sir?"

I awoke with a startled cry and cringed back away from the hand that had broken through my dreams—a hand that, to my bleary, aching, half-sleeping eye, appeared crimson with blood.

"Sir?"

Jenson. His hideous face a picture of concern—of alarm, even.

It was only Jenson.

I looked around. These were my rooms, crookedly illuminated by the fading light of the nearly two dozen candles wasted in my sorry vigil. I was at my desk. My head, which was beginning to clear, had lain among a sea of papers all inscribed in Montrose's florid hand.

This was reality. The rest was a dream. Not the familiar dream—the night had been blessedly free of that horrifying, bloody vision. Instead I had been a helpless victim to an abbreviated performance of what must have been a Black Mass, with Montrose as celebrant, and Esther Raveland, in witch's attire, at his side as demonic deaconess.

The superstition-laden scene of Catholic ritual had never held much attraction for me before. I had not thought much of it at all, in fact, and had thought that Sidney's allusions to it were mere affectations to shock any captive audience. Whatever Sidney's real association with the business, it was a source of great interest to Montrose. In his notes he described such things in lurid, obsessive detail, disclosing to my mind an intimate picture of the dark secrets of the occult. Demonic practices worldwide. Cannibal feasts. Witches' brews. Dark, primitive, animalistic, drunken, lewd rituals.

I sat up in my chair and began to gather up the scattered papers with an almost frenzied haste.

"Jenson! Please take this portfolio and have it delivered to Mr. Victor Montrose. I don't know where he lives and I don't want to know. If he can't be found, burn the filthy lot!"

"Will you not eat something, sir ..."

"No, Jenson," I said firmly, and as he appeared to be on the verge of a protest: "Jenson—*no*."

I unceremoniously shoved the mess of papers into Jenson's waiting arms and dismissed him.

I shaved that morning with an unsteady hand. Everything and nothing reminded me of that cursed novel and even more cursed dreams. I nicked myself with a blade and half expected to see Dracula behind me, his eyes blazing with blood lust. My nerves were shot. I needed a holiday. I would go away directly—perhaps to the seaside. As soon as the Kilbronson affair was settled, I would leave London and rest. In the meantime, diligent work was the best means of relief.

I went by the Lawson home on my way to my chambers.

The house was sober and anxious. It looked as if it were awaiting the tailor to measure out the eaves and the gutters for a mourning dress, as if eager to receive its allotment of heavy, black bombazine.

A red-eyed maid met me at the door. "Oh, sir!" she said and began to weep openly.

The doctor was in the hall, preparing to leave. "It won't be long now," he said, and his voice trembled with an unprofessional degree of emotion.

"Miss Lawson ...," I began.

"Is not long for this world. Poor girl. Poor girl."

"But what is it, Doctor? She was well only a few weeks ago. How can she be dying so quickly—how can you be sure?" Even to my own ears I sounded like a desperate young Lothario, begging for the life of his lady fair. I did not care—the thing was bizarre, monstrous!

"Sadly," said the doctor with what seemed to me solemn relish, "such things do happen. That it should afflict so dear, so sweet a lady ..."

"But what *is* it, Doctor?" I demanded yet again.

He looked irritated at being cut off so abruptly, but it inspired him into dry, clear revelation: "She is dying of weakness and infection from anemia—blood loss. Whether there are other influences at work, I cannot say."

"Influences?" I fixed upon the word at once. "What do you mean 'influences'?"

The doctor was startled. "I mean other factors in her illness. Hereditary weaknesses. Other infections." He frowned at me. "What other influences did you think I meant, young man?"

"Nothing. I did not think anything. I just wondered what you meant."

"Hum," said the doctor and looked at me with an eyebrow slightly raised.

I was not going to stand there and be appraised by this medical professional—like some specimen in a laboratory. I would not stay to be wept at by the grandmother or any other dependents. There was nothing for me to do. I hurried on my way.

Safe in my chambers, I determinedly endeavored to bury myself in my work.

It was a doomed determination. Try as I might, words blurred together and pages in their entirety became unclear, lost in a hazy, half-wakened dream where the world was awash with blood, and fiendish vampires were lying in wait around every corner.

Lucy was not the victim of a vampire. It was anemia. Just anemia. Did people die of anemia? Lucy was ...

Lucy—I meant "Adele", of course.

Adele Lawson. Not Lucy Westenra. Lucy Westenra was an imaginary character in an idiotic novel. Adele Lawson was real—was really dying.

I lifted a paper and, finding it strangely heavy to my hand, turned the document over to examine it.

Several minutes passed.

Suddenly I became aware of Francis Carstairs standing beside me, watching my face with avid curiosity.

"Yes?" I said somewhat impatiently. "What do you need, Carstairs?"

"It's Mr. Kilbronson, sir."

"Well? Is he here? Don't just stand there gaping, Carstairs. Are you ill?"

"No, sir. Mr. Kilbronson, sir. He sent you this note. He requests an immediate reply."

Kilbronson was eager to speak with me once again that afternoon. He had important information to discuss with me. He would wait upon my convenience.

I found it was largely inconvenient. I expected it was one of Kilbronson's usual meetings. He wanted to sit and make indirect references to the perfidy and unchaste meanderings of his wife, but to resist making any sort of concrete allegation. He felt the need to tell me once again how imperative it was that I find the errant Elisabetta. Perhaps he was hankering for that cursed ring. Really I think he only requested such meetings to hear himself talk. The man's voice could well have driven any wife into infidelity and thence into hiding. I almost had sympathy for the Hungarian wench.

I was still somewhat capable of reasoning, even without so much sleep. I deemed I was ill-filled for such interactions. I wrote back rapidly that two days hence would suit me better. Then I dispatched Carstairs to dispose of my reply as was necessary.

I waited several minutes to be sure that he was gone. Then I retrieved the page from the stack of papers under which I had thrust it and once again fell to a silent perusal of it.

There, firmly affixed by dried-out tea to the back of the paper, precisely and evenly at its center, was the visiting card of Father Thomas Edmund Gilroy.

"It's all a heap of nonsense!" I cried out angrily.

"Yes, sir?"

"Nothing, Carstairs. Have you nothing better to do than creep about?"

My chastened clerk quitted his station on my shoulder and, climbing atop the stool before his own desk with a great deal of mustered dignity, proceeded to copy out notes with a concentration and rapidity that was an eloquent rebuke of his unfeeling, ill-tempered employer.

I left my chambers by noon, confounding the whole business to perdition in my mind, and returned home, leaving Carstairs to wonder whatever the hell he liked. He was an irritating little object, and I began to consider the possibility of sacking him. Jenson too—the whole lot of them could go. I would retire to the country and spend the rest of my days settling the petty complaints of farmers and craftsmen.

"You are home early, sir," Jenson pointed out unnecessarily when he met me at the street door—I must have left my key behind at the office.

"Yes, Jenson, yes."

I hurried up to my sitting room. It may have been my imagination, but it seemed as if the residue of Montrose's scent had seeped from his papers and still lingered in my rooms. I opened a window to try and let in the comparative freshness of the London street, but found the air humid, heavy with atmospheric anticipation. I shut the window again.

Jenson was standing hesitatingly in the doorway watching me.

"I sent those papers away as you requested, sir."

"Very good, Jenson."

He did not retire, so I sat down beside the fireplace, took up the first book that came to hand—Baring-Gould's *The Book of Were-Wolves*—and pretended to be deeply occupied in reading it. He did not move. After staring determinedly at the same paragraph for at least five minutes, I begrudgingly looked up again.

His face, contorted with concern, was even more hideous than usual. "I hope you are well, sir. Perhaps I should send for a doctor?"

"Damn it, Jenson, there's nothing wrong with me. Don't fuss me, man. One might think you were my mother."

Jenson retreated back into his ugly visage immediately. I was almost suspicious of hidden tears in his eyes.

"Is there anything else, sir?" he asked, and his voice quavered slightly.

I was immediately repentant and hated myself for it. "No, Jenson ... Thank you."

He turned to leave.

"Jenson ..."

"Yes, sir?"

"You could bring me some strong tea. Please."

The conciliatory addition was as near to an apology as I could muster, but it was sufficient. Jenson beamed with revived enthusiasm.

"*Yes*, sir. Of *course*, sir."

And he hurried away to fulfill his errand of mercy.

The Stoker novel had somehow manifested itself upon the table that sat beside the chair by the fireplace. I considered reading it—hoping that now, free of the weight of Sidney's murder, and free of the absurd offensiveness of Montrose, the fictional world of Bram Stoker would be simply and wholly that—an innocent, entertaining fiction.

Finally I gave in to the temptation, lifted up the book, and continued from the page where I had left it.

I read for what seemed like hours, turning the pages rapidly and drinking in every melodramatic word.

Jenson brought my tea, supplemented with biscuits on a lacy tray. I suppressed the urge to snarl away this Nightingale-like touch. If the man needed to show his loyalty and devotion by such means, I could hardly protest when I had been such an unsavory fellow for so many days. For all I knew, theatrical feudalism might prove a balm to his long-injured domestic feelings. I myself could find no peace, no consolation. That did not mean that I needed to begrudge all such to Jenson as well. There was misery enough in the world without me flinging the whole doily presentation up into the air and cursing Jenson in decided terms.

I returned to my book.

Lucy Westenra was dying—*dying*. Even as Adele Lawson was dying. Professor Van Helsing, that unlikely knight errant, was come from Amsterdam. The poor girl was surrounded by suitors, each willing to shed his blood to save her. But what strange measures did the professor insist on taking! Endless consultations, transfusions, bedecking her room with garlands of strong-smelling garlic, all to no avail. She was dying. She was dead.

Jenson came and offered me something more to eat. I waved him away with as much politeness as I could manage. My stomach turned at the mere thought of food.

I turned another page. Now true horrors unfolded. Children, victims of a fledgling vampiric hunger. Lucy, a vampire! Lucy preying upon innocent children! Lucy, a sinister fiend that must be dispatched to hell!

It was absurd; it was disgusting. In this day and age! When reason had debunked the hysterics of religion and science was cementing man's progressive escape from the gross superstitions of dark bygone ages. The whole thing was a fiction, calculated to amuse. It was entertainment, nothing more. Only fiction. Innocent and inconsequential. The sort of thing to frighten young women and to be laughed at by well-balanced men.

So why was my hand so unsteady? Why was my heart beating with such irregularity, such intensity?

Jenson came into the room and fussed about me with a benevolent, maternal air that was ludicrous. Tsking over the curtain that I had clumsily caught in the window when I closed it, he reopened the window and closed it again. The gust of unsavory air that came in with this action stirred up the loose papers and notes scattered about the room.

A little piece of white cardboard danced lightly across the floor to settle at my feet. I ignored it and turned yet another page.

Jenson tiptoed away.

My terror reached its peak. Lucy's body was to be desecrated. Her head would be cut off, her heart pierced with a stake, and her mouth filled with garlic.

The men who would have given their lives for her, they were the ones to whose lot the fearful task fell.

Suddenly my hands were before my face. If the task were laid before me, if it were needed to cleanse the city of terrors wrought by a possessed maiden, could these hands—could I—could I bear to do that appalling deed? Could I pierce the dead body of Adele Lawson with a stake? Could I bear that blood—the scarlet, gushing, pouring, drenching blood?

Suddenly I became conscious of the lurid colors of the novel's dust jacket. The bright orange colors suddenly seemed suffused with bloody brilliance, reflecting—staining—my hands.

"Are you well, sir?" Jenson asked, startled from lighting the lamp—the sudden blaze of light that had transformed the novel into a blood-drenched mirage—at my sudden cry.

"Yes, Jenson," I said. "Quite well."

The beads of sweat stood out on my forehead, belying the assurance. But Jenson, making a prudent calculation that showed clearly in his eyes and brought wrinkles to his forehead, checked further inquiry and left, propping the door open behind him as if the crack would more readily alert him to further disturbance. Once I heard his footsteps peter off downstairs—they paused for a long time a few steps down the stair—I rose and closed the door.

It was absurd; it was insane. Men did not go about spearing and dismembering dead bodies to exorcize demoniac spirits. Dead women did not prey on silly children on Hampstead Heath—or anyone else, for that matter. Charles Sidney had been killed by a fly-eating lunatic. The girl Stella from Whitechapel—she had been killed by a fly-eating lunatic. People could not be killed by vampires, nor could they be made into vampires. There were no vampires. It was all a deluded nightmare.

And yet the reality remained. Adele was dying. She might soon be dead.

I looked down, as if nudged by a puppy impatient for attention, to retrieve the book that I had thrown from me in my horror. I lifted it and once more revealed the white face and scarlet lettering of the irrepressible visiting card of the train-bound friar, the man who had first disturbed my peaceful life with nonsensical talk of vampires. Thomas Edmund Gilroy. Vampire Slayer.

It was only midafternoon when I made my way toward St. Dominic's Priory, but the sky was heavy with moody import and the air rich with the smell of sulphur. I emerged from the underground to find myself in the midst of the settling of a soot-ridden and potentially lethal London particular.

Such moody weather is familiar to the Londoner; when the smoky yellow cloud descends, we keep to our houses. When the cloud becomes a heavy, lowering, brown mass, darkening quickly, as is its wont—a thick curtain coming down upon the city so that the very houses find it difficult to breathe—then the Londoner cannot escape. It creeps in through the windows, the doors, and even the walls, a dirty, filthy, sooty demon, unrelenting and unstoppable, and stifles him.

The density was not yet at its fullest. I choked and fought for breath, but I walked on, making my way cautiously through the streets. There was no going back now. I was far from my home. If I did not continue on my way, I would soon be lost, a drowned victim of the unrelenting fog.

A startling noise was close by me, the noise of anger, annoyance, and physical distress.

A pale light appeared suddenly a few feet from my elbow—a lantern carried by a young carter leading his horse and team slowly through the muck. The horses, faintly discernable as a mess of muscles and dark physical mass, came like ghostly beasts rising out of the mist, transforming into gross physicality to gallop wildly over a distant, haunted moor. Black, brown, gray, yellow, and red, all blurred together in a messy dreamscape. Eerie but concrete. The fog made all things ghastly.

I walked on.

A sudden scream came out of the darkness. Cries of terror followed in rapid succession, and one awful, repeated cry of pain.

A mad cacophony of confused voices followed.

"Where is he?"

"His leg! His leg!"

"Hold that horse there!"

"Who is it?"

"Damn it! Keep out of the way!"

"Fool to be out in the fog!"

"Save him! Oh, save him!"

"What's happening?"

"You can't see anything in this muck ..."

"Is he dead?"

"Call a doctor!"

"Hold that horse! Here! You! *Hold that horse!*"

I could imagine the scene, though I could not see. Bodies. Splintered wood. Torn upholstery. The wild prancing and thrashing of sweating, desperate horses. Men's faces contorted in anger, fear, pain. The road splattered with blood. Drenched with blood. Blood.

I hurried away, feeling my path along a cold, almost invisible wall. The violence of the collision—if such was the cause of so much turmoil—rang in my ears, following me on my way, the voice of chaos in that heavy, villainous blindness.

As I stumbled along my way, I thought I saw a dim light ahead. I hurried toward it as best I could. It was a streetlamp, struggling boldly toward illumination in the face of the oppressive, all-encompassing fog.

I leaned heavily against a building to read the street sign posted upon it. *Malden Road.* I must be close.

The fog, which had whistled and whispered as it gathered, had now fallen into silence. There was nothing living to be heard. The whole world could have been silent, everyone—man, woman, and child—dead. All except me.

The horrifying end of the Russian schooner *Demeter* came vividly to my mind. I could see the desolate demise of the sailors. I could see the captain, lashed tight to the helm. I could see the strange creature, rising out of the fog. I could see its eyes.

I could see its red, piercing eyes.

Its eyes. Red, glowing eyes, hellish eyes, shining through the heavy darkness at me, close upon me.

As I watched in terror, thin lips appeared and parted in a villainous smile to display a set of glistening white teeth, with two sharp, chilling fangs at the forefront.

Crying out in fear, I stumbled back against a cold stone wall, and gazed up in desperation.

The sign was there: *St. Dominic's Priory.*

I felt my way along the wall. Here were steps. Here was a door.

I knocked at the door with a real sense of urgency—and knocked again louder. And louder again. The darkness swirled ever more heavily about me. Soon I was pounding at the door, pounding so hard that the flesh of my hands stung with pain, bruises ringing through my hands and arms and shoulders and back and onward so that my entire body seemed one throbbing mass of hysterical pain. My heart caught in my throat—a throat already suffocating in the dank, close fog; my head whirled round with mounting terrors.

"Dear God!" a voice cried—and it must have been mine—"Help me!"

A rush of wind was upon us, pulling the fog along with it. I closed my eyes, blinded by the assault of swirled up dust and wet filth.

I opened them and found I was gazing upward upon a darkening sky, glittering with a few untroubled stars.

The door opened with a comfortable creak, and melodrama melted away into nothingness. A smiling pair of
bespectacled eyes looked out at me from a round face.

"Well, well, well!" said the insufferably cheery voice of
Father Thomas Edmund Gilroy, O.P. "You've reached
the putty part, have you?"

Chapter 10

2 June 1900: Camden and Mayfair

(From Dr. Seward's diary) *"Friend John. I pity your bleeding heart; and I love you the more because it does so bleed. If I could, I would take on myself the burden that you do bear. But there are things that you know not, but that you shall know, and bless me for knowing, though they are not pleasant things."*

The parlor of the priory was simply decorated, with a few pieces of religious art displayed at appropriate intervals on the bare white walls.

One picture in particular caught my eye—an image of a disembodied head on a white cloth, with eyes staring basilisk-like out at me from a highly stylized background of gold and twisted symbols. If these Papists were really capable of battling supernatural bloodsuckers, I mused to myself, it could only be because they were more strange and more gruesome even than their Draculean adversaries.

"Acheiropoieton," said Father Thomas Edmund conversationally, following my gaze. "The icon not made by hands. *Vera icon.* Popularly known as Veronica's veil. One of my favorite images."

It would be, I thought to myself drily.

He bustled me into a seat.

"And now," he said, "tea!"

I protested—my stomach was in too great a disorder to stand anything, food or drink.

"Nonsense! You're exhausted and undernourished! If we don't start feeding you, you'll start seeing visions!"

This struck rather too close to home to be answered comfortably, so I resigned myself to tea.

He scurried out the door, exchanged a few words with some unknown person, and reappeared within a matter of moments.

"Tea," he announced solemnly, "is forthcoming!" Then he chuckled. "We should hope, however, that it is not fourth coming—I should not want to wait about through three other arrivals!"

And he laughed with delight.

I was too dazed to be horrified. I do not know what sort of extraordinary powers I had been attributing to him or why I had conceived in him some sort of rescuer from the bloodsucking threat, but the reality was a severe—a traumatizing—disappointment. A stronger dose of reality could not be conceived. A few moments earlier I had been firmly convinced that a vampiric threat was even then on my heels, complete with sharp teeth dripping with blood. And here I was with Father Thomas Edmund Gilroy, my would-be savior, suffering obnoxious jokes in an atmosphere of stifling piety. However could I have imagined that this little man in his outlandish dress with his infantile sense of humor could be any help? Either there were indeed vampires or I was going quite mad. This silly little man could not help with either sorry state of affairs. I should leave immediately.

I even rose to do so, but was forestalled.

Father Thomas Edmund settled himself in the chair opposite, looked intensely into my face, and said: "Now, my friend, sit back down and rest. You need your strength. Once we drink some tea and you are revived, we will set out to see Miss Lawson."

I was so astonished to hear her name that, without questioning further, I sat back down. It must have been the confessional effect of the seasoned Papist, but I found it difficult to resist the urge to unburden my soul. Nevertheless, resist I did.

"The fog was quite extraordinary," said the priest in a chatty manner. "Dangerous too. There's nothing like a London fog to cause mischief."

I thought it a slight understatement and was unwilling to describe my own experiences in that toxic haze, and so did not reply.

"I once was caught in a fog rather like this one," he continued, untroubled by my refusal to speak. "It was all quite eerie. I almost began to imagine things."

"Things such as ...?" I asked curiously, though against my will.

"Oh, noises and goblins and ghouls and all the sorts of things one imagines in the darkness." The idea seemed to amuse the priest for he chuckled merrily over it. My stomach churned and I once again thought of escape.

Some moments passed in silence (him chuckling while I plotted routes of prompt exit—would they stop me before I reached the front door, I wondered?), then the door opened and a young man—attired, like my host, in an absurd white dress—entered, bearing a tea-laden tray. He seemed oddly familiar somehow, but I dismissed the fledgling recognition as a characteristic of this surreal scene. Indeed, the longer I sat there in that unlikely company, the more was I convinced that my visit was ill-judged. I was overtired and perhaps hysterical.

And yet he had mentioned Adele Lawson.

I drank my tea obediently. It was then I realized that I had gone for some time without truly deriving strength from food or drink, despite Jenson's better efforts. I even felt revived, and very nearly grateful toward these eccentric Papists. They were merciful and essentially harmless— I supposed.

"My dear Mr. Kemp," said the priest, "I, at any rate, do not bite. There is no reason to fear me though you do find me—and my brethren—rather bewildering." I started to make protesting noises (once again, it was a bit too close to the truth to be polite), but he continued: "That is by the way. You are here because of your concern for Miss Lawson and because of certain inchoate fears concerning her condition. These fears are not unconnected with the strange case of the death of Mr. Charles Sidney."

I must have started visibly at the name, for he nodded and went on: "Yes, the death of Mr. Charles Sidney was of great interest to me as well. A perplexing tragedy indeed. You have come to me because you are desperate. Because you can think of no one else on whom to call. You think that anyone else would think you mad. I, Mr. Kemp, do not believe that you are mad. I will not say that I can provide you with all of the answers you seek, nor would you believe many answers with which I *could* provide you. But I do promise you this: I do not believe that you are mad."

"Then do you mean to say," I blurted out, "that you believe in vampires?"

He smiled. I wondered if anything ever brought a frown to his face. "My friend, I could tell you of far stranger things than vampires. But not today. Today we have business to which we must attend, and immediately."

"Business?"

"Yes. We will go to the bedside of Miss Lawson."

I flushed. "The family ... what explanation ..."

But he simply shook his head reassuringly. "All of that has been taken care of," he said. "There is no need for concern on that score."

I did not question him further or seek to analyze the overwhelming feeling of relief that washed over me. It might well be a business of sheep leading sheep, but at that moment I was almost happy to be led. Exhaustion—physical and emotional—was so intense that I was a malleable piece of wax, a gullible follower, even for the briefest moment, of the bustling little Papist. It must be, I thought, how the Irish feel all of the time. Potatoes and priests. Priests and potatoes. Such an odd combination.

It was when we stood together in the street that I recognized the young man—it was the white-robed priestling I had seen outside Adele Lawson's home during my horrifying nighttime jaunt. Then my feelings of relief vanished, and I once again saw in the little man, with his Homburg hat, his black cloak, and a large black bag (which I offered to carry for him), something vaguely sinister.

The dramatic fog had been replaced with alarming rapidity by a cold, dreary cloudiness. The little priest set a steady southern course, bouncing determinedly through the streets, nodding and smiling at those we passed with an almost pathological friendliness. He received his fair share of blank stares and even a number of censorious English glares, but most astonishing to me were the number of people who smiled or ventured a "good day, Father". At one point, several singularly unwashed small boys determined that the white robes were an open invitation to anyone who might feel at all inclined to follow along in our wake. It seemed the cobblestones of the London roads could have stood up to ridicule us. We walked on, a merry parade of absurdity, for several streets before they became bored with the game and scurried away to wreak mischief elsewhere.

A quick trip on the underground shortened our passage, but when we emerged on the more familiar streets of South Kensington, I began to feel even more self-conscious than I had with the mocking boys behind us. I was, after all, in the company of a rather odd little personage. I wished that his bag were rather larger—large enough to be more conspicuous than I was.

Since the fog had cleared, the streets were teeming with people. I began to see faces I recognized—a few business associates, a lady whose tea shop I had visited more than once, a young man known from my schooldays, my own clerk, Francis Carstairs (who stared at us, agape, prompting me to stare back sternly with a glance that plainly asked what he was doing out at a pub at this time of the day when he ought to be tending to business in my neglected chambers), and even Jenson, laden with food purchases; the houses had opened up to send out the teeming masses of my acquaintances, holding back only those who would have marveled at the company I kept but without recognizing me to hold it against me later on. Jenson was too well-bred to stare, but I could not help but wonder what on earth he thought of his employer, who had quit the house so suddenly, now wandering the city at the side of a rotund, white-shrouded, bespectacled Papist.

As we began to weave through streets of stately homes, nearing that which belonged to the Lawsons, I felt sick, but I continued to follow that odd little man.

The hush that had pervaded the house for days had intensified so that it was almost as thick as the fog through which I had fought my way to the priory. The lights were dimmed, and the windows themselves seemed to be in anticipation of mourning garb.

We were greeted by the same teary-eyed maid, who looked startled at the sight of us—at first I thought she was startled to see Father Thomas Edmund, but then I realized that she was more surprised to see me in his company than she was alarmed at the arrival of the priest. Still, she unquestioningly ushered us up the stairs, as if she had received instructions to convey us to Adele's bedside immediately upon our arrival.

Once again, I had stumbled upon a strange scene. The boudoir of a lovely young debutante was an unexpected enough place in which to find myself, but to arrive there as the accepted companion of Father Thomas Edmund, and to be acknowledged with sober bows by three physicians and a High Church clergyman—that was absolutely bizarre.

Adele's grandmother was there as well, her face completely blanched of color. She reached out and took my arm, pressing it lightly as an acknowledgment of my presence, then she returned to her pale vigil. At the foot of the bed lay a small, golden, curly-haired dog, sprawled across the cold feet of the bed's occupant, its eyes occasionally peeking out from under drooping lids to look up at the pinched, bloodless face of the dying girl.

She was the most fantastic figure in the room—a skeletal remain of her former self, a ghastly prop in a melodramatic scene, her graying countenance peeking out from under a lacy-white coverlet that bore the stains of sickness. And all around her a host of clustering objets d'art—for the shelves and tables throughout the room were heavily adorned with souvenirs and pretty things—seemed tawdry and tired, like failed attempts at cheerfulness in a house oppressed with woe. Could bows and lacy pillows and pink vases with silken purple flowers and satin-encumbered dolls and ceramic jewel cases and garishly smiling figurines battle against the range of crusted green medicine bottles and soiled towels imperfectly hidden on the table beside the bed?

The clergyman and Father Thomas Edmund spoke aside together for quite some time. One of the physicians joined them. The dog glanced sometimes in their direction, as if to inquire as to the conclusions drawn by these wise men, then he would sigh and look back toward Adele.

The consultation finished, Father Thomas Edmund went and stood close by the bedside.

I moved closer—not too close, as the dog emitted a deep growl when I stood beside the bed, causing me to retreat respectfully a pace—and waited, breathlessly, for what I knew must come: for the priest to request his bag, and to draw from it some necessary implement for the coming conflict. Crucifix, garlic, holy water. I expected the lot.

Father Thomas Edmund prayed silently under his breath for a long time. The minutes passed and my impatience grew in direct proportion to the number of times I saw his lips move. It was all very well to babble silent prayers, but I could see no clear indication that he was vanquishing the dark threat as he was supposed to.

Sometimes the words came forth in quiet wisps, so nearly inaudible that I almost thought I imagined the words. *In manus tuas, Dómine, comméndo sp'ritum meum. Dómine Iesu Christe, suscipe sp'ritum meum ... Sancta Maria, orâ pro me.* And again a little while later: *Requiem æternam ... et lux perpetua ... Domine exaudi orationem meam ... et clamor meus ad te veniat.*

Finally his silent prayer ceased. He opened his eyes and looked at Adele—who had grown so still I had almost forgotten her.

Then he crossed the room to her grandmother, bent down, and spoke quietly to her.

The cry of anguish that rose from the bereft elderly woman struck agony into the depths of my soul. It was echoed by the dog at Adele's feet. He scurried forward on the bed to lick his mistress' hand, then collapsed with disappointment, threw back his curly head, and howled with abandon. The doctors were already clustering around the bed. I could hear—as if from far away—maids and other attendants weeping in the hallway.

I stood gazing down at the dead face of Adele Lawson, the cheeks white and thin, the mouth sagging open slightly, the eyes closed—waxen and motionless, untroubled in the midst of the mournful bustle.

It was not the first time I had seen a dead body. The first was an old man who died in my father's church. He had snored through so many sermons that the first inkling we had that he had died was his irregular silence. My father's body was next. That came later. Found dead in his bed. Dead in his sleep. How could you tell the difference between death and sleep? Then I looked again at that gentle sagging mouth, already faded in color, and my stomach turned.

It was over. And he had done nothing. Nothing at all. Nothing to stop it. Nothing to help her. He had not even opened his bag, much less produced a sprig of garlic or a cross to put about her neck. He had only mumbled a few broken prayers. And nothing had happened. Now she would be prey to the full lust of the undead, driving her to a horrific banquet of childish victims, glutted into sensual desperation by this profane feasting. And he was doing nothing to bar the path of the evil beast. Nothing. Nothing.

The last sight I had was of a doctor drawing a sheet over that pallid face. Then, following Father Thomas Edmund in a daze, I left the room.

We passed down the hall and the stairs and out of the house without speaking.

The sunlight, questionable as it was, seemed an insult to the dead.

In the street I grasped his sleeve and blurted out brokenly the horrifying question that had come to my mind: "We will not ... shall we ... what now must we do?"

"Do?"

"For her soul!" I insisted.

"Pray for God's mercy. We shall of course offer a Mass for her repose and for the consolation of her family."

"But, Father ..." He had turned to make his way down the street, but I gripped his sleeve once more. "Does that mean we need not do that horrible thing?"

"What horrible thing?"

His refusal to comprehend drove me to state it clearly, in all of its melodramatic glory: "Exorcise her body to release her soul from the undead?" And the words of Van Helsing came to me with horrifying vividness: *I shall cut off her head and fill her mouth with garlic, and I shall drive a stake through her body.*

"Oh, dear me, no!" said Father Gilroy, almost in surprise. "No, no, no! There's no need for any of that! That would be quite ... no, not at all. She is quite well now. She was already ill, I suspect, and her condition worsened by the nearness of the threat. A victim of a bloody contagion, you might say." He smiled gently. "You really shouldn't believe everything you read, my friend."

I quitted him abruptly, awash with anger and grief.

Chapter 11

5 June 1900: Briefly the Inns at Court, but Primarily Belgravia

(From Dr. Seward's diary) *Since my rebuff of yesterday I have a sort of empty feeling; nothing in the world seems of sufficient importance to be worth the doing.... As I knew that the only cure for this sort of thing was work, I went down amongst the patients. I picked out one who has afforded me a study of much interest. He is so quaint in his ideas, and so unlike the normal lunatic ...*

Some days passed without event. I worked, ate, and slept. It seemed as if the death of Adele had brought release—my dreams were untroubled and my mind clear.

Well, perhaps not entirely clear. I did not understand anything that had happened, and when the thought of that priest or of Esther Raveland rose to mind, I was filled with an inexpressible and directionless fury. So I determinedly did not think of either. And the days continued to go by with comforting monotony: I worked, ate, and slept.

Then came a Monday, less than a week after my visits to the priory and to the Lawson home. A letter was deposited on my desk amid other everyday correspondence— and something in the envelope made my stomach turn again. The drama, whatever it was, and the disruption of my peace, would yet continue. I read through all of my business correspondence and replied to those letters which required a response before I could bring myself to read that final missive.

The envelope was sealed with wax impressed with an ornate inescutcheon of pretense combining what appeared to be the heraldry of a vast range of aristocratic houses. It was practically illegible to my eye beyond this; I ascribed it to a foreign nobleman. In this I was assisted by circumstantial suspicion: I had immediately recognized my correspondent's address as that of the late Charles Sidney.

The letter, inscribed on paper so delicate it might have been lace, was framed by a border of almost rococo floridity. The ink was of an intense black, and yet for a moment, when the words reflected in the sunlight streaming through my window, I thought it had been inscribed in the red thickness of blood.

Its contents were simple enough:

10 F——Street, Belgravia

Date

To Mr. John Kemp, Esq.
——Inns of Court

Dear Mr. Kemp,

I write to you at the recommendation of Mr. Edgar Kilbronson. I am eager to consult you professionally regarding certain business transactions I wish to undertake in the city. As I am an old man and not given to travel with ease, I beg your indulgence: might I beg a visit from you tomorrow at ten o'clock in the morning? You may call at my home. If

this time is not convenient for you, please inform me when
a visit might be soonest possible. Otherwise, I shall expect
you at the time named.

Yours, very sincerely,
L. Popescu

It was not as menacing as I might have expected, with such atmospherics surrounding my life of late. A nobleman indeed, to combine courtesy and imperiousness. It was hardly the tenor of a Draculean missive, yet I did not like the task. And what on earth had possessed Edgar Kilbronson, that bizarre, cadaverous man, to recommend me? Was it possibly he truly valued my half-hearted and ineffectual efforts to track down his errant, sensual, Hungarian wife? I sat for some time pondering the situation in silence.

Then I shook myself, dismissed the thought, wrote a quick note confirming the appointment, and returned to my dull, dusty, undramatic labors.

When I arrived at the Sidney mansion the following morning, I found it strikingly changed. The details of the alteration were difficult to identify at first. I felt certain that certain trees and bushes had been removed. It was, perhaps, a deception concocted by Mother Nature—with the summer thus far advanced, the landscape might well appear transformed. Nevertheless, a few small stumps, barely visible, were enough to confirm for me that I was not imagining a tactical deforestation.

The front door was opened by a tall, suave, handsome, impeccably clean-shaven young man, with an easy manner and a charming smile.

"Do come in, Mr. Kemp," he said affably.

I did as instructed and encountered the terrifying white face and dark glasses of the carriage driver, now featured atop a butler's sober, black garb.

"Don't mind Albu," said the younger man. To emphasize this dismissive attitude, my guide took my hat and coat, handed them to the other man, and commanded sharply: "Go, Albu. Tea."

The albino left without a word.

"My name is Gregory Anghelescu. I am Count Popescu's secretary. Would you please follow me? The count is looking forward to meeting you."

I followed him, my mind busily sizing him up and his position in this (to my disturbed mind) highly suspicious household.

Anglicized given name. No accent—except a trace that, rather than demonstrating foreign extraction, seemed to reveal a conscious correction from Cockney to the king's English. The surname was as foreign as could be imagined. His dress and appearance were excellently tailored and comported with all of the richest decrees of Continental fashion. An Englishman? Descended from ... Hungarians? Romanians? Greeks? With all of the affectation of a Frenchman, I added to myself slightingly. I had no patience with cosmopolitan indistinctness.

Gregory fit in well with the house, which, like the configuration of the lawn, exhibited significant change. It was less attractive and decidedly less respectable in its decorations. More opulent. A bit gaudy, in fact. I attributed the sudden influx of vibrantly colored tapestry, grandiose furniture on decidedly modern lines, and dramatic statuary to a foreign desire to appear more English than the English themselves. Everything was of the latest mode. Up-and-coming artists had certainly found a new patron in Popescu. This was a house prepared to be a center for artistic and social event. It seemed discordant—and as thoroughly un-English as I could have imagined a place to be. The carpets were so unworn it felt positively blasphemous to tread on them. None of the familiar signs of the careful, penny-savvy Briton, who would patch holes in carpet with pieces from another carpet, not caring if the result was a discord of designs.

The house was meticulously clean, as well. And devoid of mirrors. (My knowledge of Stoker prompted me to take special note of this absence.) Beyond this, it was precisely the sort of house an Englishman would imagine belonged to a wealthy foreigner. In fact, it felt strangely to me like a theatrical scene, carved out in meticulous and highly stylized details.

What was to be the performance? I wondered.

The count received me in the library, which had been transformed into a magnificent room. Several thousand books, many of them ornamental enough to delight the wildest dreams of the decadents, covered the walls and piled upon the tables in aesthetically precise dishabille. A large round table, with an intricate design inlaid into the top, was at the center, with maps, papers, and books around it. A command station. And its master was at its head.

"Good evening," said the count, and bowed. "Welcome to my home, Mr. Kemp."

I thanked him, and tried not to look as hysterically suspicious as I inwardly felt.

Even setting aside my predisposition to consider him so, Popescu was a strange man. He was not gilded with the superficial trappings of villainy common to melodramatic literary or theatrical depictions, so my expectations there were all dashed. He was tall and thin, but neither to an inordinate degree. His eyes were vibrantly alive, but not blazing with inner fires and neither pink nor red. They were dark blue. He wore his beard and mustaches relatively short, in the manner of a German goatee. His hair was dark, but speckled with a healthy proportion of gray and white hairs, appropriate to his age.

As to that age, I would have said he was in his fifties or sixties, based upon the topics of which he spoke as if he had personal knowledge of them. (Perhaps his father had been involved in the Greek War of Independence—though this made little sense to me, as Popescu was open regarding his Romanian heritage—yet, later that day, in an aside regarding a painting I noted in the hall, he provided details of Drăgăşani that could only have been known to one who was present. Despite this clear association to the second decade of the past century, he seemed remarkably able-bodied for a man of that age.)

"You hysterical fool!" I chided myself. "Are you going to see Dracula at every turn? Haven't you had enough of that absurd obsession?" Yet my discomfort remained.

The count continued. "You have been highly recommended by Mr. Kilbronson," he noted, and bowed slightly to a far corner of the room.

It was then that I realized, for the first time, that my client himself was in the room. He received the bow of the count, which was performed as if in recognition of a unique and meritorious action, and bowed his own acceptance of the compliment.

Popescu gestured me into a seat around the table. Then he gestured Kilbronson into another. Gregory took a third, produced a notebook and a pen, and stood at attention. Popescu took the head of the table—if round tables can have heads.

If I had been concerned about making a good impression on this potential client, I need not have wasted the energy; he scarcely allowed me to speak. Instead he held forth in confident, strident tones, with a carefully modulated voice that was somehow spellbinding.

"You must be wondering why I have called you here," he began. "The explanation is simple: I have need of a legal man to supervise some of my affairs here in London. Why London? I have left my home to seek a less confining, more sophisticated land. A land of enlightenment and progress. How could I fail, then, to turn to London! ...

"In my home country I was so far advanced as to gain some unpopularity; you see, Mr. Kemp, I had this ridiculous notion that a man of great thought and sophisticated ideas could be of assistance in society, even if that man was burdened with an ancient title. I aspired to bring advanced ideas to a land backward and priest-ridden." Then he shrugged and held up his hands to illustrate his tragic frustration and disappointment. "I am sure you can imagine my feelings, Mr. Kemp. The fierce outcry and intense prejudice of the uneducated peasantry was nothing in comparison with the treatment I received at the hands of those in my own class.

"I have much money, Mr. Kemp, and consequently, I could easily respond to such unfriendliness and bigotry. I removed myself, my money, and my ideas to London, where I am confident that my ideals will flourish.

"I wish to work toward the establishment of a society—or, perhaps, a ratification of the society that already exists—a society that embraces all advances in science, all of the incredible accomplishments of man, filtered through the judgment of men of profound acumen. Mr. Kilbronson has been a valuable ally for me."

Again they exchanged profound bows.

It all sounded wonderfully lofty and impressive, I thought to myself, but I had yet to discern what it was he wanted from me. It sounded rather beyond my ken. I was a practical man, and a man of sound principles, but all of this talk of ideals for society sounded alarmingly like the sort of sermon my father would have preached (though with a higher percentage of fire and brimstone, not to mention what he referred to as "The Texts").

As I shook my head to dismiss the spirit of my father from my mind, I returned to the room and the table to become conscious of my host's eyes focused steadily, even scaldingly, upon me.

I flushed and was about to murmur an explanation, when the nobleman's anger (if it was anger) vanished and a gracious smile took its place. "Mr. Kemp," he said with a self-deprecating smile, "I wax eloquent and find I have not been clear. You are a practical man, and a busy one. I have not put my business before you. I shall do so now."

Then paperwork appeared. This was something tangible, something real with which I could engage. Wills. Bills of sale. Questions of laws regarding trade.

"I wish you to become my primary legal advisor, Mr. Kemp."

"What is to be the nature of your business here?" I asked.

"It is simple. The due professional organization and functioning of an office to support the cultivation of that higher order of society of which I spoke. As far as you would be concerned, this would involve some basic trade arrangements with other countries where I have already established an office to support my labors. It would also involve legal details regarding housing space. Some storage to support my trade. All quite simple, but I wish them to be handled by someone I can trust and you, as I said, come highly recommended."

"I am flattered," I said, but my uncertainty remained.

Kilbronson was so unlikely to be a dedicated client. As far as I could tell, I had done nothing to assist him in his situation. In fact, I was rather certain I had added to his dry frustration. (Though, looking at him now, I wondered if he really *was* frustrated. He seemed so lacking in human emotion, that cadaverous automaton—if the two could thus merge into one man.)

"Then you accept the charge of my affairs?"

"If I may," I said, with some embarrassment (as I found myself inwardly panicking by the need to decide on what was probably an important commission, but so inexplicably distasteful to me), "might I beg a day to consider my current workload, to examine these documents, and to determine how well I would be able to meet your needs, Count?"

The smile widened. (It was the spirit—or voice—of my mother now: "What big teeth you have, Grandmother ...") "Certainly, Mr. Kemp. Certainly."

I saw no movement and heard no bell, but suddenly Albu was in the room again, gazing with silent, morose attention upon his master.

I must have looked as disconcerted as I felt at his reappearance, for, when I looked again to the count, I found him looking steadily at me again. Then Popescu smiled mournfully. "In my country," he commented with an engaging note of sadness in his voice, "we are much oppressed by superstition. Strange ideas and ill-taught peasants. My loyal man was most barbarously used. A gypsy child. Sold to a traveling fair and caged like a wild animal. He once attempted to speak of his pain before a crowd of ghoulish peasants. His master cut out his tongue as punishment."

The subject of this tale did not move a muscle during the recitation. I have never thought of myself as a prig or a snob—my father, emphatic as he was regarding the limited accessibility of eternal salvation, was an advocate for passionate pity of the poorest of the poor. Perhaps prompted by the spirit of my father and roused by old memories of the endless sermons regarding "these little ones", or perhaps because the openness of this stranger to discuss such things was jarring, or perhaps because of some true, critical self-analysis, I felt sudden embarrassment and guilt for my own unspoken dislike and mistrust.

"I freed him," the old man added simply. "And now he is loyal to me."

I tried not to stare at the butler as he silently handed me my belongings at the door. He helped me on with my overcoat, and I felt as if the touch of his hand, even through the thick fabric, was icy.

Escape, I thought. Escape.

"Mr. Kemp!"

Gregory Anghelescu was again beside me, urbane and pleasant. "It was good of you to come this afternoon. May I issue the count's personal invitation to return next Thursday evening at eight o'clock? He is holding a sort of inaugural *salon de Belgravia*"—the flash of ivory-white teeth indicated his delight in his own humor—"and I believe it will be a highly enjoyable evening."

I murmured acceptance hurriedly and turned on my way.

"We shall see you soon, then," called the secretary blithely. "Good day, Mr. John Kemp!"

As I walked down the lane toward the gates that marked the limit of Popescu's domain (walking as quickly as I dared without showing my own discomfort or appearing rude), I heard my name called once again. I turned to see Kilbronson hurrying toward me. He placed a cadaverous hand on my arm.

"That ... that business about my wife," he said awkwardly. "Do know that I appreciate your efforts." He attempted a smile—a painful thing to see.

I nodded briefly in acceptance of his remarks and tried to stifle the feeling of loathing that rose in my soul at the sight of him.

When I stood again in the street outside the grounds of the former home of Charles Sidney, I found I could once again breathe with ease. But breathing was one thing; determining the right course of action was quite another.

I walked home slowly, pondering and unhappy.

Chapter 12

19 June 1900: Belgravia

(From Dr. Seward's diary) *When Lucy—I call the thing that was before us Lucy because it bore her shape—saw us she drew back with an angry snarl, such as a cat gives when taken unawares; then her eyes ranged over us. Lucy's eyes in form and colour; but Lucy's eyes unclean and full of hell-fire, instead of the pure, gentle orbs we knew. At that moment the remnant of my love passed into hate and loathing; had she then to be killed, I could have done it with savage delight.*

The stars sparkled in an unnaturally clear sky on the evening of Count Popescu's salon. So remarkable was the crisp, pleasant weather, so devoid of our constitutional English clammy chill or its summer sister, damp and inescapable heat, that every guest felt obligated to comment upon it.

"Wonderful evening. So comfortable."

"Such a clear sky. Lovely weather."

"Extraordinarily pleasant this evening."

"Have you ever seen such a sky?"

With the superstition known only to the truly modern, well-educated Englishman, this unexpected atmospheric delight was immediately attributed to the authority of our host. As if he wielded special power over Mother Nature, the clear sky and agreeable weather conditions were a point in his favor. Even before entering the small park surrounding the reformed house of Charles Sidney, guests were inclined to think well of the count. The beauty and impeccable landscaping of the grounds, the majesty of the yew tree, and the brilliant allure of the lights streaming from the house itself, cemented inclination and transformed it to near bigotry. Crossing the threshold, the metamorphosis was complete: guests became disciples.

It was all thoroughly unpleasant and baffling. To begin with, it was unheard of to witness a party on that scale after the London Season had technically concluded. There were scores of people there who by rights ought to have been out in the country visiting each other or preparing shooting parties and other diversions during the summer recess of Parliament. Nevertheless, here they all were. I looked at those faces, torn between ghoulish curiosity, greed for status (to be seen in such a place!), and a sense of self-importance buoyed by the mere invitation, and felt disgusted with society.

Esther Raveland too. That was a shock.

So was seeing Gregory Anghelescu so attentive to her needs.

He wasn't obsequious, but he was clearly even more charmingly conscious of her presence than he was of all of the guests. He and Popescu combined made an effective host. Popescu stood back graciously awaiting and receiving the floods of fascinated adorers. Anghelescu weaved in and out among the guests, speaking with everyone, engaging in an intense, highly personal manner, as if each and every person to whom he spoke should feel honored by a special attention.

Indeed, that was the real charm of the man. He had a power of imbuing every speech, every glance, with a special and deeply personal significance. There was a dark side to this automatic intimacy—the exclusion of the nonchosen multitudes. I did not see evidence of it this evening, since his attentions were widespread and even gratuitous, but I could well imagine the devastating impact of being the one person who did *not* receive those attentions.

There was also no respect for caste or position in his courtesies. I remembered the words of Popescu, his purported egalitarianism. It seemed hypocritical as he stood there, lord of the manor, showering gracious attention onto the lowly masses. Meanwhile his excellently dressed dogsbody gave each and every person a sense of being *someone*.

It was an eclectic group, with no participants completely outside the reaches of polite society, but the boundaries of social acceptability were certainly strained. The denizens of the red book, though not entirely respected, were not technically trespassed or breached. Unwashed artists and their bohemian models, lounging in this corner, legitimized chiefly through the fact that the particularly unkempt young man with the shaggy beard was in fact the dissolute second son of a marquis. Pompous university dons holding forth in another corner to an audience of one or two miserable victims. Diamond-dripping duchesses at the window, alongside a Frenchwoman of some notoriety attired in emeralds and as little else as fashion permitted. Debutantes, some innocent, most not. Scientists and leading men of the day. It was not usual to see so many of the artistic set mingling (or at least occupying the same general spaces) as Members of Parliament and other dignitaries. What attraction could the count hold to draw in such a wide range of visitors? What power or influence did he wield so that the guests accepted this bizarre mixing of their circles—and even delighted in it? For any other host, this would have been a monumental failure of a gathering. Here it was a triumph.

Except, I thought dryly, to me. I appeared to be the only person present who was not in the throes of an almost mystical societal delight.

I looked again to Esther Raveland. Even when Anghelescu was not at her side, he seemed yet to be the self-appointed minister of her care and ease. I saw a smile of gratitude on her face, and so strong was my anger—and, it must be admitted, jealousy—that I felt her to be un-womanly and even immodest.

I turned away from the sight of her, wondering who it was that truly had attended her at this party, for at first there was no sign of aunt or cousin. Then, as I scanned the crowd, I espied through the teeming sea of Popescu adorers a single, uncomfortable face.

I recognized her from a fleeting glance months before. This must be Lydia, and her unhappiness made her my kinswoman.

I walked over to her.

"Good evening," I said. "I'm sorry to push my own acquaintance on you, Miss, but you look as if you are seeking someone. May I help? The name is Kemp. John Kemp."

"Oh, I recognized you," she said hurriedly. "I know I shouldn't say it, but really, anyway, it is so good to see a face I know. Not personally, you understand. Such an odd place, don't you think? So many strange people. I've quite lost my cousin. Have you seen her?"

Her relief at my self-introduction was as clear as her discomfort, and I had not the heart to pretend I did not know whom she meant.

"Miss Raveland is in the next room, I believe. May I escort you to her?"

"Oh, yes, please. She *would* come. Mummy didn't want it, you know. She couldn't come because she was promised to Great-Aunt Agatha (and I don't think she would have liked to have come anyway, do you?). So she sent me along to make it respectable. I was quite surprised how determined Essie was. I mean, we don't even know these people really. Only that business at the gallery. Hardly enough to make one want to go to parties. Especially parties like this. Though perhaps it is because everyone seems to be here. Most everyone. Have you noticed there are no clergymen? Perhaps he is one of those Papists. Not even an archbishop, and they are usually at Lady N——'s assemblies.

"It wasn't the National Gallery, of course. Essie has seen that so many times. But she *will* go to those little hole-in-the-wall places, where the artists are so rude and the models sometimes come in—wearing next to nothing. I think it is from being American. Essie just doesn't realize that some of those places are unpleasant. Maybe even dangerous. Not the gallery I mean. Or maybe I do. Oh dear."

This was the third time she had mentioned the gallery incident, and I was finally so provoked by curiosity as to ask: "What *did* happen at the gallery?"

"She cut her hand, you see. There was a nail or something. It could fester, Mummy said. Blood got on her glove too. It wasn't a bad cut, but the glove was quite ruined. The count was there and Mr. Angel (that's what Esther calls him) was so gracious. Can't say his name. It's too bizarre for words, don't you think?"

Her voice had fallen to a whisper as we approached Esther Raveland. Anghelescu was once again beside her, and I felt my rage mounting once again.

She was indeed beautiful, and I felt she was showing her face and figure to its fullest advantage. Lush, red lips. A coy smile. A generally inviting demeanor. How could I ever have supposed her open or innocent?

"Essie," said Lydia pleadingly, "I think it is time to go home now."

"Why, Lydia. You don't mean that. The music will come later, will it not, Mr. Anghelescu?"

"Music, my dear Miss Raveland! What an appalling idea!"

Esther laughed—a ringing, charming, disgusting laugh. "Appalling? Surely not!"

"Appalling indeed," he said with mock seriousness.

"Essie," Lydia said again, looking nervously from her cousin to the secretary, "I really think we should go. It is so late and Mama ..."

"It isn't late, Lydia. If you are tired, perhaps you can rest somewhere? I am sure Mr. Anghelescu can find you a quiet corner."

I was indignant. If Esther Raveland was so insensitive, I at least was gentleman enough to champion this unfortunate young lady. "Miss ... Miss ..." I realized suddenly I didn't even know her last name. My mortification was complete when Gregory Anghelescu easily supplied my lack: "Gibson."

"Yes, Miss Gibson." I said irritably (now it seemed I had merely forgotten, and Lydia's face had flushed to reflect that interpretation). "Miss Gibson, would you please accompany me into the other room for refreshments?"

Lydia took my arm wiltingly and, with many reproachful glances at her cousin, followed me in my dignified (I hope) march across the room.

Standing before the tables of food, loaded down with sumptuous gustatory delights, and decorated with rippling mountains of flowers, fruit, and candles, I shook my head at myself in disgust. My temper was so foul that evening that everything was seen through a filter of my own annoyance. Even the rich, splendid food seemed rotten and distasteful. Fine, creamy cheeses from an astonishing range of countries. Delicate pastries that would have crowned a royal tea tray. Thinly shaved meats, heaped in decadent abundance. A cornucopia of wealth and sensual pleasure, all foul and decomposing in my mind.

"It *is* good, isn't it?" said Lydia, much cheered by the food.

I was spared the trouble of answering.

A respectful hush rushed across the room. The crowd parted, admitting a robust, middle-aged figure, dressed in the height of fashion, with an air of bored graciousness.

Lydia squealed identification (unnecessarily, since everyone in the room recognized His Royal Highness—he was no stranger to society; in fact, his close attachment to various female representatives of that society had surpassed notoriety to achieve mundanity). I bowed with the rest of the common man and removed myself from the presence as quickly as I could—not before I witnessed Popescu manifesting himself before his royal guest, but with a self-important manner of his own almost on par with the English heir apparent.

It was an interesting spectacle—to see a man whom all expected would soon be crowned a monarch (the queen could not *really* live forever) received in the house of an unknown foreign nobleman with odd habits.

Then again, I noted dryly to myself, His Royal Highness was not renowned for his discernment with regard to his acquaintance. I heard one woman whisper as I sneaked from the room (closely followed by Lydia, who strained her neck to see and savor this royal sighting, endangering the pyramid of food she had constructed on her little china plate): "That's Alice Keppel with him. Yes, she replaced the Countess of Warwick."

His Royal Highness indicated to the crowd that conversation could continue. The noise resumed, now whipped to a deafening pitch by the brief abstention in respectful silence. My follower and I worked our way through the laughing, jabbering crowd and passed into the library.

There were few people here, including Kilbronson and a few other men. They stood apart by the large round table where Popescu had held our initial interview, and paused in their conversation to turn and stare at us.

I was momentarily embarrassed to stand out thus encumbered with a young female, but the feeling almost immediately passed. Lydia, comforted by the presence of *someone*, settled herself in a chair to enjoy her spoils. She didn't even bother with conversation for several minutes. My heroic role as knight to an unattended young woman was obvious, and taken as rote by the other men in the room.

Further, it seemed that I was to be accepted into their little circle, for Kilbronson stepped forward, addressed me formally by name, and proffered introductions.

Porous, flabby-faced, and conscientiously distinguished: Mr. Braughton Lane.

Lean, ferret-like, and impeccably tailored: Mr. William Harper.

Bald, plump, and wearing a gilt monocle: Sir Douglas Wetheringdon.

Tall, lean, wiry, and aged, with an intense eye and an air of willful command: Colonel Lawrence Mattington-Brown.

"Mr. Kemp is the lawyer I mentioned," Kilbronson began.

The other men nodded in sober appreciation of ... what? What on earth could this cadaver-like client of mine have said that would be so memorable?

"I hope you live up to your reputation," commented Braughton in his deep voice.

I bowed—it seemed the thing to do, since there was really nothing I could think of to say. The whole thing felt so ludicrous. It wasn't that I imagined my reputation was a bad one. On the contrary, I knew I was respected (or, before my life had become tainted by Gothic drama, I had been), but I was no Sir Abraham Haphazard, nor even a Sydney Carton. Books would never be written of my legal triumphs. I was a stolid, reliable man of law, lacking both the charisma and the resources that might have attracted anyone's attention. But Sir Douglas was speaking ... I dragged my mind back to the room with an effort, and endeavored to focus on his ponderous tones.

"To hear what someone of your experience might have to say on the matter."

He paused, and all of the men looked at me, clearly expecting a reply.

Silence reigned for a few moments, even to the point of becoming uncomfortable. Then I made a slight bow and tried to imbue my manner with an air of sagacity and cautiousness. "I am afraid, Sir Douglas," I replied (with a disarmingly calm voice), "that I should require a great deal more information before I could express anything so dangerous as an opinion."

Braughton Lane burst out laughing. The man's voice, shrill and cackling, almost made me shudder. "You lawyers are careful devils, damn you!" And then he laughed again.

In the midst of that unpleasant hilarity, the door opened to admit our host.

Popescu's eyes were aglow with the triumph of the royal visit. He smiled at us through those remarkable white teeth.

"Capital!" he cried (quite like a character in an English novel, I thought). "Capital! His Highness has departed, but he spoke well of my little gathering." He rubbed his hands together, and, for a moment, I thought I saw soft, dark hair on his palms. A moment later, I saw I was mistaken. An odd trick of the light, conspiring with my overactive imagination primed as it was by lurid details of folklore and Stoker. I tried to remember where the notion of hairy hands phenomenon had originated, but my research was not scholarly enough to support such recall.

"Now, Wetheringdon," cried the count (effectively recapturing my attention), "stop fretting my legal man with your schemes and real-estate swindles."

Sir Douglas looked rather offended, though he tried to smile.

"Come, Mr. Kemp," continued Popescu. "We want to talk to you of business. These men are part of my plan." He smiled, as a king might in showering gratuitous gifts upon a lowly populace. The three men bowed. Kilbronson looked grim. "In fact," he continued, "their own involvement in a highly respectable English establishment—a club, shall we call it—particularly qualifies them for this. They may even simplify our processes of organization. Why establish an office when we can simply unite our efforts with one already standing? Is it not likely that my own honorable pursuits *should* unite with those most impressive and bright developments of a progressive society?"

He seemed to want an answer, so I made a noncommittal noise.

Mattington-Brown exploded. "Progressive society? How can a society be progressive with all of the appalling and criminal abuses that go on today? Church to Parliament, they're all riddled with peddlers of outdated nonsense, and they make book on it, I can tell you. That's the enemy, and we need to root them out. Destroy them in their very profligacy and—"

"The colonel," Popescu interrupted (in a biting tone that silenced the ranting, red-faced military man), "is a passionate man. While we respect such hotness of blood, we do not find such reckless expression useful."

The awkward silence that followed was broken by a snort from the colonel himself. He tossed his head, growled something I could not understand, and stormed from the room, slamming the door.

Popescu's eyes, for one moment, were fiery with emotion, then faded back into gracious, aristocratic nonexpression. The others continued to stare. Kilbronson even frowned. He opened his mouth to speak, but a dull thud startled him.

We all turned to see the girl, Lydia, sound asleep, with her head nestled into the corner of an armchair. The plate of food I had foisted upon her had slipped from her lap, cascaded down her skirt, and landed on the floor. As if she felt our eyes upon her, she awoke, stared with the frightened eyes of a suddenly awakened child, and cried in horror: "I am the only girl left!"

Then she sprang from her place of unexpected slumber with more agility than grace and raced frantically from the room.

I made a few mumbled apologies and followed to try and help the child regain herself. I was too late; by the time I found her, she was standing, still flushed with disquiet, at the side of her cousin, attired for departure. Anghelescu, their chosen escort, was there, and I received only a timid smile of thanks from the flustered young cousin and a stately nod from the older one.

I was left awkwardly standing by the door, my role usurped by that oily foreigner, caught in a limbo between continued attendance and departure. I wavered, but only briefly, then beckoned to a bright-eyed, pink-cheeked little maidservant for my hat and gloves.

"Tomorrow morning ..." Kilbronson's voice, coming from behind my back, was eerily disembodied for a moment. Then I turned to see his cadaver-like face, and the eeriness intensified (the man should go to the seaside or something, so that the color could, for once, enliven his pallid face). "Tomorrow morning. Perhaps ten o'clock? Come to this address, Mr. Kemp. We will speak at greater length."

As he spoke, he scribbled a note on an unadorned piece of paper: *The Hall. Great Queen's Street.*

I nodded and left the house, hurrying up the drive to avoid further conversation.

Thus my evening concluded with complete dissatisfaction and confusion, despite the fact that I had received so clear an assurance of the count's confidence in my labors on his behalf—for whatever it was that he hoped to accomplish.

Chapter 13

26 June 1900: The West End of Central London, in Particular, Great Queen's Street, with a Brief Foray into Maiden Lane

(From Jonathan Harker's diary) *The time I waited seemed endless, and I felt doubts and fears crowding upon me. What sort of place had I come to, and among what kind of people? What sort of grim adventure was it on which I had embarked? Was this a customary incident in the life of a solicitor's clerk sent out to explain the purchase of a London estate to a foreigner?*

As I stood before the imposing façade of Freemason's Hall the following morning, I half regretted my automatic acceptance of Kilbronson's invitation. Truth be told, I might have accepted anything in my haste to escape the Popescu party. And yet there was something in the notion of all this spiritual nonsense that discomforted me. It wasn't even the tomfoolery of the Papists, but something that Englishmen—men of reason and progress, who ought to have known better—embraced. And I didn't care for it at all.

The building was huge, dark, and grandiloquent—one of those elegant monuments to power and privilege. This was not the power of London socialites; this was the power of money and politics. That was an added irritant. I had that disgust for such things—a disgust which is the lot of most common men, and is clearly born of envy. Now that I was actually walking up the marble steps, along wood-etched corridors, summoned to speak within walls hallowed by centuries of aristocratic influence, I felt an odd mixture of awe and resentment (which was owing to the fact that I felt unworthy to enter).

Finally, it must be admitted, the voice of my Calvinist father rose in my ears, condemning even my innocent presence in that place.

Announcing my appointment to a respectably attired footman at the door, I was ushered rapidly through the building.

I had no idea of the expectations I carried with me when I walked into the hall—visions of marble halls; dignified Englishmen muttering incantations to themselves as they hurried about, incongruously attired in dark, elaborate robes; an altar of pagan sacrifice; torches, candles, and incense.

And instead I encountered the stolid, soothing, slightly musty atmosphere of a respectable English club. Marble there was, with black-and-white tiled floors in every direction, but there were no blood spatters from midnight sacrifices, and no claw marks from the fingernails of struggling victims. When I heard the rustling of newspapers in a side room—presumably the library—I felt completely reassured. For all of the mumbo jumbo of temples and circles and rites, this was at least familiar and nonthreatening. Even my father might not have objected.

I must have breathed a sigh of relief, because a thin man, still perfectly tailored, materializing at my elbow, wryly remarked, "Not quite what you expected, eh, Mr. Kemp?"

I said good morning to Mr. William Harper.

He dismissed the footman with a wave of his hand. "I shall take Mr. Kemp the rest of the way, Briggins."

The footman bowed and vanished.

As we continued to walk, Harper began a lecture in the form of a catechism: "Mr. Kemp, what do you know of the Hermetic Order of the Golden Dawn?"

"Very little," I admitted (though "nothing at all" would have been nearer the truth).

"I assume, then, that you know nothing of the Isis-Urania Temple either?"

A nervous schoolboy giggle rushed to my throat and stuck there for a moment, before sinking back into the pit of my stomach. I quietly acknowledged my ignorance with a humble nod.

Harper, this simple inquiry satisfied, now commenced his informational soliloquy, like a young student who eagerly recites a well-learned lesson when a new victim appears.

"I won't bore you with the history of Freemasonry, Mr. Kemp, nor shall I attempt to explain to you the various offshoots of its principles in the many societies and temples to be found in England alone.

"We of the Isis-Urania Temple bring something unique to that company. We go beyond petty spiritualism and the thrill of esotericism. We have united our study of scientific naturalism to something that cannot be fully captured by it—and that something is *magic*."

At that final word, he theatrically opened a heavy, paneled door, to disclose a small room, with black-and-white floor like the rest of the building, and a long, black table at its center. Seated at the table were the gentlemen I had met the evening previously, with Kilbronson at their head.

Popescu was not present, but Anghelescu sat as proxy at the right hand of the corpse-like Edgar.

The scene felt rather rehearsed, and I scurried into my indicated seat with the feeling that my own performance did not satisfy the dramatic expectations of my hosts.

"I see you have anticipated me, Harper," remarked Kilbronson dryly (and, I thought, with a touch of irritation). "I shall continue the history, Mr. Kemp, perhaps supplying information my colleague has forgotten."

Kilbronson's recitation was much more unappealing than that of Harper, for his unprepossessing appearance and voice, calculatingly precise like an unimaginative accountant, was even more disturbing when he added the tone and fervor of the true believer. The results would have been comical, if one had dared to laugh at such a humorless man.

"We follow in the footsteps of great men—standing on the shoulders of giants. Woodman, Westcott, Mathers. We believe in the advancement of man through study and awareness of the four classical elements—earth, water, air, fire. Our founders were men of great intelligence—the sort of men who are critical to the establishment of an advanced, a greater social order. They knew, as we do, that much is to be learned by such men—not the common herd, who are easily deluded by the mummery of priests—in their scholarly attention to the wisdom of the ancients. Science has done much to explain things that earlier generations must have dismissed as mere mystery. Mystery itself is not destroyed, of course. It is now clearly the province of great men to understand and wield the power of the mystical."

"Might I add a word?" asked one at the table—a woman, whose presence I had not noticed before. She was neither young nor attractive. A well-preserved woman of middle age, attired in spectacles and tweed.

"Miss Philippa Young," Kilbronson introduced her. "One of our most respected members."

I must have looked surprised (Kilbronson had never struck me as possessing suffragette tendencies). "Yes," Kilbronson added. "We allow women in our Order. They can even serve with us in perfect equality with men, and can advance like them in the hierarchy to the Second Order. We could not do less, when our very existence is derived from the charter of Anna Sprengel."

Once again, I was lost at a name. It apparently meant something to him and to his companions, for they all exchanged knowing glances and sage nods.

"You cannot dive recklessly into a society such as ours," cautioned Miss Young, who had not looked particularly pleased during Kilbronson's magnanimous explanation of her presence. "This is not some simple creed for simple *men*." (The emphasis was not my imagination, for Kilbronson flushed.)

"Indeed not," cried Kilbronson indignantly. Then he hurried along with the thrust of his sermon: "Because of this, Mr. Kemp, we issue this invitation: Come and join us in our studies. We cannot promise to initiate you into our First Order, for we know not the tenor of your mind. Could you grasp the Hermetic Qabalah? Are you one with the three parts of the wisdom of the whole universe? What do you know of alchemy? Astrology? Theurgy?"

I was about to admit that I knew nothing of any of them, but he went on (demonstrating that the question was, essentially, rhetorical).

He went on, waxing eloquent about emanations from godhead, shared divinity, the ten sephiroth, "The Book of

Enoch", the rosae rubeae et aureae cruces, and the nuances of magic such as astral travel. When he spoke (in hushed tones) of the "Secret Chiefs", my mind glazed over, and I looked around to see the effect upon the others in the room.

Some of the men were still nodding and making noises of devoted acquiescence. One man looked decidedly annoyed. A handful were clearly not listening.

Kilbronson was midsentence when the even tones of Anghelescu broke in. "Important as all of this background must be, Mr. Kilbronson, perhaps it would be better to address the practical needs of the present moment, rather than make a proselytizing effort."

Kilbronson turned red (if such a thing were possible in a bloodless man), but did not say anything further.

Anghelescu acknowledged his silence with an appreciative nod. "Now then, dear Mr. Kemp, I am delegated by Count Popescu to commission you to find a location for our meetings. A center of operations for his efforts."

"Which are . . . ?" The question, which had so troubled my mind for weeks, came to my lips almost before I could think it.

Anghelescu smiled. "The legal mind at work," he said in a patronizing tone. "Getting right to the heart of the matter. The count has chosen his advisor well."

He then launched into a series of businesslike details, delivering them in a tone of efficient management that well befitted his role as secretary. I had not considered the question of his capabilities before, but now (grudgingly) admitted that he seemed suited to the job.

"Our office is a tripartite establishment, which offers the following: scholastic opportunities for the unfortunate; apprentice training for the same; and, finally, discreet charitable opportunities for those who can benefit from neither of our other two branches."

"The count wishes to establish a charitable organization?" I asked, in some surprise.

"Indeed," said Anghelescu. "He considers this a vital first step for the proper reordering of society. The most critical body of persons is the class of the underprivileged. They require assistance and support. They also require education and training to raise them from their current squalor. For such to be accomplished, it must be the work of an organization that spans national borders. His work is based on models already established in several smaller eastern countries.

"To that end, we require the following. First: we need a building in which to center our efforts. Neither the count's home nor this location is suited to our efforts. We require rooms for a secretarial bureau (to organize all efforts). We require a room for the interview of candidates. We require a room through which charitable donations are to be channeled . . ."

I scribbled down a list. By its conclusion, I was officially commissioned to seek out and rent the necessary establishment, to investigate all legal ramifications and establish necessary connections to the governmentally established organizations that addressed the question of the poor, and even to seek out support among the ranks of highly placed and influential philanthropists.

Anghelescu suddenly looked up from his notes. "It seems this conversation will continue for some time, gentlemen. Please do not feel obliged to remain on our account."

The dismissal was undeniable. The representatives of the Isis-Urania awkwardly but obediently left the room. Kilbronson was the last to leave, hesitating at the door and staring at me with an intensity that seemed to indicate strong emotion (though who could tell with such a man).

After the door closed, I sat with my pen raised expectantly for Anghelescu to continue his catalogue of tasks.

When he did not speak, I looked up.

He was smiling broadly. "You think it is all nonsense, Mr. Kemp. Do you not?"

"Nonsense?"

"Yes," he said. "Nonsense. All of this talk of magic and secret societies. You are a skeptic, Mr. Kemp."

He seemed determined to hear my opinion of the entire business, but I wanted to remain discreet. "I am not in a position to judge the society, Mr. Anghelescu," I said coolly, "nor is it the job for which the count has chosen to employ me."

He did not appear to be at all troubled by my tone or my reluctance to engage on that topic. He smiled again and rocked back in his chair, raising his eyes to the inlaid, intricately worked ceiling, and spoke in the sort of voice that a man might use in a meditative moment with a trusted and intimate friend. "Our country is a problematic world of priest-ridden ignorance, where help to the poor is seen as an assault, both by the poor and those who tyrannize over them. The count feels this deeply and believes that your country will offer a greater opportunity for his ambitions."

"He is a philanthropist then?"

"No, he is a humanist."

"I wonder, then, what his interest must be in this temple business?"

"I said, Mr. Kemp, that the count understands all too well the hazards of a land ruled over by archaic ritual and the despotism of priests. He is not, however, blind to the dangers of this new land. No, he believes—as I do—that there must be a healthy middle ground between the tyranny of superstition and the tyranny of science which has dismissed anything inexplicable according to the rules of scientific inquiry. What is it that is said by your Shakespeare? There is more than is dreamt of in your philosophy.

"Our friends here at the temple are closer to what we need and desire in supporters than you might think. And your own reluctance is in your favor. The immediate and credulous acceptance of something so unfamiliar, so outside your understanding ... that would be the sign of a weak mind. And the count does not rely on weak minds in the achievement of his goal."

It should have been a reassuring thing to hear, especially since the association with Kilbronson (who was apparently an unbalanced spiritualist) was increasingly ludicrous and disturbing to me. Even so, and with all of the delicate flatteries Anghelescu insinuated throughout the rest of our conversation (which otherwise consisted in unthreatening business details), I could not shake my feeling of discomfort in that building and in the entire business.

I was standing on the steps of the temple when my father's voice came back to me, so strongly that it was as if he stood there beside me, glowering down under his beetling brows, with the full bent of his Calvinist indignation focused upon my unfortunate head: "And the soul that turneth after such as have familiar spirits, and after wizards, to go a whoring after them, I will even set my face against that soul, and will cut him off from among his people."

Guilt and shame were strongly upon me in that moment, but I shook them off. As I bodily shook my head to signify liberation from the censure of a man long dead, my eyes settled and focused on another form, one that was oddly familiar, and yet not immediately identifiable.

One moment later and I had it; it was old Mrs. Lawson.

Truly, she couldn't be much advanced in age—at least, I had never thought of her as being so. I hadn't thought of her at all, I had to admit, except as a hovering, clucking, hen-like figure in the background, always in the mode of chaperone and matchmaker.

Now I wondered if I had done her a disservice by so characterizing her.

She was walking slowly down the street by herself, attired in sober black, unsmiling and seemingly unconscious of all of the bustle and hurry and indifference of the London crowd.

I crossed to her and called her name.

She looked up and stared at me for a moment before recognizing me. Then she greeted me kindly enough and allowed me to continue with her on her way, but she remained distracted, as if she were not fully present to me, just as she had been absent in that busy street.

I did not yet burden her with attempts at conversation. I was not eager to escape her, though I could not have said why not. There was work to do, and serving as the chaperone for the grandmother of a dead girl whose name had once been paired with mine ... well, it wasn't a scenario I would have expected to find attractive.

We walked in silence for some time—nearly an hour, perhaps, until we were standing on the edge of Hyde Park. There were groups of people walking about. A nurse struggling with three wild, black-haired children; young courting couples maintaining a borderline respectability; a businessman standing in contemplative study of a flock of birds. I wondered which of these had attracted my companion's focused gaze.

After a moment she looked up at me, and her eyes were full of tears.

She smiled and spoke gently, but her words were acid: "Happiness is difficult to accept in others when your own world is in pieces. You go around and look like you are alive, but you are dead inside. And then you see lovers in the garden, laughing together. Smug in their joy. Children running to their mothers—mothers who are impatient and tired. So ungrateful. The children could be gone in an instant. They could be alone. How easy envy becomes in moments of darkest grief.

"I do hate happy people," she added wistfully.

I do not know that the rebuke was designed for me, but it stung. I thought of Esther Raveland, whose face, conjured up so easily in my mind, provoked a torrent of warring emotions. Then I thought of Adele Lawson, and found I could not recall her face at all.

I looked at the old woman before me, small, rigid, correct, and inwardly broken.

There was nothing I could say.

She took my arm again, and we continued to walk on our way.

I returned her quietly to her house, politely refused the offer of tea, and returned to my office. Work was difficult, but it also brought relief. I applied myself diligently to the tasks listed to me by the count's secretary. By the arrival of evening, I felt I had more than made a beginning in the execution of Popescu's wishes. I departed for home with a professional conscience untroubled. My personal conscience was quite another matter.

The night air, which was hot, sticky, and oppressive, reawoke the unpleasant feelings that professional labors had drummed into happy dormancy. Thoughts of Adele were upon me again. It might have been something in the face of her grandmother, but now I found I could see Adele's face clearly in my mind.

I remembered other things as well. I remembered pleasant moments with her, moments that had helped cultivate public expectations of our relationship. My later desire to escape such a snare was undeniable, but those earlier encounters were likewise undeniable.

She had been such a pretty, sweet, charming little thing, with a flattering attention that was not—or had not seemed to be—entirely insincere. Flighty, yes, but life encumbered with such a wife would not have been completely insupportable.

I jumped out of the way, as a cab nearly knocked me down. My abstraction was proving life-threatening. Grimly setting my mouth in a focused line, I stomped along on my way, refusing to consider any distractions, however ghostly.

Chapter 14

1 July 1900: Soho and Other Seedy Corners

(From Mina Murray Harker's journal) *She looks so sweet as she sleeps; but she is paler than is her wont, and there is a drawn, haggard look under her eyes, which I do not like. I fear she is fretting about something. I wish I could find out what it is.*

A few days passed, days that were overshadowed by nights of dark dreams, each more painful than those that had preceded it. Adele, in danger and in pain. Sometimes at my hands. I could never help her. I simply watched the dark violence, incapable of saving that delicate, girlish victim.

The nightmares made each day more exhausting, and my professional labors seemed to become increasingly dissatisfying. On the final night of a long series, the members of the Golden Dawn stood leagued in respectable array in the background, their docile aristocratic trappings resplendent beneath fur and jewel-encrusted capes, with bizarre symbols embroidered all over them. And opposite them stood, not vampires in black cloaks, but eccentric-faced Papists in ragged white—smiling, beaming, and doing nothing.

The following day, when musty legal volumes and dusty papers and purposeless cases became almost suffocating, I left my place of business early, ignoring Francis Carstairs' looks of disapproval—the little beast had become judgmental, of late. The whim was upon me. I would go and visit my godmother.

Mrs. Barbara Fitzalan was a good-tempered, aggressively tolerant woman, with a humanistic bent of mind, tinged with an enthusiasm for things spiritual. In my youth, she had been an odd, chirpy, middle-aged gentlewoman; now she was an odd, chirpy, elderly gentlewoman. Vague in her doctrine, she was yet insistent on particular points, however contradictory. For instance, she was charitable and generous to all of God's fallen creatures, but unequivocal in her pronouncements against what she considered to be dangerous ideas or people. She was also unpredictable in her plan of attack—and attack she did.

"You're unhappy about that girl, an't you, John?"

For a moment I was not sure which girl she meant. Then I remembered Adele and felt guilty.

"She was rather flighty," my godmother continued. "Not worthy of you, for all you can be such a dull fellow sometimes, John, and you know you can. But I'm sorry for her, and there you have it. She was harmless, really. I don't know what that grandmother of hers will do."

She wagged her old head in a few decisive nods, and then rang a little silver bell for her maid.

"Tea, Doris!" commanded my godmother, once again nodding vigorously.

Her servants must have grown accustomed to her wants and routine, because the little maid bustled out and bustled in only a few minutes later, bearing sumptuous midafternoon delights, all delicately arranged on silver trays with paper doilies, with an alacrity that seemed indicative both of enthusiasm and foreplanning.

"Eat up, John. You're much too thin. Have you been fretting lately? Of course you have. It really is sad, but you need to grieve and move on, my dear. You really must. And then you'll be able to figure out what you really need to be doing with your life." The nodding became even more emphatic at this point.

I knew well where the conversation was going, or thought I did, and tried to deflect the oncoming comments about my unmarried status.

"Is the shepherdess new, Aunt Barbara?"

She was a collector of china statues, particularly in the pastoral mode. Sheep were a recurring motif throughout the room, even embroidered across the upholstery.

My godmother was clearly unimpressed by my attempt. She merely looked at me wryly for a moment, then resumed her nodding.

"I've heard of a gathering, John. At the Bassington-Smith's. It's a wonderful opportunity to find the consolation you need—to have the girl herself tell you that it's all right and you should move on."

"I don't believe in that sort of nonsense. You know that, Aunt Barbara."

"Don't be such a skeptic, John. It may give you some relief. If it doesn't, well, it's harmless, isn't it? The Bassington-Smith's always have wonderful food, and the conversation isn't terribly tedious. What else do you have to do with your time except work?"

She went for me with the tenacity of a terrier, and, pinned under plates of sandwiches, scones, and petit fours, I was less than capable in my resistance.

My father's voice did not resurface in my mind—or, rather, it was drowned out by Anghelescu's, repeating that persuasive misquotation of *Hamlet*.

In the end, I simply could find no reason compelling enough not to go; so I went.

Mrs. Lillian Bassington-Smith, a highly respectable matron with a highly respectable husband, threw highly respectable parties at discreet and appropriate intervals. She attempted a Bohemian flair in a measured, cautious way— not too much (thereby to challenge her own respectability) and not too little (thereby to appear absurd and caricatured in comparison with those true souls committed to darkness, art, moral ambivalence, and sloppy fashion). She superficially advocated all of the tenets of true Bohemianism except for poverty, radical unconventionality, and aggressive tolerance for those like themselves. As a result, she represented a safe haven for those dabblers who themselves had no desire to undermine reputation for the sake of Bohemianism. Thus Mrs. Lillian Bassington-Smith was at the forefront of every thought that was new, daring, and not too objectionable, and her gatherings were usually very popular. They were also very dull.

This particular party was to be small. Spiritualism has its moments of popularity and thrill, but they are not usually conducive to large-scale entertainment. She would not sink to the level of magicians on a stage or conjurors performing parlor tricks. Her efforts always aimed for something higher.

Mrs. Lillian Bassington-Smith welcomed me in her booming voice. "Mr. Kemp! Dear Mr. Kemp! So you've come to our little evening of dabbling into eternity. Come, please, into the room and await our most honored guest."

I was ushered in with ceremony, and then duly ignored.

The room was small. Dark purple curtains veiled the windows and large sections of three of the walls. A bizarre tapestry covered the fourth wall, depicting some raucous scene in pseudo-Classical style. I tried to place the source, but its details were too vague. Ovid yet again desecrated by the burlesque.

And in the middle of the room, seated at the large round table with the green, inlaid top, covered with an ornate design around a strange symbol that was oddly familiar, was Esther Raveland.

Before I could react, a voice, with the hint of a laugh, spoke at my elbow. "It seems we are destined to meet under circumstances fraught with supernatural significance, Mr. Kemp. I had no notion our conversation would convert you into a connoisseur."

Anghelescu. The seedy, self-absorbed, foreign cad. The man really was a bounder, and now he had seen me at this ridiculous gathering, after my skeptical dismissal of Isis-Urania.

I made a noncommittal response, and he moved on, still (I thought) laughing at me.

Lydia was there as well, even unhappier and more out of place than she had been at the Popescu party.

"Essie *would* come," she wailed (it seemed to be her constant lament). "Mummy doesn't even know we are here. Essie made me promise not to tell her. I always tell Mummy everything. She is most insistent on it. I don't understand why Essie is being so horrid ... I mean, Essie is wonderful, but this whole ... this whole thing frightens me. Mummy says it is all Cousin James' fault, and I think he must have been a truly dreadful man, don't you think too?"

The room was full, now, with people standing about in awkward, nervous groups. The laws of etiquette had not yet addressed the particulars and protocols of small talk before a séance.

"Be seated," said our hostess sonorously.

We all sat obediently. Lydia beside me. Then a tittering debutante, and beside her a clearly discomfited escort. Beside him sat Esther Raveland, and beside her, retaining that proud place, as if indicative of ownership, sat Anghelescu. My annoyance was keen, though whether it was from a sense of having been made appear a fool (whatever had possessed me to accept the count's business?) or from a frustrated romantic impulse, I could not say.

Our hostess was on his other side. Then there were three others, none of whom I recognized, including a sleek fellow with well-oiled hair who simpered and sneered with the affectation of superiority. Finally, on my other side, a slender, impassive woman, simply attired in gray and without ornament.

"It's the Duchess of M——," hissed Lydia in my ear.

Some unseen hand extinguished the electric light, and we were shrouded in darkness, save for the flickering beeswax tapers. I sat down.

A female voice tittered, then sobbed—it was not Lydia, who trembled in silence at my side. I suspected the little debutante. Miss Raveland could not have made such a simpering noise. I could imagine the hand of the burly Lothario, sneaking a comforting squeeze upon the timid, lacy fingers. I did not know if I was more disgusted or envious—to have attempted such a reassurance to Miss Raveland would have been to invite prompt dismissal, and perhaps even the obliteration of my manly self-respect, so sharp would be her tongue.

Someone must have pulled a string, for the curtains parted—seemingly on their own—disclosing a figure all in black, with a vast robe embroidered cryptically in intricate gold and silver. A woman. Dark, lank black hair. Ornate makeup, imitative of the fashion depicted in the Egyptian room of the British Museum.

"Madame Fortesque," Mrs. Lillian Bassington-Smith pronounced the name in that same deep, resonant tone. "Madame has come to show to us the mysteries of the hereafter. To open for us the hidden depths of the unknown. To bring to us the souls of the dead, so that we can hear from them all that we wish to know. And . . . yes. Indeed."

With this less than compelling conclusion, she sat down rather abruptly, turning over the floor to the well-decorated medium.

Madame Fortesque brought an official air to the proceedings. She surely was a fraud, but she certainly knew her business. She was a fraud rendered formidable by the dramatic force of her presentation.

She sat down wordlessly between our hostess and the oily man beside me. Then she stretched out her hands and crooned out in a velvety contralto chant: "*Join hands . . .*"

An oily hand on one side, and an icy, trembling one on the other.

The debutante giggled.

"*Silence.*"

There were no further disruptions from that quarter.

"*Spirits,*" droned the medium in plodding tones, "*come to me, you who speak from the Great Beyond. Come. Fear not. Come.*"

As she spoke she rolled her eyes back into her head, so only the whites were visible through half-closed lids.

What a lot of rubbish, I thought with annoyance. Grown adults. Playacting. The rapping on the table would begin soon—wasn't that the ruse employed by those American women, the Fox sisters, who deluded crowds by their performance of spiritualistic revelation? A theatrical spectacle, here for the benefit of the bored, petty gentry.

Then the serene, chilly silence was broken by a single, shattering sound—a rap upon the table.

"*Come. Spirits, come.*"

Once again, silence. It seemed as if a full quarter of an hour had passed, though perhaps it was only under a minute.

"*Spirits ... You who speak from the beyond ... You who ...*"

Against my better judgment, my skin began to creep. That unearthly feeling was upon me that an invisible hand was behind me and was moving closer, ever closer toward the skin at the nape of my neck. Soon that hand would attain an icy physicality and bring my mortal body into contact with some appalling other realm. If my hands could only be free to scratch the itch of suspense ... but still the oily and the icy hands remained in mine. Lydia was holding so tightly that her nails were digging into my palm. No relief to be found. It was as if I could feel the long, sharp, animal-like fingernails brushing the delicate hairs hidden below my collar ...

I shivered, moved my shoulders as if to shake off the sensation, and cleared my throat.

For that offense, I was shushed by an irritated someone on the other side of the table. The light flickered, so I could not identify which of my companions had administered the rebuke. Even so, the effort at discovery served me well; it completed the task begun by my shoulders and effectively freed me from my momentary absorption. Suddenly the trappings of the theatre were grossly apparent, and the superficiality of the entire ritual were garish and unimpressive. It was that moment when disbelief, no longer willingly suspended, regained her throne.

Knock ... knock ...

Now we were processing through an endless series of noises and interpretive leaps. Were we really going to march through each letter of the alphabet to type out the laborious messages of our visiting spirit? Our questionable entertainment continued: "*There is one here . . . one who cries out for . . . the touch of that . . . vanished hand . . . the sound of the . . . voice . . . that is still . . .*"

I thought of the dead poet laureate. If he could hear his beautiful words, recited in tinny, theatrical tones in this absurd little charade, he might be provoked into haunting the proceedings. It would have granted the whole farce an air of supernatural significance otherwise completely lacking. His beard would help. No costume required. Did spooks wear costumes, except on the stage?

My thoughts were interrupted from this fascinating vein by the pronouncement of a name.

"*James . . . James . . .*"

A tremor rushed through the room. Before I could discern its source—was it Esther Raveland?—a shriek split through the theatrical veil of the séance.

Lydia leapt up, burst into tears, and ran from the room, knocking over chairs in her wake. I followed after her quickly—in her state of mind she might have run into the street unaccompanied.

"Please," I said. "Please wait!"

At the sound of my voice, Lydia scurried into a corner and almost crouched, like a terrified fox at bay. Tears streamed down her face, and she held up her hands to shield herself—perhaps from the mortification of being seen, and perhaps from some strange spiritual threat, conjured up by that scene.

Esther Raveland was at my elbow. I expected her to be rude and dismissive to her cousin, but she simply gathered the sobbing girl into her arms and soothed her with quiet noises.

"Oh, my dear," she said. "I should not have brought you here. I am sorry, Lydia. Come. Hush. All is well."

Lydia's crying soon subsided, leaving behind them only the occasional choking sob.

"Young ladies"—Anghelescu materialized at my elbow—"I have procured a cab. Let me bring you there at once." He reached down to offer his arm to Lydia.

The girl recoiled into her cousin's arms. "No, no, thank you, please, no," Lydia gasped, seeming to struggle between her fear of displeasing her cousin (and perhaps of annoying their would-be rescuer) and her deep dislike of Anghelescu.

"Thank you," said Esther firmly. "We appreciate the offer, sir, but I believe Mr. Kemp is already engaged to accompany us home."

We rode in silence, except for Lydia's occasional sniffling. Miss Raveland looked grim, probably (I hoped) considering her imprudence, both in attending that ridiculous charade, and in trusting herself and her cousin to the chaperoning of a suspicious-looking creature like Anghelescu.

When we arrived at the girl's home, Lydia hurried upstairs almost immediately to rest her aching head.

Miss Raveland removed her gloves and hat and fair near tossed them at the maid—who looked rather astonished by this abrupt behavior on the part of the Yankee.

I was torn between a strong desire to stay and an inchoate instinct to escape as quickly as possible. When the maid took my hat from my hands and gestured expectantly for me to follow Miss Raveland into the drawing room, I gave in to desire and followed.

Left alone with me, it did not seem that Miss Raveland was at all inclined to conversation.

First she sat, and I took a seat across the room. Silence.

Then she stood up and began to pace. I stood up at that cue, but was left, socially stranded, by her clear disinclination to acknowledge my existence.

Finally I cleared my throat. "Well, since your cousin seems to be safe and ..."

She turned, and I saw that the emotion that had kept her silent was not remorse, but anger. "I appreciate your kindness to Lydia," she said, with flashing eyes, "but you have no right to pass such a censorious judgment on me. Who are you to question me?"

"I did not question you," I cried, astonished.

"I saw it in your face. I know what you are thinking. What were you doing there anyway, you with your sanctimonious skepticism?"

"It doesn't take a skeptic to know a fraud," I replied heatedly. "Anyway, it's a dangerous business. You're playing around with things you don't understand."

"What? The thing you say is nonsense is supernaturally dangerous? Powerful nonsense indeed. You shall have to make up your mind, Mr. Kemp. Is it evil or absurd? You can't have it both ways. And either way is a severe insult to me. You in your almighty righteousness. What right have you to question me? Who are you to pass judgment on me? Are you my governess? Or my guardian?"

Her face, flushed with passion, was exquisite. Framed by that thick, luscious dark hair, and illuminated by the delicate evening light of a drawing room unadorned for this unexpected visitor, that hint of green in her eyes had blossomed into a keen, definite shade. They were like the green of spring, when it reaches that intense moment immediately before the yellow of summer tarnishes it.

A new feeling rushed over me—superseding the desire to shake her into reason. For a moment, a vision flashed through my eyes—Miss Raveland, clasped in my arms, as I showered kisses upon her upturned face.

I caught my breath. This was the result of reading novels.

"I haven't passed judgment on you, Miss Raveland," I said (and to my own ear, my tone was prim). "You are correct. I have no right to do so."

"So long as *you* know it."

A long pause followed, with her glaring eyes on me.

Another thought came to my mind and, before I could control my tongue, I started to blurt it out: "Who is it you—" But before I could finish my question, Miss Raveland had turned away as if she had not heard me, but with a stiffened back and rigid neck as if she had.

"Good night, Mr. Kemp." (And her manner added, with finality: "Goodbye.")

Thus dismissed, I left the house, with discontentment flooding my brain.

It was long past midnight, and home was not far from me. It was raining, and the sensible thing would have been to hurry home to the comforting irritation of Jenson's loyal attention.

Instead I began to walk. For hours I walked, crossing familiar streets, passing into the darker corners that, even in daylight, sanity would have prompted me to avoid. My mind was a field razed; no thought could come to harvest, even with the nurturing fall of the raindrops. Step after step. Step after step. Purposeless and emotionless I walked.

Morning came, with light not fully formed. Infant-like, it wisped delicately before my eyes, weaving through the raindrops. When I finally looked up, there was the temple of the Freemasons again, looming out of the darkness, silent and forbidding. What sinister rituals were taking place in the bowels of that strange hall? It seemed deserted enough. Probably the frequenters of the temple were all sensibly in bed and asleep. I turned on my heel and walked on.

The roads were beginning to be busier now.

I was tired of walking, tired of being wet, and tired of my very existence. I would sit.

I found I was following a small crowd of people, shuffling with eager hurry into a large door in ... where was I? Maiden Lane. Here were ecclesial markers, but I was not dissuaded from following. It was as good an option as any. My days had been punctuated of late by vivid spiritualistic experiences; perhaps it was time to turn to the stolid security of old-fashioned Christianity. It couldn't hurt, anyway, and going in would mean escaping from the rain.

I opened the door and hurried inside.

Some service was ongoing. Without looking around, I ducked into a pew at the back, next to a family with nigh on a dozen loud, unkempt children. The words of Scripture were being spoken somewhere, but I could not hear it over the bustle of that untidy crew. I closed my eyes, pretending to be contemplative—or, at least, attentive—but, in reality, futilely endeavoring to ignore their existence. And, truth be told, I was on the verge of falling asleep.

Everyone sat. A sermon was imminent.

"This is a hard saying, indeed," said a quiet, measured voice from the pulpit.

It was a voice I knew, a voice strangely and even comfortingly familiar, though of recent acquaintance.

I opened my eyes, my vision cleared, and I saw many things: the statue of the little boy; the strange stained glass with the fanatical nun.

Then the voice came again and the obnoxious children—yes, the place must be Papist to gather in such a noisy brood, and probably Irish too!—even those children faded into the background of my consciousness.

Father Thomas Edmund Gilroy was preaching his sermon.

If someone had asked me at its conclusion what he had said, I scarce could have given an account, but the gentle, rhythmic flow of his voice and the quiet precision of his argument seemed, in the moment, somehow remarkable.

Phrases lodged in the tangled web of my confused brain:

"A world drowning in the redeeming blood of Jesus Christ . . ."

"Sharers in His blood . . ."

"Deep and abiding mercy . . ."

"Sacrifice of praise . . ."

"Our most perfect worship . . ."

"Thanksgiving . . . transformation . . . sacrament . . ."

And again, and again: "*This is a hard saying, indeed . . .*"

It was as if I were listening to a foreign language, and yet found consolation in the very mystery of it.

His preaching concluded. Then, up there at the front, an odd, solemn ritual began, like a dance. The others seemed intent and prayerful (though a few old women looked distracted enough, one playing with beads, and another—was she knitting?). I felt like a spectator at a pagan ceremony.

"We sacrifice Church of Englanders sometimes," a Papist schoolmate of mine had once told me. I was eight years old at the time, and the thought had troubled me for several months. I thought of that again and felt vaguely uncomfortable.

I did not fear sacrifice, but I did not want to witness their cannibalistic theatre. Don't they disdain symbolism, I thought, and pretend to feast on the living corpse of their God? They were as bad as the vampires. Now *that* was a thought to bring chills. Silly, but there it was.

I would leave. I had found the comfort I wanted, and there was no point in prolonging my stay into awkwardness.

I wriggled as quietly as I could from the pew (how noisy such places are, especially when you are endeavoring to leave without attracting notice!), moved to the back, and, when the opportunity afforded and all eyes were trained elsewhere, escaped.

As the door closed behind my fleeing form, I heard the bright chiming of bells.

Chapter 15

20 September 1900: London, the Inns of Court, and South Kensington

(From Mina Murray Harker's journal) *The wind fell away entirely during the evening, and at midnight there was a dead calm, a sultry heat, and that prevailing intensity which, on the approach of thunder, affects persons of a sensitive nature.*

A strange period of quiet and peace followed. For over two months I slept, ate, worked, and lived like a normal, healthy version of myself. No nightmares, no bizarre encounters with supposed blood drinkers or cultish spiritualists, no white-clad Papists (smiling or otherwise). I did see Popescu and Anghelescu many times, and even saw Kilbronson in passing, but all of those meetings seemed to be business-related and unthreatening—even dull.

My social engagements decreased considerably. The London Season was finished, and many had ventured off to country houses to suffer through the long vacation of Parliament. I had received my usual invitations—including an earnest note from my godmother—and had refused them all without a pang of regret.

I had not even seen Esther Raveland. I thought of her often, wondering what she was doing, and with whom she was spending her time. It was likely she was out of town, like so many others. Either that or she was studiously avoiding me (which would be easy to do, with the Season in abeyance). I did not think she saw much of Anghelescu either—at least, he never mentioned it, and I rather suspect he would have done so if he considered himself as scoring off a rival.

The very notion of a romantic challenge between myself and that man turned my stomach, so I did not entertain it long—though it did occur to my mind more than once.

Surprisingly, my initial relief during this quiet period shifted after a few weeks into a vague discontentment. There was a lack of resolution in this new calm that I found somewhat disquieting. Nevertheless, it was a relief to rebuild myself physically and mentally with the monotony of a regular schedule. And I made great progress with work, including with my tasks for the count. These involved such plodding details that I began to wonder if my discomfort in his employ had resulted entirely from my lack of sleep and the trauma of the death of Adele.

"Another fine day ends, Mr. Kemp," said Francis Carstairs pleasantly to me one evening as we closed up the office.

I nodded absently as he retrieved my hat.

"I hope you have a quiet weekend, sir," said Carstairs.

I wished him the same, and left. Carstairs watched my back (at least, I felt his gaze on me). Such an odd little man. I wondered (for the first time in our acquaintance) what he did when he was not in the office. I rather imagined he disappeared into the ether when he stepped over the threshold at the end of the day. Or perhaps he had a secret life of danger and intrigue. A headline flashed through my mind: "Lawyer's Clerk Turns Jack the Ripper". The thing was so unlikely and so sensational—so like those things that had occupied my mind in previous months—that I burst out laughing, attracting not a little notice from passersby.

It was an oppressively hot day. The sweat gathered in my hair so quickly that I removed my hat. I ran my fingers through my hair—an ineffectual attempt to shake off the offensive moisture. In my walk home, I became even more damp. I passed men who were doffing ties and coats—a casual gesture that would have been unthought of were the atmosphere not so appallingly intense. Humidity, the great leveler of social strata, made friends of MP and street sweeper. The young man selling newspapers at the corner and the soggy Lord of the Realm who bought them from him exchanged a commiserating glance—a moment of egalitarian communion that would have warmed the already toasty heart of any observant radical.

By the time I reached my home, though I felt as if I had leapt into a pond on my way, I was eager for a bath and for a cool, uncomplicated meal. Then sleep. There was little else to do on a day such as this.

Jenson's ugly face, glowing with perspiration, greeted me with a wan attempt at a smile upon my return.

"Good evening, sir," he said. Then he paused, as if he were having trouble speaking.

His disconcertment was pronounced enough to catch my attention.

"Jenson," I said, "are you ill?"

His face was slowly turning a pale shade of green. "Sir, I regret to say . . . I must . . . If it would not be too great an inconvenience . . ."

Then he collapsed at my feet.

I dragged him to his bed (while he feebly protested, adding "sir" even to his whimpers), plied him with water, and fetched a damp cloth for his forehead. After several minutes of ministrations, he regained more of his usual pallor. He even ventured another smile at me.

"The heat, sir," he said. "It was just too much ... sir ..." He fell asleep on the last word.

I left his door open so that I could hear if he woke up, and set about caring for myself for the evening. A cool bath, dry toast, and tea. It was all I desired. I made two small plates, placing the second on a tray, along with a second pot of tea, all of which I set on the little table beside Jenson's bed. That way, if he awoke, he would find sustenance ready to hand. If he wanted something else to eat or drink, he would just have to suppress the feudal propriety of his soul and ask me for it. I would play his nurse as best I could, whether he liked it or not.

He was snoring away vigorously now, so I tiptoed out and sat down to my own little repast.

A few minutes went by in silence. Then a knocking roused me from my vague, unfocused thoughts. At first I thought it was Jenson, then I realized the sound had come from the door. I hurried to answer before the racket roused my sleeping valet.

I opened the door to find a stranger before me. A tall, dark man, with an ostentatiously foreign air about him. His brooding, Byronic profile turned toward me, and a pair of large, round black eyes, fringed with lashes that were almost feminine in their rich beauty, focused on my face. It is a testament to the heat of the day that this figure was most bizarre to me because of the fact that he was garbed in a long, heavy, black winter coat, fringed with fur.

"Mr. John Kemp?" inquired the visitor.

"Yes?"

"I must have speech with you. Might I come in?"

Still musing on the strangeness of his garb, I ushered him into my drawing room.

My visitor seated himself comfortably before the unlit fire, holding close his fur-tipped coat. I thought he must have been sweltering with the heat, but he smiled with obsequious apology.

"The dampness of England," he said. "I have not yet become accustomed."

There was the slightest trace of an accent discernable in his voice, a pleasant, softening note that to my ear felt vaguely menacing.

"I must make an introduction of myself," he said. "Else you will think me abominably rude. My name is Vadas. Vadas Radu—or, as you Englishmen would say, Radu Vadas."

It might have been a dizzying form of introduction, but I suddenly recalled the eastern tradition of putting the patronymic first. (I recalled it, not from my travels, but from the Stoker novel—an embarrassing source, the thought of which made me feel suddenly rather at a loss.)

While I struggled inwardly, Vadas continued. "You may imagine why I have come to you."

I did not reply, though my mind had raced to make a few useful clarifications: Vadas. A kinsman of Elisabetta Kilbronson, no doubt.

He confirmed my suspicions almost immediately. "I am the brother of Elisabetta Vadas. She was married some years ago to an English gentleman—a Mr. Kilbronson. He was known to our family in business. Mr. Kilbronson, I believe, is a client of yours."

Once again I did not reply, attributing my reluctance to speak to a degree of caution appropriate to a lawyer.

"I have come to England," Vadas went on, "in search of my sister. I wish to bring her home with me, to take her from her husband, who is a villain." He spoke with a strange calmness that increased my discomfort. "I have heard tales of her suffering. He has long mistreated her. Oppressed her cruelly. He is a strange man and a vicious one. In my country I would have challenged him—defended my sister's honor. But here ..." He shrugged meaningfully, a theatrical gesture of foreignness that, it seems, was taken up for the purpose of making his point more eloquent.

"I have learned that you are the legal representative of Kilbronson and that you too are in search of my sister. I would ask—though I know it is not ethical or deemed proper in your country—that if you hear of her, to let me know. I do not ask that you betray your client and inform me before you speak to him, but beg you to inform me. I would be there to defend and protect her from the wrath of a man such as her husband."

"Of what precisely do you accuse Mr. Kilbronson?" I asked in a cold, even a defensive, tone. I had found my tongue at an odd moment, perhaps, as I disliked my client enough to be willing to cast him in the role of villainous and oppressive husband.

"Of cruelty," was the matter-of-fact reply.

I waited for a moment, but Vadas did not elaborate.

"And you wish me to ...?"

"Merely to have speech with me if you find my sister."

"Mr. Vadas, I am sure you know that our laws here are quite different from those in your own country."

"Indeed, yes, Mr. Kemp. But, please. Give patience to a brother's heart. Elisabetta is ... like my own child. My ... what you say ... half sister. When I was myself very young, my own father died. My sister, she was born much later. Our mother ..."—he crossed himself in the manner of a practiced Papist—"she died in the birth of Elisabetta. Elisabetta. Yes, I have raised her myself. I am her guardian."

"And you permitted the marriage to Kilbronson?"

He shrugged. "I had no trust for the man, for any man to approach my sister. Yet, Keeeeel-bronson—he seemed not to be a dangerous man."

I changed tacks: "Can you produce a photograph of your sister that might aid me in my search?"

He shook his head and smiled. "No," he said. "My family has never been photographed—my father has a terror of photography."

"Is your father still living? I thought he had died." (The family tree of the Vadas was becoming more and more bewildering, and my notes reflected my own confusion.)

"I apologize—I am not quite a master of your language. My father, he *had* a terror of photography." Then he smiled again, even more widely, displaying a set of glistening white teeth.

For a brief moment I thought to myself that the canine teeth were rather unnecessarily long and sharp, but in a moment the teeth had vanished with the smile and Vadas was readying himself to depart, leaving me to wonder if I had imagined it all. I was beginning to see vampires everywhere. Perhaps these men from Hungary had a special diet to afford such wonderfully white teeth—enviable, considering the English tendency toward dental decay (though mine, I proudly declare, are strong and respectable enough).

"I can tell you honestly, Mr. Vadas, that I have no real leads regarding the search for your sister."

"I believe that you soon will."

"Indeed?" Suspicion returned.

"I have myself heard word that she may be in your North. Near Durham. That is . . ."—was he eager to conceal his surprising familiarity with English geography?—"somewhere in the region. I heard that place named once. Perhaps."

He smiled again, and ventured no further information.

"I can make no promises," I said, "but please do let me know where you can be contacted in London."

"It is difficult for me . . . I have not yet a place."

This was awkward. I was about to make a few suggestions, but he smiled. "I have friends here, however, and have hopes of safe haven. I shall seek you at the due time, Mr. Kemp."

He stood up, still clutching his coat with his black leather gloves. "Good night, Mr. Kemp."

He left. I stood, holding my front door, for a few moments, meditatively.

It was worth looking into, anyway. I had an acquaintance in Durham—an old school chum, now a professor of linguistics. If anything could rouse Sebastian Roubles from the library, a little search for a dark Hungarian adventuress might.

I scribbled a brief note, and addressed it to my friend. Then I set out into the heavy, hot evening to send it.

I was standing by a post office box when I saw her. Esther Raveland, standing on the side of the road, seemingly in meditative solitude.

I hesitated, then walked to her side.

"Good evening, Miss Raveland," I said. "I hope you are well."

Her face was pale—as were so many others in that heat—but, as her eyes focused on me, her glance softened, and she even smiled. "Mr. Kemp," she said with a trace of that old Yankee enthusiasm. "It is good to see you."

"Have you been in London long?"

"We are just returned. We spent a few weeks visiting in the country, and now are back here to swelter with the best of them."

Her manner was so different from that when I had seen her last, that I felt bold to offer my arm. She took it, and we walked together for a time in silence. She seemed somehow more delicate than she had been.

"I fear you have not been well, Miss Raveland."

"Indeed not, Mr. Kemp. I own that the air has not agreed with me of late. I am rather unlike myself. My aunt has threatened me with doctors and the seaside, but I am of a hardier make than she suspects, and I shall baffle her with my return to health very shortly."

"I am so sorry to hear that you have been ill. Perhaps I walk too quickly for you?"

"Indeed not. And how could I suffer with your arm on which to lean?"

There was that smile again, and my soul melted to butter. She was so beautiful, and in distress had an appeal that had been lacking in her most tyrannical moments of strength.

A moment of silence followed. "Mr. Kemp," she said quietly, "I fear I owe you an apology. Perhaps too an explanation."

I repressed the urge to utter discouraging noises. Uninterrupted, she continued after a moment. "It seems a strange thing, to explain myself to you, but I do want to. I don't want you to think ill of me, for some reason, Mr. Kemp. I am a rather silly woman, it seems. But I don't want you to think that I am wicked or ignorant or reckless."

Still, I said nothing. My silence seemed to encourage her, for she went on. "It has been a difficult business, being an heiress—and an American one, to boot! So many voices telling me what to do. And I have tried to listen. I have found, though, that I have some confusion and some regrets now. Some private griefs. And these I ..."

She stopped to stare down at a creature on the curb—a dark, huddled figure, reeking of spirits and filth. A small hat sat beside the crushed figure.

Esther Raveland reached into her purse, and I said earnestly: "Do not, Miss Raveland. He will only drink more with it."

Her face had changed again. Hard. Resentful. "I don't care what he does with it," she snapped. "I want to give it to him, and I shall."

She bent down, and as she dropped in a handful of coins, the man—for man it was, despite all appearances—sat up. He was a hideous sight, all black and dirty, with red splotches of inebriation visible on the parts of his skin that were not soiled, and a bloody bruise across one eye.

"Good evening, my friend," said the lady, her voice gentle and kind. "Are you well?"

"Aye, lady. But I pray you, do not fall in love with me, for I am falser than vows made in wine."

Instead of replying with indignation, as any respectable Englishwoman might, Esther Raveland merely laughed with good humor. "Your warning is apt, good man. I shall guard my heart. Have you money for food and lodging?"

"Thanks to you, merry angel, I do indeed."

"See that you *do* use it for food and lodging—" I began sternly, but Miss Raveland interrupted: "I told you I don't care how he uses it, Mr. Kemp. Pray do not interfere with my business with the good gentleman."

The man doffed his cap in a dramatic gesture, and spoke with a theatrical accent: "Now mercury endow you with leasing, for thou hast spoken well of fools."

"Shakespeare again," she replied, and her voice was once again gentle.,

"The Bard and I are old and dear friends," he said, and added with a saucy smile: "You wouldn't think it to look at me, my dear, but I had an Oxford education."

"Really?" she said, and without a trace of irony in her voice.

"Yes, indeed. Oxford educated from birth. My father was a don, you see. Riddled with prizes and respect. Honors fairly oozed from every pore. A monument of scholarship and English respectability. And my mother was Coventry Patmore's dream—the very Angel in the House incarnate. A prize of womanhood. A cherished daughter of the City of Dreaming Spires.

"And such dreams there were too." His voice was now wistful. "I was his only boy, you know. I had a sister. Fair Nell. Fair sweet Nelly ... Where were the traces of her early cares, her sufferings, and fatigues? All gone. Sorrow was dead indeed in her, but peace and perfect happiness were born; imaged in her tranquil beauty and profound repose. Fair Nell. Sweet, dear girl." His eyes gazed upon some invisible form in the middle distance, then he shook his head and resumed his autobiographical performance. "I conned the Greeks at my father's knee. Well, as close to his knee as I could come to the old reprobate, and 'scape a thrashing. Conning state without book. Verily. For I can cut a pretty caper. Or ... at least ... I could. The thrashing cut too."

"I'm sorry," said Miss Raveland. "How dreadful it must have been."

"He wasn't always so," the drunk assured her, "except when the honors kept him too far from his happy, hidden comfort. Drowning honors in barrel of malmsey. As my mother wept and screamed in an upstairs room. And found her own solace. Forgive me, my dear. I mix my metaphors, quite."

"What happened to him?" I asked, almost against my will. This pitiful creature, who reeked of stale alcohol and his own dank, filthy odors, had risen to a commanding pitch of pathos somehow. He was no less repulsive than before, but I found I could not look away from his reeking, filthy, disgusting carcass, so alive was his sodden eye.

"My father?" he seemed astonished at the idea. "He's dead of course. Dead and buried. And the worms have long devoured his flesh. Why, e'en so: and now my Lady Worm's; chapless, and knocked about the mazzard with a sexton's spade: here's fine revolution, an' we had the trick to see 't." He sighed. "God, I want a drink."

Silence fell, apart from the wheezing drone of the half-sleeping inebriate.

"Miss Raveland," I said with quiet urgency, "it grows dark around. Please, allow me to escort you home?"

She did not reply.

I repeated myself, gently, but with greater insistence.

She looked up with tears in her eyes. "He's in the third degree of drink," she whispered. "He's drowned."

The man in the gutter suddenly awoke: "Shakespeare once again," he declared with a strange, unnerving triumph. "Your turn, missy, and you did him proud." Then he turned toward me, his face wild and furious. "Will the madman sit in judgment on the drunken sot?" he demanded in a roar. "Will he? Will you?"

"Come on, there, Nick!" said another voice—a voice of authority. I looked up to see a constable (not one of my acquaintances, thankfully). "You can't make a noise like that. You'll have to move along."

"Oh, Davis," whimpered the sodden Nick. "Don't make me move along. I've been a-moving on and a-moving on. I'm a-moving on to the berryin' ground— that's the move as I'm up to."

"Dickens," whispered Esther Raveland.

The man turned with a smile of delight. "You are a dear," he said affectionately.

To this unseemly, presumptuous compliment, she curtsied thanksgiving and tossed a small purse to him.

Drunken Nick caught the purse easily with one hand and kissed the other one to her before turning back to the policeman. "Good sir Constable Davis," he said grandly, "I go! I go! See how I go!"

He took several, staggering steps, rendered all the more ludicrous by the solemnity of his bearing. Then he tottered and fell into the street. Davis and I rushed to his side and found he was merely snoring.

I tried to help Davis lift him, but the constable said, "Thank you, sir, but I know a place for him to stay. I can lift him, really, sir. You go to the young lady. It's growing dark now and the streets are no place for her."

I agreed too much with this statement to resent him for the direction; I stood up, wiping the mud from my clothes, to find we three men were alone. There was no sight of Esther Raveland down the silent street, not even a shadow or a hint of her movement in the flickering uncertainty of the streetlights.

Chapter 16

16 October 1900: South Kensington, Thence Northward through England, though Mostly within the Pages of a Book

(From Mina Murray Harker's journal) *There are such beings as vampires; some of us have evidence that they exist. Even had we not the proof of our own unhappy experience, the teachings and the records of the past give proof enough for sane peoples. I admit that at the first I was sceptic. Were it not that through long years I have trained myself to keep an open mind, I could not have believed until such time as that fact thunder on my ear. "See! See! I prove; I prove." Alas! Had I known at the first what now I know ...*

Over a fortnight passed. Jenson's health improved slowly. I spent a great deal of my time with him, when I was not in my office. One morning, I was interrupted in my attentions to the convalescent manservant (who had regained enough energy to be deeply mortified and annoyingly apologetic) by another knock at the door.

I wondered if it would be Vadas, still attired in his incongruous overcoat (though the weather was already much more appropriate to his attire), perhaps having slept in the park all night. Or perhaps he would be there, fangs bloody, to gloat to me of his recent vampiric conquests ...

I shook my head. Vampires. Nonsense. Was I going to go quite insane once again? Such thoughts were appropriate only to crackpot Papists and the like.

I opened the door and there, as if on cue, stood the crackiest-potted Papist I could ever imagine.

He bore the mark of many a year, perhaps even a hundred, or six hundred—his face a contracting network of wrinkles—and was attired in voluminous white garments like Father Thomas Edmund Gilroy.

"There was a girl named Daisy in the town where I lived," announced my visitor in strident tones. "She fell down a well."

Then, without further explanation, he walked past me, perched with prim, perfect posture on the end of a stiff-backed chair, blinked twice, and smiled affectionately in my direction.

"May I help you?" I asked.

"We shan't play cricket on the green," cried the elderly man. "Not without raspberry preserves."

He nodded. The matter was settled.

"Indeed not," I ventured, awkwardly.

"No use arguing now, Mr. Kemp!" the little man said with a stern shake of the head. "You'll never convince me. That's what I always say, and my belief is unshakable."

Then he fell into a ruminative silence, staring down at the cold grate in the fireplace.

After a few moments, he began to emit an odd sort of purring sound. I moved closer to discover that he was sound asleep, snoring gently and contentedly as a child might.

Another knock came at the door and I rose to answer it.

It was the post, and it contained a letter from my friend in Durham.

John,

I knew I should have been a lawyer. Such adventures you must be having! Lucky for you, I recently read all of the works of Conan Doyle and consequently knew just what to do. I undertook an official sort of inquiry and can tell you that a mysterious woman of foreign extraction did arrive a few weeks ago. I do not have a name, but she did not stay in Durham City long. She relocated to a rather mysterious place nearby—the Convent of the Most Sacred Heart in Ushaw Moor. What are you up to, old chap? Do write and tell me, or better yet come and visit and give me all the news. Elsie's in her confinement again, and the children have quite overrun the house. The noise is overwhelming. A little adventure would do me good.

—Seb.

I looked up from my letter to see the elderly Papist wide awake and looking at me with frank interest.

I hurriedly folded up the letter and turned to him.

"Yes, Father?" (I assumed he was a priest.) "What can I do for you?"

"Why," he said, astonished. "Thomas Edmund's book, of course. I brought it to you."

I was dumbfounded. "His book?" I asked.

"There's the theatre there too."

"The theatre?"

"Don't be silly, man! It's what they're always saying to me. Don't be silly, Henry. Don't."

I tried to look as unsilly as possible. The whole thing was madness, and shouldn't one humor madmen before they turned violent?

"Who is Henry?" I asked.

"Why, I am!"

My attempt to appear unabsurd had apparently failed. He even looked for a moment as if he were dubiously considering my sanity. Then he widened his eyes, as if commenting to himself that one must humor lunatics, and went on. "My theory still stands, of course," said the priest sagely, nodding. "Why else would there be that push from the thirteenth century, revolutionizing our understanding of the term? Completely illuminates the entire question."

"The term?"

"Why body? Why corpse? Why cadaver? Whence come these words? The Old High German *botah* shouldn't have had the influence it did. *Bodig. Botah. Corse. Corpus.* That's it. That's the one. *Cadere. Cadaver.* Urban IV issued *Transiturus de hoc mundo* in 1264! And, of course, *the* doctrine was widely promulgated by the end of the twelfth century."

He beamed broadly at me, having made his point, whatever that was.

"Well, now, Mr. Kemp. Shouldn't you begin packing?"

"Packing?"

"Yes. For the convent, of course. That's the next step. As well you know!"

He stood up.

"Goodbye, Mr. Kemp. Thank you so much. Remember to leave the dog out, else the curtains will fail."

And, with a smile, he swept from the room, beads rattling at his ankles.

A moment later he was back. He thrust a small book into my hand, smiled broadly again, and hurried off.

Left alone, I stood for a long time staring after him. Then I roused myself and looked down, where I held the note from my agent in Durham, alongside the Papist book. It was a tiny volume, tightly bound with black leather, with a small shield, emblazed with a cross of harlequin black-and-white fleur-de-lis, with lurid red lettering that declared it to be:

Catalogue of the Preternatural
Rev. Thomas Edmund Gilroy, O.P., D.C.L.

I considered the visit from Vadas, and now this strange descent by the ancient priest. Fairly considered, I could not have said which bizarre visit had troubled me more. I looked at the book for a few moments, then, grimly setting my teeth, I thrust the book into a bag and thereby commenced packing. I was bound for Ushaw Moor, Durham, and the Convent of the Most Sacred Heart.

My preparations for departure did not take long. As I was throwing together the last of my things, I remembered Jenson. There was a difficulty. Could I abandon him, weak as he was? A solution presented itself almost as immediately to my mind.

I tiptoed through the front hall, opened the door and shut it behind me quietly, and hurried downstairs.

On the lower level lived a retired Army colonel. He was quite deaf and lived a quiet life, occasionally receiving visitors, but just as frequently staying alone at home. He ventured out daily on a slow, marching walk down a few streets and then back home. I imagine his routine was a disciplined, regular one. In any case, he found me a quiet neighbor, as indeed I found him. We nodded at each other in passing, but were not in the habit of interacting socially or exchanging favors.

I felt this keenly as I knocked at his door prepared to ask a favor.

His cook answered the door. Mrs. Pritchard. A buxom, beaming, round-faced monument of a woman.

"Good day, Mrs. Pritchard," I said. And in that moment, I reconsidered my task.

"Good day, Mr. Kemp," she replied with jolly good humor. "The colonel is out on his constee-toot-nal. Shall I tell 'm you called?"

"Actually, Mrs. Pritchard," I replied, "my business is with you."

"Indeed, sir?"

"Yes. You know my manservant Jenson?"

To my surprise, she blushed like a schoolgirl at the question.

"Why, yes, sir. And, sir, I do assure you there's never been so much as a moment of impropriety. Perhaps he has spent a morning or two in my kitchen. Perhaps I've took tea with him in your parlor, but always with great respect and deportment. Just a body being civil, you know. Not a hint of . . . Well, since Mr. Pritchard died, I own I've been lonely, but Mr. Jenson, he has the soul of a gentleman, begging your pardon, sir, and never once has he . . . Well, sir, I just hope you know it, and took no offense. A natural friendship, you might say, with all respect to you and the colonel, and no presumption."

At her conclusion, she looked rather alarmingly as if she might burst into tears, so I hurried to interpose myself.

"Indeed no, Mrs. Pritchard, which is why I feel bold to ask you for this favor. Knowing of your friendship, as I now do."

That baffled the tears, and curiosity got the better of her.

"Favor, sir? From me, sir?"

"Mr. Jenson has been quite ill, and ..."

She gasped and turned pale and I was frightened she might faint (she was of considerable girth, and were she to fall, I was sure I could not carry her inside—perhaps she would even fall on me, and I would be pinned there in the hall, helpless, until the colonel happened to find us, revive her, and free me from such a ridiculous posture). I hurriedly added: "Mr. Jenson is much better, but still weak. I find I must travel north immediately on business, and though I have taken the better part of nursing on myself, I wonder if you might look in on him sometimes in my absence, just to be sure he is ..."

Now her eyes were alight and I prayed that Jenson's intentions had been honorable and, particularly, matrimonial, for I feared that in any case I would hear of an engagement upon my return. "Don't you fret your mind one moment, sir," she said. "Mr. Jenson will be safe as houses, sir. Never you mind."

I escaped from the machinating cook as quickly as I could and returned to my bags. I had everything staged at the door when I ducked back in to warn Jenson (who had just awakened) of his fate.

"I must go north on business, Jenson," I said. "Mrs. Pritchard has promised to look in on you."

He leapt to his feet, his face crimson with emotion. "Em'ly mustn't see me in this bed of sickness and woe! She is frail, sir! She might catch her death!"

Mrs. Pritchard seemed an unlikely casting for the role of weak heroine, but I made a few soothing noises to the apparently lovesick swain, and hurriedly left the two of them to figure out their own business between themselves.

It was disquieting indeed to discover that my residence was atop a volcano of hitherto unknown emotions, but I did trust that Mrs. Pritchard, at least, knew well how to value herself enough to protect against dalliance, and honestly I doubted that Jenson was the type of man to dally. In any case, it was their business, and I had much else to occupy my mind.

I dispatched a telegram to Sebastian, alerting him to my plan.

There was one other thing to do. I wrote a quick note to the dour Edgar, reporting that there might be a chance of his wife's presence in England and that I would be following it up. I would report further when I had more to say.

As I finished the letter and reread it for clarity, I wondered at my own reluctance to proffer any other information to my client. I did not want to tell him of my foreign visitor, and I certainly did not want to indicate in which cardinal direction I intended to take up the search. Perhaps it would come to nothing, after all, I told myself. At least I was doing my duty by alerting him to the possibility.

An hour later I was on a train headed north. The urban scene whipped away, and we entered the country winding our long way upward. The train was not crowded; I had a compartment all to myself. I gazed at the scenery until it faded away into a blur of unseen trees, fields, and shrubs. We passed through a small town. Further north I dimly recognized cows in the distance. My mind wandered, and I drifted into a nap.

I awoke hungry and irritable. I had thrown some few things to eat into my bag—in the most untidy manner, which would have horrified Jenson. As I delved into this haphazard feast, my eyes lit upon the little black volume brought to me by my other visitor of the morning. *Catalogue of the Preternatural*, indeed. Well, I would give the Papist his chance to speak at last.

I opened the book and began to read.

While the history of our Order must be familiar to the likely reader of these pages, it is not unseemly that we state, rather than take for granted, our illustrious history, as it must recall to our living memory the heritage passed on by our holy Father Dominic.

The Order of Preachers was founded in the thirteenth century to battle heresy and preach the Gospel. We continue in our mission of preaching even unto the present day. Here we focus particularly on the role of Dominicans in addressing the problem of the vampire, also popularly known as the undead—a living dead body that gathers sustenance by drinking the blood of its victims.

(I hoped to myself that he would go no further into medieval history and instead address the issue at hand—and my hope was mercifully rewarded.)

As will be discussed in greater detail below, Pope Benedict XIV ratified this authority by edict. An apparent vampiric surge later in the seventeenth century made a more formal organization necessary. A catalogue of all paranormal threats was thereby created (presented here in a new edition, with modernized spelling, and attendant footnotes).

Please note the focus here is not exclusively upon blood drinkers, though they are the primary concern of the Order of Preachers. Both flesh eaters and blood drinkers (as an anti-Eucharistic threat) are of interest to us. Other branches of the preternatural (though manifested in our catalogue here) are the concern of other Orders. For more information regarding lycanthropy, inquiries must be made to the Order of Friars Minor.

For the last two millennia, flesh eaters and blood drinkers have been primarily a concern east of Germany or south of the equator.

When need for this new organization arose, the Holy Father deemed the Order of Preachers well equipped to handle the particular vampire challenge. Some did say that it was favoritism, owing to his well-known affection for Aquinas. And still others have said it was a deliberate step to undermine the seriousness of the discourse—Dominicans would be too skeptical in their scholasticism to give real countenance to the threat of vampires.

This was perhaps overly optimistic, as has been illustrated by the brief periods of panic introduced into some Dominican houses, particularly where those tasked with the supervision of revenant operations were not fully schooled. Davanzati has asserted in his writing that the fact that so many of the fiercest advocates of the existence of vampires were uneducated members of the peasant class was proof positive that it was all born of peasant hysteria. In fact, he makes no true allowance for the singular impressionability of the well-educated man who has been schooled to believe that such creatures cannot exist, and consequently is overwhelmed with horror when he discovers that they in fact do exist.

This was an uncomfortable thought, so I hurried along.

Death itself was his next subject, and the question of the body after death. One quotation in particular jumped out at me:

As Aquinas himself noted in his Summa, *Part III, Question 71, Article 11, in reply to objection 3: "Hence, in accordance with this natural affection [for his own flesh], a*

> *man has during life a certain solicitude for what will become of his body after death: and he would grieve if he had a presentiment that something untoward would happen to his body."*

That "something untoward" made me chuckle, though I wasn't sure why.

I skimmed dense chapters regarding natural law and the stigma regarding the consumption of human flesh and drinking of blood, early Jewish misconceptions regarding the Catholic Eucharist, and a lengthy exposition on the sixth chapter of the Gospel of John. This latter portion concluded with the following acknowledgment:

> *It almost goes without saying, of course, that the complexity of the Eucharist miracle far outweighs the garish delineation of the preternatural. However, it is useful to observe the dark mirroring achieved in the logistics of active vampirism.*

I turned the page and found myself in the territory of more immediate history.

> *In the eighteenth century, a series of events caused Pope Benedict XIV, a scholar of some note, to consider the dangers of vampiric activity. He rightly feared both the effect of unrestrained vampires upon innocent souls and the effects of superstition on the alarmed peasant populace. Tales of bloody ravages, along with accounts of desecration of so many graves, caused the Holy Father to summon to his presence the then Master of the Order of Preachers.*
>
> *Consequent to their conversation, we were granted the additional task of battling recent upsurges in vampiric activity. In this, we operate under the Suprema Congregatio*

sanctæ romanæ et universalis inquisitionis, the Congregation that would have supervised the defense of the Church's earthly dominions in past centuries. As the Holy Father himself wrote (the translation is mine):

> *In recognition of the extraordinary achievements of the followers of holy father Dominic, and, indeed, as proper appreciation of the talents and strength of the Ordo Praedicatorum, we hereby give to them the task and vest them with the powers of vampiric exorcism, as well as the dispatching of other revenant creatures.*

The experience of the Ordo Praedicatorum in and through the Supreme Sacred Congregation of the Roman and Universal Inquisition particularly equipped this Order to address the new threat—new, not in its origin, but in its manifestation. For the Evil One knows well how to match his wit and his wickedness to the defining characteristics of a generation, and to become, thereby, a more effective tempter of souls.

In 1803, Father Piotr Kwiatkowski's Quaestiones disputatae dei vampiri *definitively settled the question of the historical precedent for the Holy Father's pronouncement. The author's English translation (the first completed) ...*

And, I muttered to myself, likely the last!

... appeared in print in 1889.

When operating in the role of Inquisitors, the followers of Saint Dominic battle against heresy, both in its manifestation in the light of popular superstition and contemporary thought, and in its representation after death in the form of the intrinsic vampire.

In the Order's conflicts with the Albigensians, a bloodstained habit was that of martyr, a sign that the adversaries of truth were spurred on to violence. Most remarkable in our recollection is Peter of Verona. Today, in contrast, a scarlet-stained habit is popularly conceived as one of the familiar attributes of the battle whether it ends with martyrdom or a staking. Metaphorically speaking, of course. Some have posited the theory that the bloodiness of the scapular was indicative of the ability of the supposed vampire slayer. This supposition is likely apocryphal, or, at best, gravely mistaken. The title of vampire slayer, in fact, is misleading and a popular corruption of the Latin title duellator contra lamiis. *This role is clearly seen as minor to the established mission of the Order, and to the role of ordained friar priests in the confection of the sacraments.*

Clearly, I remarked to myself with dry sarcasm.

Subsequent pages erupted into the catalogue itself, delving into the differences between the zombie and the vampire, the definition of animal souls, a ranking of different sorts of vampires—"master" or "full vampire", and those creatures who, like that of the zombie, were constrained and controlled by an oppressive outside rational force, with passing references to the place of the lycanthrope (most commonly known as a werewolf), and a host of minor spirits and sprites. Another passage caught my eye: "Such reptilian or brute characteristic are commonly witnessed in the more primitive ranks of the undead." Halfway through, I stumbled upon another lengthy discourse on the subject of zombification—its West African origins in notions of voodoo (where the dead could be controlled by a powerful *bokor* or sorcerer).

It was believed by many (the author concluded) that the soul of the zombified can be freed by Divine intervention.

To be zombified is a temporary condition during which moral culpability is suspended. Kwiatkowski has a similar understanding of the distinction between the vampire and his victims.

I noticed he spent a great deal of time addressing questions of the culpability of vampiric victims who themselves begin to prey upon new victims. I found the timeline of vampiric succession thoroughly bewildering, and was even irritated that he did not more clearly clarify for me the process by which vampires are created.

He did add this odd point (in his discussion of the nuances of an undead hierarchy):

Evil can create nothing for itself; it can only corrupt that which is. Thus, we conclude that the undead body, though preserved from corruption by the intervention of the Evil One and his breaking of the natural law, is good. Because of this, treatment of that body must proceed with proper respect.

I closed the book in disgust. "He's as bad as Stoker," I said out loud, and cared not who heard me. The whole thing was absurd. A lot of nonsense thrown together by a host of mad little followers of the Scarlet Lady.

Then I thought of Charles Sidney. Of my wild, inchoate suspicions of Popescu and his secretary. My vacillating feelings about Esther Raveland.

And Adele. I thought once again of Adele and the uselessness of the priest at her deathbed.

How dare he make light of the tragic fate of Adele? What sort of heartless buffoon was this man who went about in white robes and pretended to have the power to combat the undead, and then stood there muttering empty prayers while a young girl died before his very eyes? He probably did not have as much as a clove of garlic in his bag—and he called himself a vampire slayer! The mummery of priests! This was it all it came to! It was worse than it had been with my father—what had his harmless, befuddled, good-natured hellfire and brimstone availed in the face of real tragedy? Had it spared my mother from her death—too young, too young by far? Had it kept him from descending into pottering and fading into death himself—premature in years but long overdue in spirit?

But that was long ago. This was now, and it was much worse. What would happen? Would the vampire continue to ravage London, victimizing unsuspecting girls? Unknown, undiscovered, unstopped. I remembered the horrifying Whitechapel murders of over a decade earlier—Toby Barnes had noted it in his column. I remembered the terror that had gripped London—remembered it clearly though I was still at school at the time. We were sophisticated students and devotedly read the city newspapers, living vicariously through the printed page while exiled in our scholarly retreat. And this was worse than "the Ripper". This was an undead creature that fed upon the living, drawing them into that same, hellish, undead existence. All of the nonsensical theorizing of those silly men in their robes and their foolish religion could do nothing. They knew nothing. Nothing but theories.

It was all nonsense. If there were vampires, we would soon all be dead, and it was a far better thing when girls were going about being left to die and no one doing anything about it. Meanwhile other girls were going around pretending not to be vampires when they really were vampires and giving upstanding gentlemen nightmares and distracting them from their work. It was all quite idio-tic, disgusting, infuriating, and horrifying.

"Damn, damn, damn, and damn!" I said loudly.

The train lurched and continued humming, clacking on its way. If there were vampires. Then it came to me, as a dark, rushing memory, as strong as if it had only just happened.

It was on a train that I saw a vampire myself.

I stood up hurriedly, as if to shake off that troubling thought, dropping the book to the ground in my haste.

The door opened.

I looked up, strangely alarmed.

There stood Father Thomas Edmund Gilroy, smiling in what appeared to be pleasant surprise.

"Why, my friend!" he cried. "We do seem to come across each other on trains!"

Chapter 17

16–17 October 1900:
Still Train-Bound for the North

(From Mina Murray Harker's journal) *"Dr. Van Helsing, what I have to tell you is so queer that you must not laugh at me or at my husband. I have been since yesterday in a sort of fever of doubt; you must be kind to me, and not think me foolish that I have even half believed some very strange things."* He reassured me by his manner as well as his words when he said:—*"Oh, my dear, if you only know how strange is the matter regarding which I am here, it is you who would laugh. I have learned not to think little of any one's belief, no matter how strange it be. I have tried to keep an open mind; and it is not the ordinary things of life that could close it, but the strange things, the extraordinary things, the things that make one doubt if they be mad or sane."*

He sat. I sat opposite. He looked at me with an obviously friendly feeling. I glared at him with unveiled mistrust.

"Well, now," he said. "Here we are."

"Yes," I said.

Once again, silence fell, and I continued to bristle with unspoken antagonism.

"Take your time, my friend," he said, and his voice was gentle. "When you are ready to speak, I shall be ready to listen."

That confessional manner was the last straw. I exploded. "It's all ludicrous, you know."

"I imagine it might appear so."

"So you slay vampires."

"I would take issue with your choice of language. Much too dramatic. We do not slay vampires. We exorcise demons, particularly revenants of various breeds."

"What does that mean?" I insisted, continuing in this backward catechism.

"Yes, I dispatch vampires and other revenant—or 'undead'—threats."

Well, that was one thing out in the open at least. "How do you do it?"

"Do what?"

"Kill a vampire."

"There are prayers and rituals of exorcism for our task."

"Another prevarication," I said with annoyance.

The little priest just smiled. Such an infuriatingly gentle smile.

"I've read your book," I said, throwing this information out as if it were a strong card in my hand—a trump card to shock and challenge him out of complacency and bring him down onto my level.

Then his demeanor changed. His face turned a deep crimson—almost purple in its intensity. Was I about to see Father Edmund Gilroy roused to anger? I had seen one of their secret texts. I had an inroad to investigating their secrets. The hidden machinations of the Papists were open to me.

"Ah dear," he said, and sighed, his face still red. "Father Henry, was it? He said he might, but he says many things now, dear man, and one never knows ... He was a mentor to me in my youth. He takes a great deal of pride in it ...

and many were pleased at my little effort. But ... really ...
I had not expected ..."

And his color grew yet deeper.

Not rage then. The blush of a shy author.

I was disarmed at that thought, and I fear he knew it.

Looking at my downcast face, Father Thomas Edmund
laughed and regained his own usual color. "My friend,"
he said, "enough of the sabers of skepticism. Let's have
tea. We can discuss the matter more fully and in a civilized
manner then."

Thus it was that I found myself once again in the dining car of a train, sitting opposite a round-faced man in a
white dress.

I eschewed tea and, to the astonishment of the waiter,
ordered a round meal. Dismissed, he hurried off to the
kitchen.

Father Thomas Edmund beamed. "I am glad you
have your appetite, my friend. An empty stomach can so
bring one's mind into confusion that you might imagine horrors. There is that old tale of the Mother Superior of a convent—or perhaps it was a saint. Probably
Teresa. She was known for her matter-of-fact mind. In
any case, when she heard report that one of the sisters
had seen visions, she wryly instructed that the young
woman be given something to eat." He chuckled. "Or,
if you prefer, a less overtly religious example. What is it
Mr. Scrooge says? That witty observation to the spirit of
his dead partner? 'There's more of gravy than of grave
about you!'"

And he laughed for a good minute over this pun.

He spoke of indifferent matters for some time after
that. Weather. Travel. Observations of the geography as
we continued on our way. We were far beyond York,

now, and the sun was beginning to move lower in the horizon. It would be twilight long before we arrived near Durham.

I had finished my meal and was ruminating uncomfortably on this point when Father Thomas Edmund reintroduced our earlier topic.

"Now, John," he said—the first time he had ventured to use my first name. "Let us speak frankly."

"I wish we could," I said, "but I own that much of what you may tell me will be impossible for me to believe."

"I am not asking you for faith, John. I am simply and practically proposing a uniting of forces. I trust you. I am well aware that you do not trust me or my brethren. That is entirely within your province. I have enough respect for your intelligence and your integrity as an honorable man to know that you will give what I say a fair and balanced consideration.

"There are such creatures as vampires. They are undead creatures that prey upon the living. They are of the damned. They seek not merely the physical destruction of their victims, but the spiritual destruction as well. This latter is my primary concern, but it is closely united with the former. After death, there is no chance of further spiritual corruption—or salvation."

"Your attitude seems ... callous." The word was out before I could find a tactful synonym.

He didn't seem shocked. "I have complete confidence in the justice and mercy of a God who died to save sinners. If those souls that are lost cannot be saved by His tears, they cannot be saved by mine. I do not know the consequences that brought about the destruction of this soul. I do know that now he cannot be saved, and that he dedicates his entire undead being to the destruction of others.

And that I cannot allow, inasmuch as it is in my power to stop him."

"He?" I asked, though I hated to hear the answer.

"Why, yes, of course. The vampire now plaguing London."

We'd reached another critical point. "So you think there is a vampire now. In London."

He smiled. "Don't you?"

I shook my head. "I don't. I think it's a lot of nonsense. There's a logical, practical explanation for all of this. Something that can be reasoned out. Something that doesn't involve the supernatural."

"Technically," said the priest, "we are discussing the preternatural. We haven't even touched on the supernatural, and I am not inclined to do so with you."

This felt like being dismissed. "Why not?"

"Because I am a preacher, not a proselytizer. But you have called me callous, so let me approach this from another point. Consider moments in which you yourself have grieved. Have platitudes or nonsensical fantasies brought you comfort? Have they drawn you nearer to God?"

"Certainly not," I said.

"Then we are agreed: there is no true consolation to be imparted by flighty, errant theology. I say that the vampire is a damned creature of evil. Consequently, my concern is for his victims. That does not make me cruel or callous. It makes me ... logical and practical."

Before I could respond with fitting indignation to this remark, the train suddenly lurched and came to a harsh stop.

As we had been talking, the weather had turned sour. The sky clouded over to a dark gray and began dumping copious amounts of rain all around and over us.

"What's the trouble?" I asked the waiter as he hurried past us.

"Flooding on the tracks," he said. "Shouldn't be delayed for long, sir. Never fear!"

Then, with a face of concern that belied his words, he almost ran out the dining car.

"I think," said the little priest, "that we are in for quite a delay. Shall we return to our compartment?"

I agreed, finishing up the remains of my meal and following my white-robed companion between the tables and down long corridors, so eerily standing still, frozen in the deluge, back to our seats.

We settled in, and for some time we did not talk. The rain was enough to keep our minds occupied. It came down in driving buckets (if such a bizarre metaphor may be allowed). I recalled my father, preaching his sermon on the flood of Noah. "Forty days and forty nights," I murmured, without realizing I was speaking aloud.

"I doubt," said my companion with a twinkle in his eye, "that the employees of the railroad would alert us to the fact. They would simply assure us that all was well, the delay would not be of long duration, and we needn't fear."

I agreed that this was very likely.

The hours passed by slowly. Sometimes I dozed. At first I endeavored to maintain a quasi-seated posture, indicative of prim propriety, but I soon abandoned the pretense and stretched out across the compartment so my feet rested beside my companion. He slept more than once, quietly leaning his head against the windowsill, his hands folded together in his lap. At one point, he even took the white panel from the front of his robe and threw it across his face, veiling it from light.

In between these periods of sleep, we spoke of many things. It would have been impossible to maintain the aggressive anger that had so possessed me at the beginning of our trip—our delay was simply too long and the circumstances too conducive to relaxation. After four hours, I found myself in a comfortable and friendly conversation, and I didn't much care.

"Charles Sidney. Was his death connected with your hypothetical vampire?"

"The vampire is here in London. The death of Sidney is clearly and closely related. The police initially believed the murderer to be a madman. The fellow in question was the embodiment of that useful literary device, the red herring. He was returned in due time to the asylum and was, I understand, thoroughly frightened by it all and as eager to return to his confinement as his doctors could wish."

"Was it the vampire then?" I pressed.

"The vampire or one of his minions. And I do not think that the lunatic is officially a minion. A minor pawn, perhaps, but not a minion. Stoker overthought that business too. To great effect, of course. The madman in his novel is one of the most fascinating characters. And, of course, he perfectly represents the moral question of timing and culpability. It is indeed fascinating that the character who most clearly embodies the theological complexity of the vampiric anti-Eucharist should not even be a vampire."

"But why?" I insisted, ignoring the priest's speculative meanderings. "What earthly reason could there be for killing Sidney? He was a self-satisfied dandy and a conceited ass, but why kill him? And why with such appalling violence?"

"The logic of the vampire is a dark, twisted thing, my friend. The provocation could have been infinitesimal to our minds—either Sidney had outlasted his usefulness or was more useful dead than alive or he had resisted the vampire in some way."

"More useful dead than alive," I repeated. "Do you think then that Sidney ... that Sidney is now himself a vampire?"

"No, Sidney is not a vampire."

"But how do you know?"

"As a close friend of mine, Father Paul, might say: 'We make it our business to know such things.'" Father Thomas Edmund Gilroy delivered this in a tone that indicated that further questions were not necessary—a tone I remembered well from my father, as on the day when I inquired as to the likelihood of Jonah truly surviving his ordeal in the belly of the big fish. Then he smiled again and reassured me quietly: "We do know."

Old Mrs. Lawson arose next as a topic.

"She is a woman of faith," I said (and not a little snidely). "She will be fine."

Father Thomas Edmund, taking me at face value, shook his head. "My friend, do you imagine that these 'women of faith' do not question the mercy of God? Indeed, they often do so daily, and the battle against grief and despair that is waged in the hearts of so many of those simple, pious women can be more fierce than anything imagined or experienced by an exorcist."

That led to Adele and, indirectly, to a question that had long bothered me.

"I am not saying I accept your theory of the vampire, Father," I said, "but if that were the case, why would a vampire care so much about me and those close to me? What of Adele Lawson?"

"You need not worry for Miss Lawson—though you should indeed pray for her. We rely upon God's mercy, even as we certainly expect his justice. But—pace Stoker!—she was no vampire."

I began to protest but he shook his head.

"The whole business of 'making vampires' is a great deal more complicated and yet more simple than the novelist conceived of it. As to Miss Lawson's death—the manner of it and the comforts surrounding it—there was nothing more I could do; nothing more to be done. Her illness was not vampiric in origin. The doctors did all that they could to save her. Moreover I am always compelled to respect the wishes of her family and of their clergyman. I brought everything I would need for the final sacrament of course, but as she was not a Catholic, I could not foist them upon her. Dr. Grant assured me that everything had been done according to their rite. He is a good man—in much earlier days a friend of Pusey in fact, and an acquaintance of Newman. He is rather confused on some points of sacramental agency and entertains some very convoluted notions of ritual sacrifice in ancient cultures—but Father Matthew has spoken with him at length concerning that. He's rather an expert on the subject—Father Matthew, that is. I do assure you, my friend: every step will be taken to preserve the wholesomeness and sacred peace of her final resting place. I promise you that."

I was stubborn and not convinced. "I saw a vampire outside her window shortly before she died."

A slow smile crept across his face. "Did you, indeed, John? So you do believe in vampires?"

I was trapped, and I accepted it with good humor. "Well, then," I said. "Either you are correct, vampires are real, I saw a vampire, and he was preying on Adele, or there are no such things, I didn't see one, and you are peddling nonsense again."

His smile was delighted now. "Nicely done, John, nicely done. How shall I counter you ... let me see." He ruminated a moment, as if puzzling out a tactic in a parlor game. "You must remember that the presence of evil is not new. And simply because I tell you there is great evil in London does not preclude the presence of many forms and manifestations of evil. In fact, evil attracts and begets more evil. The creature you saw is not the creature we have discussed, but it was no doubt of the same corrupted nature. Further, had the opportunity presented itself, I have no doubt that your reptilian creature would have preyed upon Miss Lawson. But he was not able to do so."

"Why not?" I demanded.

His eyes twinkled. "Because a certain London lawyer showed up and made such a ruckus that the police came."

I couldn't help laughing with him at that. Then I returned to the topic of the vampiric motivation.

"Why me?" I asked. "I'm not that good of a lawyer."

"False modesty will avail you nothing. But, truly, this is not a matter of your skills. Whether you are a talented lawyer or not, you are Edgar Kilbronson's lawyer. And that makes you particularly well situated to assist in tracking down the one person on which our vampire is maniacally fixated. Elisabetta Kilbronson."

"Why on earth would he want the Kilbronson woman?"

"Now, that, my friend, I do not yet know. Nevertheless, the facts are clear and lead us to that conclusion. Your first encounter with one of those creatures was while you were in Budapest seeking Elisabetta Kilbronson. You had a connection with Charles Sidney—he is now dead. You had a connection with Adele Lawson—she too is dead. And all of a sudden you receive pressured invitations to enter the Temple of the Golden Dawn."

"How do you know that? Have you been following me?"

"Not following, so much as keeping an eye on. Our interests so clearly intersected on so many points, and, knowing, as I do, the ruthlessness of this enemy ..."

"So then you are on this train to try and learn ... what? I am on the trail of Elisabetta Kilbronson. You say she is important. How? Why would your vampire want to pursue this unfaithful wife? No, first, before you tell me that you cannot answer that question, you must answer another: Should you not be considering who the vampire is? How can we find him in a city as big as London? He could be hiding anywhere—*anywhere!*" (The thought was nerve-racking, and I barely restrained myself from glancing uneasily over my shoulder to see if there were red, glaring eyes staring out at us from the bushes.)

"Oh," replied Father Thomas Edmund with blinking eyes, "we are already clear as to all that."

I stared at him.

"We know who the vampire is," he said. "Now we have but to learn *who* he is."

When I continued to stare, he elaborated further: "We know his identity—we know who he is here in London. We have known that for some time."

"But you said ..."

"To battle him properly we must know more about him than merely who he is here in London. We need to know his lineage, his history, where he has come from, who his minions are, who else in England he knows, what contacts he has made in London, the plot which brought him here ..."

"Where he lives?" I asked.

"We know that already as well. And you do too. He lives in the house of Charles Sidney."

And there it was. "You say that Count Popescu is a vampire."

"It's a strong working theory, my friend. A man appeared in London as an elderly and infirm Hungarian nobleman, accompanied by at least two attendants with the possibility of a third. They all arrived one month ago. We have not yet determined all of the steps of his journey—though there is reason to believe that he made use of at least one train. An odd thing as there is a supposition that ancient fiends mistrust modern forms of transportation, but these are changing times, I suppose, and even vampires must change with them."

"But the supposed vampires I have seen and all that Stoker has written—fiction or no, the story has roots in the same history over which you claim to be an authority—and even the evidence of my own eyes, all of it makes your claim unstable."

"How so?"

"My hysterical delusion—for that is what it must be—is of pink-eyed monsters who crawl up walls and reek of their own decaying flesh. Not philanthropic socialite foreigners."

"Yes," he said with an infuriating calm. "I thought you'd try that one. This is a much more complex horror, even as it is more simple. Our modern vampire—meaning one that has originated in the last two hundred years—can exhibit the questionable sophistication you note. Such advances beyond the bestial are to his advantage, certainly. If his object is, as we know it to be, to drive men into hell, he would be best served by merely facilitating the ordinary means of damnation—man's disordered appetites. Demonic theatrics can easily have the counter-effect of inspiring faith. Better the man who believes nothing and indifferently pursues vice than the one who is petrified into the beginning of belief. And yet ... yet there is an impulsiveness in these creatures to reveal themselves. The demonic ego." He nodded with apparent satisfaction over this point. "Very often the creature's undoing. That or some other disordered desire."

He had delivered his report in a businesslike tone, but concluded with a smile and a nod toward me.

I did not smile back. The revelation was in some ways a relief, and yet I felt somehow cheated. There was no mystery here, no unfolding of clues, nothing to whet the intellectual appetite of a Sherlock Holmes.

"A great deal will be dealt with by the police—as best they can," he went on. "Inspector Harris is an able man and a good one. But this is a very serious business indeed. Very serious. For us, the delights of the hunt will be much more subtle than those which novelists would lead us to expect. I fear you think that I am talking in circles, but this is a very serious business, and the more dramatic expectations of the novelist may prove more of a stumbling block than an aid in addressing the problem as we must."

I still felt deflated, and even cheated. "Well," I said, finding solace where I could, "all of that would be compelling if there were such a thing as a vampire."

He looked patiently at me. "I told you once before, my friend, the logic of the vampire is a dark, twisted thing. If you expect a clear explanation such as might be contained in a legal brief, you will not find it. The real question you must first ask is whether or not you are, as I fear, already involved. To answer this, you must consider the evidence. First, there is your friendship with Charles Sidney, his death, and the letter you received from him hours before he died. Second, there is your relationship with Adele Lawson and the suggestion that the vampire was distantly connected with though not the cause of her death. Third, there is the interest paid to you by Victor Montrose—more concerning him later. Fourth, there is your recent trip to Budapest and your meeting with me on the train—and the subsequent first encounter with the vampire.

"To summarize the whole and present it in a compelling fifth point: there is the obvious fact that you and various members of your acquaintance are being personally hounded by a bloodsucking menace. Why have you been chosen? Only time will reveal this, and perhaps never fully to your satisfaction. 'He eat not as others,' said Stoker's entertaining professor from Amsterdam—with that outrageous accent. I would add: 'He think not as others.' But even with all of this to persuade you of your involvement, I assure you that you can nevertheless only join in our battle voluntarily. If you choose to remove yourself from danger, I shall not think any less of you for it. And we will certainly do all in our power to protect you."

There was a grating, deafening noise, and the train began to move again.

"Well," said my companion brightly, "we will make Durham by morning. Perhaps now we should try again to sleep?"

Chapter 18

18 October 1900: Durham and Ushaw Moor

(From a letter from Sister Agatha, Hospital of St. Joseph and Ste. Mary, Buda-Pesth, to Miss Wilhemina Murray) *My patient being asleep, I open this to let you know something more ... He has had some fearful shock—so says our doctor—and in his delirium his ravings have been dreadful; of wolves and poison and blood; of ghosts and demons; and I fear to say of what ... the traces of such an illness as his do not lightly die away.*

"Johnny!"

We stood on the soaking wet platform of Durham station. Father Thomas Edmund Gilroy was beside me, wrapped in a black mackintosh, with a large, flat black hat on his head, from which water poured like a torrent.

A rotund man with meager, wispy, fair hair, and glasses, professorially attired in tweeds, ran puffing up to us in the rain, pumping his umbrella with each labored step. He embraced me enthusiastically, nearly drowning us both.

"Johnny Kemp! I haven't seen you in years! Nearly a decade, even! What an awful wet day. It's a wonder your train ever made it—even twelve hours late! How much you've changed! You look ill. Too thin. You should come visit. My Elsie would keep you well fed. She has a talent for picking cooks, and does a bit of the work in the kitchen herself. Or she does whenever she isn't ... occupied."

"You mentioned she is ... expecting?"

"Oh yes. This is our seventh. Five girls and one boy. We'll see how this one turns out."

I turned toward my companion from the train to proffer an introduction: "Sebastian Roubles, Father Thomas Edmund Gilroy. Father Thomas Edmund, Sebastian Roubles."

Sebastian shook the priest's hand so strongly I wondered he didn't pull his arm out of its socket.

"Pleased to meet you, Father! Very pleased. Well, well. Well, well, indeed. Why, Johnny, you're the last one I'd expect to turn Papist!"

I started to protest, but Father Thomas Edmund Gilroy jumped in smoothly: "Alas, no. Mr. Kemp is not an associate of mine through faith. On the contrary, he provides an enduring, healthy, skeptical questioning challenge to me and mine."

"And I would expect no less!" cried Seb, as if I had been paid a powerful compliment, and he was an affectionate parent, greedy to hear such kind words said of me. "John was always our resident skeptic! Now, me, I'm in the High Church, myself. My parents were and I am too. My wife's father is a bishop down south. We're all too busy to deal with those sorts of questions, but John, here, he was always curious as a monkey." He smiled broadly.

I attempted to change the subject: "Seb, you have a lead for us?"

"And so I do!" he cried. "Come! Let me get you some tea, and then we can have a fine old chat about it."

I shook my head. "Perhaps later. We are really in a hurry. The delay of the train was unfortunate, and we have a great deal of time to make up for now."

"Well, then," said my friend, dampened, "I suppose I can tell you quickly on our way to find someone to drive you out to Ushaw Moor—"

"We are really very grateful," cut in Father Thomas Edmund Gilroy, "and I am sure you have a great deal of importance to tell us."

Sebastian brightened again. "Why, yes, yes, I do! I was rather clever about that. No training, either. I couldn't have done a finer job of it if I'd been Holmes himself. I'm quite a reader of those stories, and I know I don't have the powers of observation of the great man. I never can think through the answer to his problems. I always have to read to the end—or look at the end, if I am tired enough or Elsie needs me and I need to finish reading up as quickly as I can.

"As I said, I knew I could not track down anyone on my own. So I tapped into the most observant, all-knowing source in the entirety of Durham—the old woman gossip circles." He was talking rapidly as we hurried through the rain. "My great-aunt, Greta. She's quite an old hand. She knows everything there is to know about everything. Nothing goes on in Durham she doesn't know about. She knows about girls who get into difficulties even before *they* do!" It was an interesting notion, and one that amused him greatly. "And if you think that a foreign-looking woman, full of mystery, could debark from a train at our station, and make her way through darkened streets, turning this way and that to escape detection, then hurrying across the wilderness to the very mysterious and intriguing Convent of Roman Nuns—which, by the way, my aunt quite relies upon as being the center for all evil, mysterious intrigue in the region, so do not ever seek to rob her of that delicious belief—why, my aunt knew of it within the hour.

Her little spies hobbled in with baked goods and tidbits of news. Some of them were so eager that I dare say they left their bonnets at home!

"Why, look," he said, interrupting himself, "the rain stopped."

And it had indeed. This made our process of finding transportation much simpler. As Sebastian endeavored (in hushed tones, which he apparently deemed appropriate) to engage us a cab, I thought I could see shadows down a long street beside us—the flitting agents of Great-Aunt Greta's gossip patrol, no doubt. I hoped it was nothing more sinister.

"It's too bad," said Sebastian regretfully as he bade us farewell. "I'm thrilled of course, as always. And I wouldn't want to leave Elsie for long at such a moment. Still"—he paused, and his tone was wistful—"I don't suppose you have need of a philologist in your adventures?"

We assured him that, if the need arose, we would call him immediately.

Then we were off again. It was hard to imagine the unseasonable heat that had oppressed London the day Radu Vadas visited me. Here the dank weather had reduced the world to an intense grayscale; hills that would have been lush and green in the springtime damp were now desolate, crying out for relief from the cold and the rain in these late weeks of autumn. Fog settled in patches, adding a touch of mystery to our progress through rolling, angst-ridden hills. A few rocky promontories, which had brought variety with increasing frequency as we wound our way north, now came rapidly, one after the other. The effect was claustrophobic.

The convent was deep in a dell, an unhealthy situation, I thought, with such an ugly, twining, naked, tangled mess of trees and bushes around it. In the springtime, perhaps, it would be beautiful. A rich, comforting, nestling green. Now—if ancient myths could be trusted—I could even imagine the barren trees as souls in torment, twisted and bound together. Or, like a fairy tale, this could be the thorny thicket to conceal a sleeping princess.

But here no princess would awaken. Here was a place for the sleepless terrors of creatures neither dead nor alive, but perpetually trapped in the hell of the undead.

We stepped from the cab, and Father Thomas Edmund Gilroy paid the driver. We watched in silence as our transportation departed (was it my imagination, or was the driver eager to leave that strange place?).

"Come, my friend," said Father Thomas Edmund Gilroy. "We are expected."

He walked to a small side door and knocked.

When the door opened, and I saw the gentle, smiling face of the lady, attired in white like her priestly counterparts, with a black veil over her head, it was as if I had walked into another realm—a spiritual place loftier and yet more mundanely real than the world knew.

We walked down long, regular corridors, flanked by many doors.

As we passed a heavy, wooden double door, one side opened slightly, to allow another veiled figure to flow out and down the hall. Before the door closed, I glanced through and saw a modest chapel, surprisingly lacking in decoration, save for a garish golden monstrosity, with rays like the sun around a windowed encasement in which was their Catholic Host—a garish, shining idol, perched aloft an altar or table draped with linen of impeccable whiteness. On the ground before it, prostrate in grief or worship—or perhaps in sleep—was a figure, all in black.

It was only a glimpse, but I felt sure it was neither nun nor priest.

"Was that your chapel?" I asked our guide.

"Yes," she replied in a voice so soft it was difficult to hear. "We take turns in perpetual adoration of the Blessed Sacrament in reparation for blasphemies against His Sacred Body and Blood. Many of those who come to us find solace in this devotion as well."

"You see," said Father Thomas Edmund Gilroy, "that there is a place for those victims who survive and who even hope to escape from the toils of those creatures."

A hospital for vampire victims, watched over by little nuns. It was an idea full of Gothic potential. It struck me once again and with new violence that there was an alarming intersection between the theology of these Papists and the perverted bloodlust of the threat they purported to combat—but the thought was ill-conceived to grant serenity at a moment when I was so clearly outnumbered.

We continued on our way. Of the convalescing patients, I saw few young people, and no one advanced beyond a weary middle age. I noted this aloud.

"It is a consequence of the disease," said our guide quietly. "A man or woman ill enough to benefit from our assistance is usually physically strong to begin with. Advanced age or other illness accelerates the process. An elderly victim, for instance, is likely to die from the assault."

"And the young?"

"They first must desire our help. The young are often not equipped to resist the glittering facade evil puts on for their benefit."

It was a dark thought. I had not considered the attractive side of the question. In fact, I found the notion baffling. And yet, considered, I found myself thinking of particular instances that illustrated just that—Esther Raveland, not least among them.

Our escort ushered us into a small room, with one small window. The room was divided perfectly in half by a thin metal grate. Stools sat before it. Father Thomas Edmund Gilroy took one; I took another. Then the nun disappeared, and we waited.

When the door on the other side of the grate opened, I expected to see another of the robed women. Instead, in walked a man in black, with a disarming smile.

"Why, hello!" he said, as if we were the most delightful guests he could have imagined meeting.

"Good morning," said Father Thomas Edmund Gilroy with stern dignity. "I believe we are awaiting the Mother Superior."

I was surprised at his authoritative and unfriendly tone, but the man in black merely laughed. "Oh, I'm not one of the nuns—*obviously*. I'm one of their tame slaves. They keep us here to torture us with promises, refusing to give us the one thing we really desire."

His face was strangely, unwholesomely alight with passion. I was distinctly uncomfortable having his eyes so focused on me, and even turned to look at the priest several times to try and draw him along with me into the man's attention.

Father Thomas Edmund Gilroy listened, silent and stern.

"You ... you don't know what it's like ... and the euphoria ...," the man whispered ecstatically. His eyes glazed over and for a few moments he was lost to me, lost to the priest, lost to the very world of present reality. When he returned, his face was grayer, and his tone sharp and bitter: "Well. That's what it's like."

"And when you stop?" I asked.

Now he was livid with anger: "What sort of God—" he broke off, then shook his head angrily and walked out the door, almost straight into a tall nun with large gray eyes.

"Come now, Mr. Mason," she said. "You know the regulations. Go and report to Sister Josephine."

I thought for a moment that he would turn on her in rage—indeed, he even seemed to swell with fury for a moment—then he deflated into submission and, murmuring a quiet "Yes, Mother," he scurried away—presumably to face his punishment.

The tall nun waited until he had vanished, and watched for some moments after him. Then she turned to us, and I thought her eyes were full of tears. She came, with quiet dignity, to sit opposite us behind the grate. Then she said, as if answering the question I had not asked: "The agony is acute. There are screams. Nightmares. And the waking nightmare that is worse than sleeping. They do not sleep, in fact. Days. Weeks. Often months pass. It seems they are trapped in the hell of unending wakefulness. The madness comes upon them then. And the desire is flamed into something inexpressible. Sometimes they become violent. Sometimes they plead. Sometimes they could easily harm themselves."

"And what do you do?"

"We operate on a system of firm discipline, as the framework upon which a new and healthy life can be built. Meanwhile, we wait. We watch. We pray. We give what scant comfort we can. We grieve those who are lost."

"What a dark life," I exclaimed. "What a horror. Why not give the man what he so desires? It will kill him, but won't this cruel denial simply drag out that tortuous death?"

248

"What will it profit a man to gain his dark drug and lose his soul? It is a difficult work we do, here, Mr. John Kemp, but it is part of the battle against eternal damnation. Even this suffering of the present moment will be as nothing."

Then she looked to the priest. "What is it you are here to learn, Father?"

"We are seeking a young woman from Budapest. She has an English husband, an unhappy marriage, and is for some reason personally desired by one of the undead—desired so strongly that he has sought her throughout several countries. Her married name is Kilbronson; her maiden name was Vadas."

The nun shook her head. "We have no one of that name here, though it is oddly familiar to me."

"I expected as much, Mother. I wish to speak with Éva Koszorús, if she is well enough. I believe she will have information that can help us."

The Mother Superior frowned. "She is still frail. I know that you have been very helpful to her—indeed, she considers you as having saved her from the deepest horrors. But I do not know if it is in her best interests at this time to speak of things such as this."

"Mother," said the priest, "you have known me for many years. You know that I would not make this request were it not of vital importance."

She thought for a moment. Then she closed her eyes, and, her mouth moving almost indiscernibly in what I assumed was prayer, remained thus for several long minutes. Father Thomas Edmund sat patient and silent.

When she opened her eyes, the Mother nodded and said, "I will grant you the interview, Father. And I shall remain here with her."

"I would not have it any other way," he responded.

She left us then for several minutes.

"Who is Éva Koszorús?" I asked.

"She was a victim of the undead, but was saved before she was utterly destroyed."

"Saved by you?"

"I was one of many who served her."

The door opened again and the Mother Superior returned, followed by another nun (short and round) and a thin gamin of a girl, with unearthly eyes—light blue, they were, flashing into a deep, lush green in moments of intense emotion—set in a narrow, wasted face, and with long, lanky blank hair. She looked as if she were teetering on the brink between childhood and womanhood, or as if she were a fairy violently wrested into human form, and nearly killed in the process.

Directed by the nuns, the girl sat quietly before us.

"Éva," said Father Thomas Edmund Gilroy, "I have come to ask for your help."

She smiled softly at him and nodded.

"Can you begin by telling my friend, Mr. Kemp, who you are and where you come from?"

Then the eyes turned toward me. "My name is Éva Koszorús," she recited simply, in heavily accented English. "For many years I was under the power of that creature—no," she said, anticipating the question in my eyes, "I am not of his kind. Not yet. I could have become so. I still . . . if he finds me . . ."

She began to breathe quickly and her eyes dilated—with terror or with passion, I could not tell. We sat for some minutes as she regained herself. Then, with a deep breath, she continued: "I am not of the undead. But he did drink of my blood and forced me to drink of his." This time she closed her eyes tightly, as if struck with a sudden physical pain, and began to tremble uncontrollably. Mother Superior stepped forward and laid a gentle hand on her shoulder. The girl was calmed instantly, and after a moment she opened her eyes, now full of tears, to gaze up toward the crucifix on the wall, and then to look earnestly at my companion. "From this living hell was I spared, *Asszonyunk Szüz Mária, Istennek szent Anyja* be thanked."

Another sister stepped forward and proffered a glass of clear, bright water. Éva accepted the glass gratefully and drank deeply from it before she continued.

"I was from a poor but respectable family in Vác, a town nearby to Budapest. My father, he was a teacher of music. My mother—she was from Wales—died when I was very young. I was considered beautiful by many and expected to marry well. On this my father had based many hopes.

"When I was fifteen ..." She stopped and smiled. "Indeed, perhaps you would have thought me little older than that, would you not?

"My mother's family descends from a dead man. A witty man. He would not take this English religion—though he tried. A murder of crows chased him—a rebuke from heaven. The Evil One rushing to gather up his weakened soul."

Her mind appeared to be wandering, and the sister gently called her name to draw her back. "Éva ... child ..."

The girl started, stared at us as if recollecting our presence for the first time, impatiently shook her head to dispel some dark but familiar thought, and went on. "Perhaps it was my Welsh mother. He has some interest here. Some tie to England. I don't know what. I don't know why he is here. But I know it is some dark, horrible purpose.

"Shall I tell you my tale of seduction? Power. Passion. Lust. Awakening the senses, overpowering them, confusing the mind. He said I desired it. Perhaps I did. I don't know. It was all frightening and bewildering.

"I do not know why he is here in England. I fear he has come for me. But only as he has come for us all. There must be some dark reason."

"Can you tell us who he is?" I asked. It seemed to me the most direct point of attack.

She shook her head, and her body began to tremble with—fear? "I cannot speak his name. But he is no nobleman. No mighty lord. Many say he was the bastard son of a wicked priest. He would have all believe he is descended from the Evil One himself, when he came to earth in human form and fell in love with a peasant girl. When the people turned upon her as a witch and burned her at the stake, the Evil One carried off her child and raised it in the hidden Scholomance. His own son. He believes he is the son's son's son. I know nothing of this myself, but only what I have heard. How can we know anything of him?"

Father Thomas Edmund spoke softly. "Tell us of Elisabetta Kilbronson."

"Ah," cried the girl, her eyes now blazing green with terror. "She. She is doomed. Every day she moves closer to her doom. When she dies, she will become like him. He will make her like him. He yearns for her blood—yearns specially. For that will give him even greater power. It too will give him revenge. She has run away, turned from him. No one can find her. She has outwitted him. But, like me, she cannot escape."

"Why, Éva? Why does he desire her blood specially?"

She shook her head. "It is a secret," she moaned. "A dark secret."

Father Thomas Edmund Gilroy did not press her. He sat, immovable as a statue, watching her in silence. She wrestled within herself, the struggle rendered visible in her tossing black head, and audible in her moans. After a few moments she fell into a calm. Then she raised her eyes to us and continued her narrative in a whisper: "They say that he knew many dark things. Darker still than those who went before. That he surpassed his own teacher—and feasted on him. That he knew a way to keep the blood— the blood that was his. He imprisoned it in a dark jewel—a ruby so wondrous that any man to see it must desire it. She carries that jewel."

The notion of mysterious gems with special properties— particularly ominous ones—so strongly reminded me of the writings of Wilkie Collins that I found myself even more skeptical than usual. Why would this powerful undead (if he were indeed so) bother about a ruby, even if it did contain his own blood?

"There must be something more," I murmured, half to myself.

"What more must there be?" the girl cried. "Is that not enough? He knew a way. A way to be both himself and undead. Slowing, for a time, that dark magic. His own doom. He brought about his own death and pleasured in it. Now, with special cunning, he can make others like himself. That is his school, his art. The art of a slow death, and growing powers. But if he finds that ruby—that jewel of his own blood—it must give him new and strange powers. He must seek it above all else. And no one will be safe when he finds it."

A deafening, unexpected crash interrupted us. I looked to the window and was startled to see that the vault of the heavens had transformed from insipid gray to an intense, angry crimson, punctuated by black clouds.

As I watched, lightning split the sky with jagged violence, and an immediate explosion of thunder signaled the nearness of the storm. This was not a rain like that we had seen previously. A second bolt followed, as if thrown by the hand of a vengeful god. With that shining blast, the pierced sky gushed forth its guts and the rain, emblazoned red by the ferocity of the horizon, poured down in a bloody torrent and once again drowned the world.

When I looked back from the spectacle of the angry sky, I saw the priest praying quietly over the bowed head of the frail young woman. I did not hear the words he spoke, but I saw her tears, and her growing calm. One last little smile, and the second nun gently led her from the room.

Mother Superior looked to Father Thomas Edmund Gilroy.

"What does it mean?" she asked.

"I do not know," he said. "It is a dark thought, indeed. A ritual—or a cold, calculating process—to initiate souls into the undead. I fear that this creature will unite his own dark art to the method of our present age. This makes him doubly dangerous. He has not merely the desires of the undead; he brings to it a ruthless intellect, perhaps beyond what we have seen before."

"And the woman?"

"Elisabetta Vadas was a child raised by gypsies," he said. "Fatherless. Found cradled in the arms of her mother—a young woman found frozen to death in the snow on St. George's Eve. Radu Vadas considers her his sister—I do not know if that was the case. Perhaps a cousin? Beyond this, there is much there which we do not know. This business of the ruby does not explain his eagerness to find her. What is the ruby? Why has he not yet found her? How can she elude him, if she is one of his initiates? How did she escape—how does she continue to escape—if she is one of his victims? I do know that he must be working from the assumption that consummation of his dark desires must mean greater power. Why else would he pursue her—hunting so intensely and desperately that it even robs him of the clear cunning of evil?"

"Do you think it does?"

"I think it certainly does. It is a great asset to us in our work, in fact. Whenever this woman moves or appears, he moves more rapidly and becomes more vulnerable to us."

"And the woman herself?"

"I do not know. I do not know if she herself harbors dark passions in her heart, or if she has some special power to escape him. We only know that she has fled and continues to flee."

The tall nun shook her head. "Jesus, have mercy."

"Indeed, He does, Mother."

She looked at him in thoughtful silence for a moment, then nodded and said, "I shall call our coachman to return you to the station."

They bade each other farewell, and we went to the antechamber to await our transportation.

"But, Father," I said, when we were alone, robed in our still-damp overcoats, "is that why he is in England? To find this woman?"

"I do not know precisely why he is in England. Every day that he is here thousands of lives hang in the balance. There must be some dark reason. Elisabetta Vadas is clearly part of it. We knew that even before we came. Perhaps in time we will have a clearer vision of what part she plays."

"Do you think he knows what drinking her blood will do?"

"I don't know," he said, his forehead furrowed with concern. "I should think not. Nevertheless, he must be working from the assumption that her blood will give him some added power or deeper pleasure. And" (he smiled at his own weak attempt at humor) "he would give his eye teeth for that."

The drive back to the station was a silent one. The storm was too fierce to afford opportunity for conversation.

"Johnny! JOHNNY!"

I had quite forgotten Sebastian until we reached the station and he appeared before me, shouting my name and waving a newspaper in my face.

"It's bad news from London!" he cried—then paused for the full horror of the headline to sink in: VIOLENT ATTACK ON LAWYER'S HOME. Phrases leapt out at me: "John Kemp, respected man of law ..." "Early hours of the morning ..." "Police seek information regarding the whereabouts of Mr. Kemp ..." "Bloody carnage ..."

"O God!" I cried. "Jenson!"

Another voice broke in: "Thomas Edmund!" Here were three white-robed men, cloaked with black, their faces stern. "We must hurry," said the first of them. "There's been another one, and it is very likely to accelerate quickly. We've come to secure the convent. You're needed back in London."

Then came a third voice, an official voice, and with it came a hand—a hand that fell and gripped like a vise on my shoulder. "Mr. John Kemp? Inspector Harris would like to have a few words with you. Would you come with us, sir, please?"

Chapter 19

19 October 1900: Hyde Park Police Station

(From Dr. Seward's diary) 19 August. Strange and sudden change in Renfield last night. About eight o'clock he began to get excited and sniff about as a dog does when setting. The attendant was struck by his manner, and knowing my interest in him, encouraged him to talk. He is usually respectful to the attendant and at times servile; but to-night, the man tells me, he was quite haughty. Would not condescend to talk with him at all. All he would say was:—"I don't want to talk to you: you don't count now; the Master is at hand."

"It was a mercy she heard the noise and went upstairs to investigate. The intruder hadn't realized your man was in the house. Judging from the treatment your furniture received, if he had known there was a potential witness in the flat, your man wouldn't be in the hospital now—he'd be in the morgue."

Inspector Harris, nondescript as ever, was almost expansive in his enthusiasm to tell me the lurid details of the violent dismemberment of my home, and the near assassination of my valet. Further, he seemed to accept without question the presence of Father Thomas Edmund Gilroy (who had accompanied me on my dizzying overnight return to London by train in the company of two representatives of Her Majesty's police force). I even wondered if they had known each other previously, from their manner of greeting upon our arrival.

"She came in waving that rolling pin around like a madwoman. He was thoroughly shook up, I can tell you. Her own account is quite remarkable ..." (and the inspector actually chuckled). "He's in custody now, and glad to be so, I warrant."

All in all, considering the sternness of that call back to the city, I was surprised to find him so delighted. It seemed that Mrs. Pritchard was the darling of the force, for her daring rescue of her ailing lover.

"Inspector," said Father Thomas Edmund, "if any suspicion has fallen upon Mr. Kemp, I am here to testify that he spent the entirety of the night in question trapped in a train halfway between London and Durham, and I was trapped in the same compartment."

"Suspicion? Indeed not," Harris replied blithely. "We just were eager to speak with Mr. Kemp. Not a surprising thing, I should say, considering the circumstances. Now, Mr. Kemp. Would you follow me please?"

"Where are we going?" I asked.

"I'd like you to speak with my prisoner for just a moment. Perhaps the sight of you will provoke something more honest out of the man."

I followed him reluctantly enough.

Victor Montrose behind bars was as paunchy and damp and unappealing as he had been the last time I had seen him. Wrapped in sullen silence, he did not even look up as we approached the bars of his cell.

"Montrose," barked Harris, "we have someone here to see you."

"So I see him," he said resentfully. "So what?"

"Do you recognize this man?" Harris asked me.

"Yes," I said. "Of course. He was one of the legatees in the will of Charles Sidney. He approached me personally months ago."

"Approached!" The prisoner was piqued by this for some reason and spoke mostly to himself in his indignation. "Suffered *your* desperate pleas for assistance, you mean, ignorant little man. Weak creature. Insect. Ingrate."

Then he noticed Father Thomas Edmund Gilroy. He leapt into his feet, his face transformed into sneering glee. "You fool," he cried. "You and yours. You—too good and too high for men of greater minds and greater abilities. You'll see. You'll find out soon." He began to laugh—a raucous, cackling laugh. The laugh of a madman.

Father Thomas Edmund made no reply. He listened, quietly, his face unmoved.

The silence clearly disappointed Montrose. "I won't speak to you anymore," he said petulantly. And he turned away toward the wall, an almost comic demonstration of this determination. We returned in silence to Inspector Harris' office.

"He's a madman," I said quietly to Father Thomas Edmund.

"He's a bothersome creature, indeed," he replied. "But he really is a tragic man."

"Why does he hate you?" I asked.

He shrugged sadly. "It is not me. He hates the thought of a person such as me. He has built his life on lies and pretenses to a status of spiritual superiority. As a very ignorant, selfish man, he cannot conceptualize anyone who is unlike himself. He has even represented himself as a priest or another ordained minister."

259

"For all your charity, Father," I said grimly, "it sounds as if he is simply in need of a good swift kick. In fact, a kick might be the best thing that could happen to him. He should have received several more kicks at school."

Someone pounded at the door, and almost immediately Toby Barnes burst in. "Now, Harris," he lamented, "you can't do this to me! You can't tie my hands! What a story! It's got everything! Drama! And a love-crazed cook bludgeoning a burglar! Hello, Mr. Kemp. Would you like to give a statement to the press regarding your emotions upon hearing of the attack on your flat? Were you pleased to learn of the burgeoning romance 'downstairs', as it were?"

"Barnes," the official caution came with all of the firmness I could have wished, "I've told you. At the moment, we do not wish you to publish any details about this incident in your newspaper—*or any other*," he added as the reporter began to protest. "As soon as I have my prisoner's confession clearly and officially recorded, I'll give you an exclusive. That's as much as you can publish. Here. I'll write your copy for you. *Toby Barnes, intrepid reporter of the* Pall Mall Gazette, *is working alongside the police to investigate the mysterious assault on the personal home of a respected London attorney . . .*"

"That's as much as we've already printed!" cried Barnes in disgust. "Do you want to run me out of business? Do you want me to starve in the streets, man?"

"Well," the inspector replied with a wry smile, "perhaps not in the streets. The constabulary are kept busy enough with the drunks and tarts. We don't need them cleaning up the bodies of nagging newsmen too."

Barnes collapsed into a chair with a resigned sigh. "Ah, well," he said, "I suppose that's that."

"Yes," said Harris soothingly, "that's that. And now you can go, Barnes. We'll call you when we need you."

"Ah, no, Harris. You said I was helping alongside the police in this investigation. I'm damned—excuse me, to the parson there—if I'm going to leave until I have the exclusive you promised. Wait, you're a Papist, an't you?"

Father Thomas Edmund nodded patiently.

"What's the Vatican to do with all this?"

The priest, who looked as if he found the whole exchange singularly humorous, yet replied with an air of deep seriousness: "I do not believe that the Holy Father has a comment to issue for your column, Mr. Barnes."

"Too bad," said Barnes. "My readers like a good Jesuitical angle."

"Barnes," said Inspector Harris, "if I allow you to stay, you will remain silent during this interview. And that is a large *if* indeed."

"Not a peep," swore Barnes obediently, and settled back with an open notebook, pen at the ready.

Harris glared at him, then turned back to me.

"Can I see Jenson?" I asked. "Is he really all right?"

"I gather that, having been awakened by the noise of the burglar ransacking your flat, he was ... prudently concealing himself under his bed when the lady came to his rescue. In the struggle (though there wasn't much of it, as far as I can tell) the lady was thrust back upon the top of the bed so violently that it collapsed."

Barnes sniggered and tried to stifle it with his hand.

Harris ignored him. "The valet should survive. The cook is ministering to him right now. I am not sure how long he will remain in your employ. I suppose it depends on your attitude regarding married domestics. Now, sir, can you suggest any reason why someone would be rifling through your belongings? And destroying them, for that matter?"

"Since I haven't been allowed to see my flat," I replied, "I cannot say what the object of the search—or the destruction—might have been."

"Your perturbation is understandable, sir. But I hope, sir, you recognize that, in our initial inquiry, your complete and untraceable absence from London at this time did raise many questions."

"It could not have been fully untraceable," I said wryly, "since your men found me."

Inspector Harris smiled. "I should have said *almost* untraceable."

"Can you tell me what was damaged?" I asked.

"Everything, sir. It looked like someone went through the place with a knife, tearing open everything in sight. It's such a mess that you can't tell what anyone could have been looking for. It looks like a fit of malevolent destruction."

"Inspector Harris," said Father Thomas Edmund Gilroy, suddenly, "was there not another violent incident in the city that night?"

There was a long pause, as Inspector Harris sized up his questioner. Then he frowned. "What makes you think that, sir?"

The priest merely looked at the policeman and waited patiently for his reply.

I expected Harris to throw my companion out, but, after the silence had continued long beyond the point where I would have been (and was) deeply uncomfortable, he actually gave a rapid-fire response: "Young man. Seedy background. Found knifed in an alley by the docks. He was a familiar of some of the darker dens down there."

"Opium?"

"Indeed."

"And the knife was found?"

Yet again, the inspector paused and seemed to weigh his response carefully. "No, sir," he said at last, "the knife was not found. The murderer struck his victim several ... *dozen* ... blows. The alleyway looked like it had been painted in blood."

"Anything else remarkable about the victim?"

"Well ..."

Someone knocked at the door and, invited in by Harris, stepped through to join us. It was that dour mortician I had met on my previous visit. He looked bored and, on seeing me, perhaps a bit irritable.

"Dr. Lewis here can tell you all about it. Lewis, your report on that knifing victim?"

"Eighteen blows by a strong hand. Hitting him from all sides. I should say it was in a fury. Also the scratch marks of fingernails across his face. From the breadth of the hand, I should say it was a woman."

"Could the stabbing have been done by a woman?" My stomach was turning, but Harris still matched the doctor in the clinical brevity of his tone.

Lewis shook his head slowly. "I doubt it," he said. "Unless she was a woman with unnatural strength."

"And," said Harris with half a smile, "since Mrs. Pritchard was otherwise occupied at that time, we assume she was not the perpetrator. Now, sir"—turning to Father Thomas Edmund Gilroy—"I'd be interested to know how—"

A loud, strange commotion interrupted him—it sounded like violence, with screaming and shouting, and though it was clear it was from some rooms away, it was enough to startle everyone and bring us to our feet.

"Briggs!" ordered Inspector Harris. "Get down there and see what's going on."

The young policeman vanished obediently. He was back within a few minutes, bursting through the door, his face white and his eyes huge and alarmed: "Sir! It's Montrose! He's escaped!"

"Is that Victor Montrose?" Barnes leapt upon the name eagerly, but Harris barked out: "Barnes!" and the reporter retreated into silence (scribbling furiously into his little notebook).

"I don't know how it happened, sir. The window into the cell—the bars have been bent so far they've almost broken in half. The man who was in there with him—he's blithering mad from fright and doesn't make sense."

"What's he saying?" Father Thomas Edmund asked quickly.

After one curious glance at the questioner's white robes, the constable answered eagerly enough: "He says that a creature in black tore open the window. He keeps talking about wings and teeth and snarling."

"Does he say that Victor Montrose left willingly?"

"That's the odd part." (A quaint choice of phrase, I thought, given the fact that he was reporting the words of a madman.) "He says the man was torn out the window, screaming and struggling."

This declaration was met with a silence so heavy with meaning that I turned to look at Inspector Harris—to see that he was frowning and looking quietly at Father Thomas Edmund Gilroy. The priest once again returned his gaze calmly.

"Briggs," said Harris, eventually, "when any of our men bring in more information, send him in immediately."

The dismissal was clear.

"Let's put our cards on the table, priest," said the inspector. "We've had run-ins before. I know what you're about, and you know what I'm about. Shall we work together, or would you like to suffer the inconvenience of an official inquiry?"

"Inspector Harris," replied the priest with patient good humor, "you know full well that everything associated with me and with my brethren will stand up to any such investigation. Scandal, when it does exist in our ranks, is sniffed out by the satirical spinsters—excuse the phrase; alliteration required it—long before you and your men would be at all suspicious."

"You know to what activities I refer," said Harris. "I'm a man who believes what he can see, but I also know there are things that baffle me in my work, and those are things that generally involve *your* work."

"Are you granting me carte blanche, then?"

"Nothing of the kind. I'm encouraging you to be open with me—with regard to things that will be valuable to me in my investigation. Your theology and ghost hunting you can keep to yourself. And, Barnes, if you even so much as breathe a hint of a word of this to anyone, I'll crucify you—begging your pardon, Father Gilroy."

"As usual," said the priest, "I accept your terms—with all of the usual reservations."

Harris frowned then sighed: "I know better than to press you for more."

"You would not credit more if I told it to you," Father Thomas Edmund calmly replied.

"That is likely true," Harris admitted.

With that, the baffling exchange was at its end. The two contestants turned back and reacknowledged our presence.

The mortician had been standing in a sour, despondent study. Ignored and undervalued, I have no doubt he was contemplating resigning from the police force and retiring to some damp, depressed little hamlet, to live out the remainder of his life in despairing observation of fetid pond life. He was consequently startled when he heard Father Thomas Edmund Gilroy speak to him: "So what scenario would you suggest, Doctor?"

The invitation so clearly served Dr. Martin's deepest desires that he looked suspiciously at the priest. Assured, after a moment, that the question was honest and a response expected, he brightened and began his eager hypothesis: "Well, from my experiments, judging from the angles of the blows, and the way in which the blood on the face differs from that which issued from the knifing wounds, I would say that the scratch predates the knifing by some period of time. Perhaps as much as an hour. It would not have been longer. Consequently, I suggest that the victim found himself in a situation with a woman wherein she was held against her will. A prostitute turned against a client, perhaps. It is not an area of town in which respectable women usually wander."

"Perhaps the encounter with the woman took place elsewhere," suggested Father Gilroy.

"Perhaps so," the doctor agreed.

"Apologies," said the priest. "I interrupted you."

To my astonishment, the mortician was delighted by this courtesy. He smiled and made a genteel bow. "Not at all, sir. As I was about to say, soon after this encounter, perhaps even on the heels of it, another person appeared. Whether this person was connected with the woman or not, I cannot say. The victim only appears to have put up a weak fight. There are some bruises that seem to indicate

266

some resistance on his part. I do not"—he forestalled the question—"believe that the woman would be capable of inflicting bruises of this nature on a man of this stature."

"What stature was that?"

Each question only thrilled the doctor more. He opened a large, official-looking notebook and began to read: "Specimen was a man in his early thirties. Dark hair, dark eyes. Beard. Stood six feet, ten inches. Sixteen stone. Broad upper body strength likely. Many old scars across the body, consonant with the tenor of his life. Marks and stains on his body support his reputation as laborer. Probably dockside for his life—not a sailor. Tattoo on his chest in a foreign language. Recorded here."

He handed his notebook to Father Thomas Edmund Gilroy, who read aloud: "*Cu moartea toate dierentele dispar.*" He paused. "It's a Romanian proverb. It means, roughly: 'All will be the same in one hundred years.'"

"Heavy stuff for a violent waterside character," remarked Harris.

"What was his name?" asked the priest.

Harris supplied the answer: "He was known as Boris. He had no known surname. Well, Gilroy. That's where we stand. Now. Your turn."

Father Thomas Edmund narrowed his eyes in thought. "Inspector," he said, "I can tell you this. I believe that if you cannot find Montrose quickly, you will soon find him dead, and by the same creature who attacked Charles Sidney."

"Creature. So you credit our addled pickpocket's story."

"I do. I believe there is something evil at work here. I cannot venture names, for at this point it would be libelous. I would say: observe carefully the activity at 92 Grove Lane, Camberwell."

The inspector whistled. "Here now. That's the new little do-goodery for the posh set. That's a hefty order. I've heard the prince has been seen there. Didn't you have a hand in setting that up, Mr. Kemp?"

I acknowledged this to be the fact.

"And Charles Sidney was by way of a friend of yours?"

I nodded shortly.

"And in your absence, your home was attacked and your valet could have been killed ... Have you ever considered, Mr. Kemp, how unhealthy you have proved as an associate? I wouldn't advertise it. That sort of thing can be bad for business."

He returned to the white-robed Papist, who continued to sit quietly, with his hands folded in his lap, and his string of beads in one hand.

"Well? Anything else?"

"Additionally, if you have any news of foreigners arriving in the city, particularly women of Hungarian extraction—"

"Who might have been seen in an altercation with a burly opium addict of a seaside character, perhaps?" Father Thomas Edmund only smiled. "Well, now. That's very interesting, now, isn't it." He sat and thought it over for some time. Then, seeming satisfied with the point, he nodded. "Fair enough, Gilroy. For now, anyway. I have work to do. I have a crackpot-churchman-turned-burglar to find."

He turned back to me. "Please alert us immediately when you have your new address, Mr. Kemp—that's right. In addition to being under investigation, there's really no point in you trying to stay in those rooms at this time."

"Can I not go home and fetch some things?" I protested. "Clothes?"

He considered the question then barked: "Constable Peters!"

In came my old nemesis. His dislike of me had not decreased since our meeting some months earlier. He concealed it poorly now.

Harris continued to snap out his orders: "Accompany Mr. Kemp to his old premises. Supervise him as he rifles through for some things. And, Peters, any suspicious characters lurking about, you're to bring to me. Immediately."

I rose and prepared to depart. Father Thomas Edmund followed me, nodding courteously at the inspector. Toby Barnes stood up as well and attempted unobtrusively to make a third in our exit.

Harris' voice fell like a lead hand on the fleeing reporter: "Barnes, you stay here," he said with grim humor. "I'm ready now to dictate your column."

Chapter 20

19 October 1900: South Kensington, Especially Hyde Park, Then Camden

(Letter, Lucy Westenra to Mina Murray Harker) *Oh, Mina, couldn't you guess? I love him. I am blushing as I write, for although I think he loves me, he has not told me so in words. But oh, Mina, I love him; I love him; I love him! ... I do not know how I am writing this even to you. I am afraid to stop, or I should tear up the letter, and I don't want to stop, for I do so want to tell you all. Let me hear from you at once, and tell me all that you think about it. Mina, I must stop. Good-night. Bless me in your prayers; and, Mina, pray for my happiness.*

Inspector Harris had been quite correct; there was little purpose in returning home. My flat was an unmitigated disaster. I had never lived in opulent splendor, but the home and the things in it were all mine, and I had valued them.

I wandered, stunned, from room to room. The bed was turned upside down, the sideboards of its frame snapped and flung across the room. My clothes looked as if they had been flung willy-nilly in every direction—and many of the articles of clothing had been so manhandled that they were now unwearable. An old and rarely used legal wig looked as if every single hair had been yanked out in a frenzy.

My drawing room (which had so long served as an at-home satellite for my office) had experienced the worst of it. Books thrown to the floor, their pages ripped from the binding, papers and letters scattered wildly about, ink dumped out on the carpet—which was likewise torn into useless strips; it was a chaos of vicious destruction. Every piece of china was smashed to dust. Every picture too, including little darreograph portraits of my parents, was torn and wrenched into unsightly confusion. There were few things to salvage.

The most defaced object was at first difficult to identify. It was a heap of tiny fragments of fabric, gold, royal blue, and emerald green threads. Bent, twisted hinges. A smashed lock. *The ornamental peacock box left to me by Charles Sidney.* I had forgotten the thing existed. It had contained my notes from months earlier, when I made my amateur scholarly efforts in the British Museum. Those, I was sure, had gone the way of the rest and were now part of the dismembered papier-mâché disaster.

"Good . . . God," I said in disgust, and under my breath.

I suddenly remembered Constable Peters. I looked up in embarrassment and saw he was watching me carefully.

"Apologies, Constable," I said. "I'll see what I can gather." My search was depressing and short-lived. I was weeding through for a few things to support life and work, as he stood there, his eyes boring into my back, when the policeman finally spoke.

"It's a shame, sir." He said it with such a studied lack of emotion that at first I wondered if it was sarcasm.

I hesitated then thanked him.

We stood there for a few minutes awkwardly. Then, assuming he was finished speaking, I leaned down and continued my search. My pitiful little collection of personal belongings finished, I shoved the few items into my briefcase (it all fit with alarming ease).

I looked up at Peters. "Well, Constable …," I began, preparatory to suggesting a departure.

His eyes were narrowed. "Anything particular catch your attention, sir?"

I looked questioning, but said nothing.

"I mean, sir, anything that might help our investigation?"

I considered then gestured toward the wreckage of the box. "That belonged to Charles Sidney," I said. "It was a box."

"Was it indeed," he said musingly. He nudged the remains with his toe.

I was quite sure that his sudden garrulousness was a result of his awkward sense of pity for my plight (inasmuch as the man was capable of empathy). I found this oddly heartening, in the midst of the debris.

"What was in it?"

"Oh," I said, "just some papers. Some notes. From some research. It was months old."

"What was the subject of your research?"

My hope for the humanity of Peters had been premature. He had posed an embarrassing question to me, and I squirmed inwardly as I attempted to find a suitable equivocation. "It … was … in connection with …" Then I remembered that my visit to the British Museum was principally characterized as my dramatic first meeting with Victor Montrose. This was certainly something to think about.

I looked up and saw, predictably, Peters watching me like a hawk.

"I'm sorry, Peters," I said. "I just remembered. My notes were from a visit I made to the British Museum. That is where I first met Victor Montrose."

He became eerily still; he even seemed to stop breathing. "Is that so, sir?"

"Yes, Peters. It is so." I was feeling rather impatient now. I would happily supply the police—even Constable Peters—with the information required, but his manner was so disagreeable as to make me reluctant to say anything.

"Funny you didn't happen to mention that to Inspector Harris ...," he said next slowly.

"I didn't happen to remember it when I was with Inspector Harris. But I can tell you one thing for certain— I am telling *you* now."

He considered this for a moment. Then nodded (with self-satisfied pomposity). "And the subject of your research that day, sir?"

He was as tenacious as a terrier, damn him.

"Folklore representations of the undead," I snapped, inwardly defying him even to look a judgment at me.

To my astonishment, this revelation seemed to provoke him into further transformation into a living, breathing person. As I watched, fascinated, Constable Peters became almost friendly. "Look at these, sir," he said, eagerly. He pointed to the wall.

The deep cuts were slightly offset, but tracked in a five-line pattern.

"Fingernails?" I asked, my skin beginning to crawl.

"It seems so. And that bed. Montrose is a blubbery bit of a cad. He hasn't the strength to do that in there. That's why we're keeping it as it is—except for those things you have gathered there, sir. We've a lot of unanswered questions here. A lot of things that don't make sense."

"What ... what do you think is the answer, Peters?"

For a second, it seemed as if he had recalled himself to himself. Could Peters survive the shock of discovering that he—he!—had lapsed to the degree of speaking familiarly to someone so unworthy as me? Then the eagerness to declare his own theory overpowered his instinctive mistrust (and, alas, his dislike) of me. "Well," he said, "I believe there was another person in the flat. Someone who eluded Mrs. Pritchard. Her story is a confused mess, but she mentions noises that cannot be explained if there were simply one intruder in the flat. It might be the imagination of an hysterical woman, but then again it might not. And with so many other unanswered questions ..."

He nodded wisely. "It's quite a mystery, sir. And one we'll sort out, don't you fear, sir." His chest swelled visibly. "Leave it to the Force, sir."

I was happy enough to do this—for the moment, anyway.

"Can you tell me which hospital my valet is in?" I asked, eager to change the subject, and to escape before Peters decided once again that he loathed me.

The constable directed me and, bidding him a civil adieu, I set off, on foot, carrying the remnants of my belongings in my little briefcase.

It was early afternoon by the time I arrived at the hospital. My association with Jenson was sufficient to gain me entry and an escort to his bedside.

"The doctor says he must lie very still, Mr. Kemp," said the little nurse who showed me the way. "Several of his ribs were broken, and it is painful for him to move."

Jenson was lying back in his bed, pale and hideous as usual. His entire abdomen was elaborately bandaged. Nevertheless, when he saw me, he struggled to get up from the bed as a sign of feudal respect.

I urged him to rest.

He compromised, sitting up bolt upright in the bed, looking singularly uncomfortable and virtuously unhappy.

"Excuse me, sir, for my appearance. It really is ... well, sir, you see. Hospital regulations."

While he was speaking, Mrs. Pritchard appeared, her arms laden with packages.

"Why, Mr. Kemp!" she cried enthusiastically. "How *good* it was for you to come and visit *poor dear Eustace*." (The possessiveness of the use of his first name made *me* squirm, but Jenson seemed unperturbed; in fact, he was gazing at his protectress with something akin to adoration.)

As she spoke, she bustled about, adding dainty touches to his bed. A floral coverlet, a substantially fluffier goose down pillow (as she pounded it into shape, a cloud of feathers filled the air), a pile of books at his feet (I could not get near enough to identify their titles, though the covers seemed indicative of popular rather than edifying contents). The little nurse hurried over. She looked quite terrified of Mrs. Pritchard.

"Mrs. Pritchard," she said tremulously, "the doctor did say ..."

"*Now, now,* ducky," the cook replied, patting the younger woman's hand with crushing firmness, "don't you mind about us here. I know you've so much to do, and I'll look over the patient here for now. Go run along and get your work done, now there's a good girl."

Then she turned back to me. As Mrs. Pritchard launched on her eager narrative, the nurse hesitated, looked unhappy, then scurried away. "There was a *monster* in that flat, Mr. Kemp. That constable is a fool. He wouldn't listen. But, let me tell you! It was quite a miracle. And when I heard that racket. Oh! Mr. Kemp! My heart it fair near to stopped, it did. I could have wept with fright. But the thought of Eustace—Mr. Jenson—up there, undefended, helpless in his bed of pain. Well, then, I couldn't just *leave* him there, could I?"

She looked at me with the wide, innocent, pleading eyes of an experienced ingénue.

"Oh," I said with the gallantry that she seemed to expect (though hating myself for it), "certainly not, Mrs. Pritchard."

She shot me a coy smile then beamed with (I hope) sincere affection at her wounded lover.

"Oh, Eustace. He really is *quite* the gentleman, now isn't he?"

Jenson only responded with a tender smile at her (which was a prudent thing; if he had joined in her celebration of my character, I might have been forced to murder him).

"Well, now," said Mrs. Pritchard, hitching up her skirts inelegantly to climb onto the foot of Jenson's bed. "That takes a load off. Well, sir, as I was saying, I hurried up the stairs with my trusty rolling pin. Those villains had closed up the door behind them, but they were careless and didn't bother to lock it.

"I was cautious and opened the door nice and slow ..." She was leaning and swaying with her story, to emphasize the stealth with which she proceeded at this critical moment. "I crept in quietly. They were making such a racket that it's no wonder they didn't hear a body coming in behind them. I made it to the doorway of your sitting room and found them there. I was even able to stand there a good moment and let my eyes adjust to the mess they were making. They were working by lantern—two or three of them. It made for a strange-looking place, I can tell you.

"There they were. Two of them. One of them was an ugly, low fellow. A no-account sneak thief, I'd call him. Looked as if he could use a good washing and a good woman to give him her mind—though he's the kind no woman of self-respect would take, if you know what I mean, sir. The other one was strange and black and snarling—that was the monster—crawling about the wall and sniffing things just like some sort of strange animal. I stood there a good moment, as I said, and looked at the two of them. Then I called out in a loud voice: 'You there! I've called the police, and now you're for it!' "

"Had you called the police?" I asked, honestly curious.

"Why, of course, sir. I made the boy as comes and polishes the colonel's shoes go right away when I was going up. I told him: 'Now, Harold, you go and find a constable sharp, and no nonsense about you, or I'll tell your mother you've been visiting that girl as works at Drury Lane Theatre.' You couldn't hardly see him for the way he was running *then*!

"*Well*. As I was saying"—there was a mild reproach in her tone, for she clearly considered this another climax of dramatic action and did not desire interruption—"there I was and cried out: 'You villains! The police are on their way! You're for it, you brazen devils!' " (I imagined that this bold declaration was becoming more and more articulate with each retelling.) "They jumped up at that. The monster snarled some more and leapt like ... like a wild thing. It knocked over the lamps and we were in darkness. I swung out with my roller and screamed as loud and as clear I could. I know I hit something, and I just kept on swinging. I hit many things then, and I heard someone howling in the darkness. I just kept swinging and swinging and swinging!"

She was bouncing on the bed now as her arms flailed, and Jenson, who was becoming paler with each convulsive movement, suddenly groaned.

Mrs. Pritchard nearly fell on him in her concern. "Eustace, what is it? Let me fetch that nurse. Never here when we want her!"

She bounded off the bed and started for the door, but he gasped out: "Em'ly, I'm well. Pray don't ... pray ... continue your story, my dear ..."

Mrs. Pritchard was uncertain for a moment. The story was perhaps the most important thing in her life, but his welfare came in a close second. She pondered it, watched him for a moment, then determined that he honestly could survive a few more minutes without medical attention. She resumed her tale (and did not sit back on the bed, a fact that probably saved my valet's life).

"Well, sir, I was there, thrashing it out and doing a lovely job of it on someone. I feel sure the monster was taking care of himself. I don't imagine such a creature would give that ugly fellow a second thought if it was a question of his own skin, do you? Well, the rascal started fighting back. He pushed and struck at me and said words no lady could bear hearing, but my father was a sailor and liked his rum now and then and I've heard worse—and better said too—many a time. You can't cow me with that sort of noise. I just kept on fighting with all that is in me.

"When he finally pushed me into the ... your ... your own room, sir, which was already quite a shambles, and into Eustace ... Mr. Jenson, that is ... into *his* room, and shoved me on the bed, I quite thought he might think it was a different sort of crime, if you know what I mean, and I fair near set out to bludgeon his dirty mind. That's when he fell and went stone cold for a moment. Not dead, but knocked out. Like a prize fighter. The constable came, slow as can be, and with little Harold there too, and he was looking around and lighting lamps and seeing the wreckage of the place.

" 'Why, Mrs. Pritchard,' says the cheeky little bug ... beg your pardon sir, cheeky little pimple. 'What've you done to Mr. Kemp's flat?' I boxed his ears (once I could get back up off the bed).

" 'What've I done?' I said. 'They've gone and murdered Mr. Jenson and destroyed Mr. Kemp's everything, and you go and ask fool questions, while I've caught one of them anyhow, and he's that whimpering mess over there behind the door, and thank you for taking your time while a lady was left to do the job of four men, and none of them as weak and thankless as you, young man, and I've a good mind to have a talk with your mum all the same!'

"He scurried off then, squealing puny threats. The constable looks at me all sharpish and suspicious and asks for an explanation. I was giving it to him, and he was looking at me still, when we heard a noise and there we found poor Eustace under the bed.

" 'Help,' he says, 'I've been crushed.' Then he passes out again. And then I went down to the police station and talked to the inspector, who was a right gentleman and took everything down proper, and then Eustace was sent here to rest and see the doctor, and here we are."

She seemed dissatisfied with the anticlimactic nature of her conclusion and frowned, looking meditative for a moment, as if considering if there were any dramatic detail left unmentioned. Nothing came to her, however, so she sighed, then remembered her strong emotional attachment to Jenson, and turned to beam on him instead.

Jenson was probably attempting to gaze at her with the same intensity of affection, but the hideousness of his visage and the unprepossessing effect of grave injury on his features made any effort of that nature thoroughly grotesque.

There was little else to be gained by staying. I remained a few more minutes—only long enough to give Mrs. Pritchard assurances of my appreciation of her courage, to offer what consolation I could to the valet, and to speak briefly with the doctor regarding Jenson's likely bills.

I left thoroughly depressed.

What comfort could I give Jenson? What support? I was a homeless wanderer, with a small bag of belongings. A respectable man of comfortable means, suddenly plunged into the drama and intrigue of an absurd novel, and robbed of all his worldly goods, his flat, and his ugly valet. The injustice of my situation suddenly seemed so overwhelming that I could hardly see straight.

I stormed through Hyde Park, dragging my pathetic little briefcase, rebellious at something intangible, fleeing from something improbable, and seeking something inexpressible.

The path turned sharply and I turned with it, running straight into Esther Raveland.

When I say "straight into", I use the phrase in its literal sense. If I had deliberately set out on a course to crash bodily against her, I could not have chosen a more direct nor a more forceful path.

We both stumbled, and she would have fallen had I not involuntarily flung my little briefcase from me—it flew into a bush—and caught her about the waist.

It is a discomfiting thing to find oneself embracing bodily any woman, but the circumstance becomes especially awkward when the woman in question has been a troubling focus for months—sometimes inspiring romantic dreams that would grace the pages of the sort of novel women read; sometimes figuring in dreams in the role of a sensual, blood-splattered vampire. A part of my mind, seeing the scene from the side as an impersonal observer, wondered momentarily whether any book of etiquette had addressed the subject. And in the middle of a bushy nowhere too.

The situation was not helped when Miss Raveland drew herself to her full height (still held close in my arms), glared majestically into my face, then melted into tears and began to sob copious amounts of the said lachrymose fluid over my coat front.

For many minutes, she remained hysterical. A few words were indistinctly audible amid the tears: "So frightened ... so frightened!"

I looked around somewhat nervously, half expecting that a third party would stumble upon us and immediately misinterpret the entire situation. Was it *my* fault that she went about the lonelier park paths in a state of emotional instability?

Then I looked at her tear-streaked face once again and my heart responded with fervor: *Yes. Of course* it was my fault. Did I call myself a gentleman? I was a brute. I was a fool. I was a clod. I deserved to be horsewhipped.

Her sobs were subsiding, passing into delicate sniffs. She glanced up at me, her face full of a host of emotions, and then, to my complete astonishment, she burst out laughing.

"If you looked any more reluctantly hangdog," said Miss Raveland to me, still laughing, "you would turn into a spaniel. And it would not be an untimely transformation—I already look like a drowned rat. Novelists say that women look more pathetically attractive after a stormy bout of weeping—but, as we all know, novelists are a silly pack of creatures. It was a sort of pent-up reaction. These have been rather eventful days, of late."

I released her (somewhat reluctantly) and proffered a handkerchief.

"What happened?" she asked, as she dried her eyes and face. "I heard ... we read ... the newspaper accounts were so confused. I didn't know if you'd been injured in the attack."

"I was far from home," I assured her. "My valet was injured. The cook sat on him. He's in hospital, but he'll be well soon enough."

The explanation was highly absurd, but it seemed to satisfy her.

"But your home! Was everything destroyed?"

I nodded, but looked brave. I suddenly felt that mere possessions were not so very important after all. "I will rebuild in time," I said. "No one has died, and that's the main thing."

It was a noble sentiment, indeed, and she was duly impressed.

Then she seemed to recollect herself. "I ... I must look a sight. I'm so sorry, Mr. Kemp. Please, I'll be well after a moment. Pray, don't be bothered about me."

The scene that followed, cherished though it is on some level in my remembrance, is at the same time one overshadowed by acute embarrassment. It was hardly the province of a gentleman (and I hold fast to that old-fashioned term) to devolve into lovemaking. What else was there for me to do? The whole thing had become inevitable. But I can avoid that deeper and more shameful lapse—the fictional exposure of this intimate moment—and, indeed, for my own squirming comfort, must take refuge in summary: In the next moment, I told her in no uncertain terms that I *was* bothered about her. In the moment after *that*, I was pouring forth warm, manly assurances of the deepest affection. Almost immediately, I received shy acknowledgment that such feelings were reciprocated. A delicate (and quite satisfying) kiss seemed the inescapable conclusion—and I gave in to the impulse. In the moment after, as I realized my own presumption, I was relieved that she was an American. She blushed and smiled, and laid her head against my shoulder, but she didn't slap my face.

We sat there together for some time, speaking of many things. Almost against my will, the name of Gregory Anghelescu arose between us.

I asked her not to see the man again.

She looked surprised. "Really, he's just an acquaintance. I hardly know the man."

I accepted this, but urged her to avoid him all the same.

"I don't understand it," she said, confused. "Can't you tell me why he troubles you so?"

I was torn. I had no desire to explain further. But ... was my reluctance creating greater danger? Would it not be better for her to laugh in my face but at least be cognizant on some level of the truth? Even if she did not believe me, would she not still look askance at both the secretary and the Count the next time they crossed her path?

The moment passed. I did not tell her. The conversation moved on.

"Well, if it troubles you ... John ..."—she gave me a sweet sideways smile as she tested out this usage of my Christian name—"if it troubles you, John, of course I shall avoid him."

In that moment, I believe she sincerely meant it.

I escorted her home, in essence an affianced man.

After the door closed behind Esther—*my* Esther—I stood in the street for a few moments, considering the unexpectedly romantic turn my day had taken. Then I recalled, as if clarity came breaking through the fog, how my morning had begun. The satisfaction of that interlude in the park could not outweigh the practical problem of my present situation—such a tragic counterpoint to my emotional state. My heart was alight with songs of requited love; my home was uninhabitable.

I was about to go and seek out an inn or a hotel to stay for the night, when a cheerful voice spoke nearly at my elbow.

"Good evening, Mr. Kemp!"

A young man in those familiar white robes, with a wry smile perpetually on his face, and a lively eye for now fixed on me. "Father Thomas Edmund sent me to find you. My brothers and I were about to send out blood-hounds." (His eyes were open and innocent now, but I suspected deliberation behind that unfortunate choice of words.) "Would you care to stay with us while your living situation is settled? Our guest quarters are modest, but comfortable."

I thought for a moment then impulsively accepted the invitation.

An hour later, I stood surveying my temporary home. My escort had been quite correct; modest, but comfortable. There was an air of safety I had not felt since before my departure for Durham.

"The bars on the windows," I said to my escort (one Brother James), "when were they added?"

"Oh," he replied, "those date back to the Gordon Riots, I believe. To keep out the angry Protestant mob."

He grinned, gave a quick bow, then added: "Supper at five, if you want to come." Then he closed the door and left me to my own meditations.

I tossed my briefcase on the bed and looked around once again at the sparse furnishings of my little cell.

"Dear God," I said out loud. "I'm a willing prisoner of the Papists."

Chapter 21

6 December 1900: All over London

(From Jonathan Harker's journal) Last evening when the Count came from his room he began by asking me questions on legal matters and on the doing of certain kinds of business. I had spent the day wearily over books, and, simply to keep my mind occupied, went over some of the matters I had been examined in at Lincoln's Inn. There was a certain method in the Count's inquiries, so I shall try to put them down in sequence; the knowledge may somehow or some time be useful to me.

After such eventful days, the six weeks that followed were singularly uninteresting. I found my temporary home restful. My dreams were largely untroubled. I spent my days in the city endeavoring to attend to business. My evenings were spent in Esther's company, as often as was possible. Some few times I returned to the priory at an early enough hour to sit with Father Thomas Edmund in a little parlor. Our conversations were many and varied, but always returned to a single point—and that an unsettling one.

There was one event of consequence—and it was addressed with glee by Toby Barnes. The following morning, all of the morning papers were awash with the story. Skimming over the front page of the *Pall Mall Gazette*, it was not difficult to pick out Barnes' distinctively lurid style.

HYDE PARK HORRORS CONTINUE

*Some months have passed since the appalling circumstances
surrounding the death of Mr. Charles Sidney, and many of
our readers may have slept with growing comfort, assuming
that safety once again reigns in our fair city. Alas! Last
night witnessed once again the brutal murder of an innocent
London citizen. The victim, with face disfigured beyond
recognition, was a revolting mess of blood and gore, chest
and stomach freshly torn apart as if by a vicious beast. A
policeman made this gruesome discovery in the early hours
of Monday morning.*

We at the Pall Mall Gazette *cannot help but ask, Why
have authorities failed to take into custody the perpetrator
of these horrors—who we hope is the same man that killed
poor Mr. Sidney, else we must fear an epidemic of bloody
murderers! Why have no precautions been taken regarding
travel through our beloved streets and parks at night?*

*Those London parks are one of her most beloved assets.
A sign of civilization, cultivation, and refinement—indeed,
of social grandeur. A meeting place for peers and peasants.
Now transformed into the stage of horrifying and bloody
murder. When will it end? Are the police doing anything
to stop this? We are reminded once again of the unchecked
career of the brutal Jack of some years back, and the memory gives no assurance of the talents of Her Majesty's
constabulary.*

*Meanwhile, we take the presumptuous step of recom-
mending that our readers do not go abroad at night, unless
in company.*

It was indeed horrible. An outsider could have considered
Barnes' challenge of the police to be brazen, but given the

continuation of dark crimes in our city, I and a few others knew better.

As I read the paper, I could see all too well the scene of that early morning. Owing to a strange dream, I had awakened before dawn, and was dressed when the message arrived for Father Thomas Edmund Gilroy. I put my coat on at once and accompanied him to the police station. We stood there and looked down at the corpse of the murdered man. He was not, as Barnes later stated, unrecognizable. In fact, he was almost immediately identified by one of the constables nearby.

"Name was Philip Hammon. Librarian. In his fifties. Kept himself to himself. Worked at the British Library."

Poor Philip Hammon. A nobody of consequence. Lying there on a slab, his face transfixed in terror, his abdomen a disgusting mess, as if something had feasted upon that dead flesh.

"Could have been a wild animal," was Dr. Lewis' dry suggestion. "I doubt it. Looks like the same violent murderer we have seen several times before." He looked up at my priestly companion and added (with an unnecessary note of sarcasm in his voice): "Perhaps it's your bogeyman."

"Visit the zoos," Harris ordered one of his men, "just to see if any wild animals—any big cats or wolves—have escaped. And—you, there." A tall, dark-haired young man stepped forward. I didn't remember seeing him before. He had the look of a man who has a bad character where women are concerned. My thoughts returned from analysis of the man to hear his name and his orders: "Collins," Harris said, "go and call in Barnes. I've got a job for him to do."

The job in question was the writing of the column.

"If nothing else," Harris remarked dryly when he finished issuing his commands to the willing columnist, "you'll help us keep fools in their houses at night."

What strange and threatening things lurk in the shadows of our parks? Mothers, keep your daughters at home, lest they fall prey to the savage thirst of the vampire!

Early that evening, Esther read the column aloud and delivered this particular passage with expression (to Lydia's great discomfort).

"Don't be silly, Lydia," said her cousin flippantly. "Vampires don't have shadows. You would think that the *Gazette* would do proper research into such things."

The comment seemed so out of place, from a woman who sought some lost love through séances and mirrors. I turned so she would not see my disapproval. Much of it was self-directed; was I turning into a silly, petty, jealous man?

Since our engagement, and her docile avoidance of the company of creatures such as that Anghelescu person, she had at first been the picture of contented love. As the days passed, however, she seemed to become nervous. She was affectionate and clearly pleased when I was in her company, but prone to fits of distraction or, as on this occasion, almost feverishly high spirits. It was as if some strange concern preyed on her mind, something of which she did not care to speak to me.

"She hasn't been sleeping well," Lydia whispered to me at the door. "I think she has nightmares. She slept in my room last night. I wish she wouldn't read things like that. It just makes things worse, I think." The venturing of something so daring as an opinion nearly unnerved the girl, and she scurried away.

I left preoccupied and irritable.

When I arrived at the priory, the friars (this was the technical term, Brother James had informed me) were sitting quietly in their refectory (another addition to my vocabulary supplied by that helpful young man), preparatory to beginning their supper. It was a ritual I found fascinating. At the one or two meals I had shared with them, I had heard their litany of the names of the dead, and their solemn prayer over them. It seemed a curious way of incurring indigestion, to my mind.

"Do you think the eternal fate of your dead members is so much in question?" I asked Father Thomas Edmund after one such evening ceremony.

"The mercy of God is even more mysterious than His justice," he said quietly. "We presume nothing. We hope. And we consider it a privilege, not merely the obligation of fraternal affection, to remember our dead."

That night I tried to hurry past the refectory to my room. I had not dined, but I was not in a mood for company.

Aged Father Henry saw me and, as their prayer concluded, called out: "COME! Mr. Kemp! I beg you! I need you!"

All eyes were upon me—friendly, but inescapable. There was nothing to do but submit, short of being appallingly rude to my gracious hosts.

The old man (I had learned in my time there that he was ninety-nine and three-quarter years old) settled me down beside him, patted my leg, and foisted food on me. It was an odd thing, but one I had learned not to protest against, that they seemed to think I required as much food as a group of six men. On this particular evening, I had to wrest serving spoons from Father Henry with gentle violence, for fear the table itself would collapse under the weight of my plate.

"What did you need, Father Henry?" I asked, trying to distract him from forcing three hot, buttered rolls into my face.

"Need?" he said, blinking. "I do not require anything. My cup runneth over."

And then, as if to illustrate, he accidentally knocked over his glass. Three brothers came to our aid, and the four of us (with anxious attempts at assistance on the part of the old man) mopped up the mess.

"Good night, Mr. Kemp," said the old man when I quitted him for the night. "I recall for you the words of the poet: *"ch'i' sent" trarmi de la propria imago, et in un cervo solitario et vago di selva in selva ratto mi trasformo: et anchor de' miei can' fuggo lo stormo."*

The Italian lines, delivered in a singsong, were only later identified for me by accident. Like so many things spoken by Father Henry, it seemed thoroughly random.

It had proved a tiring meal, and Father Thomas Edmund seemed to be occupied, so there was no conversation to be had afterward. I did not really mind, because I feared I might have spoken of my present dissatisfaction with Esther, which would have felt like a betrayal. It was better to sleep, with the hope of awakening in a better frame of mind.

The next morning, as I prepared to leave for my place of business, I heard an increased rustling of robes. One of the brothers hurried by me.

"Is everything all right?" I asked.

"It's Father Henry," he said, and his eyes were red. "He died in his sleep last night."

I stammered out awkward condolences and asked after funeral arrangements.

"We shall know later today," he said. "And thank you, Mr. Kemp."

I walked off on my way, oddly sobered. Death had been such a dramatic presence of late, but here was something new, and yet familiar. The quiet death of an old man, sleeping peacefully in his bed. Just like my father. I could imagine the ancient priest going smiling to ... whatever really happens after all of this mess. The particularities of the afterlife was not a topic that had occupied my mind much. In recent weeks, the nature of death, the fate of the human body, and the due treatment of that body had been weighty topics indeed. But here was something that was after the diseased almost afterlife of the vampire. The dead, not the undead, and those dead because of the march of time, not from any sinister or violent means.

At the door to my office, I shook off such ponderous thoughts as best I could.

Of late, I had spent my days predominantly in my office, endeavoring to save my legal practice from the strain of scandal, not to mention absolute ruin.

"Good morning, Mr. Kemp," said Francis Carstairs. "I hope you've been able to return home, sir."

I shook my head. I had no intention of explaining myself to my clerk, but my flat had remained uninhabitable. In fact, I was beginning to wonder if it was a place I cared to salvage at all. The destruction had proved to be of so intrusive a nature, not merely robbing me of nearly all of my belongings, that it required substantial renovation. This I had undertaken, but with an increasing inclination to sell the place and move elsewhere. Meanwhile, there were more pressing issues to consider, and I meant to deal with one of them that very day.

Shortly after lunch, I gathered up papers into my brief-case, told Carstairs I would be out for the afternoon, and set off for the charitable establishment and office of Count Popescu.

My personal misfortunes had been a considerable excuse for my long avoidance of both Edgar Kilbronson and the count, as well as their associates. I had sent a great many vague reports in response to inquiries sent me by each man. Kilbronson's displeasure with me seemed clear. I half feared he might seek me out at my own office, but he had not yet done so.

I could not clearly see the intentions of the inspector or the priest. They seemed inclined on a waiting game, addressing each horrifying new incident as best they could, but there was no aggressive battle plan to rout out the threat—whatever it actually was. In the middle of the night, when I was standing at their side gazing down on a mutilated corpse, I was inclined to give all credence to theories of vampires and vampirism. In the light of day, especially when I heard my lovely Esther laughing over the suggestion, I felt suddenly foolish. In any case, I could sever the association for myself and be free of some of the burden of preternatural antagonism. I did not intend to quit accompanying Father Thomas Edmund on his outings in response to the inspector, of course. I had not discussed it with Father Thomas Edmund or Inspec-tor Harris directly. I just didn't want to be bothered with the expectations of clients whom I suspected of untoward behavior of any kind.

It was an interview I dreaded. I considered inform-ing my two clients by letter, but that seemed to be the coward's way. I would go even though I could make no further explanation. What on earth *could* I say? "I'm sorry, Count, but I suspect you of being a vicious blood drinker. And you, Kilbronson, are simply an indistinct form of monster no gentleman would support, because of vague but insurmountable principles of decency and gentility." The thing was unimaginable.

I would simply use as my excuse my current straightened circumstances, and that would be that. They could hardly argue with me, and they couldn't possibly take my retirement from their service personally.

That is what I told myself as I mounted the steps to the large brick residence I had acquired for the count.

The man who met me at the door was a stranger to me. I gave him my name, but it seemed to have been unnecessary, for he nodded and beckoned me in.

It was a strange house, seething with respectability, and not at all what I had expected. It was full of bustle and activity. As we walked down a long corridor, I heard several rooms full of typewriters, all of which were apparently in use. I saw women of a clearly secretarial nature, hurrying past me with their arms full of important-looking documents. The door of one room opened as I passed it, and I saw a crowd of filthy beggars, and two alarmingly competent nurses bullying them into order, preparatory to receiving the charitable support of the count's organization.

Another room, further on, seemed to be a place for the professional placement of fallen women—at least, that was my assumption, based on the line of highly objectionable-looking young women that stood, giggling, awaiting entry. It was rather like running the gauntlet, to pass by those coquettish glances, and to hear their whispering—which I felt confidently must have me as its subject, at least in part.

I had hoped we would go straight to see the count, but a second man suddenly approached the first (who hadn't bothered to speak a word to me), whispered something urgently into his ear, and we turned instead into a small room, clearly for waiting guests.

I remained there for some time, until I had become rather irritable at being kept waiting. My errand was so unpleasant that I wished to have done with it as quickly as possible. After twenty minutes, I was utterly tired of waiting. I would find my own way.

I opened the door, stepped into the corridor, and found myself face-to-face with his royal highness, the Prince of Wales.

"Bertie" looked at me coolly.

I bowed with as much courteous dignity as I could muster—and felt deeply how much I failed in my attempt. Then I stepped backward back into the room I had vacated, and closed the door behind me.

I was breathless and mortified—and much more willing to wait for escort.

Questions flooded my brain. What on earth could bring the heir to the English throne once again into the arena of Popescu's influence? The Prince of Wales was possessed of a problematic reputation, indeed, but I could not see what the philanthropic agenda of a foreigner would offer that could not be easily found elsewhere. I hoped there were not a deeper allure.

In spite of that disquieting thought, by the time the door opened again, I had regained my composure.

"I am so sorry you were left waiting so long, Mr. Kemp," said Gregory Anghelescu, smiling with all of his teeth. "Thank you so much for your patience."

I nodded briefly and moved to follow him.

I thought, from his expression, that he wished to converse on our way, but I had no intention of treating the man as an equal. My message was for his employer, and I would not increase my own feeling of discomfort by putting myself in the awkward position of repeating myself.

Anghelescu honored me with a smile clearly at my expense, then shrugged slightly and gestured me on our way.

Our goal was apparently the count's "war room", the place of all planning and organization. Here was no round table; there was a long, dark table, carved out of the most hierarchically correct ancient tree, I had no doubt. The chair at the head—Popescu's chair—was a noble creation, bearing an elaborate escutcheon. The count himself was seated there now, and I could not imagine him with a more thoroughly delighted expression on his face. He was almost gleeful.

The air in the room, indeed, was unequivocally one of triumph. All of those present—the count, his secretary, Kilbronson, Mr. William Harper, Sir Douglas Wetheringdon—were all clearly full of some shared excitement. I imagined it was their encounter with the Prince of Wales. A coup d'état of the first order. What on earth could have possessed that powerful man, representative of the future of England, to fraternize with this improbable group? That remained a troubling counterpoint to my own intended errand.

The count, who seemed to have to work hard to suppress his satisfied smile, remarked on my recent misfortunes. "I am sorry for your sad trouble, Mr. Kemp," he said with the air of an ancient king, showering gratuitous benevolence on the head of an unworthy peasant. "I trust that, so talented a lawyer, you will recover your fortunes in time."

"Perhaps you have done so already!" Anghelescu spoke at my elbow. "Indeed, we've heard that not all of your life is misfortune. We applaud you, Mr. Kemp, upon your engagement. You have captured quite a rich prize."

The words were offensive, and I believe they were intended to be. I repressed the desire to kick the man. Jealousy and frustration, no doubt. He was not worth my notice.

I turned back to his employer. "Count Popescu," I said, "I am sorry to say that I am afraid I can no longer support your legal needs, sir."

In a moment, the atmosphere was transformed. Triumph gave way to an ominous stillness. Several moments passed. Then Count Popescu spoke, and his voice was hard: "And your reason?"

I had anticipated this question. "I am simplifying my practice," I said, "consequent to my recent misfortunes. I do not expect to remain here in London long."

This declaration of intention to depart from the city, not merely from their employ, did not seem to assuage my listeners. Popescu glared at me with narrow eyes. Anghelescu was watching me too, and there was a strange look on his face, a thoughtful, expectant look, which turned my stomach.

My words certainly did not soothe Kilbronson, who, the moment I had delivered my text, had flushed with fury and fixed me with a livid gaze.

Now he turned on me, and his anger found voice. "What of my wife?" he demanded.

Concrete details were much easier to handle. "I have produced a dossier for you," I said quietly. "It summarizes all of the information I have gathered to date." (*Most* of the information would have been closer to the truth, and *some* of the information would have been even closer.) "You will see that few conclusions can be drawn from it. I believe you will have greater success in your search if you work with another agent."

"Another agent? Are you saying you failed? You claim you didn't find her?"

"Mr. Kilbronson," I said quietly, "I make no claims. I merely state the truth. And the truth of the matter, clearly outlined in that dossier, is that I have not found your wife. This strengthens me in my determination to suggest to you that you find someone else to assist you in your search."

Dour Edgar was now so horrifyingly alive with passion that he seemed like a grotesque carnival performer, aping human emotion to the point of comic absurdity. In this case, I could not laugh.

"You're hiding her," he shrieked. "You've found her and you're hiding her. How much is she paying you? Who else is paying you? I told you. She's mine. She's my wife. She's mine, do you hear me!"

He was on his feet and moving toward me.

Out of the corner of my eye, I saw someone I thought I recognized.

In a smooth, rapid move of which I could not have imagined myself capable, I leapt for the window, flung it open, and called down into the street: "Constable Peters!"

That honorable representative of the law looked up and waved acknowledgment.

"It's Mr. Kemp!" I shouted (ignoring the fact that several people stopped in the street to stare). "I'll be down in a moment. Wait for me."

He called up his agreement.

When I turned back, triumphant in the thought that I had baffled the vicious intent of that strange, cadaver-like man, my celebration was dampened by the sight of Kilbronson sitting, silent and sullen, in a chair, where he had been thrust by Anghelescu.

The count, with one withering glance at the glowering man, looked up to me. "I am very disappointed, Mr. Kemp. Very disappointed."

The words were portentous. I am sure that I appeared cool and untroubled; interiorly I braced myself for the onslaught of demonic fury and vengeance.

But that was all.

"Good day, Mr. Kemp. We shall not keep you."

I was dismissed. I bowed slightly and walked out.

A few minutes after as I stood on the sidewalk, I could hear the steady racket of typewriters through an open window.

"Everything all right, Mr. Kemp?" asked Peters.

"Yes," I said. "I think so."

He waited a moment, but I offered no further explanation.

I was too busy standing there, wondering if I were indeed a fool.

Chapter 22

7 December 1900–17 January 1901: Principally Hyde Park Police Station, South Kensington, Camden, and Hyde Park

(From Dr. Seward's journal) *When I came to Renfield's room I found him lying on the floor on his left side in a glittering pool of blood. When I went to move him, it became at once apparent that he had received some terrible injuries; there seemed none of that unity of purpose between the parts of the body which marks even lethargic sanity. As the face was exposed I could see that it was horribly bruised, as though it had been beaten against the floor— indeed it was from the face wounds that the pool of blood originated.*

"I wish that you had waited, sir, or consulted with me." Inspector Harris frowned his sternest frown at me. "You could have at least told us what was in your mind."

"With all due respect," I replied with some annoyance (I was no child for him to rebuke), "you haven't taken me into your counsel, Inspector Harris. I don't know what you are waiting for, but no gentleman could stomach that sort of employment."

He considered this. "Indeed not, sir. But what I think you fail to appreciate is that these times are not those which rely upon gentility. They rely on sense. We have no clear case that would allow us to trace these acts to the count or to anyone in his household. And now ... well, sir, I fear that soon we shall. If he is indeed the villain you suspect him to be, having you in his employ somehow kept him in check."

"In check!" I cried. "My home destroyed? Charles Sidney murdered? That girl Stella? The little librarian? And have you uncovered the location of Victor Montrose? If this is a villain kept in check, I should hate to see unrestrained activity."

"Well," said the inspector dryly, "that might be what we are all about to see."

"Well," I retorted, "I imagine there must be something respectable about the place, since the prince fraternizes there."

That stopped the inspector in his tracks for a moment. "Again?" he asked. "You saw the prince there?"

"Yes," I said.

Inspector Harris sat back down. "Well now," he said, as if to himself, "what on earth is he about *now*?"

He mused on it for a moment then looked up sharply at me. "Well, sir," he said abruptly, "we won't bother you about this anymore. Collins will show you to the door. Good day."

Escorted by that sardonic officer (who clearly found my discomfort amusing), I left the station dismissed and with a flea in my ear. I told myself that nothing could inspire me to return.

The weeks passed, and nothing happened. For the first week, I was anxious and watchful. The next week, I felt a sense of triumph—it seemed that the inspector's prediction was totally unfounded. This feeling would not be long-lived; other worries intruded almost immediately. It might have been the sudden liberation of my mind from more lurid concerns—a reaction to the shift from emotional intensity. Now that I was not caught up in the thrill of the chase anymore, my days were relatively mundane. My evenings, still spent in Esther Raveland's company, should have been delightful and relaxing.

But Esther was unwell over Christmas, and in the days that followed, she became thinner, more nervous, and more preoccupied.

"It's just a cold," she told me more than once. "Pray, don't worry about me, John. I'll be well soon enough. Truly. I just need some rest." Then she would smile so sweetly, sweeping away my doubts with that most charming brush, a gesture of affection. Each time, as I walked home in the cold darkness, the doubts would creep back with steady insistence. My nights were once again deeply troubled.

Christmas social engagements were numerous—at least, the invitations were. We attended none of them. Esther was always too unwell, or too tired, or otherwise simply and quietly unwilling to attend. It seemed such an unexpected change from her eager social fluttering from the previous Season. I did not mind avoiding so many dull parties, and the torture of society's attention regarding our engagement. Further, I had no desire to suffer ghoulish curiosity about the assault on my home or my current unorthodox place of residence.

For all of these reasons, an evening spent quietly in Esther's company was a much more attractive prospect to my mind than hours of mind-numbing small talk and insincere pleasantries. Nevertheless, there was something in the nature of our withdrawal from society that bred in me mild discontentment and uncertainty. It was as if we were hiding from something.

Or someone.

Lydia and her mother continued to accept invitations somewhat regularly. It was one such—on the eve of the new year—that provoked an even more articulate and open concern in my heart.

The following day I came by invitation to tea.

Lydia was almost gushing with her enthusiasm about the preceding evening. It was an odd thing, but it seemed as if, as her cousin grew quieter, weaker, and more nervous, Lydia blossomed. Dressed in pink lace, with rosettes scattered in lavish disregard for taste, her eyes sparkled as she told us of all the titled and influential people she had seen across the room (she was yet shy and would not have gathered up her courage to approach any of those people). I only half listened. Lydia was a dear, like a little sister might have been, and her excitement was charming. But Esther, in simple, unadorned gray silk, was sitting in uncomfortable stillness by the fire, fidgeting a tassel on an embroidered pillow. As she ruthlessly pulled and tweaked the ill-fated ornament, her eyes stared down at the burning logs, her mind clearly far away.

Her attention—and mine—returned with a jerk when Lydia spoke a single name.

"That horrid man was there too. Mr. Anghelescu."

I looked up and Esther moved sharply in her chair. Since the day we became engaged—that strange, wonderful meeting in the middle of the park bushes—we had not mentioned the Hungarian secretary.

Lydia was chatting along unconcernedly. "He asked after you, Essie. You too, Mr. Kemp. He asked particularly after you both, in fact. He even came back and asked me again about you. I really didn't know what to say. He's such an odd man, you know, Essie, though you always seemed to like him."

"I hope you told him ...," Esther began, then: "Oh!" she exclaimed. She looked down in her hand. The threads of the worried tassel had snapped, and there was nothing but a mess of disemboweled red silk. Esther looked up, her face blank, and saw we were all looking at her. "Oh," she said, suddenly irritable. "Nevermind. It doesn't matter. Go on, Lydia. Tell us more about your magnificent evening."

Thankfully, Lydia did not seem to notice her cousin's unkind tone. She went on, happily prattling.

My mind shifted instead to Lydia's mother. Esther's cousin Millicent was a shadowy figure in all of this. A tall, thin woman, with tightly curled, wispy hair, and an anxious expression. My presence in the house was a paradox: on the one hand, Esther's engagement appeared to be a relief; on the other, the regular presence of a man in her home was clearly a terrifying prospect.

At this moment, she was looking with nervous pride at her own daughter and shooting fearful, confused glances toward her distant cousin.

"You look unwell, Esther, dear," she said (in a voice that I imagined would sound nagging very quickly). "Perhaps you should go and rest again?"

"I'm quite well, Cousin Millicent," was the cold response. "Pray do not worry about me."

"Oh," said the older woman, even more nervously than before, "but I do worry, my dear. You are so pale, and seem so ... unlike yourself. So ... impatient ..."

"I'm not impatient," snapped Esther. "Or if I am it is because I really simply wish to be left alone."

She got up abruptly and stormed from the room. I was half afraid that Millicent would burst into tears. After a few moments of awkwardness, I excused myself and walked to the hall.

A little maid, with a shock of red hair and a flock of merry freckles, was hurrying by.

"Susan," I said, "can you tell me where Miss Raveland is?"

"Oh, sir," she replied apologetically, "I'm afraid she's gone out. She said she would walk in the air and return soon."

I left, hoping to find her as quickly as possible, but there was no sign of her in the street.

That night I walked home even more annoyed than before, and with all of my old anxieties and jealousies about that Hungarian bounder.

The next evening Esther received me quietly and seemed less edgy. I thought perhaps she would wish to speak of that man, but she studiously avoided anything like a personal conversation. Most of our time together was spent in an unhappy silence.

And so the days passed.

I still remained an occupant of the guest room of St. Dominic's Priory. I tried several times to leave. Father Thomas Edmund always encouraged me to stay, to wait a little longer, and allow my uncertain affairs to settle. Thus, my tenure with those peculiar Papists continued long past the time when under normal circumstances I felt I should have outlasted my welcome.

The funeral of ancient Father Henry was an interesting experience. I had never attended one of their services in full. The quiet, rhythmic prayer and gentle, well-choreographed movement of the robed men presented a curious paradox for me; on the one hand, I found it all chilling in its un-English exoticism, but on the other, there was a soothing quality to the performance. The coffin, draped in sober black. The candles, the clouds of incense, those men's voices united in uniform, practiced chanting. As a contrast to the horrifying spectacle of death that I had seen so frequently of late, this ritual was perfect and absolute.

That night I slept well, and dreamlessly.

Days passed into weeks. I began to wonder—more than I already had been wondering—how the police investigations were proceeding. I had heard nothing since my last, dissatisfying interview with Inspector Harris. Where was Victor Montrose? Had there been any other reported incidents? Any more bloody developments? I read nothing in the newspapers. Toby Barnes was eerily silent. Perhaps he had been reassigned. Perhaps he had given up. Perhaps everyone had given up.

I remained in this limbo of uneventful, inchoate dissatisfaction. If Esther's listlessness had mitigated even by a small fraction, we might have been able to engage in a direct, open emotional exchange. Even an argument would have been an improvement from our growing alienation.

Then came the day when everything changed. It did not appear, at the start, to be a day of any significance. In fact, it began with a dull, unproductive sort of morning, which developed into a dull, unproductive sort of afternoon.

After several hours of attempting to achieve something in the way of business, I gave up.

"I'll be leaving early this afternoon, Carstairs," I said. "There isn't much left to do for any of our cases—the ones we still have left. When you're finished, just hurry on home. Don't forget to lock up."

"Thank you, Mr. Kemp," he said cheerfully.

I left, cursing his pleasant efficiency. I had come so close to dismissing him—what need would I have for a clerk, when my business was so thoroughly muddled? I still could not tell if I would recover professionally from the scandal of the attack on my home and my own actions in severing the connection with two rich clients. Every time I nearly gathered together the courage necessary to inform Carstairs that his services were no longer required, I would find him working so diligently, and with such dedication, that I could not bring myself to say what I had planned.

As I made my way, as usual, to visit Esther, I wondered to myself if, in the end, Carstairs might outlast *me* in my own business.

"I'm so sorry, sir," said the freckled little maid, Susan. "Miss Raveland is resting. Mrs. Ferrier said she was not to be wakened for anyone. Would you like to leave a note, sir? I am sure Miss Raveland will be sorry to have missed you."

I mechanically scribbled an affectionate note. Then, after bidding the maid a polite farewell, I stood on the street considering what I should do next. For some minutes, I racked my brains to find some alternative, some friend or some interest I could pursue to pass the tedious hours until night. When nothing came to me, I gave up in irritation and marched to a nearby pub.

One steak and kidney pie later, I felt more braced to accept my lot in life. I determined that, the very next day, I would press Esther for a final decision regarding the date of our marriage. I loved her. I adored her. She was unwell and needed me to remain patient, and loyal, and strong. We would find a new home together, and I would rebuild my profession to a degree that would allow me to support her in the manner she deserved.

I walked back to the priory full of determinedly happy resolve.

On the doorstep, I heard my name called. I turned back toward the street, and there, breathless and disheveled from running, was Lydia Ferrier.

"Mr. Kemp ... Cousin John, that is, ... I don't mean to ... to interfere. I know Essie will be angry, and Mother would forbid it, but I just can't bear it anymore. I don't understand it, but I think there is something very, very wrong. Please."

I was not sure of the protocol of a guest receiving guests in the priory, but I ushered her in and chose one of the parlors. As I closed the door on our tête-à-tête, I glanced at the framed print on the wall behind Lydia's head. It depicted one of those white-robed men, with an axe embedded in his skull and a knife thrust through his chest. Seemingly untroubled by these unnatural appendages, he was kneeling and scribbling casually in the dirt.

I hoped Lydia would not look up.

"Oh, Mr. Kemp ... I mean, Cousin John. I am so worried for Essie. It must all be Cousin James. That's been the problem. The whole problem. She's fretting for him. I think she's been fretting for him for years. I just ... well, last night Essie was talking in her sleep. And ... she kept calling out for him. For Cousin James, I mean."

"Who is Cousin James?" I asked finally.

Her eyes were wide. "Didn't you know? Cousin James was her father. He was a scoundrel, Mother says. But Essie must have loved him. She was weeping in her sleep. And I don't know what she is doing, but I fear it must all have been about him."

"What happened to the man?"

"I ... I don't really know," she said. "I know he's dead—at least, I think so. He abandoned her, I believe. But Mother won't tell me, and I couldn't ask Essie but ..." Her eyes were full of tears. "I do so love Essie, Mr. ... Cousin John. She's so dear to me. And she's been so unlike herself, and I fear she will ... do herself an injury."

"It's all right, Lydia," I said. "Please don't worry. Let me call you a cab and send you home. I'll see what I can do."

As I watched the retreating cab, I made a quick decision. I went to the door of the cloister—that inner part of the priory from which I, as an outsider, was forbidden. I knocked at it vigorously.

I was prepared to give a passionate excuse for my rudeness, while at the same time begging to see Father Thomas Edmund, or for him to be summoned by some secret, private means of communication (I was sure they had one), but he himself opened the door.

"Father Thomas Edmund," I said, "do you have a moment?"

He looked closely at my face without speaking. Then he nodded and gestured back to the parlor. Now it was my turn to sit under the dust-drawing friar.

"It's ... something personal," I said. And then I began. I told him everything I had ever endeavored to conceal from him about Esther. Of that strange relationship with Anghelescu, and my jealousy. Of her recent illness and changeable behavior. Of every fear and every doubt. And now of the words of Lydia concerning this elusive "Cousin James".

As I told him, Father Thomas Edmund's face grew grave. Before I could finish my narrative, he interrupted me.

"My dear John, this is much more serious than you imagine. We must go at once."

In the street, he hailed a cab and loaded me into it.

"Won't you tell me what you fear?" I asked.

He looked at me, sorrow in his face. "Yes," he said, "though it will only grieve you before we know for certain. I fear that Miss Raveland is in very real danger. We must hurry to be there in time, to prevent yet another tragedy."

I shouted out the window for the cab driver to move faster, and, maddened at the thought of violence against Esther, I remained with my head out the window, frantically scanning those unlikely streets for ... for something.

As we raced through Lincoln's Inn, we passed my house. A small light was visible in the window.

I shouted again to the driver—this time ordering him to stop. Perhaps Esther was in my rooms. It was unlikely, but who knew what might be in this night of mad horrors.

Leaving the cab waiting in the streets, I hurried up the stairs.

I reached to unlock the door to my office, but before my hand could reach the door handle, it turned and the door flew open. There, white-faced and all stirred up, stood my clerk.

"Good God!" I cried. "Carstairs! You nearly terrified me!"

"Oh, Mr. Kemp!" he blurted out. "I'm so relieved you are here! I know you told me to leave, and I am sure it is none of my business, but I couldn't leave without telling you. It was the young lady, sir. Miss Raveland."

"What about Miss Raveland?"

"She came to see you, sir. She looked so anxious and unhappy. I hated to tell her you weren't here. She was so distressed. She said she needed to talk to you about something. Then we heard something—something on the stair behind her. She turned and saw a shadow. She grabbed my arm and fair near screamed. It turned out to be some man she knew. I didn't ... well, sir, I am sure I am sorry if he is a friend of yours, but truthfully, I didn't like the look of him, sir, so I followed. We went down several streets, and then ... I lost them, sir. I ran down several streets, trying to find them again. I know it was none of my business, sir, but I was so troubled by it all. It just wasn't right, sir. Something wasn't right. She kept looking over her shoulder, but he was leading her on sure enough. I think she was trying to think of some excuse or something. Anyway, there was such a flurry of traffic near Piccadilly Circus, and when it passed, they were gone."

"Quick," I said. "Which way did they go, Carstairs?"

He gestured down the road, and we almost ran along the way. Several twists and turns followed.

"I lost them here," he said, gesturing in the midst of the bustle of the theatre district.

Before we had a moment to lament, one of the young men in white appeared, gasping. "Father Thomas Edmund! Brother James was right behind her, but we lost her by the Marble Arch. We have to run. We're searching the streets now, and we sent Brother Joseph for the police." He glanced at me, but seemed to make up his mind to go on: "It isn't good, Father. There's something very wrong. She was weeping—and ... and I heard her cry out ... for her father."

Our little band of desperate men grew at every corner.

"No sign down in Soho, Father."

"The inspector's on his way, sir."

"We have two dozen men throughout Mayfair."

"It's as if they've vanished, sir. It should not have been possible for it to happen that quickly."

As we neared the Marble Arch, we heard another commotion—a man, huddled close to the ground over a heap of something that might have been human.

The man looked up, and I recognized him as Constable Davis.

He recognized us then too and shouted: "Come! Mr. Kemp! All of you! Please! Hurry!"

The young constable, the tears streaming down his face, struggled to lift up the broken, bloody body of the old drunk, that Shakespearean posturer who had so caught Esther's fancy months before.

One of his eyes was no longer visible, buried under a bloody mass of battered, swollen flesh. The other eye rolled around wildly, glassy and staring desperately without seeing.

"Who was it?" I asked. "Who did this?"

He gurgled out something, but the words were so soft and blurred that I could not understand him. I bent over his mouth and listened—I tried to stifle my own breath, to shut out the deafening beating of my heart, to hear him.

"Brute. I . . . I tried, man. I tried."

He seemed to drift then, to hurry on his way to the solace of death.

"Where did he take her?"

This question, perhaps the only one that could have roused him from that rapid descent, made that blind eye fly open again, and with one, final, mighty effort, he pointed into the chilling, oppressive darkness of Hyde Park.

"Leave me," he croaked, the blood oozing from his mouth. "Go to her. Go, man. Hurry. Save her. A plague upon you, murderers, traitors all! I might have saved her; now she's gone ... for ever!"

Father Thomas Edmund hushed him gently.

In the moment before he slipped away in the eerie twilight, below the murmured incantations of the priest, I heard a frail voice whimper for God and for whiskey.

Hyde Park. That throbbing in my chest, so loud I wondered that anyone could hear anything else. I thought I might run mad.

Hurry, man. Hurry. Run. Run to her.

I was indeed running then—running like a man possessed. Running, running, running. Running madly, but yet with purpose. And with a clear sense of direction. How could I help but know where I was going, when some inner vision was there to show me the way?

Can you not run faster?

Running as if speed were the only possible way to dispel the horror. Running, though my soul cringed inwardly at what I knew I must find at the end. This footrace of Atalanta, but, at its conclusion, not the satisfaction of heady desire and romance. Only tragedy, the gift of vengeful, malicious gods.

Have you not seen this before? Have you not received warning again, and again, and again that this would happen?

The scene rushed upon my senses with the eeriness of an all-too-familiar dream. This was not a dream. This was living and real. An appalling, inescapable, desperate present.

Down one path. Then another. Then another. Winding through the trees and bushes. Were others close behind me? I had no idea, and I did not care. I could have been running into danger, into death.

There—look there. John Kemp, you have failed.

The trees parted, and the clouds too, granting me a clear view.

Two figures appear before me: the figure in black hovering menacingly over the figure in white. This is the vision which my dreams taught me to see, made new in the half-light. Nothing sparkles. Nothing shines. The moon scarcely grants me light to see that which I know is there.

The creature in black turns—and I see the face of Gregory Anghelescu, triumphant in hate, his mouth suffused with blood—*her* blood. For a moment, the blood is all I see.

I rush forward, murder in my heart.

With a laugh, a dark, chilling sound that reverberates in hell, he calls down a cloud of confusion all around me.

The creature is gone.

And there in the grass, her dark hair loose and trailing, her face pale and deathlike, lies Esther Raveland, with blood upon her neck.

Chapter 23

18 January 1901: Hyde Park Police Station and Kings Cross

(From Mina Murray Harker's diary) *Then he spoke to me mockingly, "And so you, like the others, would play your brains against mine. You would help these men to hunt me and frustrate me in my designs! You know now, and they know in part already, and will know in full before long, what it is to cross my path. They should have kept their energies for use closer to home. Whilst they played wits against me—against me who commanded nations, and intrigued for them, and fought for them, hundreds of years before they were born—I was countermining them."*

The group of men on the heath huddled together around the cold, blood-stained figure. She was in my arms, her eyes still closed. My soul rose and fell with each shallow, halting breath.

Her eyes suddenly flew open, so full of terror that they seemed to look past me, without recognition. She held up her hands, crimson with her own blood, and looked frantically from one to the other. Then her trembling red lips parted, and her voice came forth in a shattering scream. She screamed and screamed and screamed, and the sound echoed all around us.

"Esther." It was Father Thomas Edmund who spoke. "Esther."

This new voice, speaking her Christian name, some-how calmed her. The screaming ceased, and she lay in my arms again, silent except for the occasional wracking sob.

"Come," said Inspector Harris, his voice low with emo-tion. "Bring her inside. This is no place for her."

I gathered Esther in my arms and half led, half carried her. The other men surrounded us, marching along at a slow, painful pace—a progress eerily reminiscent of a funeral procession.

A short time later, we sat, a sober council of war, in the office of Inspector Harris. He had dismissed most of his men. Father Thomas Edmund was there, of course, and a handful of his brethren in white. Dr. Lewis was summoned, though I was not sure why. The thought of a mortician as her attending physician seemed singularly grisly to my mind; yet there was something comforting in his cold, detached, clinical manner. And who else could we take into our confidence at such a moment?

As he was examining the wound on her neck, a young constable—Davis, it was—tapped me gently on the shoul-der. I looked up, and he gestured with something toward me. I held out my hand, and he dropped into it a little gold necklace, with a small locket, stained with blood.

The locket had an intricate design on it, with interlac-ing letters over a heart, crowned with roses. I opened the locket and saw the face of a man, a man with a ghostly resemblance to Esther. Dark eyes with that same intense look. A strong, masculine jaw—perhaps overstrong, as if striving to compensate for inner weakness. A mouth awry in a crooked smile, both impish and arresting. Dark thick curls. A young face, but a likeness too old to be a brother. Too like her to be a lover. A father.

"That's mine!" cried Esther, in a voice throbbing with agony. She had leapt up from the chair, nearly knocking down the doctor, and tried to snatch the locket from my hand. In my astonishment, I had reflexively closed my hand over the locket and drawn it back from her. Now we stood there in tense uncertainty, staring at each other, while all eyes fixed upon us.

She was frantic again, hysterical, but for a new reason. The sad wounds on her throat were forgotten in this desperate avalanche of a child's grief. "Do you know what it is to see the dearest man, full of charm. Affection. Devotion. To see his eyes, full of cherishing love, dim into blankness. To watch him retreat into some dark, hidden pain. To see him destroyed. Killed slowly by some oppressive inner thirst. Drowned. Unable to save himself. Unable to free himself from the oppression of his own pain. To watch the world turn against him. To be dragged from him. Kept from him. To be told to pray for him. 'Yes, Esther, pray for him.' 'Give him to God, Esther.' To pray with tears. Piteous tears. To swear everything a child can swear to God just to have back the one thing that really mattered.

"You don't know what it is," she said, her voice harsh with bitterness, her accents clipped as she angrily bit back her own tears. "The loneliness. The shame. The cruel judgment. The dismissal. Oh, I had money. I had a position that was virtually unassailable, save by the loss of my own virtue. The money came to me. And I was kept from him—my guardians felt I was untrustworthy. That I would have given everything to him. Wasted it away on a wretched creature. A lost man."

"And would you?" I asked.

Now the tears were gone. She looked up at me with eyes frank and decisive: "Oh, yes," she said. "And I would give it all now to give him one moment of peace.

"If God is merciful, then let him come to me and tell me so. Let me see his face and hear that still voice awake. Let me feel his hand upon mine. Give him back to me, so that for one single moment I can feel joy again.

"You are angry with me—as if I cared for your anger. Or perhaps you are embarrassed. I care even less for that. I have spent my life a subject of embarrassment. Spared outright social censure by money. 'Poor thing. Such a father.' 'He had such talent.' 'Pitiful man. He died, you know.' 'Good riddance. Only would have sunk the estate.' 'Handsome fellow. I never really thought him honorable, though.'

"Can't you see?" Her voice throbbed with passion, with this mad seesaw of hysteria released, then repressed and constrained by an angry will. "Don't you understand? If she hadn't died. If I hadn't been born. I am the one who killed him. Killed the one I would have given anything, even my life to save."

Tears once again, and she collapsed back into her chair, her body racked with sobs.

The rest of the men were still frozen—like stereotypical Englishmen, horrified at this unrestrained expression of strong emotion. And yet there was something more to paralyze the room—a deep, raw vulnerability in this woman, a woman we had failed to protect, despite our efforts.

I say the men were paralyzed; one was not. Father Thomas Edmund Gilroy moved silently to her side and crouched down beside her, without touching her.

"Child," said the priest gently, but with a firmness that caused her to raise her eyes to his. "Can you speak of what has happened?"

318

She raised her tear-streaked face and stared up at him. For some moments, she did not speak. Then she slowly nodded.

"That ... that dreadful man," she said. "The first time ... when we first met him. I ... I made fun of him. He seemed such a self-satisfied sort of creature. Then he began to talk and I felt confused. I think he hated me then. He would speak of things that ... that ... I don't know how he knew. And he told me of things. Of ways one could speak with ... with those who are dead. It was all so strange but so ... so much what I wanted. I just wanted to hear his voice. Just once.

"But always, just when I thought I might hear my father, that ... creature was there. Horrible, evil man. But that too was strange. Sometimes, if he were near me, I found myself thinking things. It was as if he ... as if his thoughts were in my head. I knew they were not mine, but there was nothing I could do. And then the dreams started. My father. He would come to me in my sleep and beg me to speak to him. And whenever I tried—oh, how I tried!—I couldn't. And he would leave me so grieved. I tried ... I went places a few times. John, you were at the séance. It was so absurd, but I kept hoping and thinking there would be something. Some way. And that man ... he spoke to me so infrequently, but he was always watching me.

"I became frightened to go out, because he always seemed to be there, and when he was there, I couldn't think clearly. I couldn't ... it was all such a muddle. And even when I didn't see him, the dreams continued. Sometimes he was there in the dreams. Standing there, watching me. And sometimes he spoke to my father in my dreams. I could not hear what they were saying. Oh, I would have given anything to speak.

"John—Mr. Kemp. He asked me not to see that man anymore. It was easy enough to agree. I didn't want to see that man. But so often, when I left the house for anything, even for a moment, he would be waiting for me. I would see him, lurking there in the shadows. I would run back inside as quickly as I could, but I always knew he was there. Always waiting for me." She fell silent, staring down at the ground, lost in her dark recollection. Then she shivered, involuntarily.

"What happened tonight?" Father Thomas Edmund Gilroy asked quietly.

Esther shook herself, blinking away tears, like a child who struggles to focus obediently upon a task set her by an affectionate governess. "I was resting, and no one came to wake me when John—Mr. Kemp—came to see me. There was a note when I awoke. I was so fretful and unwell that I decided to come and see him. I would not walk far— only a little ways, hoping the fresh air would revive me. Then I would take a cab. John—Mr. Kemp—would see me home. I just wanted to see him. At least, I think that was what I wanted.

"I saw his clerk, and heard he was not there, and then ... that man, that creature. He was there. He said he would help me on my way. I wanted to run from him, but there he was in my mind again, and I couldn't help going where he led. He told me that he was bringing me to my father. I knew it was a lie, but I couldn't stop myself from walking alongside him. I knew he was leading me to ... I knew it. But there was his voice in my head, and I couldn't stop following him.

"He ... he said that I ... I had drawn *him*. He said ... he said ... such filth. When he ... when he bent over me, and I felt his teeth upon my throat, only then could

I struggle, and that horrible, rank breath ... I fainted, and when I awoke, all I could see was the blood. Everywhere. The blood."

The hysteria was returning.

"My love. My dear one. My poor girl." I hushed her and leaned over her, taking the trembling girl back in my arms, and rocking her, as I might have rocked a child wakening from a nightmare.

The acute embarrassment I had felt when I first embraced her in the park seemed an impossible emotion now. My lips brushed her hair, and I murmured gently in her ear, and I cared not who saw these tender, inadequate signs of love. She cowered into my arms, terrified and broken. I loved her then more deeply than I had ever done and hated myself for failing to protect her.

"What now, Father?" I asked at last.

"She must go north, my friend," he said quietly.

I knew what that meant. I leaned once again against her dark, soft hair for a moment, then looked back to the priest, and nodded my agreement.

Inspector Harris did not question the decision.

In the end, despite the frenzied calculations I kept making in my head, we arrived at King's Cross in very good time—and with three quarters of an hour to spare. Our escort walked in silence—six constables; two heavily overcoated men who, even in this attire, exuded the air of officialdom; Inspector Harris; myself, with Esther, veiled and cowering on my arm; and four men in white robes and black cloaks. Quite a parade, I thought to myself—and yet I was glad of it.

There were few others on the platform—it was perhaps an odd time for a trip into the North country. An elderly gentleman sat some way down from us, guarding over a large trunk which he refused to release from his sight, though a kindhearted porter endeavored to liberate him from its responsibility.

A schoolboy in a gaudy blue and yellow scarf walked by holding a ticket tightly in his right fist and looking profoundly nervous until he was joined by an older man—a brother, perhaps? Too old for a brother. Father or uncle.

Three businessmen came along ten minutes later, chattering of dull details and figures. I realized that it must be nearly morning. Streaks of dawn were breaking through the sky.

A middle-aged woman with pince-nez.

An Irishman in an unnecessarily green jacket and the sort of hat one would think would only be worn to entertain tourists.

Bustling movement down the platform caught my eye; a flock of those men in white approaching, with two young women in their midst.

The group drew closer, and the women sat together on a nearby bench.

Now I could see the women more clearly, and my stomach slowly began to churn. They were both dressed in black and veiled. Young women, I would have thought. Delicate, if not sickly. I felt, rather than saw, their paleness. Every movement was nervous. Surrounded, as they were, by men in white, and a host of police constables— watchful guardians indeed—it was clear that not one man could be as watchful as those women.

But there was something in their movements that so oddly mirrored those of my own Esther, that it was almost as if I were seeing her wounded misery in dark triplicate. A memory stirred—not of something I had seen, but of something I had read. Surely there were three women in the castle of Dracula at the beginning of Stoker's novel ...

I turned away from the thought, and found Father Thomas Edmund watching me thoughtfully.

"Who are they?" I asked him, sotto voce.

Then he frowned and looked, for the first time, weary. I recalled that we had not slept all night.

"You do not think," he said, "that the vicious appetites of such creatures would tend toward a single prey? I believe we shall spend a great deal of time in the weeks ahead tending many victims."

It was a chilling thought, and one that stayed with me through the dizzying, surreal minutes that followed. The train arrived, bringing with it clouds and atmospherics that seemed more in keeping with the theatre than with a cold January morning in the real world.

I mechanically bade Esther an affectionate goodbye, and she responded dutifully.

"I shall come and see you as soon as I can," I promised.

"Please do," she said, but absently.

As I stood back, waving farewell, watching the train steam gently out of the station and into loud, determined motion, the dreamlike quality of the scene intensified to a ludicrous degree. Any observer would have delighted in the scene, which so delicately balanced tender feeling and the demands of propriety. It was as if I were simply seeing off my betrothed as she left on a rest cure.

"John? John?" Father Thomas Edmund called my name many times before I heard him. "John, we must go. Come. There is much to do. The others have already left."

I looked around us. We were indeed alone on the platform.

"Where are we going?" I asked.

"Inspector Harris. He wants us to come back to the police station."

We walked together for a long time in silence.

I was waiting for him to say something—anything—that might give me an opening to vent my mounting fury at his God. I shot him several glances, hoping he might be prompted by one of them to speak to me. But he continued on his way without opening his mouth. A picture of respect, patience, tact, and insufferable obtuseness.

"Well?" I said, finally.

He looked to me, raising an eyebrow almost imperceptibly. "Well, what, John?"

"Aren't you going to try and talk to me about it? To console me? Isn't that part of your job?"

"Do you want me to try and console you, John?"

"No," I said. (This was opening enough, and I grabbed at it.) "It would be pointless for you to try and argue with me. There is darkness and betrayal all around us. If you even tried to speak of hope, it would be a mockery."

The little priest was silent for a moment. Then he spoke quietly: "I have hope, John Kemp, because my hope is grounded in Good. For weeks, our one topic of conversation has been evil. Its varieties, its cunning. Its plans. Now it has become a topic that is tragically personal to you. But the real strength, and power, and thrilling creativity comes, not from evil, but from goodness. Stoker was wrong about that. Deeply wrong. The captivation of evil is on par with a cheap parlor trick in comparison with the awesome, fascinating wonderment of the Good. For that Goodness is Love."

"Love," I said. "Don't preach on that theme. It couldn't save Esther. How can it stand up to this bloody carnage?"

"That, my friend, is precisely what it does do. And it is the only thing that can save Miss Raveland. But to appreciate that perfect paradox, you must see with the eyes of faith. I can't impose them on you."

"I believe enough," I said. "I admit to you that I believe in vampires. If that doesn't make me a man of faith, I don't know what would!"

He shrugged gently. "So you believe what your senses have told you. You have considered with your reason if your senses are reliable, and decided that they are. That is simply an application of the same principles that have guided you thus far. Faith in God is a completely different business. I tell you again: vampires are nothing in comparison. A petty, silly mockery. Dancing paper dolls in the shadows, compared to the wonder of God. Why do you think these dark happenings ring so false? Because they are nothing new. Evil can create nothing. It can only corrupt what is and set up shadowy negative realities. Thus the vampire is a dark, mundane corruption of our sacrament."

"All of that nonsense aside—I am sorry, Father, that is what it seems to be to me—all of that aside, what sort of God allows such things to happen?"

"Do you not see, my friend? If evil things did not occur, and if man did not struggle with the curse of death, then every man would give in to vice, and in the ruthless quest for pleasure, and for power, the world would drown in blood."

"Is it not doing so now?"

"No, it is not. For there is yet Goodness, and it is far more powerful than any vampire."

"The Goodness you call God?"

"Yes. And the inherent goodness of some men who, even if they cannot or will not see the fullness of what has been revealed, resist evil and seek the good."

"You mean men like Inspector Harris," I said.

"Yes," he said slowly. "He has a great deal of virtue. But when I spoke, John Kemp, I was actually thinking of you."

That was something to silence me, indeed.

"Suffer through your grief," he went on. "I hope you will find that, though you will likely see horrors that even now you cannot contemplate, your final and lasting remembrance will be of goodness. The goodness of your fellows, which is but a tiny reflection of Goodness Himself."

We had arrived back at the police station. A few of the officers nodded as we entered, and we walked straight back to the inspector's office, unchecked. Father Thomas Edmund knocked, but there was no answer.

Collins was standing nearby, watching us. He frowned and stepped forward. "He's in there, I'm certain, sir. He had visitors some time ago, but he's alone now."

He knocked again, then tried the door. After a breathless moment, the door opened and we walked in.

Inspector Harris sat very still at his desk, very still indeed. At first I wondered if he were in some sort of fit, frozen and unconscious of our presence. In a flash, I even suspected something worse and wondered if we were staring at yet another dead body. Then I saw him breathing, saw the red color in his face, and realized that he was holding himself still by a masterly effort. Inspector Harris was, it seemed, enraged.

"What's happened?" I asked. "What is it?"

"We have had a visitor," he said through gritted teeth. "Two visitors, in fact. Your friend the count. And his close friend ... the superintendent."

I was not sure which was rankling the man more—the visit by the titled foreigner, or the presence of his superior officer.

"Yes," Harris continued. "The count came himself. He was most anxious. He wants us to find his secretary. He fears foul play. The superintendent reassured him that we will do everything in our power to support and protect so valuable an émigré to our fair city."

"Did you ..." He glared at me, and I faltered, but asked the question all the same: "I beg your pardon, Inspector Harris, but did you speak to the superintendent of the situation?"

"Of course I did, man. As far as he is concerned, there's nothing of note going on in the city—nothing to justify the overthrow of his ambitions. He has his eyes on a seat somewhere or other, there's no doubt of that."

He was standing now, glaring at a large, detailed map of the city which hung on his wall. "Nothing of note," he grumbled. "Nothing." With a rapid movement, he grabbed up a handful of little colored pins and began to stab them into the map with targeted precision. "Nothing going on *here*—Charles Sidney. Or *here*—the tart, Stella. Or *here*—that girl, the first one for Mr. Kemp. And certainly nothing *there*—just a librarian, after all. Or *there*—the alleyway murder. Nothing to worry us *here*—four other murders, minor bloody affairs, the killings of nobodies, hardly deserving of remark in the press. And *there's* your home, Mr. Kemp. And then there were those other scattered attacks—but I am sure you can add more, Gilroy. Or *there, there, there* ... No matter those little reports Peters has compiled—so many suspicious nothings. Nothing, nothing, nothing. And we can't forget last night—two for *those* nothings, with the worthless drunk and the lady. So many nothings. So let us go and help the superintendent to promotion, damn him."

When he was finished, he stood back and surveyed his efforts. Scattered constellations of pins. London, a veritable voodoo doll.

I waited for Father Thomas Edmund to speak, but he motioned to me to remain silent.

Finally, Inspector Harris spoke again.

"Collins," he snapped, "fetch Peters."

As the door closed behind the dark-haired, satirical policeman, Harris nodded at both of us with grim determination. "To hell to policy," he growled. "I'm in."

Chapter 24

19 January 1901: Brixton

(From Mina Murray Harker's journal) *Well, you know what we have to contend against; but we, too, are not without strength. We have on our side power of combination—a power denied to the vampire kind; we have sources of science; we are free to act and think; and the hours of the day and the night are ours equally. In fact, so far as our powers extend, they are unfettered, and we are free to use them. We have self-devotion in a cause, and an end to achieve which is not a selfish one. These things are much.*

"I'm very confused, Father, on one point," I said, as we sat, uncomfortably crowded together in the back of a closed police wagon, rattling through the streets. "How are we supposed to tell the difference between a vampire and someone who is just working under the influence of the undead?"

"That's one of the complicating factors in this business," he said, settling back to deliver the invited lecture. (He was sitting on that large, black bag he had carried on our visit to Adele Lawson so long before. I wondered, once again, what the strange bag contained.) "This is also where dear Bram Stoker oversimplified the situation. There are particular degrees of complicity—the primary or dominant undead; the secondary or servile undead, who yet have a demonic free will, but are clearly subordinate to the more powerful rank; the minion undead, who have little free will to speak of and serve the dominant undead before they even indulge their distorted passions (here you will find some of those bizarre, bestial characteristics that express the unnatural state of the creature—your pink-eyed reptile-like lurkers, John); the living minion, who, either in hopes of attaining undead powers or out of its own distorted passions, serves the undead, and even can indulge in practices common to the undead (such as blood drinking, flesh eating, or other victimization of the living)—these minions are heavily influenced by the mesmerizing powers of higher-ranking undead; the victims, who, contrary to popular belief, are not usually destined for a vampiric afterlife. Those who are usually fall under a minion category, for there must be some degree of choice—beyond the choice made by a severely weakened will—in pursuit of that course."

"That's ... quite a lot to think about," I said. "How do you suggest we balance all of that if we're in the midst of a full-scale battle? Are we to stop and inquire as to the degree of complicity in a given attacker?"

Father Thomas Edmund chuckled. "Of course not, my friend. All of this is to say: firstly, defend yourself nobly; secondarily, respect the inherent goodness of the defiled body of any attacker; and thirdly, leave the analysis and ... redressment ... of all such attackers, living, dead, and undead, to me and to my brethren."

Peters coughed. "I am not sure, sir, that I can promise to take into consideration the inherent goodness of anybody—or any *body*—that happens to be coming for my throat with teeth or claws or a knife or whatever it might be. I might, at that moment, be otherwise distracted."

"Why, Peters," said Inspector Harris. "I do believe you have a sense of humor after all."

At this backward compliment, Peters blinked several times and fell silent once more.

We were on our way to the first of many raids in a complex plan of operations. I call them "raids", but Harris was insistent on this point. "We are following the superintendent's orders in seeking out a lost secretary. That we fully expect to stumble upon bloody carnage, and that we are prepared for it, isn't something that needs to go into our official report."

He was armed, I knew, and, after a momentary hesitation, he asked me if I knew how to handle a pistol. I said that I did, but my experience was not impressive. I was not a notable marksman, even on the occasions when I had received and accepted invitations to hunt in the country.

He considered this honest response then quietly handed me a pistol anyway. "Just don't shoot one of us," he said with wry solemnity.

The night was silent when we arrived outside a large, abandoned warehouse, an unhappy relic of industrial strength. The owner of the attached factory had staked his life and his fortune on black bombazine. He had relied on the example of the widowed queen, and assumed that oppressive grief would remain a popular affectation for decades to come. Fashion had decreed otherwise, and bankruptcy, swathed in bolts of unused and unusable black mourning, was the legacy of a once-rich merchant and entrepreneur.

This history was told to me conversationally by Inspector Harris at a later date.

"Who owns the property now?" I would then ask.

He would shake his head at that. "It is unclear. The owner took his own life. There's a fierce battle raging in the family over it. Unhappiness heaped on unhappiness."

When I first stood outside the building in that chill darkness, I knew nothing of the tragic history of the place, and yet I felt uneasy and glanced over my shoulder against my will to see if someone—or some*thing*—were behind me.

It had seemed to me that Harris had chosen this place arbitrarily from that mess of pinned locations on his map. He ruminated aloud over them before announcing it: "No sense in beginning at the house. We're agreed it is a likely center of operations, but it would be asking for more trouble than we can handle. If we're going over the heads of those who'll make a lot of noise ... well ... it would be prudent not to storm the citadel first.

"Next obvious consideration: the do-goodery of doom." (The priest chuckled at that. The Inspector, it seemed, could creatively turn a phrase, when the mood was upon him.) "That's a nonstarter too. Begs for attention and undermines our work before we've even started.

"Next, we look toward likely outposts. Thanks to the investigations of Constable Peters"—that worthy and honorable representative of the law seemed unmoved by the commendation—"which have, it turns out, each received corroboration from Father Gilroy and his ... fellows, we list three places in particular: a warehouse in Brixton, a theatre in the West End, and a graveyard—Kensal Green."

Someone coughed rather nervously at this last. Inspector Harris continued on without comment: "The secretary may be hiding out in one of them—that's one reason to look. But more than that, I want to know what the hell is going on in those places. And we will begin tonight with the warehouse in Brixton."

Thus we planned, and thus we executed.

The approach to the warehouse was simple enough. Not a creature stirred. The only noise we could hear from the outside was a capricious wind.

After a careful inspection of the grounds, Inspector Harris chose our point of entrance. "Collins," he said, "work the lock."

The locked door thus circumvented, we crept in, single file, and stood together for some moments in silence and darkness.

"Now," said Harris in a sharp whisper, "in teams of three. Riley, Jones, Davis, go that way. Peters, Smith, Collins, go the opposite. Mitchell, stay with the priests and Mr. Kemp. Grimes and Stewart, come with me."

Two hours of searching followed, with no results.

One group reported on boxes of damp, rotting cotton. Peters nearly came to grief when a broken window fell in unexpectedly, but Smith pushed him out of the way at the last moment. I don't know what transpired between the three men, but Collins came back red-faced with resentment, and Peters looked righteously indignant.

"As useless as if his brain's addled," I heard him mutter under his breath.

Harris and his companions likewise seemed not to have found anything.

Mitchell had proved a singularly unimaginative companion, so our time had been spent in looking over a small expanse of space with nothing remarkable in it, beyond heaps of small, dead, Egyptian-looking bugs, which exuded a slight, sickening stench. I am no entomologist, but these dead creatures, which seemed to wear intricately designed plates of armor on their backs, were totally unknown to me.

"There's a cellar," said Peters, "and the door to it is bolted fast. It'll take more than a burglar's kit, Inspector."

"Break it down," was his stern response.

The splintering of the door made quite a noise.

"Well," said Harris dryly, "if there's anyone here, he knows we're here now too—if he didn't know already."

The stairway disclosed was singularly uninviting. The electric torches of the police danced around in an exploratory fashion, revealing darkness, cobwebs, and more heaps of those odd, distasteful little beetle corpses.

We made our way in silence and in single file. At the bottom of the stairs, we regrouped in a hallway. There were seven doors—three on the right, three on the left, and one at the very end of the hall.

"Come on, now," said Harris. "Forward we go, men."

The first room on the left appeared to be a rat burial ground—or unburial ground. There were carcasses in revolting abundance. I guessed there were at least eighty of them. Only one or two were moving, crawling over their dead fellows, pausing periodically to gnaw on a cold, bony leg.

The torch in front—held by Riley, I think—faltered and moved quickly away from the living vermin.

"All right," said Harris, his voice still calm. "Enough of that. Move on. Stewart and Grimes, you can take one last look and make sure we haven't missed anything."

The next three rooms revealed similar evidence of unuse and decay.

"This place must be where every rat in London comes to die," muttered someone at the back.

The fifth room was full of wooden boxes or crates. At Inspector Harris' command, the policemen broke these open, to disclose dark, moist soil, with a long, thin indentation at its center—as would be made by a body resting in the dirt. Once again, a parallel: did not Stoker's count bring with him fifty boxes of ancient earth? After we explored these silently, three of the friars remained behind. I remembered a similar scene in my reading of that strange novel and assumed that they intended to perform some sort of exorcism. The black bag, which so intrigued me, appeared once more. I would have stayed to see for the sake of satisfying my growing curiosity, but Father Thomas Edmund (perhaps reading my mind) gently nudged me along.

"Father Thomas Edmund, look." One of the young friars whispered it and shone a torch into the sixth room, which was empty except for a large pile of scattered objects in its exact center. They looked as if they had been thrown or heaped there by reckless hands.

I looked over the brother's shoulder and thought they were somehow familiar. A moment later, and I could pick out some of the effects of their ritual and sacrament. Gold cups. Small boxes—like, and yet unlike, round snuffboxes, with crosses on their lids. A sculpted Madonna or some saint, smashed now so that what remained of the serenely pious face looked mildly alarmed. A vast treasure trove of despoiled vessels, statues, and other Papist paraphernalia.

It was the first time I saw anything but serenity on the face of Father Thomas Edmund Gilroy. His forehead puckered in mild irritation, and a cloud passed over those bright eyes. He was distressed, I thought, and I looked away to spare myself the embarrassment of seeing tears in his eyes. Then he spoke and I realized that I was mistaken in interpreting his countenance thus; this was not tremulous sorrow—this was wroth.

"Brother Paul," he said, "run back and inform Father Reginald."

No one stopped or questioned him. Leaving the Papists to deal with what was, to them, a dark sacrilege, I continued on my way with the policemen.

The end of the hallway was oppressively dark—like hell, I thought, with a fleeting remembrance of Dantean cantos. I almost wished I had paid closer attention during that earlier classical training. Not that the Italian master armed his readers with anything like vampire-slaying munitions, but perhaps the *Divina Commedia* might have lent me some greater understanding that would have brought, if not greater strength, greater solace in this walking nightmare. Such thoughts were absurd, but the very absurdity made the whole thing more horrible.

"Shhh!" a voice hissed in my ear, and I realized that I was panting with anxiety in the midst of my quasi-nostalgic imaginings.

"I am not well," I told myself. "I am not well. It's only darkness, after all. What, in truth, can be lurking down here except for those rats?"

Inspector Harris pushed open the door to the seventh room.

New dampness. And a strange odor, conflating the senses into one: it smelled warm; it smelled sticky; it smelled fresh; it smelled eerily familiar and yet bizarrely foreign.

Blood.

The electric torch danced around the room. A horrifying spectacle was thereby disclosed, shown in fragments. Just that mosaic of horror was enough; the hand holding the torch weakened and dropped it. The torch rolled across the floor. Before it was lost in a dark corner, it whirled around, continuing the surreal effect of sporadic, disjointed revelation. Then darkness.

"A torch!" commanded Inspector Harris sharply to his men.

Nothing happened.

"Give us light now!" he said more urgently.

Then suddenly, as if an unseen hand had dumped a gallon of fuel on the cinders of the abandoned fireplace in the wall opposite us, a blinding flame leapt up. The room was ablaze with light. All eyes were fixed on the unholy sight, freshly illuminated, of the bloody corpse of Victor Montrose crucified upside down against the far wall. His chest had been sliced open—or perhaps torn. A strange conflation of autopsy and animal dismemberment. His face, transfixed in horror, was almost unrecognizable at first, from the pallor of death, contrasting so starkly with the dried streaks of blood crusting chin, cheeks, forehead, and hair.

The fire, so strangely roused, now vanished as quickly, and we were engulfed again in absolute darkness.

The contents of my stomach rose to my mouth. I could hear someone retching helplessly against a blood-stained wall beside me.

Several hours later, when the warehouse, its unwholesome cargo dispatched to the police morgue (a fascinating gift to odd Dr. Lewis), I turned in weary expectation to Inspector Harris.

"What now?" I asked.

"Now," he said grimly, "we take a little rest before our next foray into hell."

The police wagon left Father Thomas Edmund Gilroy, his brethren, and me back at the priory. I collapsed on my bed in the guestroom. When I closed my eyes, exhaustion at first brought on immediate sleep.

Two hours later, I found myself lying in the bright, brutal light of day, with the vision of Anghelescu bending over Esther so dramatically present in my head that I could have screamed. My hands were clenched together upon the quilt in a furious, futile attempt at vengeance. I released that stranglehold on the bedclothes and found that I had left sharp white indentations in my own flesh.

After another hour of attempted rest, I gave up. I rose from the bed and went to perform morning ablutions. After splashing my face with water from the basin, I surveyed its haggard, unshaved ruggedness. This would not do. I might have been cast, against my will, as the lovesick, tragic hero, but I need not look the part.

When I left the room, meeting up with Father Thomas Edmund Gilroy in the hall, I was shaved, neatly dressed, and presentable, though pale from my lack of sleep and from the trauma of what we had seen.

"Do you think that this will work?" I asked Father Thomas Edmund Gilroy as we made our way back to the police station together in preparation for the evening's festivities.

"There are many things in our favor," he said, "but the difficulty is that we are not simply seeking a run-of-the-mill criminal, who conveniently leaves clues for us to follow. This is a demonically clever creature, and one who, I fear, has anticipated our every move thus far."

"How can you say that?" I demanded. "We found that gruesome corpse—could he have wanted it?"

"I don't know," he said. "And yet ... there was something in that scene that felt ... staged. We were looking for horrors, so we found them."

338

"What do you think . . . why do you think . . ." I couldn't articulate it. The very thought of Victor Montrose was too sickening.

"What happened in that room?" Father Thomas Edmund frowned. "It is not an easy thing to recommend, but do not think much on it."

"Do you understand it?"

"My friend, in my work I have learned a great deal of the activities of evil creatures. I have studied many theories of the creation of these creatures—how and why the natural law can be circumvented or, to be more precise, twisted into the unnatural law that governs the creatures."

This was close again to something that had troubled me. "What about the victims? Are they . . . doomed? Doomed to become creatures of darkness?"

"Rest easy, my friend. That is yet another thing that dear Stoker muddled—drawing from folklore, of course, and that's a frighteningly unreliable source. The peasant mind can misinterpret many things."

I stopped in the street and turned, so that I could be sure I understood him. "So you are saying that Esther will not become a vampire?"

He stopped too and met my eye unwaveringly. "Not necessarily," he said. "In fact, if, as I believe to be the case, this was the first assault and not a reciprocal, unnatural indulgence—one where she was so clearly a terrified and unwilling victim . . . yes, rest easy, my friend. Truly, there must be a degree of willingness, even from the broken will of a vicious victim. She does have a long and hard path. What she most needs is healing and safety. She is not likely to suffer the lust for blood, but I fear she is doomed to horrifying nightmares. For now, she is where she is most safe and most likely of care—the care she truly requires. Meanwhile, our best course of action is to continue our quest for the dominant undead. As we make our way through each tier of the hierarchy of evil, we will come closer to vanquishing him and ending his rule."

"This all sounds rather complex," I said irritably.

"The rules—or, rather, the antirules—of the undead have a certain logic. These are helpful to our investigation, for they teach us how he is likely to behave. We cannot, however, determine precisely from those antirules what it is that has actually happened and continues to happen here in London. It has become clear that, as is his wont, the dominant undead seeks to establish himself here, gathering his minions about him and seducing new recruits to his undead army."

"Army?" I said, dismayed. "How many of these creatures do you expect we must battle?"

He shook his head. "I cannot say. I do not believe he has had enough success for it to be a full-scale war, and yet we clearly *are* at war. That does not mean you should anticipate a battlefield. Envision instead the hidden battlefield. The insidiousness of his attack comes from the fact that so much, on the surface, appears to be other than it is. Montrose's body—even that can be explained as the act of a madman. Nothing in that warehouse directly pointed to the dominant undead. Nothing pointed to the creature you yourself now seek."

"But the blood!" I protested.

"There are plenty of bloody-minded villains," he said, "and not all of them are vampires."

This was a likely truth, but it was not helpful in clarifying the situation for me.

The streets were busy now, though the cold air dissuaded many from venturing out. There were no wanderers on the street that afternoon; everyone who passed us seemed intent and focused on a particular goal, and eager to reach that goal, whatever it might be, without undue distraction or deviation. I found the cold air bracing, like a sharp whip to rouse a sleeping horse for a race.

For some time, the priest and I walked in silence. My mind was working through a line of questions, mostly derived from my vague remembrance of the vampiric rules outlined in that ridiculous novel.

"It seems," I said finally and in some irritation, "that Bram Stoker has a great deal to answer for."

We had arrived outside the police station. The door opened just as I spoke, and Inspector Harris walked out.

"Well, Mr. Kemp," he said, almost smiling, "you'll have a chance to tell him that. We're on our way to the Lyceum."

Chapter 25

18 January 1901: London's West End

(From Jonathan Harker's journal) *The great door swung back. Within, stood a tall old man, clean shaven save for a long white moustache, and clad in black from head to foot, without a single speck of colour about him anywhere. He held in his hand an antique silver lamp, in which the flame burned without chimney or globe of any kind, throwing long quivering shadows as it flickered in the draught of the open door. The old man motioned me in with his right hand with a courtly gesture, saying in excellent English, but with a strange intonation:—"Welcome to my house! Enter freely and of your own will!"*

The lights of the Lyceum Theatre shone unenthusiastically in that pale light of a waning winter afternoon. That well-loved house was then on the brink of a dramatic renovation, though the building could not yet know its fated rebirth. That day, it appeared tired, though resting on the laurels of its vast and mostly honorable history. That crowning theatre of the West End for over two hundred years could well stand upon the skeletons of her more sordid chapters—though waxworks from Madame Tussaud's earliest foray into the public eye still lurked in her basements. Was this place not home to the greatness of Dickensian theatricals? And now, was it not home to that remarkable personality, known for his ghostly theatrics and his air of perfect gentility? Had not the shade of Shakespeare himself been graced by this great man's attention? Had not the crowds come in steady adulation for decades, to gaze upon each dramatic, sweeping gesture, and to weep or laugh or cheer or applaud or shiver at his cue? The greatness of the Lyceum, even had it been swept away by a historian's critical eye, must yet remain, for now her greatness was embodied in Sir Henry Irving.

We arrived at that honorable temple to English opera at an hour of theatrical limbo, between the early morning silence and the thrilling evening bustle. It was yet too early for any but last-minute ticket purchasers; the evening's entertainment would not commence for several more hours. The actors were likely resting (too important to arrive hours before curtain call). Theatrical staff, on the other hand, must already be present, hurrying to prepare for that noble, soul-inspiring moment when the curtain would rise and Sir Henry Irving, England's greatest living actor, walked out upon the stage.

I did not quite understand why, but we ventured out in significantly reduced numbers: Harris, Father Thomas Edmund, myself, and—a late and much lamented addition—Toby Barnes.

Barnes had appeared close on our heels a few moments after we left our cab in the theatre district ("To attract less attention," Harris said).

"Well!" cried the journalist. "This *is* a delightful surprise! Glad I am to meet up with you, Harris! It's been extraordinary how difficult it has been to catch up with you busy, busy men. I won't ask for a statement now, Harris, but I'll happily follow along and learn what the police have been up to of late. I hear a rumor of Victor Montrose that I would dearly love to hear you confirm—especially considering his recent capture (and escape) ..." He trailed off invitingly, his eyes wide with a charming (and studied) look of innocence.

"Barnes," said Harris, "swallow your sweet talk. If you keep your mouth shut, you can come along. Not a word, though. Not a word. And if you so much as think of opening that little book of yours while we try to conduct our interview, I'll throw you in a cell."

Barnes grinned at me, mouthed, "Good man, Harris!" and happily joined our little group.

At the stage door, I expected Inspector Harris to take the lead. I was therefore surprised when he quietly stepped aside and Father Thomas Edmund Gilroy spoke to the grizzly, unsmiling Cerberus who barred our path with all three of his unfriendly heads.

"Good evening, Pearson," he said. "We are here to speak with Mr. Stoker."

Pearson did not seem pleased at the thought. "It's well nigh starting time," he growled. "Mr. Stoker's sure to be occupied."

"Perhaps so," the priest said calmly. "We will wait while you go and see. Thank you, Pearson."

The gray-haired man frowned heavily, drawing his eyebrows down over his glaring eyes. Then he shrugged, spryly leapt down from the tall barstool on which he perched at his gloomy little window, and hobbled off to seek the Lyceum's manager.

We stood and shivered there in the unfriendly cold for some minutes before he returned. He moved slowly, a testament to his unwillingness and displeasure at bringing good news.

"Mr. Stoker will see you," he said grudgingly, adding, as he opened the door for us: "Go down that passage and be quick about it. Sir Henry will be here soon, and he won't like to catch you all here right before curtain."

Father Thomas Edmund, who seemed to know the way, led us down the prescribed passage—dark and cluttered with props and pieces of theatrical sets, punctuated by the occasional large red door—and knocked at one of the doors.

The door opened, disclosing a red-haired giant of a man—tall, heavyset, with friendly blue eyes, and a sandy beard. Silently but smilingly, Mr. Abraham Stoker nodded, welcoming us into his little office with quiet hospitality.

As Father Thomas Edmund made the introductions, I looked at the man closely, trying to see in his face something of darkness and mystery, a sign of the lurid imagination that had created that weird novel. Try though I might, I couldn't see it.

"Well, now," said our host in a deep Irish voice as we settled into our chairs (the Irish lilt was a reassurance; weren't they all superstitious talebearers?). "And the guards with you too! This seems to be serious. Have you come to speak of the book again, Father?"

"In a way, Bram, I have."

"And to tell me I need to be taking greater care of myself? Finding a place to hide from the bogeys." He chuckled.

"I know that you are unlikely to take such a caution to heart, Bram," the priest replied, "so I don't bother wasting my breath on it."

"Why, Father," said the giant good-humoredly, "I hope you don't think I am dismissive. Florence wouldn't like that at all." He glanced with easy affection over a small framed portrait on his desk—the picture of a remarkable beauty (his wife, as Father Thomas Edmund later explained). "Florence thinks very highly indeed of you, Father. Especially now as she's turned Papist. Good enough for her. Keeps her happy. Her mother now—but I am too busy at the moment to bother with being scared off." He shook his head gently, as if soothing an anxious child. Then he grinned. "It seems to me you think more of that book than most other men."

"Such as . . . your employer?"

His smile faded. "No, he didn't like it much." At first I thought this was wounded pride; then I realized he was earnest in his defense of the man who had rejected his work: "He's made for grander things, truly. And that's the real work, you know."

"Mr. Stoker," interposed Harris, "we have reason to believe that certain criminal activity may have taken place here in the theatre."

Then Stoker frowned. "That's a fret," he said, quite seriously. "Not in my theatre. I can promise you, we're all above board here, and I keep the place—and the personnel—shipshape." He considered it, still frowning. "What sort of trouble did you suspect? Is it still that business with those murders?"

The priest responded slowly, as if choosing his words with care. "It is related to those, yes, Bram. And some circles we suspect of dabbling in some dark practices."

"Now, Father," the charm was back again (and the clear disbelief with it), "don't you be starting on the Masons again. I told you. It's just a sort of club. They do all sorts of good things. I'm not for it myself, but Sir Henry, he's one, and a nobler man you wouldn't know—or a greater."

346

Father Thomas Edmund did not argue.

Inspector Harris appeared to be perfectly at ease, if not completely distracted from the conversation. I wondered if this was a sign that he was growing impatient over this unproductive visit; I surely was.

"But ...," said Stoker cautiously, "if you were to ask me truthfully of strange things—not criminal, mind. Just strange. Well, we've had some of those lately."

Here was something. I probably looked my eagerness, for the manager glanced at me briefly, then returned to the priest. He edged his chair closer in a confessional manner and nodded. "Yes, we've had a few little things. Nothing so much that you'd notice and not, as I said, criminal. Nothing of that sort in my theatre. But we've had three people leave suddenly, and without warning. Just come in one morning and there's a note. Stagehand—though he wasn't very good and likely to go soon anyway. Girl— Winifred Fraser. She played a few minor roles, here and there. And a conceited young ass named Junius Booth, who had a few minor roles and thought he was ... well. He would have left soon too, if he hadn't taken himself off without warning."

Stoker broke off and suddenly grew still, his head raised, like a trained dog, listening carefully for a quiet, almost indistinguishable sound.

Footsteps walking down the hall.

Stoker looked up at the clock. Then he jumped to his feet, hurried to the door, and opened it.

There, before our eyes, was a tall, thin man, with a long face and a marked air of gentility. At first, we saw him only in outline, for the light hit him from behind and hid his features in shadow. The black column struck a chord in my remembrance, and I thought of descriptions of Count

Dracula in Stoker's novel. Then the figure moved, becoming more visible; for a moment, the aging lines of the face, and the less certain bearing, intensified the memory. The next moment, the sense of the count faded; I recognized the eloquent eyes, brooding eyebrows, and ascetical chin of Sir Henry Irving well enough from various Shakespearean vehicles.

He did not speak—a lesser man might have demanded to know who we were and what we were doing in his theatre at that unseasonable hour. I believe he did not do so half from gentlemanly courtesy, and half because such a petty concern was too far beneath his attention to his higher calling. I remembered vaguely that someone had told me that, when she mocked his acting (out of pique at his neglect of his family), Irving had unemotionally left his wife forever. Looking at that high priest of the drama, I could well believe it.

"Bram," he said quietly, "I need you."

Then he swept down the hallway to his dressing room.

That was the end of any possible interview that night. As I looked at the red-haired giant, I thought unaccountably of John the Baptist—this man was no voice crying out anywhere for anything; but, in the light of the inescapable greatness of Irving, Stoker became less and did so with serenity, if not open joy.

He nodded a quick farewell to us and hurried after the actor.

We remained in silence in the manager's room for some moments. Father Thomas Edmund was thoughtful, Harris watched the ruminating priest, and Barnes and I watched them both—the journalist endeavoring not to fidget, but clearly finding the entire situation exasperating to his over-curious mind.

Finally, the inspector spoke. "If you are planning to take on the Masons, Gilroy," he commented dryly, "we really will be in for it. The lists of influential men … it's really not worth contemplating."

For a moment, Father Thomas Edmund did not respond. Then he looked up and met Harris' eye. "I think," he said, "we should stay and see the play."

I do not know how he arranged it, but we were soon seated in the wings, away from the bustle, but with a clear view of the play.

Setting aside the critical worth of *Robespierre* (which, even from my limited expertise as a critic, seems somewhat questionable), it was a magnificent performance. Full of pathos. When he stepped upon the stage, Irving's age and the recent illness which reportedly had robbed the stage of his presence for a time—all of it shrank away. Irving captured every nuance of his chosen character, from the suspicious tyrant to a man crippled by terror, remorse, and deep feeling for the son he had never known, for whom he would give his own life. I wondered if anything remotely resembling historical truth had been used as the source for this inventive exploration of the Terror—but that thought came later, for there was little chance for the willing suspension of disbelief to be shaken here. When the eye could turn from that one, striking figure, or be distracted from the tender sweetness of Ellen Terry, his renowned counterpart, the dramatic spectacular effects captured the imagination in their own right. Blood, romance, and melodrama under the deft hands of the master craftsman of the drama. The curtain fell, and the applause continued.

The audience was gone, and backstage was transformed into the loud, hectic bedlam of business and craft before Father Thomas Edmund, ever watchful, rose from his seat.

"Well," said Toby Barnes (who had been stretching, yawning, and tapping his foot with nervous impatience for at least ten minutes), "that was all very fine, and thanks for the treat, but I am not quite sure ..."

Stoker hurried up, as if he had half forgotten us in the midst of all of the pressing demands on his time. Indeed, he seemed to be the busiest of the entire company, keeping everything running smoothly, supervising everything and everyone, and above all, maintaining to perfection the arena for the work of his great employer.

"Well, now, Father," he said, "I'm sure you enjoyed it."

"I did indeed," Father Thomas Edmund said politely. He glanced at Inspector Harris, who nodded in agreement of some unspoken question. The priest turned again to Stoker.

"Might we speak with one of the cast?"

The giant's eyes narrowed slightly. "Why would you be asking that?"

"We'd like to put a few questions to him. In your presence, of course."

"And who would it be?"

"Mr. Tabb."

Stoker considered this quietly. Then nodded. He turned to the company and barked out a command—not unkindly, but with an impressive and clear authority. "Tabb. Where's Tabb?"

The actors had scattered to their rooms, reappearing here and there in various stages of dishabille.

A woman still in her towering wig (rat-infested, if it were real) volunteered in shrill tones: "He was here a moment ago."

A few men were nearby, and one of them pointed off to the side of the now-abandoned stage. "There he is. Over there!"

We followed the line of his hand and saw a young man, wiry and unappealing, with feathery down for hair. He saw our eyes were upon him, and, after blinking and gazing from face to face with an increasing expression of panic in his dull little eyes, lunged into a heap of discarded props, and pulled out a sword—a sword that glinted with visible and real intent.

Before I could cry out, Father Thomas Edmund moved with an agility of which I had not thought him capable, pulled a large spar from amid the props and, swinging it boldly and resolutely before him, struck the sword from the quaking hands of Tabb.

The company stood about, staring, dumbfounded, at the little priest. But Father Thomas Edmund Gilroy simply tossed the spear aside and looked down upon the crouching, cowed, shrinking creature before him on the floor.

"Don't hurt me," Tabb whined, holding his hands over his eyes. "Don't hurt me."

"Now, you!" said Harris, who had overcome his momentary shock and hurried to the priest's side, where he now stood in the fullness of his authority. "You're coming along with us to answer questions, Tabb. Here there! Clear this stage! And Barnes, go on out and call the station to send a wagon. And be quick about it."

The journalist left with alacrity (his reluctance to depart this eventful scene superseded by his desire to remain in the inspector's good graces). The crowd dispersed unwillingly, obedient more to Stoker than to Harris. The manager rejoined us when the last stagehand had scrambled away.

Harris bent down, interrupting this grotesque feast, to bind Tabb's hand. The mewling wretch recoiled from his touch and crouched, muttering and moaning to himself,

blood staining his mouth. "He is bleeding," said someone—I did not notice who. I was too disgustingly absorbed
watching Tabb sucking feverishly at his wound. He looked
up at us, a revolting little creature, weeping and sniffling
and grossly pathetic. "Oh, sir, it wasn't me. Not really. It
was him. I won't be hanged for it—not when it was him.
Protect me from him! You must protect me!"

"You'll tell us what you know and be quick about it,"
said Harris sternly.

"It was all him—that Kilbronson. He's a fiend. I'm just
a nobody. Kept me around to do his dirty work. I never
thought I'd . . . I'd be caught up in his murderings!"

And the awful little man began to weep loud, self-
pitying tears.

"Kilbronson," said Barnes, who had reappeared at my
elbow. And he whistled for emphasis.

All of a sudden, life began to move with an eerie rapidity, as if we were racing down a path to a certain, inevitable ending. The marble was well on its prescribed course,
and we had but to plummet down to our due doom.

Half an hour later, Tabb was deposited in a cell at the
station, and Collins and Mitchell left with him. Ten minutes after that, we were again in a carriage, rattling through
the streets on our way to the Masonic temple—to the
inner sanctum of the Temple of the Golden Dawn.

Our numbers had increased; all of those familiar faces
were once again with us. As we hurried along on that
inexorable path, Peters delivered a detailed account of his
visit (which he had made with Collins, Davis, Reilly, and
Stewart) to Kensal Green.

The transformation of the little hamlet of Kensal Green
to a busy suburb had been gradual. I couldn't imagine the
place was of much importance in early days. Sheep farmers

who had always been sheep farmers lived and died quietly and, as far as London was concerned, meant little in the course of history. Some things changed. The Grand Junction Canal and the brick works. The railway came and went and came again.

But Kensal Green is known for none of these. Kensal Green is the burial ground of the great city.

I could well imagine the scene—mist settling, and garrulous birds filling the air with unwholesome clamor in the dusky eventide. The gravestones so tightly heaped upon each other as if the dead had brought the crowded rush of the London street with them to this resting place. Some of the more grandiose monuments standing out with ghostly ostentation in the misty air. The rich atmosphere of the railway station finding dramatic counterpoint in this dreary place. Imagination plays tricks on the unsuspecting. One can too easily think a tree a goblin. But I could see in my mind's eye a shadowy figure among the tombs. I would have registered its presence with conscientious cynicism ... then, as comprehension dawned, I would stand still, my arms crossed against my chest to steady the beating of my heart ...

That was my imagination, of course. Peters, who is singularly lacking in that faculty, gave his report simply, precisely, and unemotionally.

"Our investigation proceeded as follows: we spoke with ten residents of the town, names and addresses listed in the official report. Each reported some degree of suspicious activity. Repetition of certain details confirms the fact that all of this has been discussed commonly by the townsfolk. Hard to discover what has really happened, in that case, of course. Regardless of the unreliability of each interviewee, we did track down a central area for these activities, a

353

central area in the graveyard itself. Exploration of that site brought us to a particular mausoleum—that belonging to the Kilbronson family."

I started at this seemingly gratuitous confirmation of our current errand, but neither Inspector Harris nor Father Thomas Edmund Gilroy commented on it, and Barnes knew better than to risk his standing with Harris by venturing to speak. Peters continued on unperturbed. "We gained access. Inside the mausoleum, we discovered six bodies in various degrees of decay, and evidence of violent treatment of the corpses by person—or persons unknown."

For several blocks, while that droning voice went on, I walked along, unhearing. My mind was trapped in that dark place of death, imagining with nauseating detail the abuse of those lifeless bodies. And we were on our way to confront the man who could do such a thing.

And yet . . . and yet. How quickly everything seemed to be moving. After months of slow, steady work, now we were sprinting. Kilbronson, Kilbronson, Kilbronson. So many questions answered, so rapidly—almost as it might in a lowbrow novel, which seeks, without sophistication of craft or thought, to tie up all loose ends in the final chapter. Perhaps this is what police work was like. I tried to feel confident that all would soon be well, but what of Esther? What of that Hungarian secretary? For his face still haunted me. When it rose up, disembodied, in my mind, taunting, streaked with her blood . . . the mere thought washed all feelings and passions away in a thunderous, rising wave of rage.

We arrived at the temple of the Freemasons at around nine in the morning. It was already busy—I wondered if there were special occasion for so many men to be present at once at such an early hour.

"We're here to see Mr. Kilbronson," said Inspector Harris. "My name is Inspector Harris. You can take us to him now, sir."

The young, well-dressed man at the door blinked a few times, as if considering, then opened the door and nodded.

Such a surreal march was that, through those marble halls, over the black-and-white tiles. Inspector Harris and Peters, with a flock of junior constables at their heels— Jones, Davis, Smith, Grimes, and Stewart. Toby Barnes. Father Thomas Edmund. Me. Trotting along behind our guide, on our way to apprehend the villain Kilbronson. I wished I could shake that disquieting feeling that, trapped as we were in this dramatic, inevitable path, we were at the same time caught up in a gross anticlimax.

We came to Kilbronson in that familiar room where the Temple of the Golden Dawn had interviewed me so many months earlier. With him were Mr. William Harper, Sir Douglas Wetheringdon, and Miss Philippa Young. They seemed to be engaged in a business meeting of some sort, but when we entered Kilbronson stood up, something like eagerness in his manner.

"Good morning, Mr. Kilbronson," said the inspector. "My name is Harris. You may recall we spoke some time ago regarding the disappearance of your wife. Would you please come with us, sir? We'd like a word down at the station."

Kilbronson's cheeks were pink, and his eyes were shining with unhealthy brightness.

"You've come," he panted. "You've come. Tell me why."

Harris paused. "We'd prefer to discuss that at the station, sir."

"I'm ready, I'm ready. I am prepared. Now is the time." Kilbronson had closed his eyes, repeating this little mantra over and over, as if chanting it to himself. His companions were looking at each other in discomforted alarm. The representatives of the law moved with slow, but deliberate movements, spreading throughout the room—a net of constraint in case the man made any movement.

Kilbronson opened his eyes. "I shall not go with you," he said to Harris, "and you shall not seek to restrain me."

"Now, sir," said Harris evenly, "we don't want to have any trouble with you ..."

"You should do well to consider that," the man agreed solemnly, staring out at us with those wide, excited eyes. "You do not know what powers you provoke, or who it is you challenge."

"Certainly, sir. You know best. Let's go along to the station and discuss it there."

"Silence, menial!" The madness was now fully upon him, and he punctuated his raging words with gestures so overdone that Sir Henry Irving would have despaired. "The Empire itself," the lunatic raged, his eyes brilliant, "the sun does not set upon it. What of an Empire where the sun will not rise? Have you any conception of the power that now is mine? You fools. You petty little men. I shall have her in spite of you—have her and have more! And you shall not stop me."

In an instant, he leapt up on the long table, raced down its noble length, and jumped back to the ground at the doorway, knocking down Smith and Grimes as he did. I half expected him to pause at the door and make some parting declaration, but madness made him calculatingly prudent, perhaps, and he did not slack in his speed.

"After him!" barked Harris—even as he himself ran, pushing his startled constables aside in his effort to catch up with the surprisingly agile Kilbronson.

Peters was ahead of him and tracked his quarry with steady obsession. Down corridors they raced, up staircases, the constable dogging the lunatic, almost on his heels.

The group scattered; some followed Peters and Harris, some raced down other corridors to try and head the man off. Stewart and Davis remained to speak with the other members of the Temple of the Golden Dawn, who sat blinking and uncertain in the wake of the sudden descent of Kilbronson. Miss Young found her tongue first, and as I hurried along with Barnes and Father Thomas Edmund, I could hear her loudly dissociating their organization in every respect from the lunatic Edgar.

I was following Barnes, who, as the official force raced out the door, shouted: "Outside! I need to see it all!"

We reached the streets in due time and, as if on cue, a passerby shouted: "Good Lord! Is he mad? He'll fall!"

We looked up and saw Kilbronson upon the roof, as careless of his safety as a nimble mountain goat, or a drunken young Parisian engaged with his comrades in a footrace over the rooftops.

We could see Harris and Peters, too, cautiously following. Other constables followed even more slowly behind.

The crowds were gathering in the streets around us. A woman screamed. Men shouted up their horror and fascination.

Kilbronson had reached the far corner of the roof. Harris and Peters, only a few feet away, stopped sharply before him. The confrontation imminent, Kilbronson gazed down upon the crowd, his face gleeful, and back again in triumph to his breathless pursuers.

"Come now, Kilbronson," cried Inspector Harris. "There's nowhere else to go. Come with us. Step back from the edge."

The cornered man laughed shrilly and exultantly as he shook his head. "Now," he shrieked, "now you will see the full power of this creed!"

With a cry of ecstatic triumph, his eyes wild, Edgar Kilbronson leapt from the roof of the temple, his arms outspread as if in expectation of sudden, miraculous flight. As his body fell to the pavement—unchecked in its progress by intervention from heaven or hell—it was a tribute to the strength of his fanatical delusion that it was only in the very last moment, right before that sickening, wet noise of contact, that his face registered even a glimmer of surprise.

Chapter 26

19 January 1901: Hyde Park Police Station with Some Time in Camden

(From the log of the Demeter) *It was better to die like a man; to die like a sailor in blue water no man can object. But I am captain, and I must not leave my ship. But I shall baffle this fiend or monster, for I shall tie my hands to the wheel when my strength begins to fail, and along with them I shall tie that which He—It!—dare not touch; and then, come good wind or foul, I shall save my soul, and my honour as a captain.*

The following morning, I slept late. When I awoke and stretched in the pale winter sunshine, I took stock of myself. By the time I had found my way to bed, I had been so exhausted from that intense succession of eventful nights that I had fallen asleep almost before my head hit that exceptionally fluffy pillow (those friars lavished comforts on their guests—even such a long-staying guest as I!—and I rather suspected their own rooms were severely ascetical). I had not had a moment or a spark of energy left to consider my own emotions at the current state of affairs, or even really to stop and consider what that state of affairs was.

Kilbronson dead. What on earth did that mean?

In some ways, it seemed to mean everything. All of our investigations had led to him, not to the count, as I had expected—if not hoped. A megalomaniacal Englishman dabbling in demonology, guilty of dark murders across London. Nothing mysterious, nothing otherworldly about it. There we had it, and peace could now reign again in English hearts (and in mine too, as soon as ever I found a new home and removed myself from the company of addled Roman priests). Such would be the conclusion of John Kemp many months earlier.

And yet, in other ways, this death of Kilbronson satisfied nothing. What of all of those strange occurrences for which there was no clear, logical explanation? I could remember the voice of Father Thomas Edmund Gilroy—was I once again only crediting the report of my senses, however unlikely? Indeed, that was the critical, inescapable point. Kilbronson was dead, but I could still see so clearly the face of Anghelescu hovering over my Esther. And until we found that secretary, and I was able to settle that question of vengeance, the demise of my former client must remain largely inconsequential to me in my quest.

I rose from my bed then, and readied to depart, embracing my mission with renewed vigor.

As I dressed myself, I noticed a small, folded scrap of paper someone had pushed under the door. I fetched it, opened it, and read:

John,

I have been called away on an errand. I shall return in good time. In case you have regained your appetite, I have left a bag of food for you just outside the door. I shall meet you as soon as I can.

Fr. TEG

I wondered if this errand had something to do with this whole, mysterious business, but knowing the man who had written the note, I knew it could just as easily have been something in connection with his other duties (which I only vaguely understood).

I finished dressing, located the promised bag, and set off into the city, investigating and consuming the contents of the bag as I walked, as if I were a casual laborer. My appetite had indeed returned, and the bag was soon empty.

I did feel, for one guilty moment, that I ought to go and visit my place of business. But I knew where I was drawn, and back to Hyde Park station I went.

I found Harris in a terse mood.

"What can I help you with, Mr. Kemp?" he asked shortly.

It was not quite the welcome I expected, so I did not immediately respond. Then I lamely stammered out something about seeing if I could be of any use regarding Kilbronson's affairs.

"How so?" demanded the inspector. "I had understood from your own account that you no longer were his legal representative?"

That was true, so once again I said nothing.

Harris glared at me for a moment then sighed and said: "You'd better sit down, Mr. Kemp."

I did so quickly, before he could change his mind.

The inspector ran his fingers through his hair—a gesture of impatience and exhaustion. "You've caught me in a foul temper, Mr. Kemp. Everyone is so pleased with the death of that lunatic. The superintendent is happy. The chief constable is happy. I'd venture to say the prince is even happy. Perhaps the old queen too. Everyone is happy." He tapped a stack of newspapers. The *Pall Mall Gazette* was on top. "Toby Barnes is fair near delighted, to judge from his column. Everything all neatly explained away." And he shoved the papers from him in disgust.

"But you aren't happy?"

"No, sir, I am not. I don't care for loose ends, and this case is rife with them. But, as far as the powers above me are concerned, the case is closed, and it's a job well done."

He frowned then said, almost wistfully: "Gilroy isn't with you today."

"No," I said. "He was called away on some business—I don't know what. But, Inspector, can't we learn something from the man Tabb?"

He was glaring again almost immediately. "No," he said, "we can't. Not a thing."

"Why not? What does he say?"

"We will never know what he says because a halfwit who claims to be a constable left him alone and, in those few precious moments of solitude, he produced a rope out of thin air and hanged himself."

My blood ran cold. "He's dead?" I repeated, incredulously.

"Dead and truly dead. No sign of an extra dose of life in him either."

"When did it happen?"

"While we were off at the Masons'. Riley walked out for a moment for some idiotic thing, and when he came back, there was Tabb. Swinging."

"No one could have gotten to him?"

"Not unless he walked in bold and invisible and right past Collins."

For a moment, I found myself considering whether the power to render one's self invisible were a credited characteristic of preternatural fiends in any of the texts I had studied (I vaguely remembered some floating specks of dust with mesmerizing qualities)—then I realized that Inspector Harris was watching me narrowly, and I dismissed the thought. No need to rush my way into an asylum. Indeed, these sorts of thoughts seemed dangerously unorthodox without my priestly companions to bear the brunt of external judgment.

Before I could ask another question, someone knocked at the door. Without wasting energy on courtesy, Harris sharply bid the visitor enter.

It was someone I did not know—a small man, probably in his forties, with elaborate though well-groomed side whiskers, and a nervous, almost delicate air, barely repressed beneath the veneer of smooth governmental efficiency. The attaché case under his arm bore a crest I did not recognize—but I did not need to. You could almost smell Whitehall on him.

He peered at us humorlessly through his glasses.

"Inspector Harris?"

The inspector had risen and nodded.

The visitor walked in, closing the door primly behind him. After a hard look at me, he looked again to Harris. "I am Sir Kenelm Edward Digby. I'm from the home office. I'd like to speak to you on a matter of some importance ... speak to you ... *alone* ..."

"And what might that matter be, Sir Kenelm?"

Digby paused to clean his glasses. It was a complex procedure and took over a minute. Then he carefully placed them back upon his nose and said: "It is, as I said, a matter that cannot be discussed before ... civilians."

I thought Harris was going to tell off this representative of that other branch of Her Majesty's government; then he seemed to recollect my unofficial status and bid me a gruff: "Good day, then, Mr. Kemp."

"Ah," said Digby, turning. "John Kemp. Of course." He nodded, as if my name gave him some satisfaction, then dismissed me from his mind and returned his patient gaze to the inspector.

As I left the station, I saw Riley, standing at his post, looking quite miserable.

I stopped and bade him good morning.

He seemed relieved to be thus approached and gushed so eagerly into an unhappy explanation of the circumstances that had led to his extraordinary failure, that I wondered, pityingly, how severe must have been Harris' rebuke.

"I don't know how it happened, sir. I was hardly gone a moment. And I thought Collins was there, but he says he was in the filing room for something. I don't know what, though."

He looked puzzled for a moment, as if remembering some forgotten inconsistency. Then he shook the thought away and went back to being miserable in his disgrace.

"It really could have happened to anyone," I said soothingly.

"But I was there, sir. I was there when they brought him in. There wasn't an inch of rope on him. I can't think where he had it hid. It's just baffling, sir."

I left him there in ignominy.

Well, I wasn't needed at the station, and there appeared to be no Papists about to give me other excuse. There was nothing for it. I set my mouth with determination and marched off toward the Inns of Court.

Carstairs was in the office, of course, diligently laboring away at whatever work still remained to us. He was a dedicated fellow, I would give him that.

When he saw me, he leapt from his stool, grabbed a sheaf of carefully arranged documents, and practically ran to me.

"Oh, Mr. Kemp!" he cried. "You're here!"

Before I could acknowledge this to be the case, he began handing me paper after paper. Newspaper clippings. Letters from our files. It was a comprehensive casebook on Edgar Kilbronson *and* ... Count Lucian Popescu.

"I'm sure it is entirely inappropriate of me to put myself forward," gushed the clerk as he piled his evidence so rapidly before me that I couldn't clearly take it all in, "but, really, sir, it isn't right. It really isn't right. I don't care what the papers say. Mr. Kilbronson was a horrible man, and I believe *that*. But I saw the man who took away the young lady that night. He was as unlike Mr. Kilbronson as you are to me. But I do know who he *was* like, and that's the secretary of that count. Their whole enterprise is thoroughly suspicious, and I've documented it for you, sir. I'm sure, as I said, that Kilbronson was everything they say he was, but he wasn't the one who attacked the young lady, and I warrant he wasn't the one who came to your flat. And, I am sure it is presumptuous of me, sir, and I wouldn't blame you for giving me my notice, but ... but ..."—he took a deep breath and delivered this last with an emphasis that would have served well in the concluding arguments of a dramatic court case—"I just wanted you to know."

I was too stunned to process so much information and simply sat, blinking, staring first at my clerk and then at the documents in my lap.

He had drawn himself to his full height, holding himself in readiness for whatever I had to say.

"It's ... good of you, Carstairs," I said (feeling in the depths of my soul how my response must be a disappointment to this fellow, in his first passionate flush of newfound heroic fervor).

He was slightly deflated.

"It's *very* good," I amended. "In fact ..."—I found I was almost frantic not to quash the fledgling knight—"in fact, I think it may be the very piece we have been missing in this puzzle."

His chest swelled again with enthusiasm. "As you will see, sir, we can conclude there is someone else—perhaps *more than one*. And, since it would be presumptuous of me to recommend that you take care, Mr. Kemp, I offer my services, such as they are. Let me help. I don't understand what is going on, but you know I take instruction well enough." His little speech concluded, he once again drew himself up to his full height—which was, incidentally, not very high at all.

I promised to keep this in mind, engaged to meet with him later that day, and, begging the need for time to consider the dossier, escaped my clerk and my office with the papers clutched in my arms.

I do not know what I intended at that time—perhaps a return to the priory. I needed a place and quiet to consider the information produced by Carstairs. It did seem an important avenue to explore. I walked for some time, clutching the papers, endeavoring to clear my mind and make something vaguely resembling a decision.

Then I turned a corner, and there was Radu Vadas, standing directly in my path, as if he had appeared from nowhere.

"I have come to you again," he said. "To speak to you of my sister."

I was uncertain what to do; I felt I should cry out for help and expose him to some person in authority, and yet curiosity, and a queer sort of pity for the man, changed my mind.

"Come," I said. "Somewhere private."

The church was there, and it was open, so we went in. A small side chapel would serve perfectly for such an interview—there with the statue of the pretty child saint above us, clutching her pet lamb so tightly that I wondered its stony eyes did not bug out.

"You know your sister is now a widow," I said.

He shrugged. "So I have heard. The word has spread through the city of that mad monster, her husband, and his death."

"Now she should be safe, should she not?" It was a deliberately provocative question. I felt I was on the cusp of learning something I dearly wanted to know—the true reason for our villain's obsession with the elusive Elisabetta.

Vadas' face was dark as he answered: "You know well the answer I must give to you, Mr. Kemp."

"Yes," I said. "But I want to know why. Why does this creature hunt her? We have heard of some ruby—a fair gem all men desire, and his blood within it. Is that it? Does he want the ruby? What other power does she have over him—or what power can she give him? Why would her blood be any different for him than anyone else's?"

"Because," he said, angrily, "it is not her blood he seeks. It is his own blood."

A strange thought indeed, and yet, with it came some glimmer of comprehension.

Vadas quietly continued, his anger growing as he recollected for himself this sorry tale. "Elisabetta is the gem herself, the dark beauty all men desire. And in her is his evil blood. I call her my sister, and, indeed, she is of my blood too—though that other blood rages against it and

367

would consume it. But the relation is a strange one indeed. My mother, she is dead. A cousin—a young woman—was known throughout the land for her extraordinary beauty.

"This bastard son of a false priest, he learned a way, I know not how, to make himself a creature such as this—a slow method of dark, self-death. When he made himself into the creature that now assaults your country, when he was not yet undead, and yet fully of the Evil One, in limbo between this world and the other—he . . . got her with child. Vicious creature. But he knew not of the child. Now undead, he has heard of her. And he has deep desire for her."

"Desires his own daughter," I murmured, with an ill feeling in the pit of my stomach.

"Not desire as you think it. Not love. Hate."

"You knew of this?" I asked.

"I found her among the gypsies—for they found her dead mother. From stories I heard, and from the gypsies' own account, I learn the truth. I would not tell her. We left that country. Our names—those too, I changed. I would not tell her. I raise her as my sister and give her everything she deserve—everything to try and keep her from that doom."

He moistened his lips with his tongue. "Then, when she is in her sixteenth year, he came in the night. She wakened. He did not attack her. Instead he told her—assaulted the young innocence of her heart. He invited her to come with him. To fulfill all that she has in her from him. I heard the noise and came to her aid, and he fled."

"Why would he flee?" I asked. "Why not kill you then?"

"A willing victim to him would be more delicious, and perhaps he had some hope of her service—service before his feast upon her. After that, she was changed. She knew her fate, or thought she did. Every day, she felt she moved closer to it. When she dies, she will become like him, maybe. But if he drinks her blood—her blood, which is his—then will he not be a darker and more evil power? We left once more. We ran from him and together we could hide—and hide with greater cunning than I alone, for she has cleverness like him. But her greatest fear, even if she runs far way, is he will find her.

"Then . . . ," his voice fell, and his eyes, "then came a night, when the moon was full, and she . . . it was not herself that did it. She turned upon me suddenly, and over-powered me with the strength of such creatures. I felt her teeth upon my throat, but then she stopped and drew back from me in horror. She left, and I have sought her ever since."

"And Kilbronson?"

"Kilbronson," Vadas spat out the name. "I do not know but can guess well how that came about. We had met him, she and I. He seemed to her so unlike that creature, her demon father. She would go to him, I know. I saw his lust for her long before and told her of it. She argued, said he was a man of coldness and quiet. It was some years before I knew that she had gone to him—*him*! And in her hope for safety. I know Elisabetta. She has a spirit of truth. She would tell a husband her dark secret. And he, with his own so-dark desires. What would he do?"

I did not answer at first, though my mind and heart were heavy with questions, with fledgling thoughts that required time and gentle consideration to grow and take wing as understanding.

"What now?" I asked, finally, though more of myself than of him.

"My quest, it continues," he said. "I cannot rest until I find her, and until the creature is dead—true dead. Then she will be free."

"But," I said, "how can he be killed? How can we, here in England where laws forbid us from driving stakes into visiting nobility—even pseudo-nobility?"

"I cannot tell you," said Vadas sadly, "but I shall wait and watch and, when you go to fight this creature, I shall be there, and I shall help you."

He looked up, peering into the shadows of the silent church. "I must go," he said. "You must go too. Even these walls may bear some dark spirit that reveals to him our words."

He rose then bowed to me. "Goodbye, Mr. Kemp, *áldja meg az isten!*"

I listened to his hasty, but cautious, footsteps as he left the church. He opened the door slightly and waited several seconds before opening it fully and sweeping through to be lost from sight in the crowded streets.

I waited alone for some minutes then picked up Carstairs' dossier once again, left the church, and made my way back to the police station.

I found the entire department on full parade in Harris' office, and the inspector was clearly in the middle of an angry harangue of someone or something. Toby Barnes was there too, and three white-robed men. Father Thomas Edmund was not present. I slid in beside Barnes quietly.

"So before you all congratulate yourselves on the death of Edgar Kilbronson," growled Inspector Harris in brooding frustration, "we have to stop and consider several other deaths, including that of our prisoner Tabb. Since I don't believe all of that nonsense about creatures with special sight into the minds of sane men, I come to one, inescapable conclusion." He narrowed his eyes. "We have a traitor in our midst."

His was a valid enough hypothesis, but, for a moment, as I saw his eyes scan over the group of men by the door, my heart misgave me, and I hoped that he was mistaken. These were men with whom we had already faced such horrors. How could one of these men ... be one of *them?*

Riley's face was red and swollen, as if the man had been crying. He was staring dully at the ground, refusing to meet anyone's eye.

"Collins," growled Harris, "step forward."

There was a flash of movement, and the betrayal became an all-too present reality. Constable Collins, glowering as usual, had stood without moving as Harris built up to this denouncement. Now he lunged across the room, scattering his astonished former associates, flinging all in his way to the ground with frightening strength, to leap at the inspector's throat, teeth and claws murderously pointed.

Before anyone else could react, Dr. Lewis grabbed at the nearest weapon to hand—a fire ax—and with one swift expert movement decapitated the traitor.

As the severed head fell to the ground, spurting crimson filth in its wake, the astonished mouth opened and a large, deaths-head moth flew from it. One young man in white jumped forward, extracting a glass jar from beneath his robes, and captured the moth. The imprisoned creature flew about with frantic, angry, violent movements. Then he slowed and finally fell still, curled up in death.

Few people noticed this little side drama. I was focused on it as a sort of shocked reaction away from the bloody chaos. Inspector Harris, his face ghostly pale, continued to issue calm, rapid-fire orders. In addition to his pallor, the single indicator of his disturbed feelings was a slight, involuntary tremor of the small finger on one hand.

Toby Barnes was helping to scrub away at the bloody mess—like a frantic automaton.

Three young constables and the young medical attendant were dealing with the remains of Collins.

And Dr. Lewis ... remembering his gallant action, his resolution, I looked around to find him.

There he was. In the far corner. Crouching like a cowed dog, his body racked with hysterical sobs. His hands, stained with blood, were before his eyes, and the look of terror on his face sent chills up my spine.

It was at this moment of traumatic aftermath that the door opened and Father Thomas Edmund Gilroy stood before us.

He asked no questions but quickly scanned the room. When his eyes fell on Lewis, Father Thomas Edmund nodded and went to him. I could not hear his voice, but for several minutes his focus remained upon the traumatized mortician. Finally, Lewis looked up and seemed to see the priest for the first time.

He tried to speak. "His ... his name ... was Timothy," he gasped out. And the trembling renewed, quickened.

I became aware of a presence beside me, and looked to see Harris. He was mechanically (and ineffectively) attempting to wipe blood stains from his clothing.

"What tipped you off?" I asked, the question suddenly coming into my dazed mind.

The inspector wordlessly handed me a piece of paper. It was a scribbled note, in Father Thomas Edmund Gilroy's hand:

Received word of Tabbs' death. Under no circumstances leave Riley alone. Keep Collins under guard. Coming as soon as possible.

— TEG

Chapter 27

20 January 1901: Police Station and a house on Jermyn Street, Piccadilly

(From Dr. Seward's journal) *Under the circumstances, Van Helsing and I took it upon ourselves to examine papers, etc. He insisted upon looking over Lucy's papers himself. I asked him why, for I feared that he, being a foreigner, might not be quite aware of English legal requirements and so might in ignorance make some unnecessary trouble. He answered me:—"I know; I know. You forget that I am a lawyer as well as a doctor. But this is not altogether for the law. You knew that, when you avoided the coroner. I have more than him to avoid . . ."*

Several hours later, we once again sat in that office, a council of war over a tray with a large, brown pot of scaldingly hot tea. We were a strange triumvirate—Father Thomas Edmund Gilroy, affectionately nursing his cup, and smiling encouragement to me over its brim; Inspector Harris, grim and glowering in his blood-stained shirt; and I, neither grim nor smiling, but somewhere resolutely in between. The dossier provided by Francis Carstairs lay disemboweled on the desk before us.

In the aftermath of that bloody scene, time had at first been dedicated to triage—cleaning, soothing, and removing both the dead and the living. Next had come consideration of the immediate crisis.

Collins' locker and all of his belongings were subject to rigorous search. It was an unpleasant business from beginning to end. In addition to the expected "kit" of a constable, we found filthy French pictures—not simply the cheap entertainment of a coarse man, but with an aesthetic of strangeness and perversion. I saw them for a moment as they slid across Harris' table. The inspector made a noise of disgust, flipped rapidly through, and threw the lot on the fire.

I was rather concerned that this display would shock Father Thomas Edmund, but he seemed both untroubled and uninterested, though I believe he felt, like me, that the air was cleaner when they were burnt to cinders.

When it was quieter, and we three sat alone, before I presented the fruits of my clerk's labors or described my strange encounter with Radu Vadas, I looked again at the scribbled note that had so alerted Harris to the perfidy of Collins.

After a moment's hesitation, I held it out to the priest, my question in my eyes.

"My dear John," said Father Thomas Edmund, "if a man dies by hanging, and he didn't have a rope, it must have been brought to him. If the man is in a prison, and not in the cell with the as-yet unrepaired hole in the wall, it must have come to him from inside the prison. If the man possesses the strength of will of someone like Tabb, he is as unlikely to commit suicide as he is to withstand the violence of someone stronger. And if you have two constables on guard, and one of them happens to be a thoroughly questionable character, whose actions—both with regard to this case and in general—cannot stand up to even a cursory scrutiny ..."

"So you have had your eye on Collins for some time? Why didn't you say something?"

"My concern, John, is for the salvation of souls. I thought I discerned in Timothy Collins a man of disordered passions. An unreliable policeman. Someone to watch with concern—less as a clear slave of that creature we are fighting, and more as a man who is a danger to himself and to others because of his own disorder. When I heard of Tabb's death, I knew it was clearly an issue of possession or oppression. That is why I wrote my note. There are many men whose disordered passions make them dangerous, but they are not all reportable to the police."

Harris (who had been engaged in giving the order to one of his men for hot tea, "and plenty of it") made a comment under his breath—I could not catch the words, but the world-weary bitterness they expressed was clear.

They were a fascinating pair. Each had a personal experience of the depravity of man. Harris seemed the harder for it, and Father Thomas Edmund seemed gentler.

I second-guessed this thought almost immediately, remembering moments in the past weeks, moments when I had seen strong emotion in his face too, and even anger. In his mercy (if that is what it was), the priest did not forget justice or the rigid morality of his code.

I explained the circumstances surrounding the dossier, neglecting nothing, even Carstair's offer of assistance. It sounded theatrical as I described it, but I strove to present him in a favorable light—his self-initiated efforts warranted it, I thought.

Then I spoke of Radu Vadas. It was such a striking counterpoint to my clerk's carefully documented legal investigation—this tale, half folklore, half sordid drama.

Father Thomas Edmund frowned in concentration, and as I described the meeting in that church, the frown deepened. When I finished, he sat for some time in silent thought.

Inspector Harris remained in watchful silence, looking at the priest's face.

Finally, Father Thomas Edmund spoke, almost to himself, ruminating over the facts as if to discover in them a clearer sense of the problem: "If she is indeed the child of such a creature, and if his descent was not complete when he fathered the child ... I do not know what it means. I have never heard of such a thing. For to feast upon her blood—the blood that once was his—would ... would it grant him special strength or power? Perhaps. I am inclined to believe he is driven by that expectation of special pleasure over any ambition. What we are dealing with is, after all, a dark culmination in vice. His disordered passions rule over even his cunning."

"His own child," I said, the horror still upon me.

Father Thomas Edmund Gilroy shook his head gently, as if he were preparing to speak to a child. "Such desires go against nature, my friend. But is that any less perverse than the desire to drink another man's blood?"

"All that aside," interrupted Harris, "we need to know what we are to do. You spoke of his cunning. Well, we have a case. A clear case. Kilbronson the madman, responsible for all of the horrors that have beset London. Even Tabb and Collins—that can't be traced back. Unless there is some clear link, some legally justifiable connection in this stack of papers, we're done for."

The priest nodded, then chanted out in a sober monotone: "*Cuius autem in caprum emissarium statuet eum vivum coram Domino ut fundat preces super eo et emittat illum in solitudinem.*" Then his tone changed. "Leviticus 16:10. Yes," he nodded again, "Kilbronson made a fitting scapegoat. That clear lunatic was no undead. I don't think he had the mental wherewithal or the unholy prowess. He was an unschooled dupe of that more powerful creature. That entire business, even roping in the dubious society of the Freemasons—it has all been a carefully calculated plot."

"How on earth was he convinced?" I asked, more to myself. "What on earth could have possessed him?"

"We can't know precisely what was promised," said Father Thomas Edmund, then added with a dark touch of humor: "but I think we can safely say that the ability to fly was one of them."

"What's the legal answer?" Harris demanded, persistent. "This is all very well, but we must have a clear legal case to pursue. Otherwise, as far as my superiors are concerned, we can't do a thing."

"Can't do a thing?" I said, outraged. "Even now? What of Esther? What of that creature Anghelescu? What of all of the other unsolved murders? Is this going to continue to go unchecked, because of political influence?"

Harris uttered an oath and struck the desk with his fist so that the teacups rattled. "Kemp, I'm telling you how things stand. We need a clear case or we can't take a step. The law is engaged—you cannot try and sidestep me."

We might have descended into a more heated argument, had not Father Thomas Edmund gently and silently interposed by parceling out a stack of papers to Harris, a stack to me, and a stack to himself.

Some time passed in meditative silence as each of us read.

I found in my pile a strange casebook, with the names and some personal details regarding a half dozen persons whose entry into Count Popescu's charitable establishment was noted by Carstairs. (Had the man spent his days lurking in the streets, I wondered? He always seemed to be at my place of business, and I had not imagined him capable of existing elsewhere, without expiring in a cloud of self-indictment for his ingratitude and perfidy.) At the bottom of each report, Carstairs had written this chilling comment: "Disappeared." And he affixed a date in each case. I itemized each discovery for my two companions.

Father Thomas Edmund's pile disclosed records of shipments and purchases, many of which had been made by me or through me for the count. Gathered there together, the whole business became more and more sinister. Was the count shipping in weapons? What on earth would possess such a man to invest in so much medical equipment? There were few details on the invoices, but enough to seem to point in many directions at once—a church? A hospital? A scientific laboratory? An asylum, full of the latest torture devices, designed to keep a man mad?

"If," the priest commented, "as Vadas attests, this creature has determined some means of slow death that cultivates creatures like him for an unholy harvest, it seems he has every intention of continuing that work on a professional scale here in London."

Inspector Harris was grimly satisfied by his pile. A few times, as he read, he commented on things to himself, and once he even barked out a laugh, a humorless enough noise, and said (addressing his unseen adversary): "I'll have you yet, and damn the super!"

His pile, it seemed, introduced a number of associations between the organization established on the count's authority with wanted criminals—a few men wanted for violence, a swindler, a bigamist, and two women associated with a dark trade in stolen children.

"It isn't much," I said, "and nothing connects directly to Popescu himself."

The inspector clearly disagreed: "It is enough for our purposes. With this and with Kilbronson's death, we have a good enough reason to justify a look into that house where he does his business. Lucky enough, we'll find more to go on there. What say you, Father?"

Father Thomas Edmund was listening, his head cocked to one side like a thoughtful robin watching a squirrel as it busily digs about in the soil, burying its winter harvest of acorns.

"It isn't enough," I protested, before he could speak. "We have to outwit him. His daughter—that's the way to do it. Perhaps ... perhaps we can dress up a constable to pretend to be Elisabetta Kilbronson or Vadas or whatever we want to call her, and ..."

I broke off, shaken by the obvious amusement of my hearers.

"My dear John," said Father Thomas Edmund Gilroy, chuckling, "what a lot of work and nonsense that would entail, and so likely to fail. No, my friend. Remember: evil is not original. It can create nothing. It can only pervert. It lacks imagination. We need not overthink this. In fact, I agree that we have everything we need right here to make a new beginning. We will begin there on Jermyn Street. There we will find guidance to our next step."

"And let Popescu run free?"

"Not at all. I have told you not to overthink, but also do not underestimate. Look at these names. These records. Where have all of these victims gone? We have not found them. We need to understand his goals and his desires.

They are disordered—driven toward power and pleasure. Nothing else inspires him. Further ... and I suggest this with only a touch of irony ... I suspect that our count has done his own research."

"Meaning?"

"Meaning he has read Stoker's novel himself—or knows of it. And he has seen and seeks to avoid the mistakes of his literary counterpart."

"What mistakes?" asked Harris (less, I believe, out of interest in the novel, and more in reference to the machinations of Popescu).

It was clearly something Father Thomas Edmund Gilroy had considered carefully. "Principal among the failures of Count Dracula is his failure to establish a due hierarchy of minions. Why are there no other evil, preternatural creatures to support Dracula? It's really ludicrous. A child could have planned better the overthrow of English society. And Popescu. He is indeed clever."

"What are you suggesting?" I asked, resuming my role as interlocutor.

"I suggest that, as we near this supposed count, we will uncover more and more troubling events. And possibly more creatures. We will require a smaller band of men for this, Harris. And one consisting of men we can absolutely trust."

"How ..." The question was on my lips, but I swallowed it back, not wishing to seem to be expressing doubt in Harris (though the Collins debacle was so fresh in all of our minds, and its bloody traces on the brass buttons of the inspector's uniform).

"I know my men, Mr. Kemp," said Harris calmly. "I would not have known Collins for a traitor on that scale, but ... well, sir, I never put him forward for promotion.

He was the scapegrace son of a man whose title was the only thing keeping him from penury. An unwholesome apple from an unwholesome tree, dumped on me through the influence of the old school-days friendship of someone or other. He was still on the force because I had not yet discovered a means of removing him. But it was a project dear to my heart, I can assure you."

In the end, there would be twelve of us: Inspector Harris; Constable Peters; Constable Davis; Constable Stewart; Dr. Lewis (at Father Thomas Edmund Gilroy's insistence); and Father Thomas Edmund Gilroy himself, with three of his brothers (Father Vincent, Brother James, and Brother Peter—who carried the ominous black case). I made an uneasy tenth. Our last two additions were even more unorthodox than the men in white.

As we left the police station, Toby Barnes appeared in Inspector Harris' path. Beside him stood Francis Carstairs. For once, the newsman said nothing. Then Harris nodded shortly and stepped into the back of one of two police wagons. We all followed suit, Barnes and Carstairs as well.

Our drive was a silent one and seemed to be over much more quickly than my stomach could accept.

The brick edifice of the count's establishment stared down at us in unfriendly stolidity. From all appearances, the house was alone in facing us—not a creature appeared to be stirring in its darkened depths.

Harris was quick, and his men were eager to serve. Within a few moments, they found a point of entrance through a side door, jimmied the lock, and ushered us all through.

We moved slowly and methodically through the rooms. I do not know what it was that I expected. There was something strange about it—for now it was early morning, and we ought to have encountered business at its commencement. Even as the minutes passed, it remained silent, empty, deserted. And yet there was a sense, hanging heavy in the air, that the rooms had only been very recently vacated. I could half imagine the members of the secretarial pool, having spent their night in vigil, now hurrying out a hidden back door as we came in the front.

Nothing sinister in any direction. Each room withstood our rigorous search. Three hours later, we stood together in the count's own office, a wondrous room of dark mahogany paneling, pooling together our respective nondiscoveries.

"Nothing," said Inspector Harris in disgust.

His loyal men, united even more by the recent, ignominious death of Collins, now looked both disappointed and mildly shameful. It seemed as if there had been a desire to regain some vague sense of honor for their corps, a desire now cruelly dashed by the mundanity of this place of philanthropic endeavor.

"Don't despair," said Father Thomas Edmund Gilroy. And he pointed to Francis Carstairs. My clerk was methodically walking along the far wall, placing one foot before the other, like a man who measures distance by footprint.

He concluded his exercise and nodded his head in satisfaction. "Of course," he said. And he grinned openly at the priest.

Father Thomas Edmund stepped forward and began to run his hands along a panel of the wall.

"A secret door?" I said, dubiously.

"Remember," said the priest, "I said he is unimaginative. He *ought* to have a secret room and ..."—his hand struck a hidden knob, evoking a soft "click", and the door swung open—"so he does."

The door led to a narrow, circular, metal staircase. It proved an uncomfortable and precipitous descent, circling around and around until I felt slightly sick from vertigo. We must have passed down several floors, and even beyond, below the street. Here we found ourselves before a giant metal door, carved with intricate symbols and swirling crests.

"A heraldic nightmare," remarked one of the friars dryly.

They did not pause at the door—though I, for one, wondered what we would find on the other side.

The constables' electric torches revealed a bizarre laboratory, fully equipped, yet eerily dormant. A wall of books, most of them ancient and decaying, with their bindings slowly falling to dark brown dust, and titles in strange languages. Urns and test tubes side by side, nearly all stained in crimson. Wires. An array of medical cutlery, lying beside strange tools of a more ancient, darker craft. Half scientific, half sorcery. A place of dissection, perversion, and experimentation. Dark bottles of red, one of them tipped over to spill out into the pool that dripped ... dripped ... dripped on the floor.

Someone had found a light and switched it on. In the sputtering light, my eyes scanned the room to see all of the strange, troubling details of the sinister workshop. Then I saw her, and I forgot everything else.

She lay upon a medical examination table, strapped down tight, but sprawled beneath the constraints in an unnatural position—a coarse-looking woman, with frizzy red hair that might have been arranged in some semblance of order, but now bore all of the marks of frantic flailing. Her attire (minimal undergarments, grossly stained, and of cheap quality) and her general appearance were alike suggestive of street work of the most immoral breed. Pinned like an insect, subject to who knew what dark tortures. Her white skin had an almost translucent hue—a strange shade, even for death.

But ... was she dead? As I looked closer I realized her chest moved—irregularly, but definitely.

I was about to speak of this, when revelation stepped in ahead of me.

The woman's eyelids flew open, exposing two wide, light gray eyes, which darted about the room, as if seeking someone in particular from among our ranks. Failing to find the one she sought, fright gave way to vicious, though uncertain, fury. Her mouth, framed in lips that suddenly appeared darkly crimson, opened wide, disclosing the sharp teeth. The creature shrieked at us and fought desperately at the constraints that pinned her to the table.

This lasted only a few seconds—shrill, sickening seconds. Then she fell back, the unholy light vanished from her eyes, and tears swelled. She whimpered, a broken, ravaged animal, then fell back into the frozen inanimacy of death.

Whatever the strange process, here it was incomplete.

The rest of us were too startled to react for a moment, but Dr. Lewis hurried to the side of the unconscious woman. "She's still alive," he said in crisp, almost angry tones. "Tell me"—he was speaking to Father Thomas Edmund Gilroy now—"tell me what to do."

The two men—the mortician and the priest—were bent over the woman, speaking in low tones. Words were barely audible to me—I had no desire to move closer and invade that conference.

"There is time," said Father Thomas Edmund, "though not much. And much to do if she is to be saved."

385

"Here?" asked the other.

"No, it is not a safe place. Send for an ambulance coach."

"Where?"

"For now, Meadowvale Asylum at Waug's Hollow. I shall write the directions. The doctor there knows me."

"What shall we do?"

"Father Vincent shall go with you. I must stay."

Father Vincent had moved to their side and, for a few moments, had rummaged in that fascinating black bag, and brought out a handful of tools, including a small syringe, which had in it a light pink liquid. He whispered something in the doctor's ear, and Lewis nodded. A moment later, and the drug was administered. The woman did not even move as the needle entered her arm. Until the ambulance carriage arrived (and, I am sure, after it departed with its unhappy cargo), the priest and the doctor bent devotedly over their patient, administering their peculiarly conglomerated care.

After that, things began to move quickly. Command, which of late had entirely seemed to belong to Inspector Harris, now seemed by joint decision to be shared equally between him and Father Thomas Edmund Gilroy. In fact, as the moments passed, I began to wonder if the latter in fact bore the greater part of the authority.

As Dr. Lewis and Father Vincent focused on their patient, the rest of us received sharp (though never discourteous) instructions. While several men investigated and dismantled the laboratory framework, the rest of us delved through the books that ranged the shelves. Most of them were completely incomprehensible to me (I suspected Latin in a few of them, but the script was so exotic and our search so hurried that I could not verify). The inspector and the priest prowled around, watching over our shoulders and consulting together on their own rapid summary of our discoveries.

"I don't understand this mess," I said at one point, more to myself than anything.

"Do you not?" responded Father Thomas Edmund (who always seemed to be standing behind me at moments when I spontaneously spoke aloud). "He has developed a special procedure for his own craft. Remember what Vadas told you—some means of creating the undead in a methodical way. It is half-science and half-occult ritual. Seduction. Then drugs to sustain life through the adoption of unnatural practices—drugs that may also subdue victims. Next, the cultivation of the art of blood drinking and murder, that the new creature may develop a taste for the one while learning an almost medical precision with the other—for, as we know, living blood is key. When the initiated undead has been fully weaned from natural, life-sustained practices like eating, drinking, and sleeping—that is when the contract with the Evil One is complete and self-death is sought in bloody sacrifice. Then the creature of the undead rises ..."

He had delivered this, as was his wont, as a calm, clear, and even cheerful academic recitation, but the words still conjured up for me dark and alarming visions. I looked back at the papers before me and pretended to be busy with the search. As my eyes scanned the pages, I saw nothing of their contents. My mind rushed on, frantic and calculating.

I recalled his assurances as to Esther's fate—or tried to recall them but felt much less certain than I had earlier. The sight of that last victim, half woman and half creature, had unnerved me entirely. Another woman came into my mind—the elusive Elisabetta. What on earth could go on in her mind? Did she flee her undead father or seek to find him? Did she battle inwardly against her own dark desires? Was she bent on vengeance? Or frantic for escape?

I was about to ask the priest's opinion when another thought flashed into my mind. The train. Why was he on that train? Searching for answers. Searching for this creature. Tracking down ... No. Could it be that his true object was Elisabetta? Or—darker thought—could he have found her already?

My mind began to make even more feverish connections. Elisabetta, seeking asylum with these strange Papists. Elisabetta, concealed and protected by them. Or ... no, not imprisoned by them against their will. That was impossible. I would not lapse to that degree of mistrust of these men whose goodness I had seen tried time and time again. Still, all that I knew of her was through Kilbronson, through her brother, and through these men in white. I imagined—and felt it to be true—Father Thomas Edmund Gilroy as her father confessor. Discretion, concealment ...

I looked up again, and there he was, frowning down at a book through his glasses, which had fallen to the tip of his nose. His face was such a picture of openness and sincerity—and studious care—that I shook away my thoughts and returned to my own work. Perhaps he did know where the woman was. Perhaps she had sought his help. Perhaps he had found her and brought her—willingly or unwillingly—to a safer place. If so, whatever the circumstances, I felt sure he had done for the best. I would continue to trust in Father Thomas Edmund Gilroy.

Time continued to pass, each man bent over his portion of that unhappy, dusty work.

"It's nearly one," said Father Thomas Edmund suddenly.

I looked up, startled, from the sheaf of maps I had found behind a bookcase. "In the morning or afternoon?" I asked—and not at all facetiously.

"Afternoon. We must go. If at all possible, we must try to avoid meeting him at his home in the dark." He stopped and reached out for one of the maps before me—a small, rough sketch, of much more recent vintage than many of those I had seen already.

As he examined it, his eyes narrowed and he drew in his breath sharply.

"It looks like a church," I remarked. "I don't know where."

"I know it," he said slowly. "And this does not bode well. I think I know one thing we will not find when we enter that house."

"What is that?"

"Our elusive count," he replied, frowning.

Chapter 28

21 January 1901: Belgravia

(From Jonathan Harker's journal) *I am glad that it is old and big. I myself am of an old family, and to live in a new house would kill me. A house cannot be made habitable in a day; and, after all, how few days go to make up a century. I rejoice also that there is a chapel of old times. . . . The walls of my castle are broken; the shadows are many, and the wind breathes cold through the broken battlements and casements. I love the shade and the shadow, and would be alone with my thoughts when I may.*

Despite our efforts, it was nearly dusk when we arrived at the gate that would admit us to the grounds surrounding the house that had belonged to Charles Sidney. The gate was unlocked and open.

"Does he expect us?" asked one of the younger constables, a hint of alarm in his voice.

"He'd be a fool not to," replied Harris dryly. "Considering the mess we've made of his queer laboratory, he must expect some sort of official questioning."

I looked at Father Thomas Edmund Gilroy, and he shrugged noncommittally. "You must remember," he said, "the creature is a mixture of evil cunning and a staggering lack of both common sense and imagination. We must not underestimate him, but it is also likely that his dark pride is so overblown that he cannot conceive of the possibility of his own failure. Such was the case with Lucifer himself. Having gazed upon the Divine, he yet devised an impossible rebellion. His pride outweighed even his necessary knowledge of the consequence of his sin."

This was a little beyond my ken, so I returned to what seemed to me to be the most critical point: "So you think he expects us."

The priest smiled. "Yes, John. I think he has prepared for the onslaught. And I don't think he feels particularly threatened by it."

This hypothesis seemed to be confirmed by what followed. Our unease mounted as we made our approach cautiously down the drive. The landscape, so perfect when I had last seen it, was now ravaged by cold and winter's harsh neglect. It seemed more foreign somehow, as if by passing through the gate we had traveled vast distances to a land of shadow, mystery, and darkness.

When we turned the bend and the house stood revealed, we were frozen together as a group for one moment in shared horror and astonishment. There, before us, stood, not the silent, forbidding, deserted mansion that we had come to expect, but a defiant citadel, ablaze with light. Every window was illuminated—a wide, bright eye staring out at us. Most troubling of all: the front door was open, a mouth waiting to devour us. *What big eyes . . .* The folktale, rendered all the more terrifying in the Irish lilt of my childhood nurse, was suddenly strong in my memory. *What sharp teeth you have, Grandmama dear . . .*

Only two men appeared unperturbed.

"Move along now," muttered Inspector Harris gruffly.

And Father Thomas Edmund Gilroy took up the lead, walking without hesitation closer, ever closer to that blazing, strange house.

At the open door, he stopped and knocked three times sharply. He was muttering something under his breath—I hoped it was a prayer, and a powerful one. Then he gestured us in through the disquietingly welcoming door. The house, like the grounds, was strangely transformed since the last time I had seen it. At first I could not see the more substantial changes, because the most striking attribute of the décor was the candles—thousands upon thousands of lit white candles of every size covered every free surface. They lined the floors as well. Tables, chairs, bookcases, floorboards, mantles, window ledges, window seats, decorative shelves—every square inch groaned under the weight of burning, shining wax.

"Call the fire brigade," muttered Constable Peters. At first I suspected him of sarcasm, but realized quickly that he was merely responding to an instinctive prudence. He took a few quick steps into a parlor and began systematically to extinguish candles.

"Well, come on, you lot," barked Inspector Harris. "Help Peters. Look lively! Don't want the house to go up before we've a chance to look around."

As the intensity of candlelight decreased to a less theatrical glow, I could notice other aspects of the house—dust, decay, and neglect.

"It was so well kept before," I noted, more to myself than anything.

"Good help is hard to find," whispered a voice at my elbow.

I turned to see Brother James—a young, impish fellow. He nodded with mock solemnity and continued in the voice imitative of the prim wisdom of those moneyed elderly gossips one encounters in society: "It's especially difficult to keep up one's staff to an appropriate degree when you are prone, in a moment of boredom, to suck the life out of a less than stellar maid, or, on a whim, tear your cook to shreds."

I could not bring myself to smile at his wit, because the situation brought me so much disquiet. The Season was already quickly approaching—in fact, in many houses, it was nearly upon us. Had the count not intended to continue his triumphant conquest of London? Perhaps he had lost his royal patron because of the scandalous death of Edgar Kilbronson. Perhaps his mood was changeable, and his focus. Perhaps he was whimsical in his villainous intent. Perhaps something else had distracted him from his campaign of political intrigue. I thought of Elisabetta Kilbronson and thought it likely.

We continued our careful exploration of the house. Each room was a shadow of its former glory. There was no sign of active carnage in the first few rooms, but a strange, unused feeling throughout. It was as if, except for this ritual of candles, the rooms had been undisturbed for months.

The double doors into the south parlor were closed. Constable Peters opened them with a steady hand then stumbled back as clouds of strange, sweet-smelling smoke rushed out around him. We struggled through a shared coughing fit among the billowing wafts then looked, anxiously, through the clearing air.

No living creature could we spy in the room, which was, like the others, bedecked with lit candles, but, unlike the others, was shrouded with heavy, black curtains. This funereal oppression threw into stark relief the extra touch of eerie illumination in the middle of the room: a cauldron of smoking coal, on which burned mounds upon mounds of incense-exuding sticks, bound together with thick red cord.

"Douse it," ordered Harris, hoarse from the smoke.

As his men hurried (though with uncertain glances at the red coals) to do his bidding, the rest of us attended to the candles.

"Perhaps he hasn't been here," suggested Toby Barnes, still coughing. "Perhaps he's been in town the whole time."

"That's absurd," said Francis Carstairs. "Candles don't light themselves. And anyway, I know he's been here frequently."

"And what are you, little one," sneered the newsman with unexpected rudeness, "his social secretary? Or perhaps you fancy yourself a detective?"

Carstairs turned bright red. "No, sir," he said, drawing himself up to an unimpressive height. "I'm training as a lawyer, and I know how to amass evidence and draw logical conclusions from them, which is more than you cheap hacks in Fleet Street can claim."

"I'll box your ears for that one, boy," cried Barnes, and he jumped at my clerk.

Carstairs armed himself with the closest thing to hand—a small table, laden with golden ornaments which he unceremoniously dumped onto the floor—and, swinging it as an amateur golfer might when attacked by a frenzied wild boar, struck his assailant to the ground.

"HERE NOW!" roared Inspector Harris, grabbing the enraged Barnes by the collar with one hand and the hair of my clerk with the other. "That's enough of *that!*"

To my astonishment, even thus restrained the two pugilists continued to struggle to reach each other, hurling threats and epithets of which I would not have considered Carstairs capable. Three constables joined the fray, and still it remained a furious jumble of maddened men.

I stood back, too surprised to be of any use. Father Thomas Edmund Gilroy walked calmly past me, pulled back a curtain to display a large window, then stepped back to pick up a chair, which he unhesitatingly and forcefully hurled against the glass.

The window shattered into glistening fragments.

The noise startled the combatants and their would-be restrainers, and everyone stood back in shock as the little priest systematically moved from curtain to curtain, releasing the thick, intoxicating smoke from the room. He seized the last of these and called over his shoulder: "Brethren!"

Brother James and Brother Peter were at his side in a moment and, joining him, pulled down the black curtain. With their six hands wrapped together in the cloth, they picked up the villainous cauldron and, struggling, bore it out of the room, down the hall, and out into the drive, where they left it smoldering into the open air.

When they turned back, their white robes soiled with black, and their faces clouded from the smoke, Father Thomas Edmund's face was set firmly. "Enough of this nonsense," he said. "To the chapel, and quick."

We followed him quietly, like ducklings hurrying to keep up with their mother.

Toby Barnes, his eyes wide, staring, and starkly defined by deep, dark circles, put his hand on the arm of Francis Carstairs. "Lord, Carstairs," he croaked out, as if each word pained him, "I must have been mad."

The clerk stared back at him, with eyes as strange and as alarmed. "It's this house," he said, his voice cracking. "This cursed house."

Their reconciliation concluded, they continued along with us, though with more frightened, uncertain steps.

As we hurried along, I remembered an earlier visit to that house, where I had wondered about the rumored existence of the chapel. So it does exist, I thought to myself. Somehow this architectural detail seemed to be extraordinary—more extraordinary than the probable presence of vicious, undead creatures within those haunted walls. What a strange world this is after all, I mused.

There was indeed a chapel, and Father Thomas Edmund Gilroy seemed to know exactly where it was. He wound without hesitation down staircases and through the underutilized lower rooms of the house. As we passed the kitchen, I noted its cobwebbed cleanliness. Not a crumb could be seen, even under the untroubled dust. If there had been remnants of food once, the mice had harvested them long since.

Constable Peters looked over my shoulder and remarked on it as well: "Whoever enjoys lighting all those candles doesn't seem to care much for regular meals."

"Or ...," replied Toby Barnes (though in a dampened tone after his recent altercation with my clerk), "his food is rather different from ours."

Down a staircase, through a corridor, wending our way through to the secret bowels of the house. For a moment, when we stood inside the open door of that hidden place, the dark, heavy silence was broken only by the scurry of vermin feet.

"Can there be vampire rats?" I asked under my breath—a rhetorical question, insofar as it mattered.

"Certainly not," hissed a voice—that of one of the young brothers. "Animal souls are not immortal."

"Unless, of course, we are speaking about demonic possession," whispered the other brother (James, the flippant one). "It's very likely we could have demonically possessed vermin, and the present circumstances would be conducive."

Something seemed to run across my foot, and I barely stopped myself from screaming. As the terrified utterance fell back into my throat, Brother James laughed good-naturedly. "Never fear, Mr. Kemp. We are here."

There were no lit candles to aid us here. A flurry of electric torches danced about the large, crypt-like space. I wondered that it had ever truly been a chapel. Could such a place of death and decay have been chosen even by the Papists for their odd rituals?

Tapestries hung about the walls, but the images they bore were so ravaged and torn—as if with claws—that they might as well have been inspired by French Symbolism. I thought I could see the ruins of an altar toward the front, and perhaps a place where statues might have stood at one time, but all was confusion, fetid stench, dust, dead bugs, and ruin. More remarkable than any Papist shrine was the vast assembly of large boxes throughout the room. There were at least two dozen of them.

I could easily recognize that coffin-like shape. I thought I knew what they were and what was in them.

"Open it," commanded Harris to his constables.

"No!" I cried in my alarm.

Constable Stewart, his hands hovering over the lid of the closest box, faltered at my cry. Then one hand brushed against the wood. In an instant, the door behind us slammed closed, and a loud bolt was thrown.

"Trapped," gasped Toby Barnes. "Trapped."

Constable Stewart staggered back, pointing in horrified astonishment. One by one, the lids of the boxes lifted, thrust upon the floor by unseen hands. Then, from each, one after another, rose a host of rotting corpses, gasping and groaning for our blood. A strange assembly of creatures—a few so ravaged I could not clearly discern whether they had been men or women—decayed into nearly identical impersonality.

The battle was upon us in a moment. Grappling with one frenzied corpse, who stared at me with one pink eye— and in the place where the other must once have resided, worms writhed and trembled in revolting contortions—I had little freedom to consider the fates of my fellows. But, from shouts and groans and the sound of blows, I assumed they, like I, fought against those undead foes.

It was several minutes before I realized that we were surrounded by thick smoke, heralding fire.

With a mighty effort, I pushed away my assailant so that it fell against a stone and lay without moving.

Then I looked, wild-eyed, to Father Thomas Edmund Gilroy, who had knocked down three of the living corpses and stood looking around—as if to assess where best to focus his efforts.

"The smoke!" I cried. "We'll suffocate!"

He nodded, his brows heavy with concentration. (Two creatures rose up, and he knocked them to the ground once more with his chosen weapon—it appeared to be the skeletal remains of a chair.)

"And they ... they'll be destroyed."

He nodded again and batted down his three undead creatures (who were struggling back to their rotting feet), and added a fourth.

"But ...," I panted out, "has he no sense of loyalty to his own creatures?"

"Not at all," the priest replied, in the tone in which an Oxford don might deliver a treatise on an abstract and obscure philosophical point. "Nothing is more important than his own desires. These ruined creatures are expendable." (Once again, his victims rose and fell by his hand.)

The one-eyed combatant rose and stumbled, roaring, back toward me. "Are they redeemable?" I asked, pausing to strike the creature a rough box on what had once been an ear.

"No, they are fully undead, though fully servile. The lowest rank of revenant, controlled by his will and his mind."

"There is no way out, then?" I asked, despairing, as that same unintimidated cyclops rose against me yet again. Father Thomas Gilroy (knocking his own collection of creatures back down for the fifth time) shook his head. "Remember. His is a raw intellect. He lacks wisdom. We have been led down to a trap, and within it comes total destruction. Unless you have the sense to see beyond the puerile connivance of the creature." He nodded, satisfied with his own conclusion, then bellowed: "JAMES!"

The brother in question had leapt into the center of the room and cried out in a piercing tone: "In the name of Jesus Christ, I command you all to cease!"

All movement ceased. The smoke still curled around us, but the creatures fell back cowering.

I was deeply impressed and would have said so. I saw Father Thomas Edmund's stern face, and, for a moment, that sight checked my enthusiasm.

"Theatricality," he remarked quietly under his breath, "is ..."

Then he fell silent and even smiled. Brother James was not laughing now. In that brief stillness, he hurriedly rifled through the bag with focused intent. Gathering together his selected armaments, he brought them all together with a rapidity and ingenuity that I had not realized he possessed.

Wires, some strange putty substance, a fuse—the contraption was assembled and ignited before I had time truly to understand his intention.

"Guard yourselves!" he cried and flung his weapon—not at the assailant creatures, but into a back corner of the ruined chapel.

As we ducked to huddle together behind the altar, covering our ears against the assault to come, the explosion rocked the room, flinging beams, stones, and the shrieking, newly fragmented corpses of the undead around us, swallowing up the red fury of the fire in its own maelstrom of destruction.

After that moment of horror—relief.

"Come!" cried Brother James, and we leapt to our feet, groaning and deafened, to follow him through the new, blessed door, hewn in rock, as if by the hand of an avenging angel. One man—Constable Stewart—struggled to rise to his feet and was immediately picked up by two of his fellows and bodily carried.

Battered, bruised, blackened, we, the living, ran through the house, sure of the undead fury at our heels.

There was the door. We were nearly free.

Then the breath of relief stifled in my throat. Four figures barred our path. They wore strange, colored robes, elaborately embroidered with a large red rose and a golden cross covered in pentagrams, Hebrew script, and other symbols. Hoods hid their faces from us.

"Stand aside," cried Harris in a voice of command.

The four neither moved nor spoke.

A fiercer note entered the policeman's voice. "I am Inspector Harris of Her Majesty's police. Stand aside there."

Still, the four neither moved nor spoke.

"I charge you in the queen's name," shouted Harris deafeningly in my ear, "make way."

One of the four stepped forward, drew a shining sword forth from its scabbard at his side, and threw back his hood.

The face, thus disclosed, caused Harris, that unmovable, stalwart defender of civic stability, to step back involuntarily in surprise and, I think, dismay.

"It's the super," gasped one of the constables in my ear, elucidating the scene.

"You should have heeded my command, Harris," cried the superintendent. "You should not have interfered in matters which do not concern you."

His three companions now doffed their hoods as well. Two of them were unknown to me, though I later learned that one was a world-renowned mathematical scholar, and the other a little-known Member of Parliament. I recognized the last after a few moments as Mr. Bassington-Smith, the highly respectable husband of that highly respectable matron who presided over such absurd spiritualistic gatherings.

All high-ranking practitioners of the Golden Dawn, now standing before us, swords drawn in defense of the Popescu stronghold.

"Are they all then vampires?" demanded Toby Barnes incredulously.

Bassington-Smith laughed condescendingly. "We need not be of his nature to appreciate the Power of the One, nor to share in that power."

No one had time to respond to this, for Harris leapt forward suddenly within reach of the superintendent and planted his fist so soundly into his superior officer's face that we could all hear the angry, bone-shattering contact. The superintendent collapsed upon the floor, blood erupting from his smashed nose and his broken cheek already darkening with painful blue.

Before Harris could subdue his cowering quarry further, the door beside them flew open with a crash, and a fifth and most grotesque figure joined the four Freemasons: Albu, the hideous, tongueless albino, staggering like a drunken man, roaring voiceless rage, a firebrand in his hand, and his eyes, no longer concealed behind dark glasses, blazing red with painful fury.

He struck Harris upon the jaw with an effortless backhand that sent the inspector flying back into our midst. We caught him in our collective arms and collapsed beneath the weight, like pins knocked down by a well-aimed bowler.

We struggled back up to our defensive posture, even as the chiefs of the Golden Dawn dragged their whimpering leader to his feet. No further threats or explanation were needed. Even had we attempted such an exchange, it would have been drowned in the noise that followed on the heels of Albu's appearance and we would have realized the full potential of the torch in his hand.

All around him, the house was alight. The vengeance of that willing slave was complete. We would die, engulfed in that inferno, before we could stop his master, and he, maddened in his devotion, would offer himself in sacrifice to that demon god.

"Stand fast," growled Harris, his chin now providing swollen, purple punctuation to his angry face.

"No!" shouted Brother James. "Run!"

Since this seemed the better suggestion by far, we turned to follow him back through the house, where the fire burned fiercest, into that strange room that had contained that insidious cauldron. Each man held the arm of his fellows, a chain of life and brotherhood, an enduring fellowship before the gates of death.

Brother James was right. Here was true wisdom—even as hell licked at our heels and nearly blinded our eyes, we could see the window the friars had broken earlier that evening.

Almost as a body, we leapt together though, bringing glass, window frame, and broken fragments of the house with us, and fell, heaped, bruised, and broken, onto the blackened grass outside. We did not remain there, but, each man—Papists, police, lawyer, clerk, and reporter— still holding tight to the others, scrambled to his feet and ran from the shadow of the house.

A crowd had already gathered, and the fire brigade stood, frozen in alarm.

As we watched, the staggering figure of the possessed albino, still silently roaring in rage, appeared in the doorway. At his heels stumbled the four, sword-wielding initiates, encumbered by frustration and capes.

Then the beams of the house gave way, and it collapsed, crushing his insane fury into impotent dust.

The work of the fire brigade was well underway in minutes, and the crowd still gathered in frantic attention.

I could not draw my eyes away from the steaming wreckage of the house. It was as if my heart yearned to see the removal of those creatures—some chance of weeding the irredeemable dead from the oppressed living. It seemed a bizarre moment to learn special empathy. Perhaps so many close encounters with death—or the lack of sleep—bred such feelings. Whatever the cause, when Inspector Harris and his men stood over the body of their dead superintendent, and I felt the waves of conflicting emotions in that new betrayal of brotherhood, I wondered to myself why God had promised never to destroy the world again in water. Better to drown than to face such desolation, and such uncertainty. For who knew what others around us could be practitioners of the dark arts, ready to betray those closest to them.

Then a voice spoke at my elbow, responding to my silent thought. "It is this that is so often forgotten in the thrill of the hunt," said Father Thomas Edmund. "The vampire does not merely pit his wits against ours; he is an agent of Satan and seeks the absolute corruption of souls."

"It's odd," I said aloud involuntarily. Then I flushed, afraid of giving offense to the silly little man.

He smiled. "Yes, my friend. I know well that you find us odd. And, indeed, we are a baffling breed—unto the Jews a stumbling block, and unto the Greeks foolishness. And to the English, a veritable monster."

Harris, almost rudely rejecting the ministrations of one of the doctors who had rushed to the scene, marched back up to us.

"What now?" he demanded.

"Now," said Father Thomas Edmund grimly, "Westminster."

Chapter 29

21 January 1901: Westminster Cathedral

(From Dr. Van Helsing's memorandum) *By this time I had searched all the tombs in the chapel, so far as I could tell; and as there had been only three of these Un-Dead phantoms around us in the night, I took it that there were no more of active Un-Dead existent. There was one great tomb more lordly than all the rest; huge it was, and nobly proportioned. On it was but one word:* DRACULA. *This then was the Un-Dead home of the King-Vampire, to whom so many more were due. Its emptiness spoke eloquent to make certain what I knew.*

Twilight was once again well upon us as we weaved our way through the streets toward Westminster—not the abbey, whose Gothic stolidity and splendor was as familiar to me as it must be to any British subject. For the first time, in that strange company, I wondered if it were a place of grievance for the Papists. Must they not loathe England for casting off Roman shackles? Must they not lust for so beautiful a building? I nearly asked Father Thomas Edmund Gilroy but could not discern a way tactfully to phrase such a question.

Whatever his answer might have been, that architectural representative of throne and church was not our goal.

Nor, despite his seeming interest in the heir apparent, was it the haven of Count Popescu.

No, we hurried along toward a bizarre, exotic, and thoroughly un-English place. There it stood, suddenly towering above us, the unfinished behemoth of Westminster Cathedral, a vast Byzantine monstrosity, a provocative exotic introduction even to our eclectic London cityscape.

"It was a soggy marshland," whispered a voice in my ear. (Brother James—the talkative, mischievous one.) "Bulinga Fen. It's been many things since. Pleasure garden. Fairground. A maze. Even a bull-baiting ring. And now this hideous beauty of a building. It's still a bit of a cross between a prison and a wasteland, don't you think?"

As we mounted the steps, my heart misgave me.

"Why would he come here?" I asked. "It seems the last place he would want to come."

"There are strong reasons for him *to* come," Father Thomas Edmund replied quietly. "It is not yet consecrated, yet it will be. In its consecrated state it is both unbearable to him and perversely enticing. If he has the opportunity to fix himself here before the consecration, to carve his niche of darkness into the space itself, he may have ample opportunity for desecration, corruption, and the destruction of souls. A man with a heart of faithfulness, twisted and drawn instead to evil—those are the most delicious prey to such a creature. And here is a fit place to lie and wait."

"But why here? There are other churches in London."

The priest did not answer. He merely looked at me with a slight, enigmatic smile then reached out, gripped the handle of the massive, heavy door, and opened it with an unwavering hand. A rush of cold air greeted us, and a thick, rich darkness.

I blinked several times before my eyes cleared. A mixture of brick and marble framed the heavy darkness of this strange place. Vaulted ceilings and pillars, the empty shell for space that some might eventually call sacred. I could hear water dripping somewhere—it sounded as if a large pool were collecting inside the unfinished building.

Inspector Harris pushed something into my hand—a torch—and lit it. Soon we all bore similar flaming brands. No one produced an electric torch, and the omission seemed somehow appropriate. It was as if we had passed into another place and another time to battle that centuries-old evil.

"Come, you lucifers," said Brother James, chuckling.

We came, an awkward, unpracticed procession, growing in resolution if not in grace.

As I peered about, frantically searching for our enemy in twisted shadows, I heard someone's sharp intake of breath—Inspector Harris, I think—and turned to see what had arrested his attention. My eyes came almost immediately to rest on a solitary black figure standing where the altar would someday stand. Lucian Popescu. Taller than I remembered him. Standing there, wrapped in a cloak of dark, meditative silence, watching us.

Our grim, steady march faltered under his unwavering eye. After so much seeking and searching, this quiet expectancy was somehow anticlimactic. We came to a halt with awkward uncertainty before him, like delinquent children checked in their attempt at a patricidal overthrow. Or, I thought with inappropriate whimsicality, caught by the nurse on our way to rob the cookie jar.

When his voice came to us out of the darkness, it had a sharp edge in it that pierced through the soul of his hearers.

"So it has come to this. Even in London, the tyranny of prejudice reigns. I am not of your race, so you have made me a monster. Your science, your armies, your vast accomplishments in art, politics, enterprise—what have they done for you? Have they raised you above the common herd? It seems not. Whipped into a frenzy of bizarre nightmares, you have come here, you righteous defenders of English soil, to do ... what?

"Against what do you think you are defending yourselves? Of what can you accuse me? I sought to serve the poor. Many men joined me in my efforts. Some were good men. Some less so. And some were mad men, vicious creatures lusting for power. Am I to be blamed for this? You must remember," he spat out, "you English heroes, that Edgar Kilbronson was one of your race—not mine.

"And you, Mr. Kemp ..."—hearing myself denounced, I felt a strong urge to crawl away into the utter darkness, a humiliated creature, no longer worthy of the name of man—"Mr. Kemp, whom I thought my friend. With whom I trusted my private affairs. You have brought these men here. Your reason? I can well imagine it. You have cast my secretary in the role of a vicious, heartless wolf who devours innocent young women with his dark appetites.

"But may I not ask, though you Englishmen will quiver in hypocritical ire at such a suggestion, if another story might be told? A story—not of seducer and innocent— but of deep and shared desire, embraced in a way that might make many a pompous churchman sneer? Do not be so eager to find your villain, young man, unless you are willing to look more closely at the worth and loyalty of that American girl. Can you truly say that you have never questioned her free manner? Her strange openness to ...

others? Take care lest, as this perfect judge of virtue, you come to see in sharper reality this 'pearl of great price' of yours."

Still humiliation reigned in my heart. I waited for rage to take its place, and just indignation at this gross casting of aspersions at the woman I loved. It was all a lie, and I knew it. I did not for an instant suspect Esther of anything. And yet there was something in his voice, a strange thrill that almost halted breath; a siren's song to lull reason. It was as if each wave of sound carried with it an invisible basilisk, transforming resolve to stony uncertainty. And memories came back to me—shameful moments when ungentlemanly thoughts and suspicions had indeed crossed my mind. In that indictment, my humiliation was complete. How could I have set myself up as a defender of goodness and light, when I had so easily given way to such thoughts?

The count opened his arms, holding out his hands in a dramatic gesture, expressive of indignant sorrow. "A worthless girl. A mad Englishman. For this I am now homeless. Hunted. For this you murdered my loyal servant—a poor wretch who spent his life a victim of the cruelty of all around him. I imagine you will say he resisted you—was it not engrained in his very soul to resist or perish?

"You consider yourself the heroes of all that is good and decent. So have the frenzied architects of every perverse witch hunt through the centuries. I have seen peasant mobs before. You do not have pitchforks, perhaps, but your intention is the same ... and your ignorance."

With an effort, I turned my head from gazing at him. Throughout his impassioned soliloquy, our band of men stood motionless. Inspector Harris stood frowning. Toby Barnes' mouth was slightly agape, as if he were frozen in an attempt at speech. Constables with blank, even nervous, expressions. Francis Carstairs quietly attentive, as if taking notes in his mind.

The Papists in white, with black cloaks about them, alone seemed to have the power of movement. I could see and hear the rustle of their robes, and their glances toward Father Thomas Edmund Gilroy, as if seeking his direction and guidance.

I looked to Father Gilroy next and found his eyes were on me. When our eyes met, he gently arched one eyebrow at me. It was a tiny thing, but a gesture that somehow broke the spell of the incanting voice of the vengeful count.

It seemed as if the count himself felt this, for his focus now changed.

"What have *you* to say, priest?" he cried, and his tone was ominous.

I have often wondered what Father Thomas Edmund Gilroy *might* have said in reply. I believe he likely would have remained in silence—for to respond would have seemed to have given credence to the count's tirade, or at least elevated it to the level of things deserving consideration. But, in truth, I shall never know—and I do not know if Father Thomas Edmund can clearly recall himself what (if anything) he had intended to say.

It was at this moment that the scene changed radically.

There was no noise to alert us to the presence of another person, but the Count, responding by some sharp, animal-like sense, jumped suddenly and turned to look off toward the right-hand side of the church, where a shrine to their Madonna might someday stand. "And again," he cried, in a trembling voice newly enriched with rage: "This *peasant*?"

A dark-haired foreigner sprang from the shadows and hurled words of righteous fury and heroic challenge at

Count Popescu—at least, I interpreted the sense of his words from his manner and delivery; Radu Vadas spoke in his native tongue.

The effect was like the sudden unfurling of a stage backdrop from an entirely different play—a classical tragedy, perhaps—in the midst of the third act of a light, drawingroom comedy. We, the actors, stood in shock, as interlopers upstaged us and stole our very performance.

While Radu Vada and the count faced each other, but before their threatening words and looks could descend, out of the shadows on the side opposite, another actor appeared—Gregory Anghelescu, roaring out scorn upon Vadas. I must have stepped forward at the sight of that vile monster, my anger in defense of my assaulted love roused once more in my soul, for Father Thomas Edmund's arm rose to restrain me.

Once again, Vadas made his passionate declaration—or denouncement.

The count nearly shrieked back his reply and shouted what was clearly a command to Gregory Anghelescu.

The secretary leapt without pausing even for a moment. One of the friars started forward, but not before Vadas, brandishing a wooden stake and crying out an impassioned battle cry, pierced the attacking body of Gregory Anghelescu with the weapon.

For one moment, only Anghelescu moved. He staggered to his feet, only a yard from his intended victim, the stake standing out with unnatural rigidity from the wound. Then the secretary's mouth curled wickedly in something like a smile. Vadas began to stumble back with a look of shock and dismay upon his face—so in conflict with his heroic determination of the moment before that it was almost darkly comical.

From the gaping hole in the secretary's breast a strange liquid flowed—like and yet unlike blood—full of small wormlike creatures that dried and fell to dust before our eyes.

As we watched in horror, Gregory Anghelescu clenched the stake, and with a cry of fury that was insufficient to drown out the horrifying sound of wood and rotting flesh in violent discord together, ripped it from his body.

Now snarling like a maddened dog, red eyes blazing, the secretary turned on the brave figure of Radu Vadas and leaped upon him. In the instant before he struck—confusion. Once again, the scene was interrupted—this time, by a blur of rustling robes, a flash of crimson, a cry of pain.

The two figures parted—Vadas, from his would-be assassin—to reveal a third.

A young woman, of exquisite, unearthly beauty, a large ruby ring still flashing upon her finger. Elisabetta, concealed in the dark recesses of the unfinished cathedral secreted even from the heightened powers of sense in her undead father, had leapt before that undead creature as he set upon her brother, and now fell to the ground, stone dead. Even from where I stood, I could see the striking peace, the perfect serenity of her face. A smile was on her lips. I thought of Éva. No doom here. Freedom.

Vadas cried out in grief and fell to his knees beside her. One of the priests had hurried to their side. He must have commenced a prayer or sought to bring them some sort of consolation. I heard *kyries* and *ora pro nobises* and saints and angels quietly called upon. Or, at least, I think I did. I honestly could not say what happened in that corner with the priest and his ministrations upon the body of Elisabetta, for the drama had yet again shifted, and with it we

412

were all finally freed from the immobility into which the voice of the count had cast us.

The walls rang with an unearthly shriek, as if from the bowels of hell.

Lucian Popescu, his blue eyes flaming and teeth suddenly revealed as razor-sharp fangs, gazed at the dead Elisabetta, the long-sought target of his lust. His face radiated his tortured rage—not born of the horrified, grief-stricken love of the undead father, but of his vicious, frustrated warped desire.

In that moment, he was transformed into an indescribable creature, more beast than man, claws for fingers, teeth like knives. The roused vampire pounced, snarling, shrieking—not for blood, but for furious vengeance— upon the throat of his secretary. The brutal attack lasted only a few moments, as he tore his victim to pieces. In a cloud of dust and dismembered flesh, the vampire feasted upon his own bloodless, undead slave.

Then everything seemed to happen at once.

Inspector Harris lunged from the midst of our stunned group, two revolvers in his outstretched hands. Gunshot after gunshot volleyed as if from every side, filling the air with the smell of cordite. As the bullets ricocheted from the body of the count, scattering across the floor, Popescu, revealed in his true form at last, laughed and laughed and laughed.

Laughing still, he turned slowly, the bullets still radiating about him. As he turned, the room filled with dark, suffocating clouds, and the vampire, a wrothful white face with blazing red eyes, his body augmented with fire and fury and blood, leapt toward our little band.

A new confusion was this. The blood pounded in my brain, and the fire grew so intense that, for a moment,

I could see nothing. There was a second—the merest instant (though it could well have been born of my own imaginings)—when the blackened clouds parted and revealed a tense scene in the midst of the chaos and smoke. I thought I saw the creature turning toward the lifeless body of Elisabetta. Was there a chance? Could there be one last breath? Could he still possess and consume the woman he had so long desired?

But there was Radu Vadas beside her and—a greater barrier—the white-robed form of Father Thomas Edmund Gilroy.

The little priest looked up, and though I could not see his face, whatever it showed was enough. The creature recoiled and, turning away, lost himself again in the smoke.

Once again, all was suffocating, blinding, oppressive. I acted as I am sure the others did, swinging about, fists flailing in the shadows and the smoke, hearing the creature all around me, and yet finding it nowhere.

Once again a scene opened up in the midst of the fire. In that moment I saw Constable Peters, lying prone and stained with blood. I moved with a rapidity that would have been impossible had I been capable of thought—rushing into the flames, grabbing his unconscious body, and dragging him into an open space where air might revive him. The flames licked my clothing and took hold, and I felt the excruciating sting of burning on my arms and legs, and smelled my sizzling hair.

I placed the wounded Peters on the ground. The flames might then have consumed me—they were spreading along my clothes—then suddenly arms closed around me and flung me headlong into a large rain barrel that, overflowing into standing water, I had heard dripping upon our entrance. With a mighty crash, my unlikely baptism brought a tidal wave against the melee. The fires quenched, and my head strangely cleared, I gazed about to find my fellows.

Peters, still lying where I had left him, hovered over by Toby Barnes. Constable Stewart and Constable Davis each crouched against a column, revolver in hand, scanning the darkness for a target, and my rescuer, Francis Carstairs, a soggy, exhausted wreck of a boy, looking every second of his youth, looking down at me.

"Are you all right, sir?" He panted.

Before I could thank him for saving me from fiery death, one of the constables shouted: "There he goes!"

I looked up through the partially open ceiling to see the rickety, incomplete bell tower, half scaffold and half brick-work, a craggy, dagger-like protrusion piercing the night sky. Three forms were vaguely discernable, wriggling and writhing in the midst of the bars and planks: Count Popescu, lithe and rapid as a lizard, easily outdistancing his pursuers; Inspector Harris, close at the heels of the fleeing villain; and Brother Peter, encumbered by his robes, but striving heroically to keep up.

We gathered together at the foot, almost breathless in our effort to see, as if silence could aid sight.

I heard—or imagined I heard—the sounds of manly struggle, and someone (Harris, I thought) swearing articulately under his breath.

The climb seemed to run on endlessly. For a moment I wondered if they might continue on, smaller and smaller, crawling up that tower into eternity, some bizarre, terrifying illusion that we sane men, unsatisfied in our need for denouement, might run mad.

Then—a triumphant cry. That was Harris' voice, surely. Once again, words I could not clearly comprehend, but the meaning of which was all too clear. Here was the exultant confrontation we awaited. The creature, crouching upon the pinnacle, brought to bay.

In a moment, triumph gave way to bafflement.

A new sound—the chilling echo of Popescu's laugh, growing in strength as the villain crowed gleefully over Harris. He struck at the inspector, thrusting him from safety out into the open air. Then Brother Peter's arm shot out from beneath and caught Harris by the ankle before he could plummet to his death. Salvation, but not without price. Even from that distance, I clearly heard the snapping of bone and the groan of sudden pain.

Popescu did not wait for a second assault. Instead he launched himself from the tower, arms outstretched, legs tightly together. The cruciform body fell, head-downward, with appalling and mounting speed. A cry of horror, stifled, suffocated my throat.

As we stood there, helpless, transfixed by the sight of free-falling death, the memory of the end of Edgar Kilbronson so vividly renewed in every mind, the creature lurched, suddenly, bending backward with amphibian dexterity. Drawing its arms together in a graceful, unhurried movement, it then parted the arms ... but they were not simply arms. These were the black, webbed wings of a bat.

The zenith of metamorphosis was the shrill, almost inaudible shriek, and with that sound came a wave of hot, noxious wind, buffeting my face and turning my stomach.

"James." It was a terse command from Father Thomas Edmund Gilroy, whom I suddenly recalled, realizing that he had stood there beside the body of Elisabetta— unmoved, even as the fiery, bloody drama unfolded upon him. Now, his eyes fixed upon the transformed creature, his voice called to action his young lieutenant.

The white-robed novice, whom I had also forgotten, standing there beside the misshapen black bag of the Papists, stepped forward, drew forth a contraption of iron, wire, and tense cable, and a thin, wooden stake. He coolly nocked his unlikely arrow in the contraption, raised it, and unemotionally fired it at the winged beast.

The stake struck its mark with unexpected accuracy. The creature shrieked once more and fell, this time a less appalling distance, to land with a crash into the impromptu font. A second wave of unholy water erupted across the unfinished nave—nearly drowning me for the second time.

When I looked again, blinking my drenched eyes, the creature that had been Popescu lay writhing and screaming, pinned down beneath what seemed a mere fisherman's net.

Father Thomas Edmund Gilroy stood above him.

The world seemed to stop, pausing with him as he looked down upon the writhing creature of evil.

Constables stood back, pistols held limply at their sides. I sensed the return of Harris, leaning heavily upon the shoulder of Brother Peter, who delivered the nearly crippled inspector to his men, then hurried to the side of his brethren.

A voice spoke in my ear and I turned, oddly bewildered.

"Go," said Father Vincent—whom I had imagined far away with Dr. Lewis—and he spoke with a quiet firmness that would brook no disagreement. "This work is not for you."

And I went. Carstairs limped along behind me, and Barnes nearly ran.

Behind us, in the dim, candlelit expanse of that unfinished space, I could hear the rustling of white robes, the creature hissing and shrieking as he flailed in futile fury, and the stern, calm, chanting voice of Father Thomas Edmund Gilroy addressing his prey: *"Exorcizo te, omnis spiritus immunde . . ."*

Chapter 30

22 January 1901: Westminster

(From Mina Murray Harker's journal—the original ending
of *Dracula*) *Then there was a stillness in nature as the echoes of
that thunderous report seemed to come as with the hollow boom
of a thunder clap—the long reverberating roll which seems as
though the floors of heaven shook. Then down in a mighty ruin
falling whence they rose came the fragments that had been tossed
skywards in the cataclysm.*

As the door of Westminster Cathedral closed behind us,
the wet and bedraggled remains of John Kemp, Toby
Barnes, and Francis Carstairs collapsed together on the
church steps.

For a long time, we said nothing. The night sky was
there, black and serene above us. The air was freezing,
especially in our wet clothes, but it was some time before
I could sense it. When I returned to myself, it was with a
shiver of realization.

"We're going to freeze," I said.

"No," said Carstairs. "Not if they can help it."

I looked up and followed his pointing finger to the
middle of the wide street that stood before the unfinished
cathedral.

Several dirty street urchins were busily occupied in building a small fire. Their dark skin and outlandish garb labeled them as gypsies, but the Cockney accents I could discern in their occasional conversation rendered them clear kinsmen. They must have been working at it for some time, even while we sat there. Just as we had ignored them, they had obviously deemed us not worth their tribal concern.

We three rose and stumbled toward them—cautiously, lest we fright them.

I felt sure they were aware of us, even as we approached. This was confirmed when the door of the cathedral opened and Constable Peters appeared—a frightening and official silhouette, I have no doubt.

At that sight, the tallest of the boys—posture and demeanor, even more than height, identified him as the leader—cried out strange words that must have been a warning. The boys scattered. The shortest of the boys was too slow. Peters, reenlivened by the chase, had his quarry in moment.

The boy sputtered weak defiance and then, shaking with fear and cold, burst into tears.

Constable Peters silently led the boy back to the small fire.

"Now, boy," he said quietly, "that's not how you start a good blaze. Here. Watch me."

In a few moments, we had a hearty fire, carefully and safely constructed. The other boys slowly reappeared and joined us, eying Peters with a healthy degree of distrust and the fire with unabashed admiration. We were soon warm, and I even had hopes of my clothes drying.

We sat there, a motley crew, watching the fire and looking up at the night sky, ever silent, and sometimes looking in anxious hope toward the far horizon, waiting for the hinting, pastel light of dawn to crest the edge of the world and bathe London in the redemption of a new day.

The door opened and Inspector Harris, leaning on Constables Davis and Stewart, hobbled out. They joined us silently. The boys sized up each new member of our band but seemed to accept our ragged appearance and clear indifference as a sign of security. The coppers weren't a comfortable addition, but they seemed inclined to be peaceable. We didn't mind them, so they wouldn't mind us.

Silent, still, unhurried, we sat there in the dark.

"Dawn will come soon," Carstairs remarked after quite some time.

We all considered this point, but no one replied.

"It's so ...," Carstairs ventured timidly, looking at me, "so ... quiet."

I nodded.

This silent vigil with the unseen beggars of the street was a stark counterpoint to the fascinated crowds that had gathered outside the ruined house of Count Popescu—that desecrated ancestral home of the Sidneys.

"All for the best," grumbled Harris, without looking up from the fire. "Scandal will come soon enough."

I could not resist the urge to look at Toby Barnes then. The sight of him almost made me burst out laughing—though such hilarity seemed to demand an impossible degree of effort at that moment of crippling exhaustion.

He was sitting down heavily on the stones. With a look of desolation that was almost comical, he systematically (and ineffectively) wiped the mud from his face and arms.

At the brush of my gaze he looked up and grunted. "Don't look at me, Kemp. I won't be writing anything."

I raised an eyebrow quizzically (though even my brow felt sore and weathered).

"What kind of story would it be?" he lamented. "I can't write that. I'll be laughed out of the business. NEWS BULLETIN: *Hateful Hun Vanquished! Popescu, New Leading Figure of London Society, Is—or Was—a Vampire.* Can you imagine the outcry? Can you imagine the mockery? Vampires? Papists with stakes? Blood and dust and drama? No, I shall simply recount—as briefly and with as many ambiguous hints as possible—that Her Majesty's police force, working alongside certain remarkably heroic members of the public, including a humble representative of the press, have exposed and foiled the sinister plots of a villainous foreign nobleman, who likely was no nobleman at all. More clarity is sure to come in the months ahead, as this team of dynamic heroes continues to labor for the cause of all that is right and good and decent and thoroughly English."

"And then ...?"

"And then I shall endeavor to speak of as many other things as I possibly can to distract my readers from expecting any of those details—which, you will notice, I never promised to produce."

"There is a great deal of cunning in that," I remarked.

Barnes shrugged. "Priests and newspapermen. We both have to maintain a degree of art and discretion in our delivery, or we might lose the Everyman."

"Your experiences," Inspector Harris said dryly, "seem to have turned you philosopher, Barnes. Just remember—I want to see that copy before it goes to press."

Toby Barnes bowed his head, a theatrical gesture of submission. "Your will is law, good inspector."

As I looked around the slowly wakening street, a cold wind blew across my face, bringing with it stark refreshment, and something more. Some strange sixth sense.

"Something *has* happened," I said. "Something is different."

Toby Barnes shrugged. "Not likely," he said. "Nothing changes."

"That's a cynical attitude for a newsman," I commented.

"Not at all. I know how to make the news. The thrill doesn't come from any change. It just comes in the delivery."

"And will you deliver?"

He smiled ruefully. "I always do. Ee-i, tiddly-i, the farmer went to hell."

With this bizarre twist on the nursery rhyme, we fell together back into meditative silence.

No one seemed inclined to leave, though I am sure none of us could have explained why we waited. Periodically, one or another of us glanced back to the mute, imposing doors of the cathedral. No one spoke of what was happening inside—and likely none of us knew or wanted to know.

Finally, after what seemed like hours, the door opened and Father Thomas Edmund Gilroy walked out.

He was clearly tired and as filthy as we all were, but there was a serenity about his countenance that might in the past have irritated me. Now it impressed me and calmed the disquiet in my mind and stomach.

He smiled down at all of us, including our newfound companions in his appreciative look.

"What a capital idea," he said, joining us at the fire. "These January nights can be brutal."

I half expected the boys to take fright at him, but they nodded with a growing ease, and even friendliness or familiarity—though this might have been my imagination, which had been so active in recent months.

The silence seemed ready to fall once again, but Father Thomas Edmund Gilroy was not, it seemed, of our brooding humor.

"Well, now," he said encouragingly, as if he spoke to those children and not to us men, "I think it is time we all moved along. There is more work to be done here, but it is of the slow, steady variety, and I am sure we could all do with some rest and a cup of tea. And we'll need a carriage, of course."

Harris started as if awakening from a dream and looked up from the fire. "Of course," he said. "Quite right. Stewart ..."

In a few minutes, the constabulary hurried off to fetch transportation.

Almost immediately, I heard the rumble of a carriage in the streets. Too soon for even the intrepid Constable Stewart. In the growing half-light, I could see it was no police wagon. This was a black, sober carriage. The hearse of an undertaker.

The priest was on his feet to greet the driver and direct him, in a low voice, into the building. They disappeared into the cathedral and, after several minutes, returned. Radu Vadas and the undertaker bore the weight of a shrouded shape on a stretcher, walking with slow, solemn steps appropriate to that funeral march.

We rose to our feet—even Harris, leaning on Barnes— and the gypsy boys doffed their caps.

Their cargo safely stowed, Vadas said something briefly to the driver, then turned and walked toward our group. He nodded without speaking to the others then addressed me.

"Mr. Kemp. Goodbye. And thank you."

"I am sorry," I said. "Sorry for the death of your sister."

He shook his head gently. "There need be no sorrow. She is free. It is the freedom she so dearly desired. I think that is what must have brought her here. In that creature was to be found either her doom or her salvation. But, truly, we cannot say. What a hidden path has been hers." He jerked his head toward the others. "There is one there who may know, but he will not say. And he should not."

I knew whom he meant, and as I looked back thoughtfully at that strange, eccentric, little man in white, with his round glasses and his cheery manner, I felt a certain solace at the suggestion that he knew the true story of Elisabetta, and perhaps played some secret part in leading and protecting her.

I turned back to Vadas. "What will you do?" I asked, thinking to myself of the dark, heavy despair the man must feel at such a moment of failure. Then I looked again and saw that he was smiling, and his eyes, though they streamed with tears, were alight with something—with peace, and, I felt sure, with joy.

"Now, Mr. Kemp. I shall live until I die. Then I shall live forever, reunited with her."

He bowed low before me, before returning to the carriage, seating himself beside the driver, and, with him, disappearing with his sister's body into the burgeoning light of the morning.

As they vanished from our sight around a corner, the world seemed to awaken, as if on cue.

"Scat!" cried one of the boys, and they disappeared down side streets in an instant, returning to the hidden byways and gutters that had made them.

"So long, gents!" called the shortest boy, the one whom Peters had captured.

"Be good, Billy!" called Father Thomas Edmund Gilroy (and I wondered where he had learned the boy's name).

After so much silence, the noise seemed deafening. London, rolling and tumbling about us in carts and carriages and on foot, rambling and chattering, shouting and bumping and tapping and rumbling, continued as before—blind to the sinister darkness that had been routed or the light that had triumphed over it.

Frowning a little, I remarked to Father Thomas Edmund upon this pressing theological paradox.

He smiled but shook his head. "Evil was vanquished at Calvary," he said in that characteristic matter-of-fact tone. "We have routed this infernal agent. There will be others. They too must be routed."

"But what was his purpose? Was he all along simply chasing that woman?"

"Without wasting too much time hypothesizing about the unknowable—the particular motivations of an evil creature—we can say that his aim was always power and pleasure. His actions seemed to indicate a larger, or political, purpose, as well as a more personal one. We've seen the ending of the latter, and with his destruction, I assume we have seen the end of the former. What that was, we cannot say for certain, nor need we. But think of the evidence we can amass—it was likely something to do with England, her government, and even her crown. Who rules him who will someday rule? That is a question to ponder."

We stood uncomfortably considering this fact. Then the inspector cleared his throat.

"There are my boys," he said. "Good morning." And he tipped his hat as if he were parting from us after a simple Sabbath service where the minister had preached for too long a time, leaving our joints sore and desperate for the relief of movement.

The inspector limped away. Barnes, Carstairs, a priest, a brother (and soon a second, as Brother Peter appeared beside us, quietly lugging that large black bag)—only we remained.

"Come now, my friends," said Father Thomas Edmund gently. "Off you go to rest. There's nothing more to be done now, and too much thinking on this point will make you run mad. The foe is routed for now, and your work is complete. You have lives and labors of your own."

I thought of Esther then. I would go to her—I must go to her. To see her freed of that dark shadow, and to do my part in nursing her back to life, health, and, if I could give it to her, happiness.

The priest read my thought in my eyes. "Yes, John. Go to her. Even as you go, remember. Her healing will come. In time. For now, your cause must be merely sleep—even sleep on a train as you wind your way north. Sleep long, deeply, and peacefully, or you'll start seeing visions."

That brought memory flooding back.

"Before you go," I said, "I do have one final question, Father."

He nodded expectantly.

"When I saw the fiend on the train—when he woke me and would, I think, have attacked me—" I described the scene once again, eagerly putting forth each detail, and watching as Father Thomas Edmund Gilroy noted each word calmly, as if assessing my account with Thomistic precision that any chance or carelessness might not lead to sloppiness or heresy.

"Was it your card?" I demanded. "He knew you were a slayer of vampires. Was it your card?"

As I spoke, his round face had assumed a dark, rosy hue that was hard to interpret. Some heavy emotion was upon him, but I knew not what.

"Oh dear," said Father Thomas Edmund, turning ever pinker and seeming to speak with an effort. "That is not at all what my visiting card is supposed to say."

"But I saw it," I said. "I truly did. I know I did. I had it for weeks, and every time I read it, it said the same thing!" I began to feel rather alarmed, as if this was a sign of special lunacy on my part (a slightly disproportionate response, given recent events, but I was exhausted and overwhelmed, and thus might be pardoned for irrationality).

I grabbed my clerk by the arm and began shaking him, as a lawyer in a case might loudly rustle papers containing conclusive and damning evidence. "Carstairs must have seen it. Tell him, Carstairs!"

Francis Carstairs, himself scarlet with embarrassment, admitted: "Yes ... yes, sir. You kept leaving it in awkward places, and though I tried not to see—for you so clearly did not want me to see it—but ... Father, that's what it said."

"You see!" I almost shouted it. "I'm not mad! I didn't imagine it! It *did* say you are a slayer of vampires, as indeed you are!"

Father Thomas Edmund only turned pinker. "My dear John," he said, "my dear Mr. Carstairs, this is most embarrassing. I ... my visiting cards look like this ..."

REV. THOMAS EDMUND GILROY, O.P., D.C.L.

St. Dominic's Priory
London, NW5 4LB

He had reached into a hidden pocket and produced one.

"But ..."—I stared down at the card in my hand—
"Father, I know what I saw!"

"Indeed," he said, now a lovely shade of scarlet. "I must
have mistakenly mixed my true cards with one that one of
the brethren ... well ..."

A strange, constrained, gurgling noise interrupted us,
coming from behind me, around the region of my right
elbow. Brother James collapsed upon the stones, his body
contorted as if in pain, his arms tightly about his waist.

"Is he ill?" I asked, horrified.

Then I heard more clearly and could diagnose the
cause—the young man was struggling with imperfectly
silent laughter.

"The card!" he almost hooted.

"Yes," said his senior sternly (though I thought I could
detect a smile). "See what a lot of anxiety your little joke
has produced, Brother James. I hope you have learned
your lesson." The priest looked back to me. "John, for
all we deal in these dramatic and sordid matters, we do

not advertise our labors to the unsuspecting public. Think of the terror it might inspire among Englishmen if they thought that rabid followers of Rome teemed the streets with stakes and other paraphernalia popularly believed to be employed in the handling of preternatural creatures? Why, you know as well as I do—the Papists would inspire more panic than the vampires!"

Brother James was still chuckling to himself, and even Brother Peter was grinning.

"They're all quite insane," said Toby Barnes with a shrug. "As we all must be by this time."

"Why did he run from my room then?" I demanded.

Father Thomas Edmund was pensive for a moment, closing his eyes as if to meditate upon his response.

He opened his eyes. He smiled then laughed.

"My dear boy," he said, "if you were struck in the eye by something as horribly sharp as my visiting card—would not you run away? It must have hurt . . . monstrously."

At this half pun, that would have better suited a discussion of Shelley than of Stoker, he joined the two brothers in an unnaturally hearty laugh.

"Well," I said, clinging to my point as if for very life, "what happened to the vampire on the train?"

"Oh," said Father Thomas Edmund Gilroy serenely, "he had come for me."

I waited, but he offered no further explanation. So I pressed: "Well then," I said, "what happened to him?"

Father Thomas Edmund Gilroy looked surprised at the question. "I dealt with him, of course."

And that was that.

"Well," said Toby Barnes, "you're all mad, as I say. If I never see a vampire or a Papist—begging your pardon, Father—again, it will be too soon. I'm off to try and rebuild the shreds of my reputation. But I can promise you one thing. This *will* be the last time that Toby Barnes is robbed of a top headline story."

He nodded for emphasis and shouted, "Cheery-o, my friends!" and sauntered off along the pavement, whistling a self-satisfied tune.

As he walked down the street, a boy came running past him, so bursting with hysterical energy that he catapulted against a wall and into the newsman.

"The queen is dead," he squealed in the falsetto of excited adolescence. "Long live the king!"

EPILOGUE

3 June 1911: Durham

(From Jonathan Harker's concluding note) *We want no proofs; we ask none to believe us! This boy will some day know what a brave and gallant woman his mother is. Already he knows her sweetness and loving care; later on he will understand how some men so loved her, that they did dare much for her sake.*

Ten years have passed since these events transpired. Early reports and analysis, based as they were on incomplete information and lack of imagination, would have been amusing in another context. They were easily and swiftly overshadowed by other national concerns. Perhaps that was for the best.

After some time, Esther and I married. We no longer live in London, the climate being unhealthy for my wife.

My legal practice in London suffered greatly. It is not likely that it could survive, when so many prominent members of my clientele were proved so ostentatiously corrupt. I left its sorry remains to Francis Carstairs, who has done exceedingly well for himself. He has made a name as a criminal defense lawyer who has never lost a case. In due time, I fully expect to hear he has been made a judge of His Majesty's courts, or a Member of Parliament—if for no other reason than to transfer his undefeated record to the credit of judgment rather than acquittal. A grateful monarch might someday bestow a title upon that head.

Inspector Harris is a superintendent, or perhaps even holds a higher rank. He is celebrated by all who know him (and even by those who do not) for his scientific mind, untarnished by superstition or imagination. Constable Peters is now an inspector, and I have no doubt he tyrannizes over his men. I also have no doubt that he inspires unshakeable loyalty in them, especially when he is most strict regarding discipline.

A recent letter from the South has informed me that Dr. Lewis has given up medicine, swum the Tiber, and lives an ascetical life in a monastery in some infinitesimal village in Spain. I think this must be nonsense.

Jenson and Mrs. Pritchard wed very soon after our dramatic adventures concluded. They now own a pub in Suffolk, and I have heard that nowhere can one enjoy a better shepherd's pie. I have also heard Jenson called a boisterous, gregarious keeper of the bar—but as I have not seen it for myself, and the very thought of it makes me quite dizzy, I once again am inclined to disbelieve rumor.

Esther remained for some time at the Convent of the Most Sacred Heart.

By then, my assessment of the remains of my legal practice confirmed what I had already begun to hope: London was no longer a fit arena for my labors, and we need not—we dare not—remain there. Where should we go? Sebastian Roubles provided the answer. I accepted his enthusiastic invitation to visit, and, during my stay (which was largely defined by my daily visits to the convent), he introduced me to Sir Cedric Potheringsby, who became my first client in Durham.

We make no attempt to compete with Roubles, who boasts a round dozen children (rather to his bewilderment); we have three children, two boys and a girl. The boys are as healthy and as wild as any father might expect. Our girl, named after her mother, is small, delicate, and quiet, with wide black eyes. When she smiles, though, the world is alight with a special beauty.

I have not turned Papist—not yet, at any rate. I have also not stopped Esther from doing so. It appears to give her consolation, and even hope at her more troubled moments. She goes often to the convent and sometimes stays there for several days at a time.

When I see that look in her eyes, the look of remembered pain, I am grateful for the little string of beads she holds so closely in her hand—though she conceals it in her pocket, I know it is always there. And I have even stammered out in my heart an awkward thing that might be prayer. Perhaps that is the beginning of what you call faith, Father Thomas Edmund Gilroy. And perhaps it is quite enough for me. For now, at least, it seems so.

There you have it, my friend. You may do with it what you will.

Yours affectionately,
"John Kemp"